PRAISE FOR

Singapore Sapphire

"Skillfully and seamlessly weaves actual people and events of the time with rich, multidimensional fictional characters. . . . By the end of this sharp, satisfying novel, you'll be anxious to find out what happens in the next adventure."

—*Kirkus Reviews* (starred review)

"My favorite new mystery series! Set in a unique and compelling setting, and filled with fascinating historical research, deft characterization and thrilling suspense—readers will devour *Singapore Sapphire*. One of the best books I've read this year. I can't wait to read Harriet's next adventure."

—Anna Lee Huber, bestselling author of
the Lady Darby Mysteries

"*Singapore Sapphire* is a gem of a story! You will love the intrepid heroine and the exotic locale that bring this twisty tale to life. I loved every minute of this steamy adventure."

—Victoria Thompson, *USA Today* bestselling author of
Murder on Pleasant Avenue

"Filled with all the hot, decadent splendor and sultry danger of colonial-era Singapore. Rich, atmospheric and fascinating!"

—C. S. Harris, *USA Today* bestselling author of
Who Speaks for the Damned

"*Singapore Sapphire* is a remarkably sensitive look at life in Singapore in 1910, with a wealth of historical detail as well as rich characterization. Harriet and Curran are terrific leads."

—Criminal Element

"Stuart brings both early-twentieth-century Singapore and her characters vividly to life in this first in the Harriet Gordon series."

—*Booklist*

W9-BOB-264

REVENGE IN RUBIES

♦ *A Harriet Gordon Mystery* ♦

A. M. STUART

BERKLEY PRIME CRIME
New York

BERKLEY PRIME CRIME
Published by Berkley
An imprint of Penguin Random House LLC
penguinrandomhouse.com

Library of Congress Cataloging-in-Publication Data
Names: Stuart, A. M., 1959– author.
Title: Revenge in rubies: a Harriet Gordon mystery / A. M. Stuart.
Description: First Edition. | New York: Berkley Prime Crime, 2020. |
Series: A Harriet Gordon mystery; 2
Identifiers: LCCN 2020011999 (print) | LCCN 2020012000 (ebook) |
ISBN 9781984802668 (trade paperback) | ISBN 9781984802675 (ebook)
Subjects: GSAFD: Mystery fiction. | Suspense fiction.
Classification: LCC PR9639.4.S78 R48 2020 (print) |
LCC PR9639.4.S78 (ebook) | DDC 823/.92—dc23
LC record available at https://lccn.loc.gov/2020011999
LC ebook record available at https://lccn.loc.gov/2020012000

First Edition: September 2020

Printed in the United States of America
1   3   5   7   9   10   8   6   4   2

Cover illustration © Larry Rostant
Cover design by Judith Lagerman

This book is dedicated to the memory of my father,
an officer of the British Army from 1945 to 1957.
I think he would have enjoyed this story.

REVENGE IN RUBIES

∞ ONE

St. Thomas House, Singapore
Friday, 12 August 1910

". . . *Beneath the floor of a cellar in . . . Hilldrop Crescent, Camden-road, the mutilated and battered body of a woman which had been buried in quicklime was found. The body was that of Mrs. Cora Crippen, a music hall singer of American nationality, professionally known as Belle Ellmore. Her husband, Hawley Harvey Crippen, an American dentist, is suspected to be the murderer, and a full description of him and a young Frenchwoman named Le Neve, with whom he disappeared, was circulated . . .*"

Harriet Gordon paused in buttering her toast. "We know all this," she said.

"Yes, get to the exciting bit," Julian and Harriet's ward, Will Lawson, put in. "How did Inspector Drew arrest him?"

The Reverend Julian Edwards regarded the boy from over the top of his glasses. "Stop feeding the cat under the table, Will," he said. "I can see what you are doing."

A slight color stained the boy's cheeks and he picked up the spoon to crack the top of his egg, without making eye contact with his guardian.

Julian took a bite of his toast, shook out and refolded the morning's copy of the *Straits Times* to continue reading the article headed *Sensational Arrest on an Allan Liner.*

He scanned the article and continued, *"Disguised as pilots, Inspector Drew, accompanied by two policemen, boarded the Montrose from a rowing boat. Crippen was walking the deck with the ship's surgeon. He exclaimed: Three pilots are coming on board. Isn't this unusual? The doctor did not reply. Inspector Drew walked past Crippen and made sure of his man. Then he said, Crippen, I want you—"*

A frantic rapping at the front door interrupted the dramatic account.

"Oh bother," Harriet grumbled. "Please see who it is, Huo Jin."

Huo Jin cast her employer a baleful glance. She too had been listening to the gripping account of the arrest of the notorious Dr. Crippen. The household's amah never hurried anywhere and it seemed an age before she returned with a note in her hand.

"Who was at the door?" Harriet asked, returning to the serious business of finishing her own rapidly cooling boiled egg.

Huo Jin shrugged and handed Harriet a sealed envelope. "For you, mem."

Harriet broke the seal and withdrew the single sheet of paper, embossed with *The Cedars, Blenheim Road, Singapore.*

"It's from Priscilla Nolan," she said.

Julian returned to studying the newspaper. "Is she the one from the tennis club?"

"Yes," Harriet said without looking up from the missive. "I occasionally partner her in doubles. Oh my!"

Julian looked up. "Problem?"

"Pris writes: *My dear Harriet. Please come at once. There has been a tragic accident and I would welcome your advice, and the spiritual comfort of your brother, as we must see how best to break the news to Jack.*"

Julian pushed his glasses back up his nose. "Oh dear. Do you suppose Jack's father has fallen ill or met with an accident?"

"She doesn't say. We should go to her, Julian."

She passed her brother the note and he scanned it. "The summons sounds urgent, Harri. Let me fetch my bag—I may be called upon in a professional capacity." He left the following words unspoken—generally a minister of religion would be called upon to administer the sacraments for the sick or dying.

Will, who had been watching them with wide eyes, said, "Jack Nolan's staying with Mitchell and his family at their beach villa in Katong for the month."

Harriet cast her ward a sharp glance, detecting the underlying note of envy in his voice. Unfortunately for Will, no invitations to pass a few weeks at a beach villa during the long holidays had come his way, and his best friend, John Simpson, had sailed home to England for the break, making it a long, lonely time for the boy. Julian and Harriet had talked about a few days' sojourn at the beach before school resumed in late August but the weeks had slipped away and along with them, Will's hope of a summer idyll by the sea.

Julian folded the paper and rose to his feet. "Huo Jin, please can you ask Aziz to hail down a gharry for us?"

The amah rolled her eyes and assumed her expression of long suffering before leaving the room, muttering to herself. Harriet and Julian exchanged amused glances. The grumbling was all pretense. Huo Jin had proved time and again that she had a good heart and an unspoken loyalty to everyone at St. Tom's House, but only Will regularly saw the softer side of the amah.

✖ Two

The colonel's lady lay spread-eagled on her bed almost lost in the meringue confection of white linen, lace and net, now made grotesque by the dark, reeking bloodstains that marred the pristine bedclothes.

Inspector Robert Curran of the Detective Branch of the Straits Settlements Police Force had been a soldier and a policeman for most of his adult life, and he thought that nothing could horrify him. However, the sight of Mrs. Sylvie Nolan's half-naked corpse turned his stomach.

She wore a nightdress of expensive muslin, a once-pretty thing trimmed with ribbons and lace, but the fight that had wrecked the room and claimed her life had seen the flimsy garment ripped almost in half. He didn't need the police surgeon, Dr. Euan Mackenzie, to tell him that Sylvie had died from a blow to her head, several blows, rendering the question of which one had actually killed her, academic. Whoever had committed this act had hit her repeatedly and with great force using some sort of heavy object.

Steeling himself, he leaned over to examine what was left of her face. He had never met Sylvie Nolan in life, but there had been photographs on a table in the front hall of the house and he had taken a moment to study what looked to be a recent wedding photograph: Lieutenant Colonel Nolan, magnificent in his regimental dress uniform, and his much younger wife, in silk and orange blossoms. She had been beautiful, a beauty that went beyond mere youthful prettiness. Even in the sepia tones of the photograph, Curran had been struck by the classic bone structure of the face, the perfectly proportioned nose, the large heavy-lashed eyes, the perfect complexion and a full, sensuous mouth.

Now all that loveliness had been reduced to a bloody pulp.

Her hand lay palm up on the ruined sheets, the fingers curled in a curiously vulnerable gesture. He picked her hand up and it hung limply in his grip, the skin devoid of warmth. In this climate the presence, or not, of rigor mortis told him very little. There were bruises on her arm, clearly visible on the pale skin beneath the torn, filmy material of her nightdress. The lobe of her right ear, which had escaped the battering, was torn and bloodied as if something, probably an earring, had been ripped from it.

He gently laid her hand back on the bed in the position he had found it and straightened. He had seen enough and the doctor could verify the rest.

"Cover her," he ordered.

Constable Ernest Greaves set his photographic equipment to one side and used one of the large bath towels, which lay neatly folded on the washstand, to cover the bloody mess. Even the phlegmatic Greaves had gone pale, his lips tightly compressed and a sheen of sweat, not due entirely to the humidity, shone on his brow.

Curran blew out a breath and stepped back from the bed. With the body now hidden from view, the room resumed some semblance of normality or at least as normal as it could be, given the upended furniture and broken ornaments and the presence of the late woman's husband, Lieutenant Colonel John Nolan, commanding officer of the First Battalion South Sussex Infantry.

The soldier, a man of about forty, still dressed in blue-spotted pajamas covered by a light silken dressing gown, sat on a white-painted rattan daybed furnished with pink velvet cushions, his hands hanging limply between his knees and his eyes glazed with shock. A big man in height and breadth, with a bristling brown moustache, now flecked with gray like his hair, he looked older than his years and shrunken, diminished by the horrific death of his young wife.

Curran laid his hand on the man's shoulder. "Colonel?"

When he got no response, he hunkered down so he was looking up into the older man's eyes. "Colonel Nolan, can you tell me what happened here?"

Nolan shook his head, his eyes regaining some focus. "I . . . I found her . . . this morning. Thought I'd bring her tea in . . ."

Curran left an encouraging silence, allowing the man time to gather his thoughts.

Nolan swallowed. "I went to the mess dinner at the barracks last night—regimental birthday . . . no wives. She kissed me good-night and that was the last time I saw her until . . ." His gaze flicked to the bed. ". . . until this morning."

"You didn't see her when you got home?"

He shook his head. "We don't share the same bedroom. She hated to be disturbed and my hours are irregular." He pointed at a second door that stood slightly ajar. "I sleep through there. I got home after one. The adjoining door was locked and there was no light in her bedroom, so I assumed that she was asleep and didn't want to be bothered, so I went to bed."

"Go on," Curran said.

"This morning, I heard the maid knocking on her door so I went out into the hall. The girl had mem's morning tea and the mail. I thought I would surprise her so I took the tray from her. When I tried the door, I found it was locked so I set the tray down and knocked. When I didn't get a response, I used my key to unlock the adjoining door." His voice cracked and he swallowed, his Adam's apple rising and falling. "Then I saw her." His gaze returned momentarily to the bed and back to Curran. "Dammit, Curran, you must have seen some sights. I've been a soldier . . . served in South Africa. There are things I've witnessed, but this is different. I've never seen anything . . . not someone you know . . ." The man lowered his head and the next words were barely audible. ". . . and love."

Like Lieutenant Colonel Nolan, Curran had been a career soldier and had also served in South Africa. He had witnessed grisly scenes during his time serving with the Mounted Military Police and worse as a policeman, but the broken bodies had not been someone he knew and cared for. So much easier to view such scenes dispassionately when there is no emotion.

Curran dragged his thoughts back to the present.

"Who else lives here?"

Nolan looked up and blinked. "Apart from the servants, my sister, Priscilla. Sylvie's brother, Nicholas Gentry, is a junior officer in the battalion. He lives in the mess but stays up here sometimes."

"Was he here last night?"

Nolan shook his head. "He was at the mess dinner. I was the dining-in president and he had been assigned the role of the vice president. My son, Jack, boards at St. Thomas during the term. It's holidays now and he would normally be here but he is staying with a friend for a couple of weeks at their beach villa. Apart from Sylvie and the servants, Pris—Priscilla—would have been the only one at home."

Priscilla Nolan must have been the hysterical woman Curran had glimpsed in the living room being comforted by an Indian amah.

Curran rose to his feet. "Colonel, I must ask you to leave this room. I'll deal with everything here. I suggest you retire to your bedroom. Do you have a batman who can assist you?"

"Not at the moment. Sylvie didn't like having a batman in the house. She said there was nothing he could do for me that she and the servants couldn't, so I sent Corporal Billings back to the lines. He's been looking after young Gentry."

Curran made a mental note to speak with Corporal Billings. "I will ask the doctor to look in on you when he gets here."

Nolan frowned. "The doctor? Why have you sent for a doctor?" He glanced at the bed again. "Nothing to be done for her . . . not now."

"Dr. Mackenzie is our police surgeon. I need him to verify death and the injuries she sustained."

The soldier nodded. "Of course. Good man, Mackenzie."

Curran nodded. "Constable Greaves will see you to your room."

Constable Greaves had retreated to the doorway, and looking at his pasty face, Curran realized Greaves needed an excuse, any excuse, to leave the room.

Nolan shuffled across to the door through to his own bedroom, his shoulders stooped, his eyes averted from the bed. At the doorway, Curran stopped him.

"Just before you go, is there anything out of place? Anything missing from the room?"

Nolan turned and blinked at Curran. "What do you mean?" He looked around the room. "It must be plain even to you, Inspector, that my poor Sylvie fought for her life. That chair by the desk"—he indicated an object of walnut and ebony with a pink velvet seat, which now lay upturned with a broken leg on a pretty floral Persian rug—"that cost me a fortune in London."

"I am wondering about particular objects. If it was a burglary, something would be missing."

Nolan's gaze scanned the disordered room, settling on the small, elegant desk that matched the broken chair. He pointed with a shaking finger. "One of the candlesticks is missing. A silver candlestick. She said she liked to write in her journal by the light of the candle, rather than the lamp. She said she found it more conducive to collecting her thoughts." His lips twitched. "One of her little fancies."

Curran's instincts prickled. "She kept a journal?"

Nolan nodded and he gave a hollow laugh. "She was still such a girl at heart. She kept it locked in the desk."

His hand dropped to his side and his gaze fell on an upended gilt box beside the desk. "Her jewelry box. Looks like the bastard took all her jewelry."

"Did she have anything of value?"

He shrugged. "A few bits and pieces but nothing of great value. You will have to ask Pris, she would know more than me." He glanced back at the shrouded figure on the bed. "Who would do such a thing for a few trinkets?"

"Thank you, Colonel. You have been most helpful. Do you have your keys on you?"

Nolan pulled out a set of household keys from the pocket of his dressing gown and handed them to Curran. "Why do you need them?"

"I need to secure this room, Colonel."

Curran gave the young constable a nod.

Greaves touched the man's arm and Nolan shambled out into the corridor.

Alone with the body, Curran put his hands on his hips and surveyed the room. The windows were open, the white muslin curtains fluttering in the breeze. Tasteful, feminine furniture consisting of a dressing table, the small walnut and ebony desk and the daybed. Watercolors of English pastoral scenes hung on the walls. No doubt the young bride had brought these delicate objects from home and it was too soon for the white ants, wood borers, mold and mildew to have set in. In another year they would all disintegrate.

Nothing fragile or beautiful survived long in this punishing climate.

Saving the desk till last, he turned his attention firstly to the bed. In the struggle the bedside table had been overturned. The lamp lay shattered in a pool of potentially dangerous paraffin, which had soaked into a second oriental rug beside the bed. The novel Sylvie Nolan had kept on the nightstand lay open on the carpet, the pages soaked, and a glass flask that probably once contained water also lay in splinters.

He crouched down to examine the shattered lamp and flask, dismissing either as potential murder weapons. Whatever had killed Sylvie had been substantial and weighty, like the missing candlestick, and the ferocity of the attack would have left the perpetrator spattered with blood.

The morning sun, streaming in through the windows, caught a glint of something beneath the bed. Curran reached under the bed and retrieved a single tarnished silver button. He held it up, recognizing it as the button from the uniform of an officer of the South Sussex Regiment, his father's regiment. He recalled sitting on his father's knee as a small child, entranced by the silver buttons on the scarlet uniform jacket. The lozenge shield and fleur-de-lis were still recognizable, as was the motto . . . *Honorem ante omnia*—"Honor before all."

In the bedroom of the wife of an officer of that regiment, the object was not surprising. He placed it in an envelope and on the front scribbled in pencil where and when the button had been found, adding it to the pile of evidence to remove to South Bridge Road.

An attempt had been made to wipe the knob on the door leading through to the colonel's bedroom and a close inspection revealed smears of blood caught behind it. Using his handkerchief, he opened the door and found a short, narrow corridor with an identical closed door on the far side. No doubt Nolan's room. A second door opened into a utilitarian bathroom.

Curran stood in the doorway of the shared bathroom. Nothing untoward struck him. A couple of used towels hung on a wooden rail. The colonel would, no doubt, have used the conveniences on his return from the dinner. Curran pulled the cord on the electric light and took the time to inspect the washbasin. His breath caught when he spotted a dark droplet on the floor beneath the basin. Blood . . . Was it possible the murderer had stood here calmly washing himself as Sylvie Nolan lay dead or dying in the room next door?

Back in the short corridor, he locked the door leading into the colonel's bedroom, pocketed the key and returned to Sylvie Nolan's bedroom, where he started a methodical search. He began with the dressing table. Pots of creams and cut glass bottles of perfume stood in ordered rows on its top, but if there had been a mirror or hairbrush, they had gone. Only a tortoiseshell comb with heavy silver tracery on the shaft still remained. A cursory glance of the drawers revealed stockings, handkerchiefs and other trappings of a woman's life. Nothing of interest leaped out at him so he shut the drawers. They could wait for a more thorough search.

Using his handkerchief, he picked up the gilt jewelry box and set it on the dressing table. The lock had not been forced, the key still in the brass lock, but it was empty. Only a single pearl earring that had rolled under the desk remained.

He moved on to the desk, a lovely piece of walnut furniture with ebony inlay, which would have been more appropriate in Curran's childhood home than here. A single silver candlestick stood on the right-hand side and Curran could only suppose its pair had stood on the left. The servants were too diligent to allow even the faintest trace of dust to mark the spot where it had stood. The silver lid of the inkstand was open, the matching pen and the leather blotter with its green blotting paper lay on the ground. He crouched down beside the broken chair and wondered if Sylvie had been surprised while she sat writing at her desk.

The single drawer in the center of the desk, which Nolan had indicated had been where Sylvie secured her journal, had been pulled out and also lay broken in splinters on the floor. Curran sifted through the scattered contents: good quality writing paper embossed with *Mrs. J. L. Nolan, The Cedars, Blenheim Road, Singapore*, expensive pens and paper cutters. He set aside some letters, evidently from friends and family back home, to judge by the stamps on the envelopes, for reading later.

He added a green leather address book, which matched the blotter, to the letters but could see nothing that fitted the description of a journal.

He straightened and gave the contents of the room one final scan before turning his attention to the open windows. The shutters on the three sets of windows were open to catch the breezes, and being careful not to add his fingerprints to the window frames, he leaned out one of the windows. A gravel path ran around the side of the house, some ten feet below him. He could see no convenient gutters or ladders, but the heavy well-developed branches of a substantial rain tree, probably planted to provide shade from the afternoon sun, came within a foot of the next window.

Strong and substantial enough to hold the weight of an agile man? Curran wondered.

"I didn't want to believe it was Sylvie Nolan." Dr. Euan Mackenzie's voice, tinged with regret and a strong Scottish burr, came from the doorway and Curran turned too quickly, bumping his head on the window casement. The doctor stood in the doorway, his gaze on the bed, his black bag in his hand.

"Mac, you took your time."

"I do have living patients that demand my attention," Euan

Mackenzie replied. The chief surgeon at the Singapore General Hospital, Mackenzie doubled as the police doctor.

Mac strode to the bed and turned back the towel. In between the usual round of babies and tropical disease, he had seen some unpleasant sights, but for the first time in their acquaintance, Mac physically recoiled and, reaching for his handkerchief, mopped his brow, an undisguised expression of grief mingled with revulsion on his face.

"You knew her?" Curran asked.

"Not well but we'd met on a couple of social occasions at Government House," Mac said.

Although he counted Euan Mackenzie as a friend, Curran did not move in the exalted social circles of the elite colonial society that would have welcomed the new bride of the commanding officer of the military garrison.

"I take it they've not been married long?"

Mac looked up at him. "Nolan came back from home leave about six months ago with this pretty little thing on his arm. Have to say there were a few raised eyebrows but anyone who met Sylvie Nolan couldn't fail to be charmed. Louisa called her a breath of fresh air."

Curran said, "Nolan discovered the body and he's in shock. Can you check in on him after you've finished here?"

Mac nodded. "Aye, his sister is near hysterical. She just about fell on me when I walked through the door. She'll be needing something to calm her down. But first things first."

He bent over the corpse, examining the injuries from different angles.

He straightened and replaced the towel, restoring some dignity to the woman. "I need to get her back to the morgue, Curran. I can't tell much here except that the cause of death appears to be trauma from a heavy, blunt instrument. The mortuary wagon is on its way. They will deal with her."

Curran regarded his friend's pale, sweat-sheened face. "Are you all right?"

Mac mopped his face again. "Doesn't matter how often you tell yourself you've seen it all, there is always something else to shock you, isn't there, Curran?"

Curran clapped Mac on the shoulder.

"As Nolan said, it's hard when it's someone you know."

Mac shook his head. "I didn't know her well, but she was so young, so full of life . . ." He shrugged.

"Unfortunately I need your professional detachment, Mac. I want to know when she died, what was used to kill her and if she was . . . interfered with."

"You don't ask much, do you?" Mackenzie said with a sardonic smile. He looked around the room. "I take it you've got no weapon?"

"Not at the moment, but I suspect it may have been the pair to that candlestick." Curran raised his voice. "Musa?"

Constable Musa bin Osman, on duty at the door to the crime scene, looked around the doorjamb. "Sir?"

"Keep a guard on this room. No one to enter except Dr. Mackenzie, Constable Greaves and the mortuary attendants. Nothing, I repeat, nothing is to be touched. Once the body is removed, lock the door and stay put."

He handed the keys to the young policeman and Musa nodded, his normally cheerful face grave. He'd only been with the Detective Branch a few months and this was his first cold-blooded murder. It must have felt a long way from the police outpost at Changi where Curran had found him.

Curran returned to the room and walked over to the window. Pulling on the riding gloves that he always carried, he climbed onto the window ledge.

"What the hell do you think you're doing?" Mac demanded.

"Testing a theory."

"Well, try not to break your neck. I've enough on my hands already," the doctor grumbled.

Curran braced himself, cursing as the leather soles of his boots slipped on the painted surface of the windowsill. He considered the eighteen-inch gap between the window and the solid branch of the rain tree. The ground seemed a long drop below him. He'd certainly break something if he fell. He jumped, easily catching a lighter branch as his feet scrabbled for purchase. For a heart-stopping moment he thought he had misjudged the jump but he took a steadying breath and regained his balance. He glanced back at the window. Getting in by this method would be well-nigh impossible, but as a means of getting out, an agile individual would manage it easily.

"Curran, what on earth are you doing up there?" A familiar female voice broke his train of thought and he glanced down at the ground.

A woman stood on the path below him, looking up, one hand holding on to her hat and the other on her hip.

"Mrs. Gordon, good morning," he responded automatically, although there was nothing good about this particular morning. "I'll be right down," he added.

With the long practice of a childhood spent climbing trees in the park of Deerbourne Hall, Curran descended to the ground. He stood for a moment looking up at the window while he peeled off his gloves. The flimsy curtains fluttered like white flags above him.

"At least the mystery of the locked door is now solved," he said aloud, and turned his attention to the ground around the tree, but the hardy grass that passed for a lawn in Singapore did not retain the memory of any useful footprints.

He gestured for Sergeant Singh, who waited by the front door, and issued orders regarding the searching of the grounds before turning his attention to the Detective Branch's stenographer and typist, Harriet Gordon, who stood watching him, a bemused smile on her face.

She gestured at his head. "You've a leaf . . ."

He ran his hand through his hair, conscious that he had left his hat upstairs.

"What's happened?" she asked. "Is someone dead?"

He narrowed his eyes. "More to the point, what are you doing here?"

Harriet gestured at the front of the house. "Pris . . . Miss Nolan . . . sent for us. Julian's just paying off the gharry."

"Miss Nolan? Why would she send for you?" Curran asked.

"Morning, Curran." Harriet's brother, the Reverend Julian Edwards, headmaster of St. Thomas Church of England Preparatory School for English Boys, joined them.

Curran returned the greeting, adding, "I still don't understand why Miss Nolan would send for you."

Julian and Harriet exchanged glances.

"The colonel's son, Jack, is a boarder at the school and Miss Nolan is a friend of Harriet's," Julian said.

Curran frowned. "So, when exactly did she send for you?"

Harriet checked the gold watch neatly pinned to her blouse. "Half an hour ago. We came as soon as we could. She didn't say what the problem was, only that she had some bad news that concerned Jack and needed our advice."

"So, what's happened? Has to be bad to involve you. The note just said a tragic accident in the family," Julian said.

A tragic accident? So pukka, so polite . . . Nothing could describe the horror that lay upstairs in this pleasant house.

"The colonel's wife is dead," Curran said.

"No!" both siblings chorused.

"An accident?" Julian asked.

Curran shook his head and glanced up at the window he had just climbed through. "No. Murder. Rather violent and bloody,

I'm afraid. The colonel's in shock and Miss Nolan is greatly distressed."

Julian removed his pith helmet and mopped his forehead. "Bad business, Curran."

"Very," Curran agreed. "I haven't spoken to Miss Nolan yet, perhaps it might be easier if you are present?" He gestured at the front door. "Shall we . . . ?"

❧ THREE

The Cedars
Friday, 12 August

As commanding officer of the First Battalion South Sussex Regiment, Lieutenant Colonel Nolan lived in a grand double-story house on Blenheim Road, just a short walk from the Blenheim Barracks, bearing the inappropriate English name of "The Cedars." No cedar tree grew in the garden. The front door with its porte cochere was flanked by traveler's palms and approached by a circular driveway with a dilapidated central fountain that had probably not spouted water for many years.

Harriet had visited The Cedars for tea with Priscilla Nolan on several occasions and had always been struck by its gloomy atmosphere. Now a miasma of something dark and evil closed in around her as she stepped into the cool, black-and-white-tiled hallway with its round rosewood Chinese table dominated by an enormous vase of tropical flowers.

No servants greeted them. From somewhere in the back of the house came the doleful whine of a dog and from above them, the subdued tones of men's hushed voices and heavy boots on the wooden floor echoed down the stairs.

Thin, heartrending sobs drifted through the wide-flung double doors that led into the living room.

Harriet glanced at Julian. His lips tightened and he nodded.

Priscilla Nolan lay curled up on a daybed beneath the window, her Indian amah, Indira, hovering over her.

"Chai, mem," the woman pleaded, but Pris just buried her head deeper into the cushion. The amah looked up and, recognizing Harriet, said, "I cannot get her to eat or drink anything, Mrs. Gordon."

Harriet took the tray from the woman and set it on a table beside the daybed.

She sat down beside Pris and reached out, stroking the strands of sodden hair back from Priscilla Nolan's forehead.

Under Harriet's gentle hand the sobbing stilled. "That's better," Harriet said. "We got your note. How about you sit up and Julian will pour you a cup of tea? And, Indira, would you be so good as to fetch a damp cloth?"

The amah bobbed her head and hurried off.

Priscilla Nolan raised her head. Her normally pale freckled face was now blotchy and red, and her eyes swollen and bloodshot from weeping.

Pris, as everybody at the tennis club called her, was much of an age with Harriet and had probably never been described as beautiful, having her brother's heavy features and dull mousebrown hair that now hung in disordered locks from a half-made bun at the back of her head. She had never married and had, as far as Harriet knew, followed her brother on his postings, keeping house, looking after her nephew, Jack, and generally filling the roles of lady of the house and hostess when required.

It may have been the lot of the spinster sister, but in the few months Harriet had known her, Pris had always seemed happy enough. She wondered how much the woman's comfortable routine had changed with the colonel's remarriage. She never spoke about it and certainly never complained. Harriet had never met Sylvie Nolan. The new Mrs. Nolan, apparently, did not play tennis, her interests being more of the indoor variety—cards and soirees and the like.

Pris took a deep, shuddering breath and accepted the cup and saucer Julian held out for her. The china rattled as she took it and she gulped down the tepid liquid, returning the crockery to Julian's outstretched hand.

"Oh, Harriet, Reverend Edwards . . . it's too awful. Sylvie . . ." Her eyes rose to the ceiling. "Sylvie is up there, dead . . . murdered."

Harriet murmured comforting aphorisms until Indira returned with a cloth and towel. Pris obediently wiped her face and hands, and when she was quite composed Harriet looked up and nodded to Curran, who had entered quietly by the front door.

"Pris, this is Inspector Curran of the police. He would like to ask you some questions."

Pris's lower lip wobbled and her eyes began to water again. Harriet squeezed her hand. "Be brave, dear."

Curran pulled up a hard straight-backed chair and sat down across from Pris. He leaned forward, his hands loosely clasped together, his gaze on Priscilla Nolan, his light-gray eyes filled with apparent sympathy, although Harriet knew this masked a steely determination to get to the truth. She had been working with Robert Curran for six months now and she admired his ability to put a distressed witness at ease.

"I'm sorry we have to meet in these circumstances, Miss Nolan, but you understand that we must ask questions to find the killer of your sister-in-law."

Pris nodded. "Poor Sylvie. Everyone loved her. I can't even begin to believe someone would want to kill her and so . . . so horribly. It must have been an intruder?" She looked at Curran pleadingly.

"Everything indicates a burglary," Curran said.

"And I was asleep in the room across the corridor. It could have been me!" Pris's hand went to her throat and the tears dribbled down her cheek again.

Curran cleared his throat and glanced at the ceiling, where a thump and the sounds of heavy footsteps on the landing caused the china displayed on a side cabinet to rattle.

"Reverend Edwards, do you mind closing the door?" Curran said.

Julian complied but not before Harriet caught a glimpse of the mortuary attendants carrying a stretcher with a blanketed form at the head of the stairs. Fortunately Pris's attention seemed to be entirely on Curran's gray eyes, as if in a hypnotic trance.

Harriet gave Pris's hand a reassuring squeeze and handed her a dry handkerchief.

"Tell me about your sister-in-law," Curran said.

Pris dabbed her eyes, blew her nose and swallowed. "What do you want to know?"

"She was the colonel's second wife, I believe?"

Pris nodded. "John's first wife, Mary, died when Jack was two."

"Jack is a student at St. Tom's?" Curran glanced at Julian.

"Young Jack's a weekly boarder. His father wanted to get him used to boarding school before he goes to Rugby next year. I believe he's staying with the Mitchell family at their beach villa in Katong," Julian said. "Is that correct, Miss Nolan?"

She nodded.

Julian's lips tightened. "In the circumstances it is a blessing he is not here, but he will need to be told."

Curran turned back to Priscilla Nolan.

"How long have the colonel and Mrs. Nolan been married?"

The hand Harriet held jerked, Pris's fingers stiffening, but when she spoke, Pris sounded quite calm. "Sylvie is . . . was . . . the daughter of the regiment's commanding officer, Colonel Gentry, so John has known Sylvie since she was a little girl." She cleared her throat and withdrew her hand from Harriet's to blow her nose on her sodden handkerchief. "He married her on his last leave to England."

"Was that a surprise?"

Pris looked down, her fingers twisting together in her lap. "It was to me, Inspector. I had no idea John had gone with that intention, but he told me that they renewed their acquaintance when he arrived just before Christmas and were married in the New Year. A whirlwind courtship." In her grief Pris could not hide the bitterness in her tone as she added, "Since Mary's death I have looked after his home and Jack. He said nothing to me, just said it would be a short trip to England to see Colonel Gentry on a matter of regimental business. He didn't even do Jack or me the courtesy of telling us what he had done. The first we knew of the marriage was when his ship docked in March and down the gangway came Sylvie and her brother."

"Her brother?"

"Nicholas Gentry. He's a subaltern in the battalion, the assistant adjutant. He's only nineteen but really rather sweet."

Pris looked at Harriet. "A subaltern is an officer below the rank of captain."

"I know that," Harriet replied. She did so hate being patronized.

"Does he live here?" Curran asked.

Pris shook her head. "No. He has quarters in the officers' mess, although Sylvie keeps a room for him and he stays up here when he is off duty."

Curran straightened in his chair. "That concurs with what the colonel told me." With a quick glance at Harriet, he said, "I know this will be difficult, Miss Nolan, but what can you tell me about last night?"

Pris nodded and swallowed as she composed herself. "John had a dinner in the mess. James Hawke, the adjutant, came to escort him, and they left about seven thirty. Sylvie and I shared a light supper about eight but I wasn't very hungry. In fact I had a terrible headache so I went straight up to bed."

"What time was that?"

"About nine. That's right. The clock in the hall struck the hour as I climbed into bed. I'm afraid I took a sleeping powder, Inspector. Quite a strong one. I didn't know another thing until this morning when I woke to Indira screaming."

"Indira?"

"My maid. She's been with me for years, but when Sylvie came, John suggested Sylvie could share her services. She takes tea and the mail to Sylvie in the morning."

Harriet caught the slight note of resentment in Pris's voice. Not only had she given up her place as the doyenne of the household but also had to share her longtime amah with the interloper.

"Which is your bedroom?" Curran asked.

"I have a front bedroom, across from my brother. Sylvie has the bedroom next to his." Two large tears trailed down her cheek. "When it was clear that John and Sylvie would not be sharing a bedroom, I offered her mine, but she said . . . she said . . . she wouldn't dream of taking it away from me and the two bedrooms she and John occupy are connected so it seemed sensible."

"And the fourth bedroom?"

"The one across from Sylvie's is shared by Nicholas and Jack when they are at home. For other guests we have a guest bungalow."

The tears started afresh and Harriet put her arm around the woman, drawing her into her arms while Pris wept on to the shoulder of Harriet's crisp white blouse.

Curran waited for her to recover before he said, "I'm sorry, Miss Nolan, but I do have one last question for you."

Pris gave a shuddering gulp and looked up.

"Do you know what Mrs. Nolan intended to do for the remainder of the evening, after you left her?"

Pris frowned. "She said she had some letters to write and I know she liked to keep her journal up-to-date."

Curran nodded. "Ah, the journal. The colonel has mentioned it. Can you describe it?"

"Red calfskin with her initials embossed in gold on the front cover. Her uncle had given it to her when she left England. He told her life in the Far East would be so exciting and she had to record everything she saw . . ." Pris's face crumpled again. "And now she's dead."

Harriet squeezed her friend's hand. "Pris, you can't stay here," she said. "Is there a friend you can go to for a couple of days while things are sorted out?"

Pris looked around the room with its stiff, formal English furniture and nodded. "Lavinia will take me in."

Harriet glanced at Curran, who shrugged.

"Lavinia?" she asked.

"Lavinia Pemberthey-Smythe. She has a small villa in Scotts Road. She's the widow of John's predecessor, Albert Pemberthey-Smythe, who was killed in South Africa. I've known her forever."

"Do you have any further questions for Miss Nolan, Inspector?" Julian asked.

"Just a quick one. Can you describe Mrs. Nolan's jewelry for me?"

Pris frowned. "She didn't have much. Some pretty paste pieces, a diamond and garnet engagement ring from John, several strings of pearls and pearl earrings and the ruby earrings she wore all the time."

"Was she wearing them last night?"

"Yes. They were quite plain, a ruby drop from a diamond stud."

"I need to search your room, Miss Nolan."

Pris's eyes widened. "My room? Why? I had nothing to do with it. I was asleep. I could have been murdered in my bed . . ." This last thought provoked a fresh waterfall of tears. "I don't want men going through my private things. Harriet, do I have to?"

Curran rose to his feet and cleared his throat. "There is nothing to be concerned about, Miss Nolan. We have to be thorough, and I'm afraid in cases like this, all rights to privacy vanish."

Pris waved a hand at the door. She took a couple of deep shuddering breaths and looked up at the tall policeman. "I suppose so," she said. "I will need some clothes to take with me if I'm going to Lavinia's but I can't . . . I can't go up there."

Harriet rose to her feet. "Then I shall do it. Would that be all right, Inspector?"

Curran nodded and Harriet sensed his relief. "I think that's an excellent idea. Mrs. Gordon will see that propriety is observed and there is nothing upset or broken," Curran said.

Pris relaxed. "Oh please, I don't mind Harriet going through my things. I trust her discretion." She blinked, her hand going to her throat. "What about John? Where is he? Should I go to him?"

"He has retired to his own bedroom," Curran said. "Dr. Mackenzie was going to look in on him. Ah, here he is now."

Mac walked into the room. He acknowledged Harriet and Julian with a cursory nod, and it struck Harriet that he looked tired and drawn, his face almost gray in the gloomy light of the drawing room. The normally phlegmatic Scot did not allow violent death to upset him but it seemed that the death of Sylvie Nolan had reached beyond that professional exterior.

"Miss Nolan," he said, taking her hand. "I am so sorry."

Pris sniffed. "Did she . . . did she suffer?"

The faintest hesitation before the doctor replied gave Harriet the answer to the question but Pris didn't appear to notice as he said, "I doubt it."

Pris sighed, hearing the answer she wanted to hear. "Oh, that's a relief. I couldn't bear to think she suffered at all."

"What about you, Miss Nolan? Is there anything I can do for you?"

Harriet said, "We thought it prudent to be away from this sad place, so we are taking her to Mrs. Pemberthey-Smythe."

"An excellent idea," Mac replied. "Lavinia Pemberthey-Smythe is a sensible woman." He set his bag down, opened it and handed Harriet a brown paper packet. "I prescribed a mild sleeping draught for the colonel. I suggest the same for you, Miss Nolan, but maybe wait till you are away from here."

Harriet thanked him and rose to her feet. "I will see to your packing, Pris."

Pris looked up at her. "Thank you, Harriet. You are very kind. Indira knows what I need."

"I'll find her," Harriet said with a reassuring smile. "She'll need to accompany you."

Harriet and Curran left Pris in the care of her doctor and Julian. They found Indira hovering beside a magnificent grandfather clock in the hallway. Its ponderous ticktock followed Harriet up the elegant staircase that dominated the center of the house.

Constable Musa bin Osman stood guard outside the half-open door to what had been Sylvie's bedroom.

"Constable, close that door," Curran ordered—too late.

Indira shrieked, and beyond the constable, Harriet glimpsed a large, airy bedroom with wide-flung windows, the disordered bed liberally stained with dark splodges.

She shuddered and glanced up at Curran. He frowned but before he could say anything she said, "You know very well I am not squeamish, and it's not like I haven't seen violent death before."

Curran's mouth quirked. "Then you are a stronger man than I am, Mrs. Gordon. The day I see a scene like that and not feel something, is the day I know it's time to retire," he said.

Harriet nodded. "I don't suppose you ever get used to it."

Curran glanced at the now-closed door and said, "Let's concentrate on the job in hand."

Curran ordered the amah to wait in the hall and joined Harriet in the doorway to Pris's bedroom.

The windows opened on to the surrounding verandah, which had its striped awning pulled down, intensifying the gloom. The practical, solid furniture revealed very little of Pris's inner life. Her bed had not been made, the mosquito net bundled in a heap on top of rumpled linen.

"Did you know Sylvie Nolan?" Curran asked Harriet.

"No. We moved in very different social circles, Inspector. From what I hear, she seemed very popular with the younger wives, and to someone her age, Pris and I must have seemed ancient. Louisa Mackenzie may have known her better through the church ladies' committee."

"So how do you come to know Miss Nolan?"

"Pris plays tennis at the Ladies Tennis Club. We've partnered each other a few times and she has invited me here for tea, in the company of others, on a couple of occasions. I would describe her more as a good acquaintance than a close friend."

"And yet you are the first person she turns to?"

Harriet shrugged. "I have a convenient brother, who happens to be a priest as well as Jack's headmaster."

"Did she ever say anything to you about her new sister-in-law?"

Harriet shook her head. "The only time I heard her talk about Sylvie Nolan, it was in glowing terms." She paused and lowered her voice, conscious of Indira's presence in the wide hallway outside. "There were more than a few raised eyebrows at the tennis club when Nolan brought her back to Singapore— the twenty-year age difference, to begin with. Mind you, Pris was very quick to point out how wonderful it was for her brother to have a fresh chance at love."

"I understand," Curran said. "Let's get on with it. Do you mind looking through her nightstand?"

As Harriet picked up the books and bottles beside Pris's bed, it felt like a violation of the woman's privacy, and Pris was a woman who valued her privacy.

"What are we looking for?" she asked as Curran set to work, methodically riffling through the drawers of Pris's rolltop cedar desk.

Curran straightened. "To begin with, Sylvie Nolan's journal and the murder weapon."

"Which is?"

"It's possibly one of a pair of candlesticks but we have yet to search the whole house. It could turn up."

Harriet stared at him as she pictured the terrible crime, imagining a slight, terrified woman and a shadowy figure wielding a heavy candlestick. She swallowed and pushed the image away. "Why is her journal missing?"

"If I knew that, I wouldn't be looking for it. You're a woman . . . what would a young woman like Sylvie Nolan use a journal for?"

"A girl may write about parties, young men, hopes and fears . . . but a married woman . . . ?" She shrugged.

Curran regarded her for a long moment. "What did you say the age difference between Mrs. Nolan and her husband was?"

"Twenty years, I believe," she said. Her gaze met Curran's. "What are you thinking, Curran?"

Curran shook his head. "I don't know. Her jewelry is missing as well, so perhaps a thief thought it might be of some value."

He turned back to the contents of Pris's desk, flicking through a pile of letters before returning them to the drawer. "Nothing here. Miss Nolan, it seems, does not keep a journal herself."

Harriet picked up a packet of powders and a glass from the bedside table and showed them to Curran. "This is a sleeping draught," she said, "and in the bottom of that glass, there are white grains."

Curran nodded. "Seems to support her story. Get the amah in to do the packing and I'll do a more thorough search after she's left."

He paused at the door and looked back at Harriet. "Just who is this Pemberthey-Smythe woman?"

"I've never met her. She gave a talk on orchids at Victoria Hall a few months back, which I attended," Harriet said. "She struck me as somewhat eccentric but I'm afraid that is all I can tell you. Indira?"

The amah appeared at the door. "May I do mem's packing now?"

Curran turned to the maid. "Who was Mrs. Nolan's maid?"

"I was, sahib."

"When did you last see her?"

Indira frowned. "Miss Nolan went to bed." She gestured at the bedside table. "I mixed the powders for her. She does not sleep well. I heard the memsahib coming up the stairs. She asked I help her get dressed for bed. This I did but I do not know what time I left her."

"Had she gone to bed?"

"No, sahib. She was sitting at her desk, writing in her little book."

Curran smiled at the maid. "Thank you, that was very helpful. I'll leave you ladies to do what must be done."

Curran left the room and crossed the wide hallway to what had been Sylvie Nolan's bedroom, his boots echoing on the highly polished floorboards. Harriet could hear him talking to Musa but their words were muffled.

When Indira had completed her task, Harriet told the woman to pack her own things and meet her downstairs. Clutching the small suitcase Indira had packed, Harriet left the room. She paused for a long moment, her gaze on John Nolan's shut door. It was not unusual in their class for husband and wife to occupy separate bedchambers and, given the difference in their ages and interests, it seemed quite sensible. But something niggled at the back of Harriet's mind. Sylvie and John Nolan were newlyweds. The separation seemed odd.

Curran joined her on the stairs and took the bag from her. "I'll be here for some time. Can I offer the use of the motor vehicle?"

Harriet nodded. "Thank you. I don't think Pris would manage a gharry."

At the door to the living room she paused. Euan Mackenzie had left, leaving Julian alone with Pris, and as they appeared to be in prayer, Harriet and Curran stood by the door waiting until they were noticed.

Julian looked up first and touched Pris on the shoulder. "Time to go, Miss Nolan."

Harriet handed Pris a broad-brimmed straw hat and Julian, the suitcase.

"What about Indira? I can't go without her." A note of panic rose in Pris's voice.

"She's waiting outside," Harriet replied. "Now, let's get you away from here."

Pris looked around the room. "Wait . . . Pansy," she said. "What will happen to Pansy?"

Harriet and Julian exchanged puzzled glances. Did Pris have another servant she wished to accompany her?

"Who's Pansy?" Harriet asked.

Pris looked at Harriet, her swollen, red-rimmed eyes bleary with exhaustion and weeping.

"Sylvie's dog," she said.

Harriet looked at Curran and he nodded. "There's a dog tied up on the back verandah. Do you wish to take it with you, Miss Nolan?"

Pris nodded and Curran strode out of the room, returning shortly with a rotund Cavalier spaniel on a leash. As he proffered the leash to Julian, the little animal jerked free from his grip, scampering out of the room and, trailing the leash, dashed up the stairs with Julian in hot pursuit. From upstairs came an unearthly howl and Julian, flushed and his glasses askew, returned, holding the animal in his arms.

"He made straight for Mrs. Nolan's room," Julian said. "Poor beast."

"She . . . Pansy is a she. She always slept on Sylvie's bed," Pris said.

Curran stiffened. "Always? But not last night?"

Pris shook her head. "She was with her when I went to bed. This morning . . ." She frowned. "I don't know. I didn't see her."

Julian handed Pris the dog and she snuggled her face into the wriggling brown body. "I'm so sorry, Pansy," she said.

Harriet took Sylvie by the elbow, steering her out into the bright, hot morning, away from the horror of The Cedars.

Lavinia Pemberthey-Smythe's house on Scotts Road was a strange confection, built up on piles, to allow the airflow beneath the floor, with something that resembled the sort of round turret with a pointed roof one would expect to find on a fairy-tale castle tacked on to one corner. A riot of bougainvillea and orchids of every description in pots and sheltered nooks filled the garden with color.

A European woman dressed in a blue *salwar kameez*, the northern Indian costume of tunic and loose trousers, her face shaded by a large straw hat, knelt in the shade of a pergola, engaged in repotting a large orchid. Hearing the motor vehicle she looked up, groping for a convenient garden chair to assist her to stand. She came forward to greet her visitors, removing her gardening gloves and brushing dirt from her knees.

She pushed strands of graying brown hair back up under her hat, her eyes widening at the sight of a policeman behind the wheel of the motor vehicle.

"Pris! Whatever—"

Before she got any further, Pris had thrown open the door to the motor vehicle and run to the woman, burying her head in her shoulder and dislodging her hat, which fell to the ground.

"There, there, dearest. Whatever is the matter?"

Over Pris's head, Mrs. Pemberthey-Smythe raised a questioning gaze to Julian and Harriet.

Julian helped Harriet down from the vehicle and came forward, holding out his right hand. "Mrs. Pemberthey-Smythe, we haven't met. I'm the Reverend Edwards and this is my sister, Mrs. Gordon."

"You're the principal of St. Tom's. Jack has spoken of you."

"I am but that's not why we're here. Miss Nolan needs a friendly place to stay for a few days. There's been a—"

"A murder!" Pris thrust herself out of Mrs. Pemberthey-Smythe's embrace. "We may as well call it what it is. Sylvie's dead, Lavinia. Murdered in her bed while I slept in the house."

"Murdered? Oh, my dear!" Lavinia Pemberthey-Smythe's hand flew to her throat. "How simply dreadful."

"The police are all over the house and John is distraught," Pris continued.

Lavinia Pemberthey-Smythe looked from Harriet to Julian, her distress and a hundred questions written on her face.

"We felt Miss Nolan should stay with a friend," Julian said.

"There's no question . . . of course you can stay here." Mrs. Pemberthey-Smythe put an arm around Pris's shoulder. "Now, come up to the house and we will have a cup of tea. Mrs. Gordon, Reverend, you will stay awhile?"

Julian touched Harriet's arm. "I'll tell Tan to return the motor vehicle to Curran. We can summon a gharry to take us home."

While Julian spoke to the police constable, Harriet lifted Pansy down out of the motor vehicle and set her on the ground. Pansy cowered at her feet, looking up at Harriet with large, sorrowful eyes.

Lavinia Pemberthey-Smythe glanced down at the little dog. "Is that poor Sylvie's dog? Do you mind bringing her up to the house, Mrs. Gordon, and we'll get Pris settled. Indira, please take Miss Nolan's bag."

Pris drooped against her friend and Julian and Harriet, leading a dejected Pansy, followed them up the stone stairs to the broad, cool verandah.

Mrs. Pemberthey-Smythe clapped her hands and, at the appearance of an elderly female servant dressed in a neat dark-blue sari, gave orders for tea and a bowl of water and some food for the dog.

Pris collapsed onto one of the brightly cushioned rattan chairs and covered her eyes with her right hand. Indira, carrying Pris's suitcase and her own small bundle, followed the servant into the house.

The servant reappeared a few minutes later with a tray and Mrs. Pemberthey-Smythe poured tea into once-elegant Wedgwood teacups. The pattern had faded and the cup handed to Harriet had several chips in it.

The dog lapped greedily at the bowl of water and Pris drank the tea as if it were the elixir of life, the cup clutched in both hands.

Lavinia Pemberthey-Smythe leaned over and patted Pris on the arm. "You look all done in, my poor dear," she said. "Amira is just making up the spare bed for you and then may I suggest you retire for a rest?"

Pris set her cup down and ran a hand over her eyes. "I would like that, but every time I close my eyes, I keep seeing . . . her. It was dreadful, Lavinia. I'll never forget it."

Harriet fumbled in her handbag for the packet of powders

Dr. Mackenzie had given her. She handed this to Lavinia, who read the instructions written on the packet and nodded.

"I'll come with you and see you settled, my dear," Lavinia said.

Harriet glanced at Julian. This seemed an appropriate moment to take their own leave, and as Pris roused herself and rose wearily to her feet, Julian stood.

"We'll leave you in peace, Miss Nolan. If there is anything more my sister or I can do for you . . . ?"

Pris held out a hand to him. "Thank you for your kindness, Reverend Edwards," she said with something that passed for a smile. "There is one thing more. Jack must be told and I don't believe either his father or I are in a position to break the news. Will you do that for us?"

Julian patted her hand. "Of course. Leave it with me, Miss Nolan."

Lavinia Pemberthey-Smythe held up a hand. "Let me just see Pris to her room. Please don't hurry away. Amira, more tea for my guests."

There seemed little alternative but to stay. Lavinia Pemberthey-Smythe's long years as the wife of the commanding officer of the battalion gave her apparently simple request the effect of an order, so Harriet poured herself another cup of tea and sat back in the comfortable chair, looking out over the riotous garden.

"I wonder if Mrs. Pemberthey-Smythe would be willing to give me some advice on what to do with the garden at St. Tom's House," she mused.

Julian blinked at her behind his glasses. "Harri, this is hardly the time to be thinking about gardens."

Chastened, Harriet set her cup down and distracted herself with petting Pansy, who had fallen in a heap at her feet. "Why was Pansy shut out of the house last night?" she asked no one in particular.

Julian gave the animal a baleful glance. "Probably a damn nuisance in the house," he said.

Harriet smiled. "You're not really a dog person, are you?"

Julian shook his head. "Ever since that awful beast next door bit me. Do you remember? I still have the scar." He rubbed his leg. "Just lucky it wasn't rabid."

Harriet laughed. "It was an extremely spoiled Pekingese. Unlikely to be rabid, particularly in Wimbledon." She paused. "Besides, it was the other leg."

Julian glared at her. "You're missing the point. Give me a cat any day."

"Are you disparaging dogs?" Lavinia Pemberthey-Smythe rejoined them on the verandah. She poured herself a cup of the now-tepid tea and sank into her chair. "Poor dear was asleep almost as soon as her head touched the pillow." She shook her head. "This is a terrible thing to have happened. Between us, I thought at the time that John's marriage to such a young girl would never end well."

"Did you know the new Mrs. Nolan?" Harriet asked.

"Of course I did. Sylvie's father is Colonel Gentry, the commanding officer of the South Sussex Regiment. I remember her as a babe in her mother's arms and, of course, I knew John's first wife, Mary, too."

Not coming from a military background herself, it always seemed a mysterious and closed community to Harriet. She understood enough to know that a regiment consisted of a number of battalions, and while Colonel Gentry commanded the entire regiment, Lieutenant Colonel Nolan and his predecessor, Lavinia Pemberthey-Smythe's late husband, commanded the First Battalion, currently posted to Singapore. There would be a Second and a Third Battalion floating around the empire somewhere.

Even she could see that the marriage of John Nolan and his

commander's daughter carried a greater significance than had previously occurred to her.

"Was it her choice to marry him?" she blurted out.

Lavinia Pemberthey-Smythe cast her a curious glance. "I have no reason to think otherwise," she said. "Why would you ask?"

"The age difference?" Harriet ventured.

Lavinia Pemberthey-Smythe considered for a long moment. "By all accounts it was a happy match," she said with no warmth in her voice, and Harriet noted that she had not used the words *love match*. "Age is no barrier to attachment, Mrs. Gordon."

"How old was she?"

"She turned eighteen on the boat out from England."

So young! But then again James Gordon had been ten years her senior and the age difference had felt like nothing at all.

Harriet returned to petting the dog as the full significance of Sylvie Nolan's death sank in.

"Who is in charge of the investigation?" Lavinia Pemberthey-Smythe asked.

"Inspector Curran of the Detective Branch of the Straits Settlements Police," Julian replied.

"Ah, Curran. Did I hear he had been a military policeman? That augurs well, but of course, he is not one of the family, if you know what I mean," Lavinia said.

"I'm not sure that I do," Harriet said.

"The regimental family," Lavinia Pemberthey-Smythe replied. "We like to take care of our own."

"You mean that any official investigation by a civilian is going to be difficult?" Harriet said.

Lavinia Pemberthey-Smythe shrugged. "I have no doubt the military police will take over." She paused. "They will certainly want to keep it in family. Tell me, how did poor Sylvie die?"

"We understand she was bludgeoned with a heavy implement in her bedroom," Harriet said.

The woman stared at her, all the color draining from her

face. "Who would do such a thing? She was vapid and silly but all girls that age are. I certainly can't think of anyone who would want to kill her and in such a brutal manner." She shook her head. "Did Pris see the body?"

"I think she might have glimpsed the scene. It was most unpleasant," Harriet said, avoiding her brother's horrified eyes.

"How simply dreadful," Lavinia Pemberthey-Smythe said. "Now, may I offer you more tea?"

Harriet declined and rose to her feet. "We have detained you long enough, Mrs. Pemberthey-Smythe. Julian, we should be going. I believe there is a gharry stand at the end of the road."

"Do you want me to fetch one?" Julian said.

Harriet shook her head. "We'll walk together." She extended her hand to the older woman. "Thank you for the tea and for taking Miss Nolan in without notice. Would it be inconvenient if I were to call tomorrow morning and see how she is faring?"

Lavinia Pemberthey-Smythe took her hand. "Not at all. I think Pris will need all her friends. Come about eleven and take tea with us." She turned to Julian. "Thank you for bringing Pris to me. She certainly could not have stayed in the house." She shuddered. "Do the police have any notion of the perpetrator? An intruder? A robbery gone wrong?"

Harriet shook her head. "It is far too early to say," she said. "I look forward to taking tea with you tomorrow morning."

Lavinia Pemberthey-Smythe nodded, pushing her wayward hair back behind her ear. "And I look forward to getting to know you, Mrs. Gordon. I have heard a lot about you."

Harriet let her gaze rest on the woman's enigmatic smile. "From whom?"

"You will be surprised. Until tomorrow, Mrs. Gordon."

❧ FOUR

Lieutenant Colonel John Nolan stood by the window in his bedroom, his hands behind his back, looking down at the garden where Curran's men were conducting a search. Curran concluded his search of the room and cleared his throat. Nolan turned to look at him.

"This is intrusive, Inspector," he said.

Curran met Nolan's cold gray eyes. "I am afraid murder is, Colonel."

This man bore no resemblance to the shattered, broken man of a few hours ago. Fully dressed and shaved, he had reassumed his persona as a commanding officer in one of the finest regiments in the British Army.

Although he was probably only a few years older than Curran, those years seemed like a lifetime. His service in the army had left their mark on the policeman and he felt his inferior rank under the colonel's sharp, critical gaze. Three stars on his shoulder did not equal the star and the crown on the colonel's uniform. In military terms he sat two ranks below this man and he felt it.

"Your name is familiar," Nolan said. "Have you served in the army?"

A prickle of uncertainly ran down Curran's spine.

"The name may be familiar to you. My father was an officer in the South Sussex, sir. He died in Afghanistan."

Nolan's eyes widened. "Edward Curran?"

"The same."

"If I were you, I would not mention that in your dealings with others."

Curran frowned. "Why?"

Nolan ignored the question. "What about you, Curran? Have you seen service?"

"I had ten years as an officer in the Mounted Military Police," he said. "I left after I was wounded in South Africa."

Nolan said nothing for a long moment, and when he did, his lip curled. "Traffic management not to your taste, Curran."

If the remark had been intended to get a rise, Curran refused to play that game. He adopted a tight smile as he said, "We both know there was more to the role than that. I saw things in South Africa I wish never to see again."

Nolan broke the gaze and looked away. "I lost my best friend, Bertie Pemberthey-Smythe, in that campaign. I won't tell you what those bastards did to him."

The name resounded. "Lavinia Pemberthey-Smythe—?"

"Is his widow. Odd woman but she's good to Pris."

"Odd? In what way?"

"We all expected her to settle back in England after Jack's death but after a couple of years she turned up here in Singapore. Said she had always wanted to grow orchids." He shook his head. "Can't fathom her myself."

"Mrs. Gordon and the Reverend Edwards have escorted your sister to her home. It seemed sensible for her to stay with a friend."

Nolan nodded. "Best place for her. What about young Jack?

He's staying with friends on the east coast. Perhaps Reverend Edwards could be prevailed upon to tell him . . . tell him what has happened?"

Curran nodded. "If you like, I'll ask him to do that."

Nolan's shoulders sagged. "Thank you, that would be a kindness. He would do it better than me. I think it preferable Jack stays on where he is for the time being. I don't want him here until . . ." He faltered, and as if remembering who he was, straightened again. ". . . until the house is restored to normality, if it ever can be." He turned back to the window. "Where is she, Inspector?"

"She's in the care of Dr. Mackenzie at the hospital."

"I don't like the thought of her alone in a . . . in a . . . place like that. I want her back and buried as soon as possible."

"You'd not been married long?"

The man by the window coughed. "No. We were married on my last home leave. I brought her back with me in March." He gave a hollow laugh. "You probably think me an old fool, Curran, but I loved her and, despite the age difference, she loved me."

"Yet you maintained separate bedrooms?" Curran ventured.

Nolan whirled around. "That's not unusual for people of our class. If you were a gentleman, and you sound like one, you should know that. I keep erratic hours and she liked her feminine things around her. Not one for lace and muslin myself."

Curran kept his peace. "I have to ask these questions," he said.

"Why? She was killed by a bloody intruder. Surely that's obvious?"

"Nothing is obvious, until I make it so. Now, do you mind recounting your movements last night?"

The colonel's eyebrows rose in fury but he took a steadying breath and his shoulders relaxed. "Of course you have to ask these questions. I told you we had a mess dinner. I last saw Syl about seven thirty. She and Pris were taking sherry on the verandah and Hawke had called to escort me—"

"Hawke?"

"Captain James Hawke, my adjutant. We live so close to the barracks it was hardly worth summoning the carriage but it was proper I be escorted."

"And the dinner?"

"Began at eight. We rose from the table around eleven and adjourned to the anteroom. The junior officers were keen for some mess games and"—he shrugged—"you should recall how these things go."

Curran remembered the long, tedious dining-in nights in the officers' mess that always culminated with "mess games," drunken romps in the anteroom. He had once sprained an ankle trying to circumnavigate the room without touching the floor. The key ingredient to any of these "games" was alcohol, plenty of alcohol.

To make it even more tedious, no one could leave until the senior officers departed, and if they were in the mood for sport, the evening dragged well into the early hours of the morning.

"What time did you leave?"

Nolan considered the question. "Well after one. I left by the main gate and walked home—"

"By yourself?"

"Yes." Nolan sounded testy.

"Did you see anyone on your walk?"

"No. Just the guards on the gate."

"What time did you get home?"

"About half past one. The clock in the hall had just struck the half hour. I heard it as I turned the key. See here, Curran, what's the meaning of all these damn questions? I didn't kill her."

"I have to ask them, sir. Were there any lights or movement in the house?"

Nolan shook his head. "No. The house was dark and quiet. The servants had all retired. I lit the lamp Abdul had left out for me and went upstairs. I told you I knocked on the adjoining door into Sylvie's room but got no answer."

Curran narrowed his eyes. "You only knocked?"

A muscle twitched in Nolan's cheek. "Very well, I tried the door but it was locked, and before you ask, that was not unusual. I told you before, Sylvie hates . . . hated to be disturbed. I thought nothing more about it and went to my own bed."

"Did you try the door into the hall?"

Color stained the colonel's cheeks. "As a matter of fact, I did. It was locked too. I took the hint and retired to my own bed."

"You heard nothing else during the night?"

Nolan shook his head. "No. Slept like the dead . . . Unfortunate figure of speech." The color drained from his face and he took a deep breath as he composed himself. "Abdul woke me at seven with tea and the paper as he always does. I heard Indira out in the corridor knocking on Sylvie's door so I rose and took the tray from her. Used my own key to open the door. The rest you know."

Curran nodded. "Thank you, Colonel. With your permission of course, I need to interview the officers present at the dinner last night, starting with Mrs. Nolan's brother."

Nolan huffed out a breath. "Of course, I doubt anyone's told him yet. Best coming from you. I'll write you a chitty. My second-in-command, Major Pardew, is up-country at the moment with his family enjoying a spot of leave in the Cameron Highlands, so I suggest you present yourself to Hawke and he'll give you every cooperation. My desk's downstairs."

They met the majordomo, Abdul, coming up the stairs. "Colonel, sahib," he said. "Major Goff is waiting in the library."

Curran's step faltered on the stair. Nolan didn't appear to notice anything amiss and clattered down the stairs, striding into a room behind the dining room. Curran followed, every step an effort.

Major Percival Goff stood at ease in the middle of the fine oriental rug. He had not changed since he and Curran had served together in South Africa. He'd been a captain then. Captain Goff of the MPs, the military police. At first sight he hardly presented a fearsome aspect. In height he probably barely touched five feet six inches, but his solid build and blunt, pugnacious features told of a man who would not be crossed and who did not forget.

His gaze met Curran's and his eyes narrowed. No, Goff had not forgotten.

However in the presence of a superior officer, he drew himself up sharply. "Colonel Nolan, sir. My deepest condolences on your loss."

"Thank you. Inspector Curran, I'd like to introduce you to the provost marshal, Major Goff."

Goff glared at Curran. "Captain Curran and I are acquainted, sir."

"Of course, South Africa," Nolan said.

"Word reached me, sir, about poor Mrs. Nolan and I am here to assume the responsibility for the investigation into her death." Goff's gaze slid across to Curran.

The muscles in Nolan's jaw tightened. "I've telephoned the inspector general of the Straits Settlements Police to clarify the situation. My wife was a civilian and he informs me that investigation of her death comes under their jurisdiction."

"With respect, sir, this is a military matter—"

"As Cuscaden explained to me, it is *not* a military matter, Goff," Nolan said. "I am certain she met with foul play at the hand of an intruder and once the perpetrator is discovered he will be dealt with in a court of civilian law."

Goff's jaw jutted in the direction of Curran. "And Cuscaden is putting this man in charge? With the greatest respect, sir, I do not believe that this man is capable of finding a needle in a stack of needles, let alone a murderer."

Curran tensed as if Goff had physically assaulted him.

"His father was Lieutenant Edward Curran." Goff paused for dramatic effect. "The Coward of Kandahar."

Curran drew a long breath. He'd never heard his father referred to as the "Coward of Kandahar." How like the army to saddle the dead and defenseless man with such a disparaging epithet.

"This is nothing to do with my father, sir. In South Africa Major Goff and I had certain differences stemming from the treatment of prisoners in his custody but I have put that time behind me. If you have any doubt about my capabilities with respect to the investigation of your wife's murder, Colonel Nolan, I suggest you take the matter up with Inspector General Cuscaden."

"My wife is not a bone to be fought over by scrapping dogs," Nolan said. "Goff, I will speak with Cuscaden again, but in the meantime, Curran here has my confidence and support. He will continue with the investigation and I expect him to be accorded the full support of all military personnel."

"But Colonel Gentry would expect—"

"The colonel is not here and I will be the one to deal with Colonel Gentry. In the meantime, Goff, you may escort Inspector Curran to Captain Hawke with my compliments."

He turned to the teak desk that stood facing the door and scribbled a few lines on headed notepaper.

"There you are, Curran. Just present that at the gate and you will be accorded entry into the barracks without hindrance."

Curran thanked him.

"You are dismissed, gentlemen. Curran, I expect a daily report on progress."

Outside Curran saw that the car had returned. He paused to give instructions to Tan to take a message to Reverend Edwards and his sister and, if required, drive them out to the east coast to break the news to Jack Nolan. At the end of the driveway and out of hearing of the house, Goff rounded on Curran.

"Don't think I've forgotten, Curran." He jabbed a finger in Curran's chest. "As far as I am concerned, you have a week. If you haven't brought the man to ground by next Friday, I will raise hell. Understood?"

Curran drew on his aristocratic upbringing and looked down at Goff. "Don't threaten me, Goff. We're not in South Africa now."

Harriet and Julian returned to St. Tom's House to find Curran's motor vehicle waiting by the front steps. Constable Tan stood on the verandah, spinning his hat in his hands.

"Tan!" Julian hailed the constable as he walked up the drive. "I thought you'd gone back to the inspector. What brings you here?"

Tan held out a folded paper. "I have a message from the inspector."

Julian scanned the note and handed it to Harriet. On a page torn from his notebook, Curran had written:

Edwards, the boy has to be told about his stepmother.
Nolan is not up to it and I can't leave the crime scene yet.
Nolan has requested you and Harriet should be the ones to
break the news. You know the lad and the people he's
staying with. The motor vehicle is at your disposal.

Curran

Julian glanced at his watch. "We'll go now. Harri, can you tell Huo Jin we will be late for luncheon? Now, what is the address of the villa where the Mitchells are staying?"

"It is just out of Kampong Katong," Tan offered. "The inspector asked the colonel."

In other circumstances, it would have been a pleasant drive but Harriet harbored bad memories of Kampong Katong, the once-sleepy fishing village that now serviced the beach villas and hotels that ran along the southeastern seashore of the island. She still had nightmares of her time held captive in one such villa during the affair of the stolen sapphire back in March.

They found the Mitchells' bungalow without a problem. Unlike the secluded house where Harriet had been taken, the Mitchells had rented a pleasant villa across the road from a beach fringed with palm trees shading the white sand. As they alighted from the motor vehicle, Harriet could see the distant figures of two European boys dressed in heavy woolen bathing suits, whooping in the shallows. How wonderful to be so free of care, she thought.

Harriet and Julian were greeted with alarm by Mrs. Mitchell, and a servant was dispatched to fetch the boys. While they waited, Mrs. Mitchell plied them with yet more tea and cakes, and did her utmost to ascertain what had occurred of such importance it required the attendance of Jack's headmaster and his sister.

Julian firmly resisted her entreaties, saying it was a matter for Jack.

The syce entered the airy, pleasant living room, shepherding Jack Nolan and Michael Mitchell. The barefooted boys dripped water from their bathing suits onto the tiles, their fair skin red from the days in the sun.

Already large for his age, Jack Nolan had his father's blunt features and solid build, and at school as one of the seniors, he commanded a following of boys such as Michael Mitchell. In any walk of society, Jack Nolan would always be the leader and Mitchell, a follower.

Seeing Julian, he narrowed his eyes and lowered his head, his hands behind his back, shuffling his feet, his gaze fixed on his bare toes. He had been hauled before his headmaster enough times to sense trouble, and for the headmaster to come and seek him out during the school holidays, it had to be serious.

Mrs. Mitchell told her son to leave the room and turned to follow, but Julian held up a hand to detain her.

"Mrs. Mitchell, please stay."

At that Jack looked up, his gaze flitting from Julian to Harriet. His normal, bluff bravado seemed to leech from him.

"I'm not in trouble, am I?" Jack's chin jutted in a show of belligerence belied by his worried eyes. "Because Jones . . ."

Julian shook his head. "I don't want to know what you and Jones have been up to. No, Nolan, you're not in trouble. I'm afraid I have some rather bad news for you. There's been an accident—"

"Papa . . . Aunt Pris . . . ?" Jack straightened his shoulders, bracing himself for what was to come.

Julian shook his head. "They're both fine. It's your step-mother. I'm afraid she was found dead this morning."

Jack blinked. "Sylvie? Dead?"

"Yes—"

"Good!"

Harriet stifled a gasp. Of all the reactions she had expected, this emphatic exclamation took her by surprise—took them all by surprise. Julian took a step back and Mrs. Mitchell let out a soft cry.

"Jack," Mrs. Mitchell began, "that's not—"

Jack drew himself up and turned a hot, angry gaze on Mrs. Mitchell. "I hated her and she hated me. It was her idea I should board at St. Tom's so she had Papa all to herself."

"Jack, she died in the most awful way," Harriet said, torn between some sympathy for the boy and angered by his reaction. "She was murdered."

Jack stared at her. He blinked and looked at Julian as if seeking confirmation. "Murdered? You mean someone killed her?" he said in a very small voice. "How?"

Julian shook his head. "You don't need to know the details, lad."

The boy's mouth twisted. "I . . . I didn't mean what I said. It's just that she killed my dog."

"Your dog?" Harriet glanced at Julian.

"She said he was horrid and smelly and he attacked Pansy. He didn't! He would never but she told Papa he had and he took Rufus away and shot him."

A large tear trailed down Jack's cheek and in a very soft voice he said, "Mama gave me Rufus before she died. She found a pye-dog and her pups. They were all dead except Rufus so she picked him up and brought him home."

A lump formed in Harriet's chest. How did one provide any form of solace to a boy who had his mother supplanted by a stranger, not many years older than him, who, in a few short months, had removed the last link the boy had with his own dead mother and banished him from his father's house? Little wonder his tears were for a dead dog, not his stepmother.

Julian placed a hand on the boy's shoulder. "I'm sorry, Nolan. I really am."

Jack sniffed away the shaming tears and straightened, once more a proper English boy. "How's Papa?"

"He's very upset," Julian said carefully.

"What about Aunt Pris? Is she all right?" The boy's eyes widened. "She wasn't hurt, was she?"

Harriet managed a reassuring smile. "She's staying with a friend. Mrs. Pemberthey-Smythe. Do you know her?"

Jack nodded. "She's nice."

Julian looked at Mrs. Mitchell, who had sunk into one of the rattan armchairs, her face drained of color, tears in her eyes. "I suggest, Mrs. Mitchell, that Jack stays with you for another few days, just while matters in town are sorted out."

Mrs. Mitchell rose to her feet and folded a resisting Jack to her maternal bosom. "Of course, poor lamb, we'll look after you."

Julian glanced at Harriet. "We better get the police vehicle back to town. Thank you, Mrs. Mitchell. The family will send word when it is appropriate for Jack to come home."

The woman nodded. "Do the police have any idea who would have done such a thing?"

Julian shook his head. "No."

"Poor Sylvie. Such a lovely girl. She didn't have an enemy in the world." Mrs. Mitchell's lip wobbled again and Harriet cast a glance at the boy she held folded in her arms.

"Was she a friend of yours, Mrs. Mitchell?"

The woman sniffed and nodded. "This is a terrible thing. I hope the perpetrator is caught."

They waited until the motor vehicle had turned back onto Beach Road before Julian sank back against the leather squab, rubbing his hand across his eyes, and Harriet let out a long sigh. She hadn't been conscious of holding her breath.

She glanced at her brother. "Despite what Mrs. Mitchell might say, it would seem the perfect Sylvie was not that perfect after all."

Julian shook his head. "Who is?"

❦ FIVE

Captain James Hawke, adjutant of the First Battalion South Sussex Regiment, received Curran in his office. He rose from behind his desk and looked Curran up and down, a supercilious smile lifting the corners of his neat moustache. Curran met the man's gaze and returned the inspection.

A handsome devil, Curran concluded, from the heavily pomaded black hair and trimmed moustache to the tip of his well-polished boot, he carried himself with a confidence and swagger that Curran had encountered before among the professional army officers of his acquaintance. They carried the expectations of an empire on their shoulders, and they knew it.

"You wear an officer's rank." Hawke indicated the three pips on the epaulette of Curran's khaki jacket.

"I am an officer and entitled to be addressed by my police rank or my former military rank, which was captain. We are equals, you and I, Hawke, so as brother officers, I expect to be accorded every cooperation by you and the members of this regiment."

He hated to admit it, but the encounter with Goff had thrown him off-balance. The regiment was a world he knew but to which he no longer belonged. He wore a soldier's rank but would never again be one of them or accepted by them.

The moustache could not quite hide Hawke's thin lips and these tightened, but he nodded and gestured at a chair across the desk from him. Curran noted that the visitor's chair was slightly lower than that behind the desk, immediately putting any incumbent at a disadvantage.

"Thank you, I prefer to stand," he said.

Hawke resumed his own seat, picking up a pencil and twirling it between the fingers of his left hand like a baton. "What regiment?" he asked.

"I served with the Mounted Military Police for ten years."

Hawke's lip curled in the same supercilious smirk. "The MMPs? Hardly a choice for a gentleman of breeding."

Just for a moment Curran toyed with playing his societal rank, after all he was the grandson of an earl, but decided against it. Given his relationship with his uncle, the current Earl of Alcester, it would be the height of hypocrisy and Curran did not like to think of himself as a hypocrite.

"I know why you're here." Hawke straightened in his chair. "The battalion is like a family. The colonel only has to sneeze and the whole barracks knows it. Is it true she was found dead in her bed? Murder?"

Curran watched the man carefully as he said, "Yes, murder."

The pencil stilled. "No chance it could be an accident?"

"Her head had been stove in with a candlestick. Hardly an accident."

"No!" The pencil snapped between the adjutant's fingers.

He spoke with such vehemence, Curran wondered if the man believed that by denying the act, he could pretend it never occurred.

He let a long moment of silence pass before Hawke cleared his throat. "How is the colonel?"

"Badly shaken."

"Sylvie Nolan was the daughter of our commanding officer. Did you know that, Curran?"

"Yes."

Hawke began to rise from his chair. "Colonel Gentry must be told. He will want Goff to take over the investigation."

Curran held up a hand. As it was, it had taken some difficulty to prevent Goff from accompanying him to this interview. "I have already had that discussion and the inspector general has confirmed with the colonel that, as Mrs. Nolan was a civilian, this is a matter for the Straits Settlements Police, not the provost marshal. It is in that capacity that I now have questions for you, Captain Hawke."

Hawke subsided, a frown forming between his dark eyebrows. "Me? I can't tell you anything."

"Let us start with the recent marriage of the colonel and Mrs. Nolan. What do you know about the circumstances of the marriage?"

Hawke shook his head. "Nothing. Absolutely none of my business, you understand? The colonel took home leave just before Christmas and returned in March with Sylvie—Mrs. Nolan—as his bride. We were surprised, of course, but delighted. A regimental wedding . . . keeps it in the family, so to speak."

"Did you know Mrs. Nolan before her marriage?"

Hawke picked up the broken pencil and began doodling on his blotter with his left hand. "We had met on a few occasions back in England, but the battalion has been away from home for years, Inspector, and of course, she was still a very young girl on those occasions." He shook his head. "She was only just eighteen. What a waste."

"And did you have much to do with her since her arrival in Singapore?"

Hawke looked up from his doodling. "Of course. She was

born to the role of the colonel's lady. She was a wonderful hostess and invited the officers to dine on a regular basis. She is—was—the kindest, sweetest woman. Everyone who met her could not help but be enchanted by her."

"And what of her relationship with her husband?"

Hawke's brow furrowed and his eyes narrowed. "What are you implying, Curran?"

Curran shook his head. "Nothing. There was an age discrepancy of many years, I am merely curious about your observations about the Nolans as a couple."

Hawke's chin jutted. "That is an impertinent question, Curran." When Curran didn't respond, he continued, "They were devoted to each other."

"So a love match?"

"Absolutely, and if you imply otherwise, I . . ." He threw the stump of the pencil onto the blotter to emphasize his point.

Curran changed the subject. "Tell me about last night?"

"It was a dining-in night in the officers' mess. The regimental birthday."

"Who was present?"

Hawke sneered. "Call yourself an officer? If you've attended such an event, you would know that every officer of the battalion was present and guests from general command and other units. Colonel Nolan was the dining president and Lieutenant Gentry the vice president for the night."

"Did anyone leave the mess during the evening?"

"No one left during the meal. You know the rules, Curran. No one leaves the table, for any reason."

Curran remembered the excruciating agony of dining-in nights when it was not uncommon for the officers to pass a receptacle under the table in which to relieve bursting bladders. He had hated those events.

"Who else was present?"

The question seemed to genuinely confuse Hawke. He frowned. "I told you . . ."

"Oh, come on, I am not talking about the men at the table," Curran said. "What about a band, mess staff, punkah wallahs?"

"Well, yes, the regimental band played us in to dinner with the regimental march and the national anthem, and of course, the mess staff."

"Good. I want a complete list of every single person present in the officers' mess last night. What time did it finish?"

"Late." Hawke grimaced. "Or should I say, early. The junior officers were in a lively mood and we played mess games until well after two. As duty officer I couldn't leave until it all concluded. In the end I pulled rank and sent them on their way."

"I believe you called on Colonel Nolan last night to accompany him to the dinner?"

"Yes. I called on him at seven thirty as arranged. Mrs. Nolan and Miss Nolan were taking sherry on the verandah. I stopped to bid them both a good evening."

"How did Mrs. Nolan seem to you?"

Hawke considered this question for a long moment. "Her usual bright and charming self," he said at last. His mouth twitched. "And that, Inspector, is how I would like to remember her."

"Do you live in the mess?"

"All the single or unaccompanied officers do. Major Pardew and Colonel Nolan and a few of the accompanied officers have married quarters outside of barracks, further up the hill."

"What about Mrs. Nolan's brother, Lieutenant Gentry?"

Hawke ran a hand across his eyes. "Oh God, poor Gentry. He won't know what's happened. He has to be told."

"Is he on duty?"

Hawke shook his head. "No. Once his duties as Mr. Vice were over, I'm afraid he hit the port and whiskey rather hard. I excused him from duty today. He's probably still in bed."

Curran opened the door. "I would be grateful if you could take me to him."

A low, double-storied building with a heavy thatched roof, surrounded on three sides by a wide verandah amply populated with planters' chairs, formed the residential accommodation for the officers of the battalion. Curran had seen enough of these standard official buildings to know that downstairs would be a living room, referred to as the *anteroom*, and a dining room and upstairs the bedrooms.

Hawke opened the doors into the wide, tiled hallway that lay between the dining room and the antechamber. A dark wooden staircase led to an upper level. Through the door into the anteroom, Curran could see three officers lounging in comfortable rattan armchairs, beside the double doors that stood open to the verandah. The building smelled of tobacco and port. It reminded Curran of the gentlemen's clubs in London and the Explorers and Geographers Club here in Singapore.

"There are plans to build a new mess," Hawke said as he gestured to the stairs. "This one just isn't big enough."

At the top of the stairs, a long corridor with rooms opening on either side ran on both sides of the stairwell. Junior officers would occupy the rooms to the right and Hawke turned in this direction. Heavy wooden doors lined the long corridor with patterned openwork ventilation above each one.

"We accommodate two to a room," the adjutant said as he scanned the names neatly inscribed on cards and inserted into brass holders on the doors. "Here we are."

The names on the door read: LT. N. GENTRY, LT. G. COX.

"Captain Hawke, sir." A thin man of short build and graying, thinning hair, came out of a room at the far end of the corridor, hastily pulling down his shirtsleeves as he hurried toward them.

"Gentry still in bed, Billings?" Hawke asked.

"Yes, sir. Left orders not to be disturbed, begging your pardon, sir."

Curran turned to the man. "Billings? Were you the colonel's batman?"

Billings straightened. "Yes, sir. Been his batman since he was a subaltern, sir."

"Inspector Curran, Straits Settlements Police. I would like to talk to you at some point."

The man blinked. "Me, sir? What about? I ain't in trouble."

"No—"

Hawke cut across him. "You'll hear soon enough. Get back to your work, Billings."

The batman glanced at the door and back at the adjutant. "Yes, sir."

As Billings returned at a snail's pace to his room at the end of the corridor, Hawke rapped on Gentry's door and without waiting for an answer opened it. The room was in darkness, blinds drawn on the windows and the double doors to the outside verandah firmly shut.

It took Curran a moment to adjust his eyes to the gloom. Two beds stood on either side of the central door to the verandah. Each man had a wardrobe and a small table and chair on their side of the room. A lump in the bed on the right-hand side indicated the presence of one officer still firmly abed. The other bed had been neatly made, the sheets and coverlet pulled tight and firm with a familiar military precision.

Curran's nose twitched at the stink of stale alcohol and vomit that pervaded the stuffy room.

"Go away, Billings. I told you I don't want a blasted cup of tea," said a voice from beneath the covers.

Hawke marched over to the window and pulled up the blind.

"Time to get up, Gentry," he snapped.

The bedcover was pushed back and an unshaven, tousled head emerged, eyes blinking in the daylight. Seeing Hawke, Gentry sat bolt upright. "Sir!"

Hawke considered the young man. "You look like hell, Gentry. You have ten minutes to tidy yourself up and present yourself to me in the dining room."

Curran bit back his annoyance. It would have suited him to have questioned the lad while he was still befuddled from his alcoholic stupor, but he had no choice but to acquiesce, and while they waited for Gentry in the cool, hushed atmosphere of the officers' mess dining room, Curran took a moment to inspect the scene of the festivities. Sometime during the night, an army of servants had cleaned and polished the long wooden tables and restored the battalion silverware to the locked glass-fronted cupboards, leaving no evidence of the dining-in night.

The tables were now set neatly for lunch. Several pairs of double doors opened out onto the verandah and a single servant's door led to the covered walkway and the kitchens and servants' wing. Two rows of stationary punkahs were suspended above the double row of tables. These would be operated by unseen punkah wallahs, whose posts on the kitchen side of the wall were currently deserted while the room was not in use.

The door from the hall opened and Gentry entered, shaved and dressed in his working uniform. Heavy circles under his eyes still bore testimony to a hard night.

The young man came to attention. "You wished to see me, sir," he said.

Hawke waved a hand. "Relax, Gentry, you're not in trouble. This is"—he paused as if wrestling with the decision about how to introduce Curran—"Inspector Curran of the Straits Settlements Police."

Gentry turned troubled, red-rimmed eyes on Curran. "Civvy police?" He frowned. "One of the chaps in trouble?"

There was never an easy way to impart news of a sudden, violent death, and short, sharp and blunt had, in Curran's experience, proved kindest.

"I am afraid I am the bearer of bad news, Gentry. Your sister was found dead this morning."

The young man's mouth fell open and he swallowed, his Adam's apple rising and falling. "Sylvie? Dead?" He looked from one man to the other. "No! There must be a mistake. Sir?"

Hawke's attention seemed to be distracted by a spider's web in the far corner of the room as he said, "It's true, I'm afraid."

"Not Sylvie . . ." Gentry looked from one man to the other. "How?"

"She was murdered, bludgeoned in her bedroom," Curran said.

Gentry sagged at the knees, his hand groping for the back of the nearest chair, his face already gray from his hangover blanched of all color. He ran a hand through his freshly combed, damp hair.

"Dear God," Gentry said, "I'm going to be sick."

Hawke waved at the door to the verandah and Gentry rushed outside.

"That was harsh," Hawke said.

Curran shrugged. "Had to be done."

Gentry returned a few minutes later, pale and sweating but composed. Hawke sat him in a chair and a mess steward produced a glass of whiskey, which the young man downed with one gulp. Some color began to creep back into his face and he swallowed.

"How's the colonel?" he asked.

"Shaken," Hawke replied.

"Oh God, Father," the young man said faintly. "He must be told."

"Colonel Nolan will attend to that, Gentry," Hawke said.

Gentry stood up. "I better go to him."

"I have to speak to you first." Curran took control of the situation. "Let's both take a seat."

Curran turned a second chair to face the young man as Hawke walked over to the cabinet of regimental silver and stood with his back to them, apparently absorbed in an inspection of the objects in the case.

Gentry lowered his head, his shoulders shaking as he pressed his hands to his eyes in a vain attempt to stem the shaming tears.

"I'm sorry," Curran said, "but you understand I must ask you some questions?"

Gentry nodded. He sniffed and took a breath, bringing his face up to look Curran in the eye. He looked so much younger than his years.

"You came out to Singapore with your sister?"

"Yes. Sylvie and John were married in the regimental chapel and we sailed the next day. We docked here on"—he frowned, glancing at Hawke's back as if he expected the adjutant to assist—"March fifth, I think."

"And the marriage was a happy one?"

Gentry stiffened. "Of course it was. I know people talk but let me assure you, Captain Curran, that John—the colonel— and Sylvie were very much in love. She made a splendid officer's lady."

"And children?"

Something flickered in the young man's eyes, gone in a flash. "Of course she wanted to give him children but these things take their own good time, don't they?"

"I believe you maintain a room at the colonel's residence?"

Gentry nodded. "Sort of. I have to share with Jack if he's at home, and it was understood that I only used it when I was strictly off duty. I may have been the colonel's brother-in-law and the CO's son, but to the regiment I'm the assistant adjutant, just another officer of the battalion."

"Assistant adjutant?"

The adjutant of the battalion was the main administration officer, a sort of assistant to the commanding officer. It was a desk job with few direct reports beyond the orderly room staff. A safe, comfortable job, if that was what you wanted.

Gentry glanced at his boss and Hawke turned around, his arms crossed. "That's right."

Hence the indulgence of a morning off to nurse a hangover, Curran thought.

"Tell me about last night?" Curran asked.

Gentry shuddered. "I was the vice dining president," he said.

"So you had to behave?"

Gentry licked his lips. "Up until port and cigars and the mess games."

"Was that after you all retired to the anteroom?"

Gentry shrugged. "Everyone made a rush for the conveniences and after that . . . who knows? Damned if I can remember a thing after my fourth whiskey." He looked down at his hands. "I don't remember how I got to bed."

"That task fell to your roommate," Hawke said.

"Lieutenant Cox?" Curran verified and Gentry nodded.

"George Cox. He's a good sort."

"Getting back to the dinner itself. Did anyone leave the room at any time?" Curran asked.

Gentry frowned. "No one's allowed to leave the dinner." His face brightened and he glanced at his senior officer. "Only Hawke here."

Curran turned a questioning gaze on the adjutant, who had the grace to color.

"Captain Hawke, when I asked you the same question, you didn't think to mention it?"

"I didn't think it was important. As duty officer, I got called out to an altercation between a couple of private soldiers. They're up on a charge this evening."

"What time was this?"

"About ten. I got back just after everyone had risen from the table."

"Which was what time?"

"Just after eleven," Gentry supplied, indicating the large grandfather clock at the end of the room. "It strikes every quarter hour and I'm pretty sure it had just struck eleven fifteen."

Curran looked at Hawke. "As duty officer did you remain sober?"

Hawke grimaced. "Lemonade all night. It was hell."

Curran rose to his feet. "Thank you for your time, gentlemen."

Gentry stood up. "Are you going back to the house?" When Curran nodded, he said, "May I come with you?"

Curran glanced at Hawke, who shrugged. "He's family. Take whatever time you need, Gentry."

"I will have more questions for you, Adjutant," Curran said.

Hawke nodded. "You know where to find me."

Gentry thanked the captain and returned to his room to fetch his forage cap, the peaked cap worn by army officers.

"We can go out by the back gate," Gentry said. "It cuts out the walk around by the road."

The barracks area was delineated by a wire fence topped with barbed wire. The main gate opened on to the lower part of Blenheim Road but Gentry led Curran up the hill to the back of the barracks area.

They reached the back gate, a single narrow entry on to a lane running behind the barracks. A solitary guard loitered in a hut, springing to attention at the sight of the officers' uniforms.

"What's the security at night?" Curran asked.

"We have a regular patrol of two armed soldiers who walk the perimeter every hour," Gentry said. "This gate is secured at night," Gentry said, returning the man's salute. "It's used during the day for the servants, gardeners and civilian staff coming up from the town."

Curran considered the heavy metal gates.

"What is it secured with?"

"A chain and padlock."

"Who has the key?"

"It's kept in the orderly room but the duty officer has a set of keys to the whole barracks."

"And where would they have been last night?"

"With Hawke and then he would have hung them in a cupboard back at the mess."

"Is the cupboard locked?"

Gentry looked at him. "No. Doesn't need to be."

The narrow, rutted lane at the back of the barracks ran into the highly respectable Blenheim Road, along which the married-quarter bungalows, whose design and size dictated the rank of the resident, had been constructed. The nearest neighbor to The Cedars was the slightly more modest home of the absent Major Pardew. Gentry reiterated the story Curran had already heard. The second-in-command had gone up to the Cameron Highlands, taking with him his family and his entire household staff. The house stood empty.

At The Cedars, Curran found the colonel sitting in the drawing room, an untouched cup of tea on a table next to him and a glass of whiskey in his hand. He looked up as Gentry entered and some animation returned to his face. He rose to his feet, setting the glass on the table.

"Nicholas, my boy. They've told you?"

"John—sir . . ." Gentry's voice faltered and the tears welled in his eyes again, a reminder that despite the uniform he wore, he was no more than a boy who had just lost his sister.

Nolan rose to his feet and crossed to the young man, taking him in a fatherly embrace. He thumped the subaltern on the back.

"Buck up, man. Sylvie wouldn't want you to go to pieces over her."

"Nnn . . . no, sir," Gentry covered his distress with a cough. "Where is she? Can I see her?"

Nolan shook his head. "They've taken her away and its better you remember her as she was, not . . ." His own voice cracked. "The bastard beat her head in."

Nicholas Gentry made a choking sound and reached for the nearest piece of furniture to steady himself. Nolan crossed to a cupboard and opened it to reveal a neat row of crystal decanters. He poured a glass of what Curran presumed to be whiskey and handed it to the young man. He did not offer a drink to Curran.

Gentry straightened and shook his head with an apology. He had gone an alarming shade of gray and Curran suspected that on top of the drink Hawke had given him and the young man's hangover, the first sip of the whiskey would have come straight up again.

"Is Pris all right?" Gentry asked.

"Yes, thank God. She took one of her sleeping draughts and slept through the whole thing. You can imagine she's in a terrible state so she's gone to stay with Lavinia. Jack's still down at the beach." Nolan glared at Curran. "The bloody police are all over the house and grounds. How much longer are you going to be, Curran?"

Curran shook his head. "As long as is necessary, sir."

Nolan scowled. "You better find him, Curran. I want this madman hanged."

❧ Six

Harriet and Julian returned from their unhappy visit to Jack Nolan about two in the afternoon. A familiar carriage had been drawn up under a tree, the horse grazing on Harriet's shrubs and the syce sitting with his back to the tree, chewing betel.

Harriet glanced at her brother. "Visitors," she said.

Seated in the shade of the verandah, a tray of sandwiches between them were Harriet's friends Louisa Mackenzie, wife of the chief surgeon, and the *Straits Times* journalist Griff Maddocks.

Griff had the morning's paper open, one ankle propped on his knee and, in between bites of sandwich, appeared to be reading aloud the newspaper article on the spectacular arrest of Dr. Crippen that had been interrupted by the message at breakfast. His rapt audience included Will and Huo Jin, both of whom were sitting on the front steps. The only disinterested member of the audience appeared to be the half-grown cat, Shashti, who lay curled in Will's lap.

"*. . . Crippen was charged before the Magistrate at Quebec*

on August 1, with murder. Mr. Drew made a brief statement to
which Crippen did not reply, but he said he did not oppose ex-
tradition. He was remanded for a fortnight. Miss Leneve was
not present. She was suffering from nervous prostration. The
Magistrate visited her at the house of the Chief of Police where
she was temporarily accommodated and charged her with be-
ing accessory after the fact. She did not object to a remand and
was afterwards moved to hospital. Subsequently she was com-
mitted for deportation and . . ."

"Oh, there you are, chaps." Griff lowered the newspaper as
Will gave a squeak and jumped to his feet as his guardians
climbed out of the police vehicle.

"I see you've made yourselves at home," Harriet remarked.

Louisa kissed her friend on both cheeks. "I only came to ask
you something and found Griff installed, telling Will all about
the Crippen case," she said. "Huo Jin didn't seem to know
where you had gone, only that you'd disappeared in the police
vehicle, and then Griff told me that there had been an incident
up at Blenheim Barracks . . . So, do tell?"

Harriet turned to Maddocks. "I assume that's why you're
here?"

The journalist folded the newspaper he had been reading
from and dropped it on the table, presenting a picture of complete innocence that broke down under a ferocious glare from
Harriet.

"The rumor went around the office that there had been a
death at the barracks, and as anything to do with the army is a
closed door to we gentlemen of the press, I thought perhaps one
of my close contacts with the police may know something?"

"You know very well we—I—can't say anything." Harriet
dropped into her favorite chair and removed her hat. Shashti,
deposed from Will's lap, immediately jumped onto hers. Harriet
fanned herself with the hat.

"Tea, mem?" Huo Jin inquired.

Harriet stared at her amah in horror. "No more tea! A gin and tonic would be heavenly."

Everyone else agreed that the sun had gone over the yardarm and gin and tonics all round would be perfect.

"So, what is this business at the barracks? You may as well tell me. Euan will be full of it when he gets home and it will be public knowledge by this evening," Louisa said, shooting a glance at Griff. "You know he'll just make something up, if you don't tell him."

"Louisa! I never make stuff up," Griff protested.

Julian glanced at Harriet, who shrugged. "Mrs. Nolan, the wife of the commanding officer of the First South Sussex, was found dead this morning," he said.

"No! Not Sylvie Nolan!" Louisa said. "I only saw her a couple of days ago. She is on the organizing committee for the St. Andrew's bazaar. How did she die?"

"It looks like murder," Julian said. "She was attacked in her bedroom."

Louisa gasped and Harriet glared at her brother. "That's enough, Ju! *Pas devant l'enfant.*"

They had forgotten about Will, who sat quite still, his eyes like saucers, all interest in Dr. Crippen banished by the thought of a murder on his own doorstep.

"So, the rumors were right," Griff Maddocks said. "The *Straits Times* has ears everywhere, but as I said, any chance of getting anywhere near the barracks is almost impossible. I suppose you're going to tell me to go and talk to Curran?"

"Of course I am. You're not getting anything more out of Julian or me," Harriet said as Huo Jin handed her a glass and she took a thankful sip of the refreshing cocktail.

"You know I'll just ask Euan." Louisa sounded sulky.

"Do that," Harriet said, remembering Mac's gray, drawn

face and wondering how much the surgeon would be inclined to share with his wife. "Now, what did you want to ask me?"

"I came to see if you and Will wanted to come down to the beach for a few days. We've taken a villa on the west coast and I thought it would be such fun if you could join us." She glanced at Will. "Roddy could do with some company his own age."

Harriet looked at her ward and Will met her gaze, his eyes huge and pleading. Roddy Mackenzie was a year younger than Will, but the boys got on well and it had been a tedious holiday for Will, stuck at St. Tom's House.

"Unfortunately I doubt I will be able to get away," Harriet said. "Not with this new case. I'll be needed, but if Will could still join you?"

"Of course," Louisa said. "Would you like that, Will?"

If Will had not been a properly brought-up English boy, he might have thrown himself at Louisa.

"Thank you, Mrs. Mackenzie, that is very kind of you," he said.

"I too had another reason for being here," Maddocks said. "We have a new chap in the office, and I thought he should meet some of the more sensible people in Singapore."

"I have an idea," Louisa said. "Harriet, Julian, why don't you bring Will down to Pasir Panjang on Sunday after church and Griff, you bring your friend down, and we'll have a luncheon party by the sea."

Harriet nodded, regretting that she would not be able to spend longer at the beach villa. "That sounds an excellent idea, Louisa."

"My friend has a motor vehicle." Griff brightened. "What say we call about twelve thirty and collect you?"

"Who is your friend?" Harriet asked.

"An Australian journalist—Simon Hume. Cracking chap and very keen to play a bit of cricket, Edwards. He's also a dab hand at tennis. Does this villa have a tennis court, Louisa?"

Louisa shook her head. She did not play tennis. "Maybe Harriet can inveigle him down to the Ladies Tennis Club," she suggested with a sly smile in Harriet's direction.

Harriet ignored her. "Seeing as you two have eaten all our sandwiches," she said, "might I suggest you both adjourn and let Julian and me find something to eat? It has been a very long morning."

Louisa smiled. "I see we are not wanted, Griff. Would you care for a lift back to town?"

Griff accepted and Harriet waved the visitors off. She subsided on the verandah with a second gin and tonic and considered the Sunday outing. After the grim day of death and grief, it made a change to have something to look forward to.

Curran's day ended at the morgue at the Singapore General Hospital. He should have been in attendance for Mrs. Nolan's autopsy but he was waylaid organizing the necessary clearances required by the regiment to allow his staff to interview witnesses at the barracks the following day.

He arrived at the hospital to find Mac standing outside the morgue, leaning against the post of the verandah, smoking his pipe.

Mac removed the pipe from his mouth and pointed the stem at Curran. "You missed the fun," he said without the slightest trace of humor in his grim tone or strained face.

"Dealing with the regiment," Curran said. "Not the most cooperative witnesses I have ever encountered."

"Ah, they're a law unto themselves," Mac said, pushing himself off the post. "I suppose you had better come in and I'll tell you what I've found."

Steeling himself, Curran pushed open the heavy door. He swallowed a wave of nausea in reaction to the unmistakable miasma of death and decay that hung in the cloying, humid air.

Sylvie Nolan lay on one of the marble tables in the center of the room. Her slight form barely seemed to make an impression on the sheet that covered her. Small in stature in life, she had been diminished by her violent death.

Mac flicked the cover aside to allow Curran the opportunity to identify the victim. Even the clinical surrounds of the morgue did little to lessen the horror of the force that had been inflicted on her face and head.

He shook his head and looked up at the doctor. "Well?"

"Several interesting things you need to know about Mrs. Nolan," Mac said. He picked up the remaining candlestick that Curran had sent with the body. "Silver with a square-edged lead base. I have no doubt that this one's pair is your murder weapon."

He demonstrated, holding the base of the candlestick against the wounds. "She was struck first on the side of the head with the base," Mac indicated. "That would have knocked her flat, if not killed her outright. The other injuries were inflicted after she was lying on the bed. At least six other blows delivered with what I can only describe as ferocious anger." He shook his head. "Different angles." He swallowed. "It's as if her killer wanted to obliterate her face."

"Did she struggle?"

Mac shrugged. "There are bruises on her arms." He grasped Curran's forearms. "Someone held her hard, but I can't tell you if they are connected to the final assault."

"That's interesting." Curran mulled this information over as he tried to imagine the scene in Sylvie Nolan's bedroom.

Someone had held her arms. There had been some sort of fight or argument. The first blow probably knocked her back on the bed and then the beating had begun. This had not been a random act by an anonymous intruder. The obliteration of her lovely face had been personal. Sylvie Nolan had known her late-night visitor.

"Just a small observation. She had been wearing earrings."
Mac turned the woman's head and pointed to her torn earlobe.
"They were wrenched from her ears with some force." Curran
shuddered.

Mac restored the sheet, giving the woman back her dignity
and Curran took a breath.

The difficult question still had to be asked. Curran swallowed. "Had she been interfered with?"

"No, but . . ." Mac hesitated. ". . . there's something else you
should know."

Curran swallowed. "Go on."

"She was pregnant."

Curran's stomach lurched. The killer had taken two lives.
"How far?"

"Six weeks, give or take a week, but there is more, the child
was not her first. Sometime in the last couple of years Mrs. Nolan gave birth."

Curran stared at his friend. "That can't be right."

Mac gave a hollow laugh. "I assure you I am not wrong
about these matters."

"But she's only been married less than a year."

Mac cast him a scathing glance. "Don't be so obtuse, Curran. Marriage has nothing to do with it."

"But it may explain the marriage," Curran mused.

Mac shrugged. "I don't need to tell you how sensitive that
information is. If it's not relevant, I can leave it out of the report
for now?"

"It could be very relevant to her death." Curran ran a hand
through his hair. "What a mess."

Mac blew out a breath. "If you've seen enough, let's get some
fresh air."

The two men stood in silence in the comparative cool of the
verandah, both considering the implications of what Mrs. Nolan herself had told them about her life and death.

Mac toyed with his unlit pipe as Curran lit a cigarette.

"Do you have a time of death?" Curran asked at last.

Mac frowned. "When was she last seen alive?"

"She dismissed the maid about nine thirty at the latest. Her husband returned home about one thirty and went straight to his own room. He knocked on her door and got no response so I think we are safe to assume she was dead by then."

Mac nodded. "If he didn't kill her?"

Curran shrugged. "I can't rule him out."

Mac blew out a breath. "I would have said she died around midnight, but you know how hard it is to judge these matters, Curran." He stowed his pipe in his pocket and straightened his tie. "Over to you. I have rounds of living people to make and then home to Louisa. When can I release the body?"

Curran glanced at the door behind him. "There's nothing more to be gained from keeping her on ice," he said. "She should be buried as soon as possible."

"I'll let Nolan know," Mac said. "See you later, Curran."

Curran remained, finishing his cigarette as he watched the tall, spare figure of the doctor striding across the courtyard to the General Hospital wards. He needed to return to his office and brief the inspector general on the details of the investigation.

It had gone dark by the time he returned to the South Bridge Road Police Headquarters. Nevertheless he found Cuscaden still at work, in the large, airy office overlooking South Bridge Road.

Cuscaden listened to Curran without interruption, leaning back in his chair, his fingers pressed together.

"Bad business, Curran," he said. "The military don't take kindly to what they see as interference from the civil authorities. The provost marshal, Goff . . ." He brought his chair back to earth with a thump and leaned his forearms on the desktop, his hands clasped together, fixing Curran with a steady gaze. "What's your history with him?"

Curran, who had mentioned Goff only in passing, cursed his

superior's perceptivity. "Why do you ask, sir?" he began cautiously, wondering how little he could get away with.

"I'm not a fool, Curran. You were both in the military police in South Africa and I can see in your face that there is something between the two of you. If he is antagonistic to you ten years on from that conflict, I want to know why."

Curran blew out a breath. "A couple of incidents. Goff was in command of an escort of Boer prisoners of war. One made a break for it. He was recaptured and brought back and that should have been an end of it, but Goff ordered the man to be shot on the spot in front of the other prisoners. A warning, he called it."

"And where were you?"

"I was part of the escort. It was one of my men who recaptured the Boer and brought him back to his death. Goff and I had . . . a rather public difference of opinion."

"And the other incident?"

"He had command of a small prisoner of war camp. I lodged a formal complaint about his cruelty to the men in his care. An investigation ensued and he was demoted."

Cuscaden grunted and straightened in his chair. "I see. Then Goff will not make it easy for you, Curran."

"No, he has made that quite clear."

Cuscaden narrowed his eyes. "Is there anything else I should know?"

Curran hesitated on the point of confiding his other issue with the South Sussex Regiment—that of his father's history—but decided against it.

"No, sir."

"Watch your step with this Goff chap. We mustn't allow ourselves to be distracted by the past, the priority is to find this poor woman's killer. If you strike trouble and need to escalate the issue, let me know. In the meantime, any theories?"

Curran shrugged. "Too early to say, sir. Despite the missing jewelry, I am not convinced it was a random intruder. There are elements to the killing that make me think it was someone known to her."

Cuscaden nodded. "I would appreciate a daily update, Curran. This is a tricky case. Tread carefully."

By the time he had finished at South Bridge Road, it was past ten before Curran made his way back to his bungalow on Cantonment Road. As he approached, his instincts prickled. Something felt wrong. No light shone in the windows and Li An's favorite chair on the front verandah beside the frangipani was empty. Normally she would be sitting there waiting for him.

Curran threw open the unlocked front door, his heart hammering.

"Li An?"

She came at him from out of the dark, throwing her arms around him, holding him to her. She shivered in his arms, like a wild bird, caught in his hand.

He pulled away and held her at arm's length, searching her face in the dark. "Whatever is the matter? Why are you in the house, in the dark?"

Her long, unbound hair fell forward across her face. "I am afraid, Curran."

He shook his head. "Afraid? Why? What's frightened you?"

She took a deep, shuddering breath. "A man followed me from the market today. I saw him watching the house."

The cold hand of fear grasped Curran's heart. "What sort of man?"

"An Indian man. I thought . . . I thought maybe . . . Zi Qiang . . ."

Khoo Zi Qiang, Li An's murderous brother, had not, as far as Curran knew, left Penang but they both lived with his shadow over their lives. As long as Khoo Zi Qiang continued as head of his Penang-based opium ring, neither of them would ever be quite safe.

Curran drew his lover into his arms again and kissed her hair, drawing in the scent of frangipani and jasmine that was so intrinsically part of this woman. "Zi Qiang would not send an Indian to do his bidding," he said.

Zi Qiang's business dealings were strictly within the Chinese clans.

"Then who?" Li An murmured.

"I don't know," he said. "Wait here. I'll check outside."

Drawing his service revolver, Curran stepped out into the night. It still lacked a few days to a full moon but it was a cloudless evening and there was sufficient light to see by. He prowled the perimeter of their little bungalow, pushing into the *ulu* that gave them privacy but also shut them away from their closest neighbors. Apart from startling the resident troop of langurs who swore at him from the treetops, he found no evidence of Li An's stalker.

He holstered the Webley and returned to Li An. She still cowered in the dark, and even after his assurance that there was no one watching the house, she continued to tremble. He took her in his arms again.

"Zi Qiang made it plain, he has no more interest in you," he said. "We are safe here. It was probably nothing more than a man entranced by a beautiful woman."

"I am not beautiful," she murmured.

He cupped her scarred face in his hands. "To me you are."

He kissed the long, ugly scar that marred her perfect face, the legacy of her last encounter with her brother.

"I will ask Mahmud to stay up here," he said. "Will that help?"

She nodded. Mahmud, the syce who helped with the garden and Curran's horse, the chestnut gelding Leopold, would probably be of little assistance in a dangerous situation, but Curran's offer seemed to calm her fear. She nodded and relaxed in his arms with a deep sigh and he kissed her hair.

"Let's light a lamp and have a drink?" he suggested. "It's been a long day."

She pushed away from him, lit a lamp and poured them both whiskeys. "So tell me about your day, Curran."

He collapsed into his chair, suddenly impossibly weary. He had woken with a heaviness behind his eyes, which now seemed to be developing into a headache of monster proportions. Probably just the heat. He rubbed his face and took a sip of the whiskey as he recounted the life and death of Mrs. Sylvie Nolan, the colonel's lady.

Li An listened without interrupting him.

"Someone hated her very much," she said when he had finished.

Curran nodded. "I agree. I don't think a casual intruder would have inflicted quite such damage on her. Poor woman. I can only hope it was quick."

Li An had recovered her composure with his return and they ate a light meal together before collapsing into bed. Long after Li An had fallen asleep, curled up beneath the mosquito net, her long hair spread out across the pillow, Curran sat in her chair on the front verandah, smoking a cigarette, the Webley loaded and ready on the table beside him. The creatures in the *ulu* around him filled the night with their chirps and crackles, and the langurs screeched at each other. He preferred langurs to the more invasive macaques, who were not above breaking into homes and stealing food and anything else that intrigued them.

Despite his assurances to Li An, her fear and the possibility that she had been followed and watched alarmed him and sleep had eluded him. He knew Zi Qiang confined his dealings very much within the clans. Nevertheless the sense of unfinished business with Li An's brother kept tugging at his conscience. He had failed that assignment. Failed it dismally.

When Zi Qiang had left them both bleeding, but alive, in the stinking shed on the Georgetown harbor, it had been his way of saying *Live with the knowledge you have failed. Look at your scars and weep, knowing I could have killed you but I chose not to. You are nothing to me.*

Curran had failed to protect Li An then and he knew he couldn't now, not if Zi Qiang had determined to finish what lay between them.

Li An was not a woman to show her emotions, but in the last month, word had reached her that her mother, the formidable matriarch of the Khoo clan, was ill. Despite her mother having publicly disavowed her daughter, Li An had wept inconsolably and since then her nerves and emotions had been strained.

The humidity of early morning closed in around him. Some days the air felt so thick, he could barely breathe. The slightest change in the quality of the dark told him daybreak was not far away and he had a long, long day ahead.

He stubbed out the cigarette and stretched his arms above his head and thought regretfully of the cricket match he would be missing. The Singapore Cricket Club would have to manage without him today. Sylvie Nolan demanded his full attention.

The seventh lunar month marked the Festival of the Hungry Ghosts. Li An had explained that on the fifteenth day the gates of hell opened and the spirits of the deceased were released to visit with the living. These spirits required veneration and propitiation, and already the scent of burning incense hung over Chinatown as he rode Leopold to the South Bridge Road Police Headquarters in the early morning.

Li An had set up a brazier in their own garden and every night she burned incense and threw the propitiatory incense papers onto the small fire. She had told him that failure to display appropriate filial piety had dire consequences for the living, who would be haunted throughout their lives by the unhappy spirits, and the last thing Li An needed was the angry spirit of her dead father haunting her.

The fug of burning braziers added to the already heavy air of Chinatown, an overcrowded warren of dark lanes and alleyways. Tailors, traders, medicine halls and opium dens jostled together along the five-foot ways as street traders, carrying their braziers on poles across their shoulders, shouted their offerings.

Curran stopped to buy a couple of steamed buns from one of the street traders, mindful of having skipped breakfast. With Leo's reins looped over his arm, he propped against one of the supporting pillars of a five-foot way in Temple Street and watched the passing crowd as he ate.

Mindful of Li An's distress, he found himself searching the faces of the men, looking for the round, cherubic face of Khoo Zi Qiang. Surely, he wouldn't have come to Singapore unless he was planning on expanding his opium empire, which was always possible.

Curran dismissed that notion. He was looking for ghosts. Zi Qiang had too many enemies here. In Penang he might rule the Khoo clan, but here, he had crossed too many of the other clans, particularly those involved in the illegal trade of opium.

Curran finished his bun and straightened. On the corner of Temple Street and South Bridge Road he passed the Sri Mariamman Temple, a Hindu temple that seemed out of place in the middle of Chinatown, but it had been built long before this area had been designated for the Chinese population. Its whitewashed walls and tall *gopuram* of brightly colored Indian gods, who looked down on the bustling street, seemed as much a part of the fabric of the society as the traditional Chinese temple in Telok Ayer Street, just a few streets away.

Curran paused, watching the Indian population pass through the heavy wooden doors into the sanctuary beyond, scrutinizing each face. Some gave him curious glances but he saw nothing out of the ordinary and no one showed any particular interest in the tall policeman. Leading his horse, Curran quickened his pace to the Police Headquarters and another long day.

⚬ SEVEN

St. Thomas House/Scotts Road
Saturday, 13 August

Harriet dressed with considerable thought for her engage-ment with the formidable Lavinia Pemberthey-Smythe. She eschewed her usual day dress of blue drill skirt and plain blouse in favor of an elegant beige linen walking-out suit, one of several fashionable additions to her wardrobe chosen by her older sister, Mary, on a shopping expedition in London before she had left for Singapore.

As she stepped out onto the verandah, Julian, dressed in his cricket flannels, looked up from the newspaper. Will lay on his stomach on the floorboards, reading the June issue of the *Boy's Own Paper*, which had arrived that week. At sixpence it was an extravagance but Will adored it.

Julian looked her up and down. "I say, is that you, Harri? I thought you were just paying a quick visit to check up on Miss Nolan?"

"Too much?" Harriet asked.

"I think you look lovely," Will said.

She smiled at her ward. "And you can always be relied on to say the right thing, William."

"Are you playing tennis this afternoon?" Julian inquired.

Harriet nodded. "I will have time to come home to change, I hope."

"You're not coming to the cricket? It's going to be a cracking match against Johor." William failed to hide his disappointment.

Harriet shook her head. "What a shame I have to miss it," she fibbed, "but Griff and I are playing for a championship this afternoon."

Julian jerked his head at the driveway, where Aziz waited with the pony trap. "Off you go. Hope you find Miss Nolan in better spirits."

Harriet climbed into the trap and raised the beige lace parasol. She had little opportunity to wear the new clothes and she hoped she hadn't overdressed.

They turned into the driveway of the Scotts Road villa with its eccentric turret. Aziz helped her down from the trap and Harriet ascended the front steps into the lush coolness of Lavinia Pemberthey-Smythe's verandah. Lavinia and Pris were seated in the amply cushioned rattan chairs, a tea tray on the low table between them.

Lavinia rose to her feet. Today she wore a colorful local *sarong kebaya*, fastened with intricate gold brooches. She wore her graying hair loosely piled on her head and held in place with gold pins, decorated with cutouts that danced as she advanced toward Harriet, her hand held out.

Constrained by the unfamiliar corset and the narrow cut of the walking-out suit, Harriet regretted her choice of clothes, envying Mrs. Pemberthey-Smythe the comfort and eccentricity of her choice of dress.

"Good morning, Mrs. Pemberthey-Smythe," she said.

"Mrs. Gordon . . . Harriet . . . What a charming outfit. You will find I do not give much for pomp and ceremony. Had too much of that in the army days. To you I will be Lavinia. Now, do come and sit down. Pris, dear, pour Harriet a cup of tea."

Pris obliged with a smile. She looked pale but composed, her slightly protuberant eyes still red-rimmed and circled with dark smudges. She wore a simple black gown that looked several sizes too large for her and of an old-fashioned cut. Probably something from Lavinia's wardrobe, Harriet supposed. She had not found anything in her quick search of Pris's wardrobe the previous day appropriate for mourning.

The Cavalier spaniel, Pansy, sprawled on the boards between the two women, apparently quite at home in her new surroundings.

Harriet took the cup Pris proffered.

"How are you today, Pris?" Harriet inquired.

"Much better, thank you, Harriet. A good night's sleep works wonders."

"Helped by Dr. Mackenzie's sleeping powder," Lavinia added.

"John came by earlier to see how I was. He looked simply dreadful, poor man," Pris said. "He said you and your dear brother had the difficult task of breaking the news to Jack. The poor boy would have been devastated. He adored Sylvie."

Harriet nearly choked on her tea. There had been nothing in Jack Nolan's response that indicated he had any feelings for his stepmother other than complete contempt.

"He took the news bravely," she managed, and set her cup down. "Although Julian and I were left with the impression that he harbored some resentment toward his stepmother concerning the treatment of his dog."

Pris took a decorous sip of tea. "Ah, that . . . he would have got over it, but Sylvie could be high-handed." She sniffed and reached for a handkerchief she had tucked in one sleeve and dabbed her nose. "I suppose if I can be honest among friends, it is true that Jack did not take kindly to Sylvie's invasion of our home and the supplanting of his mother in his father's affections."

"Invasion" struck Harriet as a word with a particular meaning. It implied a hostile takeover with no quarter given. "She made changes?"

"Oh yes," Pris said with a bitter laugh. "She was the colonel's lady in every sense of the word. She dismissed John's batman, Billings, who had been with John for over twenty years. Fortunately John found him a new position as batman for her brother, Nicholas. And it was Sylvie who insisted that Jack become a boarder at St. Tom's. As Jack would be going to boarding school at the end of the year, she felt it would be good for him to experience living away from home. When I protested, she said I was too overprotective and she pointed out that as I was merely Jack's aunt, it was none of my business." Her mouth quirked. "You must understand that I have looked after Jack since he was a baby and I found it difficult having my views completely disregarded."

"And what happened to Jack's dog?" Harriet asked.

"Dear Mary had such a soft heart, and while they were still living in India, she found an abandoned pup and took him in. When Mary died, Rufus was all Jack had of his mother. He adored that dog. Unfortunately, Rufus, despite his advancing years, still had an eye for the ladies." She glanced down at Pansy, who snoozed at her feet. "Pansy objected to his amorous intentions and Sylvie ordered Rufus be destroyed."

"No!" Lavinia set down her cup. "Surely John . . ."

"Jack said she killed his dog," Harriet put in.

"She left that to John but he could never have killed the animal. He found Rufus a home with one of his sergeants but, for some reason best known to himself, thought it would be easier on the boy if he believed the dog had died. He knew Jack would go looking for him if he thought he was still alive."

"Oh dear, poor boy!" Lavinia said.

Pris stooped to scratch Pansy's ears. "Pansy isn't a bad dog. She's just spoiled."

Like her mistress? Harriet thought uncharitably.

She looked at Pris. "What about you?"

Pris's eyes widened. "Me?"

"It must have been hard for you, after all those years of looking after your brother and his son, to relinquish your place to another woman."

Pris straightened. "I was delighted for John, of course. He loved Mary deeply but I could hardly begrudge him finding happiness again. He will be the next commanding officer of the regiment and Sylvie would have been a wonderful asset for him."

"Sylvie was a true daughter of the regiment," Lavinia put in. "She knew exactly what was expected of her."

"Her arrival freed me to think about a life beyond the regiment," Pris said.

Before Harriet could inquire as to what that life entailed, Lavinia cut in. "Enough of this talk, I am delighted that we have this opportunity to have you to ourselves, Harriet." She glanced at Pris, who nodded.

"Ask her, Lavinia."

Harriet ran through a list of possible entreaties.

"I have heard a lot about you from a friend of mine in London," Lavinia began.

Harriet inquired as to who they might be. She did not expect the answer.

"Emmeline Pankhurst," Lavinia replied, her gaze fixed hard on Harriet's face, watching for her reaction.

For a long moment the breath stopped in Harriet's throat. "How are you acquainted with Mrs. Pankhurst?" she inquired, her voice high and tight.

"We have been correspondents for a number of years. Like you, Harriet, I returned to England for a short time after my husband's death and I joined the Women's Social and Political Union. I found friends and like-minded women there. And like you, I couldn't escape the place fast enough. Apart from anything else, I missed the battalion so I came to Singapore."

Harriet cleared her throat. "And like me, you now live a thousand miles away from London and the WSPU," she said.

"Indeed, but that does not prevent us from remaining sympathetic to the cause. Suffragists, if not suffragettes." She laid a hand over Harriet's. "I know about Holloway. I know what they did to you and we"—she glanced at Pris—"would like to ask you to speak to our branch here in Singapore."

Harriet drew her hand back and looked from Pris to Lavinia. "You have a branch of the WSPU here?"

"Not exactly a formally constituted branch. But although we are not active in the political sense, we raise money to send to our sisters in England."

Harriet resisted the sudden urge to rise and run. Her heart hammered against her corset stays and her breath seemed to have stopped in her throat.

"I . . . I am delighted to hear that the good work being done in the name of women's suffrage is extending this far," she said, the words coming out in a staccato fashion, "but I am afraid I can't help in this instance. My work . . . keeps me busy."

Lavinia Pemberthey-Smythe leaned forward, her eyes bright. "Indeed, you are a wonderful example of what a woman can achieve. The first woman to be employed by the police!"

"That is necessity, not suffrage," she said, "and frankly, I think the whole notion of women's suffrage has many, many decades to go in this society. Just as in the European society, let alone our sisters in the Chinese, Malay or Indian communities. Women like Sylvie Nolan who serve no other purpose than to decorate their husband's salon and . . ." She broke off, appalled by her outburst. "I've said too much. I do apologize."

"Not at all. Pris and I are in perfect agreement over this. No one would know better than us what the role of the colonel's lady entails, and make no mistake, Harriet, a woman can wield significant influence in such a position, both positive and negative. Unfortunately Sylvie could not be brought to the cause. She saw her role, as you observed, as decorative." She straightened. "But I have not invited you here to discuss the Sylvie Nolans of our community. Harriet, we have upward of a dozen women who attend our meetings and we would like to invite you to our next meeting to share your story. We believe it would be inspiring to our sisterhood—"

Harriet rose to her feet. "Thank you for your invitation," she said, "but the answer must be no. I nearly died as a result of what happened to me in Holloway. I find the memory painful in the extreme and I have no wish to retell it."

Lavinia stood up. Harriet was tall but Lavinia topped her by a good couple of inches. She took Harriet's gloved hands in her own. "And it is your pain that is our inspiration. I am aware of what you must have suffered but we have sisters in Holloway enduring exactly what you went through, if not worse. Sometimes, my dear, talking openly about such experiences to a sympathetic audience may ease the burden." She squeezed Harriet's fingers. "Do think about it. Our next gathering is here on Tuesday. You are most welcome to join us."

Harriet withdrew her hands. She had broken out in a sweat, struggling to breathe.

Lavinia eased her back into her chair and poured a glass of water. "Drink this, my dear. I'm sorry to bring back such unpleasant memories."

Harriet couldn't bring herself to speak. She forced her breathing to return to normal and blotted her face with her handkerchief.

"The heat," she said. "These ridiculous clothes. May we change the subject?" She forced a smile, turning her attention to Pris. "I presume you won't be attending the tennis tournament this afternoon."

Pris shook her head. "I plan to return home this afternoon. John will need me. He said they are releasing Sylvie's body today, but tomorrow being Sunday, the earliest we can bury her is on Monday. Please give my apologies to Mr. Morris and the others." She smiled. "Although I have every confidence that you and Mr. Maddocks will take the championship."

Harriet shook her head. "It is dangerous to be overconfident, but we do make a good team." She tucked her handkerchief back into her reticule and rose to her feet. "Thank you for tea, Lavinia. I really must be getting back for luncheon if I am to be in any state to play tennis this afternoon."

Lavinia smiled at her. "I am afraid we have startled you, Harriet. Believe me, we are not so very fearsome. Just a group of like-minded women with much in common."

Harriet ignored the further reference to Lavinia's group of suffragists and bade both women farewell.

As Aziz turned the trap out into Scotts Road, she gripped her reticule in both hands, conscious that she had begun to shake. How dare they make such a presumption about her willingness to participate in their group? What did they want of her? Were they planning to chain themselves to the gate of Government House? Throw themselves in front of racehorses? She doubted it, but she recognized the gleam of political fervor in Lavinia's eyes and felt herself drawn to it in the same way the WSPU had spoken to her on her return from India.

She bit her lip and cursed herself for being such a fool as to think that by coming to Singapore she could escape her past. It had been a year since she had been incarcerated in Holloway, a year since . . . She closed her eyes, willing the terror and pain to go, but it came back with stark clarity and she dashed at the tears that came without bidding.

Nothing would induce her to relive those days. Nothing.

"What's bothering you, Harri?" Julian asked over luncheon as Harriet poked at her uneaten meal.

It went with the clerical collar he wore, but she had always found it hard not to confide in Julian and she told him about the involvement of Lavinia and Pris in the women's suffragette movement.

"They want me to tell them about Holloway," she said.

"I see," Julian said.

She looked up at him. "Enough people on the island already know that I have a criminal record," she said. "If I start talking publicly about my experience, how soon will it be before the school's governors or Cuscaden hears about it? A convicted criminal working for the police department?"

Julian nodded. "That is true, but if we lived our life in fear, where would that get us? Have you considered that the women may have observations about the death of Sylvie Nolan that could be useful?"

"In what way?"

"The regiment is a closed door. Curran is going to find it hard to get anywhere with anybody associated with the South Sussex, but you could—through their ladies."

Harriet attacked a slice of bread with her butter knife with such ferocity the bread crumbled. "That's ridiculous."

"Is it? I'm sure Curran would be glad of your help."

"But they know I work for the police. Won't they be suspicious?"

"Ah, but they don't see you that way. You are their decorated heroine. Their martyr to the cause. You know, better than me, what these women are like and don't tell me that you no longer believe in their ideals. Votes for women? Harriet, you can deny it all you like but I know that lies in your heart."

Harriet's knife clattered onto the plate. "Perhaps I should talk to Curran. If he thinks it is worth my while, then I will do it."

"Harriet, have faith. I believe things happen for a reason and this opportunity has come your way." He paused. "I also think that you need to talk about Holloway. You carry it bottled up inside you and it will continue to eat away at you. Maybe more people knowing what you suffered will help prevent others enduring the same ordeals and, more importantly, free you from this burden of guilt you are carrying. Things will work out for the best, you'll see."

She chewed her bread without tasting it. In his way, Julian was right. There was a good reason he had taken holy orders. He had an uncanny ability to see into people's souls. Despite what had happened to her, she still believed in the cause of the WSPU—universal suffrage. It galled her that she did not have a say in government, that her father had not considered it worth his investment to let her pursue the career in law she had so desired and that her mother had thought marriage was the one ideal she should strive for and, having achieved that, she should spend her widowhood looking after her elderly parents. That had been Priscilla Nolan's fate. All Priscilla's youth and promise had gone in caring for her parents and then her brother and nephew. No wonder she had found the suffragists.

And more fundamentally, the shame and guilt of turning her back on the cause and fleeing London did nag at her. Force-feeding had become a policy and it would continue until public abhorrence at the practice was brought to bear and that would never happen while the victims stayed silent.

Harriet never bounded anywhere, but after her conversation with Julian, she had a lightness of step as she entered the neat pavilion of the Ladies Lawn Tennis Club. Membership in this respectable establishment did not come easily and she was grateful to several of the "mamas" from the school who had put her forward as a suitable member. In this august club, run by a committee composed predominantly of women, with men only permitted to join as subscribing members, Harriet felt completely happy.

Unfortunately the necessity of earning her living precluded her from the leisurely weekday games but she now had an excuse to avoid Julian's tedious cricket matches on Saturdays. She had persuaded Griff Maddocks to subscribe to a membership, and as a doubles partnership, they were formidable. The only downside to such vigorous exercise was the infernal climate and she cursed the club rules that required a tennis outfit consisting of a plain gored skirt no more than four inches from the ground, a plain white blouse with no bows or furbelows (neat tucks permitted), a stiff collar and black tie and matching belt. White canvas plimsolls were permitted but it made for a hot and restrictive outfit.

Griff had already arrived, and she envied him his neat white slacks, white shirt and waistcoat, but like the women, men had to wear a collar and tie. She joined him at the table where he sat with a man who had his back to her. Both men stood and Griff waved at the spare chair and summoned the waiter with an order for a lime juice. The two of them had a private rule of no alcohol before a game.

"Harriet . . . Mrs. Gordon . . . allow me to introduce you to my colleague, Simon Hume," Griff said.

Harriet had to stop herself staring. The man had to be several inches above six feet, broad shouldered and tanned, his brown hair tipped at the ends with gold as if he spent his days in the sun. His smile revealed even white teeth and the corners of his eyes had a fine spiderweb of laugh lines.

She took the strong brown hand he held out to her.

"Mrs. Gordon," he said. "A pleasure to meet you. Griff here has been singing your praises."

An unfamiliar heat rose to Harriet's cheeks. "Good heavens, Griff. What have you been saying?"

"I've been telling him about your prowess at tennis," Griff said. "Hume here is the Australian I mentioned yesterday."

Harriet took the lime juice from the waiter and smiled at the man. "Welcome to Singapore, Mr. Hume. Are you here for long?"

"At least a year," Hume replied. "My paper likes to have someone in place for the Southeast Asian reports."

"Mrs. Gordon?"

Harriet tore her attention from the Australian to the less prepossessing Clyde Morris, secretary of the club's social and fundraising committee. Mr. Morris had been Pris Nolan's regular doubles partner over the last few months and they made a good match for Harriet and Griff. Clyde was probably in his late thirties, slight of build, balding with round tortoiseshell glasses and a straggly moustache. He held a straw boater in his hands and had an apologetic look on his face.

"Pardon me for interrupting but I just wanted to inquire if you knew how Miss Nolan was today?" He shook his head. "I read the news this morning and couldn't believe it. What a terrible thing to have happened." He blinked behind his glasses. "I thought you, of all people, might know something . . . ?"

Harriet smiled. "She is shaken but holding up, Mr. Morris. She sends her apologies for this afternoon."

Morris's eyes widened. "Oh, I wouldn't have expected . . . I've told the club secretary that we will forfeit our match." He smiled faintly at Griff and Hume and turned away.

"Funny little man," Hume said. "What does he do?"

"I believe he is an accountant in one of the banks," Harriet said. "Sorry, Mr. Hume, you were saying you have been sent up here to staff the Southeast Asia desk for the Melbourne *Argus*. How are you acclimatizing?"

Hume blew out a breath. "It takes a bit of getting used to. I'm from Melbourne. It gets hot but not this humidity. I believe I'm driving you to luncheon tomorrow?"

"There will be three of us and luggage," Harriet said. "I hope your motor vehicle is large enough?"

Hume glanced at Griff. "Three? Is there a Mr. Gordon?"

"No," Harriet said. "I'm a widow. It will be myself, my brother and our ward."

All the humor drained from Hume's face. "I'm sorry, Mrs. Gordon. I didn't know."

Harriet swallowed. "You weren't to know. My husband passed away a few years ago in India."

"Gordon and Maddocks?" A voice called from the steps.

"We're up," Maddocks said.

Harriet and Maddocks rose to their feet and picked up their racquets. "Do you play?" Harriet asked Simon Hume.

"I do, and in normal circumstances I would be happy for a game, but I'm glad to watch for a little while," Hume said with a smile. "I believe you are the team to beat."

"Come on, Harriet," Maddocks grumbled. "We'll be disqualified."

Harriet hurried after her partner.

"What do you think?" Maddocks said as they walked out onto the court.

"About what?"

"Hume."

"He's . . ." A number of superlatives danced around in Harriet's head. She confined herself to, "Quite charming."

Maddocks grinned. "I knew you'd like him."

"I've never met an Australian before. Are they all like that?"

Maddocks frowned but the need to give his concentration to the game cut off any response he may have had.

Their opponents had won the serve and Harriet set herself to receive but not without a furtive glance up to the pavilion where Simon Hume sat by the verandah rail. He raised a hand and Harriet let the first serve fly past her.

"Fifteen–love," the umpire said.

❧❧ EIGHT

South Bridge Road/The Cedars
Saturday, 13 August

After a morning spent reviewing the evidence and the state-ments obtained by his staff the previous day, Curran rode out to the barracks to interview the officers who had attended the mess dinner. Before facing the long afternoon of interviews, he thought he should pay a courtesy call on Lieutenant Colonel Nolan.

As he rode past the barracks, it struck him that on a Satur-day afternoon, the barracks took on a different, almost deserted atmosphere. Only distant cheers and yelled abuse marking a rugby game being fiercely contested on the sports field disturbed the somnolent atmosphere. Along Blenheim Road, the married quarters were silent, the recent death hanging over the area like a dark cloud.

The windows of The Cedars were closed and shuttered, and a black wreath hung on the door. He left Leopold in the shade by the gate and, drawn by smoke and a strong smell of burning, walked around to the back of the house. Nolan stood beside a large pile of smoldering embers, evidence of a sizable bonfire, smoking a cigarette. In his hand he held a silver photograph frame. Enough remained of the twisted, burned remnants of the pyre to identify Sylvie Nolan's elegant writing desk. Poignantly a small pink satin shoe had escaped the conflagration and lay at the edge of the fire among the ashes.

Suppressing his annoyance at this wanton destruction of potential evidence, Curran came to stand beside the colonel.

"I gave orders for her room not to be touched," he said.

Nolan looked like a man who had not slept in days, the skin on his face gray and sagging with exhaustion.

"It's my house. I can do what I damn well like. Besides, she's gone. Can't bring her back and I don't want to be reminded on a daily basis of her presence." He kicked the desk farther into the center and it caught and burned anew. "Couldn't bear to think I won't see her sitting at that desk, that she won't turn and smile at me." He tossed the stub of his cigarette into the flames. "Besides, the servants are talking about bad spirits and ill omens and who knows what sort of bunkum. Best to clear the room completely."

"That's not the point," Curran said. "We hadn't finished with it."

Nolan glared at him. "You have your photographs and I take it you took everything you wanted. The rest is just ephemera. Goff didn't seem to think it would be a problem."

"That's not how it works, Colonel," Curran said slowly. "I'm in charge of this investigation, not Goff. It's my decision, not his."

Nolan pulled a silver cigarette case from his trouser pocket, offered one to Curran, who accepted, and took one himself, lighting both cigarettes from a box of safety matches. The two men stood side by side, smoking and watching the fire, and the last of the evidence, die down to embers.

"We have authorized the release of her body," Curran said.

Nolan nodded. "I had a chitty from Mackenzie last night. We'll be burying her on Monday afternoon." Nolan inhaled and coughed. "Did Mackenzie have anything to say about how she died?"

"He thinks the blows were most likely delivered by the candlestick," Curran said. "We haven't found it yet."

"Did she suffer?"

Curran shook his head. "After the first blow, it would have been quick." He hesitated. "There was something else you should know."

Nolan turned to him, interest flaring in his dead eyes.

Curran cleared his throat. "She was carrying a child."

John Nolan emitted a sound somewhere between a cough and a groan. His hand shook as he put the cigarette to his lips again.

"How far . . . ?"

"No more than six weeks. Had she said anything to you?"

He shook his head. "She'd been a bit under the weather, but I put that down to the bloody heat. It can get anyone, if you're not used to it."

Curran took his courage in both hands and asked, "Was it yours, sir?"

Nolan brought his gaze down to meet Curran's, his eyes hot and angry. "Why on earth would you ask a question like that, Inspector?"

"Just a routine question, sir."

"It is insulting and impertinent."

"I know, but it has to be asked."

"Of course I am the father." Nolan tossed the stub of his cigarette into the fire and reached for another but his hands shook and it took several broken matches before the cigarette was lit. He took a long drag and said, "She was my wife. Who else . . . ?"

When Curran did not respond, Nolan picked up the garden rake and stirred the fire.

As he turned over a smoldering piece of the desk, Curran

spotted something scarlet in the ashes. He swooped on it, pulling out the charred remnants of a red leather-bound book. It had been burned almost to the spine, the pages no more than blackened leaves that crumbled to his touch and yet on the cover he could distinguish the gold initials . . . S A N . . . Sylvie Anne Nolan.

He held it up, keeping his anger barely under control. "Is this what I think it is?"

Nolan didn't flinch. "Yes, it's her journal. There were things in there . . . private things . . . that no one had the right to read except her. I pocketed it yesterday morning before you arrived. I knew it would be brought up by someone because the whole household knew her routines. Better for you to think it missing."

"This is evidence," Curran spluttered. "Crucial evidence. I told you, there are no private matters when it comes to a murder investigation!"

Nolan's eyes blazed. "There was nothing in there that concerns you. A young girl's life of shopping and tea parties, nothing more."

"If there was nothing of importance in it, that was for me to decide, not you."

Nolan met his angry gaze without blinking. "I had to destroy it before it destroyed her."

This contradicted his assertion that it contained only the trivia of a young girl's life. Curran tossed his cigarette into the ashes, seething with anger. Of course Nolan would have read it and it must have contained something important, something he didn't want the world to know.

"I loved her, Curran." Nolan heaved a sigh. "And I was foolish enough to think she entertained feelings for me."

"Did she?" Curran asked.

Nolan blinked. "Who knows a woman's mind?" he replied.

The majordomo, Abdul, came hurrying down the garden path. "Colonel, sahib. Captain Hawke wishes to speak most urgently with you. I have shown him into the library."

Curran thrust the charred remnants of the journal into his pocket.

"I'm coming with you. I'd like to speak with Hawke," he said.

Thrusting the silver photograph frame at his majordomo, Nolan strode down the path. Curran almost had to run to keep pace with him.

Hawke was not alone. He stood in the center of a fine Persian rug with Major Goff beside him. Goff cast Curran a narrow-eyed glance of pure malice.

In the presence of a superior officer, Goff drew himself up sharply. "Colonel Nolan, sir."

Nolan's gaze flashed to Hawke. "Goff. What brings you here?"

"This, sir." Goff handed over a telegram to the colonel.

Nolan unfolded it and read aloud. *"Colonel Gentry's compliments to Major Goff. You are to assume the investigation into the death of my daughter. I believe this man Curran to be the son of the Coward of Kandahar who brought disgrace on the regiment. He is not, I repeat not, to be involved in this matter."*

A red fog of anger over this interference in his investigation, mingled with the renewed insult to his father's memory, roared in Curran's already aching head.

"My father died when I was six years old," Curran said, barely holding the words together. "I am not responsible for whatever he did or did not do in his military career and neither am I here to defend my own honor. If you have any doubts as to the latter, I suggest you speak with Inspector General Cuscaden. As to the former, you take me as you find me. I am not my father."

The three soldiers stared at him. Goff wore an insolent grin, pleased that his duplicity had embarrassed Curran. Hawke shifted from one foot to the other, clearly uncomfortable. Only Nolan's face remained unreadable, his formidable brows drawn together.

The colonel folded the paper and pocketed it. "Curran, I do not as a matter of a lifetime's practice, judge a man by his antecedents.

None of us were serving with the regiment at the time your father was an officer and the facts of that matter are buried in the dust of the Afghan desert. Whatever Colonel Gentry's feelings on this matter, I am forced to accept that the civilian police have responsibility for this investigation." He rounded on Goff. "I have told you before, this is not a military matter, Goff, and I do not appreciate you overreaching your authority in respect to the commanding officer. Dismissed."

Goff's face darkened and for a moment Curran thought he might argue the matter with Nolan, but the provost marshal had been a soldier too long to risk that. He snapped to attention and with a snarled "Sir" that bordered on insubordination, he left the room.

Nolan's staunch defense of his right to investigate Sylvie Nolan's death puzzled Curran. Nolan had been caught destroying key evidence. Wouldn't it be easier simply to concur with his commanding officer's request and hand the investigation over to Goff, who would keep it nicely in the family? Or did he genuinely want to get to the truth of the matter and recognized the impartiality of the civilian authorities?

Nolan turned to Hawke. "Was there anything else, Hawke?"

There must have been something in Nolan's tone that Curran, not knowing the man, did not pick up. The color drained from Hawke's face. "No, sir. I just thought it prudent to accompany Goff once I knew he had been in contact with the CO."

Curran's anger had calmed and he held up his hand to detain the adjutant, who had turned to go. "Captain Hawke, I will conclude my business with Colonel Nolan. If you would be so good as to wait outside, I have some questions for you."

Hawke inclined his head and left the room. Nolan turned and opened an elegant Chinese cabinet, revealing a row of crystal decanters. He poured himself a measure from one but did not offer one to Curran.

Glass in hand he turned back to Curran. "I apologize for

Major Goff's interference," he said. "Unfortunately, I am not in direct command of the man."

Nolan took a drink. "It's a pity the two of you have a history, but I meant what I said, Curran, I will judge you on how you handle this investigation. I don't care a jot for who your father was or what he may or may not have done."

Curran resisted the urge to admit that he had no idea what his father had allegedly done that had brought such disgrace on his name and the regiment. Until recently, he had always believed Edward Curran had died in the Battle of Maiwand. The question that his death may have been otherwise had been raised only a few months earlier by a man who claimed to have served with the older Curran at the time, but Charles Kent was dead, hanged for murder without ever saying anything more, and Curran had dismissed his passing remark about his father as a ploy to unsettle him in the middle of a complex interview.

Pushing the memory of Charles Kent to one side, Curran said, "My father was never a part of my life."

Nolan lifted the glass to his lips but paused before he took a sip. "Then I am sorry for you, Curran. Every man should know his father and you are lying to me. It does matter to you. I can see it in your eyes."

"Thank you for your time," Curran said, abruptly terminating the uncomfortable interview. "If you'll excuse me, Colonel, I don't want to keep Hawke waiting any longer." At the door he turned and looked back at the man. "And please do not destroy any more evidence."

Something that may have been a smile quirked at the colonel's lips and he raised his glass in acknowledgment.

Curran found Hawke waiting alone on the verandah, lounging on one of the well-cushioned rattan chairs. The officer rose to his feet as Curran came through the front door.

"Sorry about that, Curran," he said. "Goff served directly under Gentry and may possess an overblown loyalty, which allows him to think he has a right to jump proper chain of command. I have the officers you wished to interview waiting for you in the mess."

Curran shrugged. He had no desire to discuss Goff. "I also want to speak with those involved in the altercation that took you away from the dinner on Thursday night."

Hawke stiffened. "Why? Just a couple of private soldiers with one too many beers under their skins."

"The thing is, Hawke, I understand you are the only officer who left the dinner." Curran let a couple of beats pass before he added, "The only one without an alibi for around the time Mrs. Nolan was killed."

Hawke paled. "Now, wait a minute, are you suggesting I—"

"I'm not suggesting anything," Curran replied. "I just need to verify your account of your whereabouts. That should be easily done if I can speak with the soldiers concerned and any other witnesses who can verify your story, such as their sergeant and corporal."

Hawke's gaze moved to a point somewhere over Curran's right shoulder. "That could be difficult. The whole platoon left yesterday afternoon to go up-country."

Curran counted to ten. "Where have they been sent?"

"Seletar. They are on punishment detail, digging defenses for a new fort."

Seletar. Fifteen miles north through thick jungle via rugged tracks. Curran ran a hand over his eyes.

"Then bring them back."

Hawke's jaw set. "If you want to speak to them, you will have to go out to Seletar."

Curran's strained patience reached an end. "I am in the middle of a murder investigation, Captain. If you want to clear yourself of suspicion, then I strongly suggest it is in your own interest to make the relevant witnesses available to me at your earliest convenience."

Hawke looked down at the toe of his well-polished boot. "I'll see what can be done but I doubt that we'll get them back for a couple of days."

"Do that and do it sooner rather than later," Curran snapped.

"Captain Hawke, sir," Abdul hurried out of the house. "I am pleased you have not left. There is a matter to do with the arrangements for tomorrow, the memsahib's funeral, I wish to discuss with you."

Hawke's neat moustache twitched. "I'll just be a few minutes. Wait for me and I'll walk with you back to the barracks."

Curran left the adjutant in discussion with the majordomo and strode down the drive to where he had tethered Leopold.

He paused, leaning his aching head against the horse's warm neck to catch his breath and regain his equilibrium. Leopold looked around at him with his ears pricked.

"You're right. I'm not well," Curran said to the horse. "Let's hope it's just the consequence of a bad night and not anything else. Hello, what's this?"

A paper had been carefully tied to the left stirrup with red string. Curran undid the knot securing the string and unfolded the paper. It was a joss paper . . . a golden square of rough bamboo paper printed with red and gold figures, a common sight particularly during the month of the Hungry Ghost Festival when such papers were offered to the spirits as financial propitiation.

His breath caught. On the reverse side, in a crabbed almost illegible pencil someone had written:

TCK. Sri Mariamman Temple. Monday 10 P.M.

TCK? What the hell did that mean?
Curran eyed his horse. "If only you could talk," he said as he

stuffed the joss paper into the pocket of his jacket. Leopold jerked his head up and down in agreement.

Hawke strode down the driveway toward him. "Sorry to keep you waiting," he said.

Curran found Singh and his constables waiting for him in the motor vehicle at the front gate to the barracks. The normally unflappable Singh's eyes blazed. "They will not admit us, Curran. Even with your chitty from the colonel sahib."

Curran glanced at the gate, where two soldiers lounged; a lance corporal and a private soldier. He strode over to them.

"My men have the authority of Colonel Nolan to enter this barracks," he said, keeping his tone low and icy. When they didn't straighten. He came to attention. "Stand up in the presence of a superior officer," he said.

"You ain't our superior officer," the lance corporal retorted, "and I told your man there, they was to use the back gate."

Hawke stepped forward. "Corporal Brown, isn't it? Well, I am your superior officer and you are to accord Inspector Curran and his men every courtesy."

The man's insolence slipped. "But they're natives, sir," he said, jerking his head at Singh and Tan. "Standing orders, all natives enter by the back gate."

Curran had no time for this nonsense. "Adjutant," he said. "I demand an immediate apology to my men, and failing that, I want these two men charged."

Brown's lip curled in a sneer, but when he looked at his adjutant, he saw no mercy in the officer's face. He took a visible breath and pushed open the gate. "Didn't mean nothing by it . . . sir."

As an apology, that would be as good as Curran could expect. The man was probably on sentry duty as punishment to begin with.

He gestured to Tan to drive in and followed on foot, leading Leopold.

"Sorry about that," Hawke said as they strode toward the administration building.

"I don't have the time or energy for that sort of nonsense," Curran said. "Singh, I want you and Tan to interview the mess servants and bandsmen. Hawke, who is the mess president?"

Hawke shrugged. "I am in the absence of Major Pardew."

"Good. I will interview the officers in the dining room."

Hawke escorted him down to the mess, where the officers waited at their ease in the comfortable anteroom. They were all present with one exception. Hawke informed him that Gentry's roommate, Lieutenant Cox, had been sent on the detail to Seletar.

Curran set himself up in the dining room and one by one interviewed the officers of the South Sussex. They all concurred that the dinner itself had finished about eleven and they had adjourned to the anteroom, where a great deal of alcohol had been consumed and mess games played. The only person to leave the dinner had been Captain Hawke, although there didn't seem to be any agreement about when he had returned, except that he had been back in the mess well before midnight for a round of "boat races." Given the amount of alcohol imbibed it came as no small surprise that anyone could remember anything after midnight, let alone who had been present. Curran hoped that Singh might have more success with the mess servants.

The afternoon dragged on and the last person on Curran's list entered the dining room. Captain Mayhew, the regimental quartermaster, was a man of around his own age with the sallow skin and bloodshot eyes of a habitual drinker. Mayhew's age and embitterment bore testimony to a disappointing career.

"Copped one in the leg in South Africa," Mayhew said as he sat down, his right leg stiffly out in front of him. "That was the end of my career as a field officer. Bloody lucky they kept me on as QM." Mayhew sat back and pulled out a cigarette case. He offered it to Curran but one look at the vile French cigarettes and Curran declined.

"Rumor has it you've been in the army, Curran," Mayhew said as he lit his cigarette.

"Mounted Military Police. Like you I was wounded in South Africa and took the opportunity to get out and try something different," Curran said, adding quickly, "Left the army as a captain."

The shared rank and experience gave them an instant comradeship.

Mayhew made an interesting witness, partly because, like many habitual drinkers, he remained remarkably sober for the evening, unlike the succession of young lieutenants who had passed through Curran's questioning.

"Bloody dinner dragged on till just after eleven," Mayhew said. "Hawke would have left about ten. I remember thinking what a lucky blighter he was to miss the jollities."

"When did he return?"

Mayhew blew out a smoke ring. "I reckon it would have been closer to eleven thirty. We were in the anteroom. He seemed a bit out of sorts so I offered him a whiskey. He knocked it back in one gulp. Not bad considering he was duty officer and supposed to remain sober."

"Did he tell you where he had been?"

Mayhew shook his head. "Just some altercation between a couple of lads who should've known better."

Curran changed the line of questioning. "Were you acquainted with Mrs. Nolan?"

Mayhew snorted. "That cow. To hell with not speaking ill of the dead. She was leading the CO a right dance, batting her eyes at every handsome man who came into her circle. Like moths to a candle, they were."

"Anyone in particular?"

Mayhew shrugged. "She cultivated a circle of admirers, Curran. She had a couple of the young subalterns hanging on her every whim."

Curran raised an eyebrow. "Names?"

Mayhew gave him the names of a couple of the youngsters Curran had already seen. Mayhew stubbed out his cigarette in a well-polished silver ashtray decorated with the regimental crest. "She liked to play the colonel's lady, did Mrs. Nolan. She dictated who was in and who was out of the social circle."

"I take it you were out," Curran said.

Mayhew grinned. He had a wide gap between his two front teeth that gave him a curiously endearing look.

"Oh yes, the memsahib took against me the first time we met when I declined her request to redecorate the house and I didn't like the way she treated poor old Billings either. He'd been batting for the colonel for twenty years, but no, the mem didn't want him cluttering up the house so he was out."

"Who else was on the outer?"

Mayhew frowned. "I'd say Cox was one, for all he shares a billet with her brother. She didn't like Goff much either. In short anyone who was not, by her definition, a gentleman."

Curran privately agreed, Goff was no gentleman. "What about Cox?"

"Came up from the ranks. His father was the battalion sergeant major until his heroic death in South Africa. By way of reward Gentry commissioned his son. Not sure he sees it as much of a reward. He'll always be the sergeant major's son no matter how many pips he has."

"What time did you leave the festivities?"

Mayhew shrugged. "You know the rules. Couldn't leave till the old man went."

"What time was that?"

"Not until well after one. I purloined a bottle of whiskey and left straight after him."

The smoke from Mayhew's vile cigarette had made Curran feel nauseous and did nothing for his headache. He thanked the quartermaster for his help, making a mental note to talk to him again if he needed questions answered without the regimental varnish.

He found Singh and Tan waiting for him outside the mess. They had completed their interviews of the servants, including the punkah wallahs, but none of them had anything useful to add to the picture Curran had already formed. It had been a typical dining-in night of too much food, alcohol and testosterone. Curran dismissed his men for the day and swung himself into Leopold's saddle, letting the horse take him home to Li An, a cool bath and a decent meal.

But despite Li An's best efforts, he spent another night tossing in sweat-soaked sheets and midnight found Curran once more sitting on the verandah with a glass of whiskey in his hand. It did nothing to alleviate his throbbing head. The front door opened and Li An crept outside, wrapped in a flimsy silk nightgown.

"Come back to bed, Curran," she said.

"Can't. I'll just keep you awake," he replied.

Li An slipped onto his lap, her slender hand brushing his forehead. "You are burning, Curran. Are you ill?"

"No. Just hot. If you haven't noticed, we live in the tropics."

Li An leaned her head against his shoulder, her fingers tracing patterns on his bare chest that did not have the normal effect such activity produced.

"Did you see any more of the man who followed you?" he asked.

"No," she replied. "I was probably just imagining it. You are right. It is not Zi Qiang's style to send an Indian."

Curran leaned his head back against the wall of the bungalow and closed his eyes, thinking about the note he had found tied to the stirrup.

TCK? He opened his eyes, his breathing coming rapidly.

TCK . . . The Coward of Kandahar?

The ugly words jangled in his mind . . . such a hideous description of a person. *Coward* was the worst epithet a soldier could be given, and whatever his father had done, surely there must be some explanation.

His blood ran cold and despite the heat he shivered. Someone who knew his father's story was playing a prank, a tasteless joke. He wouldn't put it past Goff to try and unnerve him.

Li An stood up and held out her hand. "Come back to bed, Curran. You must sleep. This murderer must be caught and you will not do it if you do not rest."

He took her hand and hauled himself to his feet, moving like an old man, aching in every joint.

✣ Nine

When your guardian is a minister of religion, Sunday morning means church—without exception. With the prospect of a holiday by the sea so tantalizingly close, Will could hardly sit still and Harriet had to reprove him for fidgeting several times during matins at St. Andrew's Cathedral.

She loved the soaring airiness of the cathedral and the long rattan-backed pews, but the memorials on the walls saddened her. So many young lives lost in this fearsome climate.

Will chafed through the social chitchat that inevitably followed the service and it was half past eleven before they returned to St. Thomas House.

As soon as they arrived home, Will rushed inside and was seated on the verandah with his small cardboard suitcase at his feet before Harriet and Julian had time to draw breath. The glorious day promised a pleasant dry heat, the hint of a sea breeze and not a cloud in the sky. Harriet took some time to dress in a pretty white cotton tea gown with sleeves to her elbow trimmed with broderie anglaise. With Huo Jin's help she arranged her hair in a loose roll at the nape of her neck, allowing several tendrils to fall around her face as she pinned on a wide straw hat trimmed with blue flowers and a matching broderie anglaise band. Her sister Mary's choice again and Harriet had to concede, as she twisted and turned in front of the long mirror in her bedroom, Mary did know what suited her.

"Cor," said Will.

"Very nice, Harri," Julian said as she stepped onto the verandah, clutching her parasol in her white-netted-gloved hands. "Is that new?"

Harriet rolled her eyes. "No. I just don't get many opportunities to wear it."

Julian jumped to his feet. "I almost forgot something," he said, and ran into the house, returning with a bright-red pail and matching spade, which he handed to Will.

"You can't go to the beach without a proper bucket and spade. Remember our summer holidays in Wales, Harriet?"

Harriet smiled. They had been happy, carefree times when their parents took a house in Barmouth for a month and the three of them had run wild along the wide sandy beach, clutching their spades and buckets in search of pirate treasure.

Will grinned and thanked his guardian. He sat cradling the present as they waited, reminding Harriet, with a pang, that this was a child who had probably received few presents in his life.

On the dot of twelve thirty, a dark-green automobile turned into the driveway, announcing its arrival with a honk of its horn that set a troop of macaques in the nearby *ulu* chattering in fury.

Julian and Will gaped. "It's a Maxwell tourer," Julian, who hankered after an automobile of any description, muttered in awe.

From the passenger seat beside the driver, Maddocks waved his hat as the Maxwell drew to a dignified stop at the steps to St. Tom's House.

Maddocks fumbled with the catch of the door and stepped out.

"Harriet, you look splendid," he said.

The driver, hidden beneath a wide-brimmed pith helmet and driving goggles, vaulted effortlessly over the door on the driver's side and came around the car, removing his hat and pushing the driving goggles up.

"G'day." Simon Hume held out his hand to Julian before Maddocks had a chance to affect the introductions. "Simon Hume. You must be the Reverend Edwards."

Julian, who had decided to attend the lunch party out of his uniform of clerical collar, spluttered, "Julian Edwards. Pleasure to make your acquaintance. Splendid motor vehicle."

Hume put his hands on his hips and cast a fond eye over the tourer. "She's a beaut. Got her for a song from some cove who was, shall we say, in need of some readies."

It took Harriet a moment to translate what the man had said, by which time his attention had turned to her. He took her hand in his. He had a strong workman's hand, marked with tiny scars. This was a man who had worked hard in the outdoors so not always a pen pusher, as Maddocks often described the profession of journalism.

As if he read her thoughts, he looked down at his hand, spreading the fingers as if he hadn't seen them before. "My family has a property out in the Western District. Spent all my holidays redoing fences and chasing sheep."

"Western District?" Harriet found her voice.

"The Western District of Victoria. Prime sheep country but my older brother's welcome to the property when Dad goes. I couldn't get off the place fast enough." Hume turned to Will. "And you must be William." Simon Hume shook the boy's hand with due gravitas, picked up the small suitcase and strapped it to the back of the car.

"All right, everyone, pile in. It will be a bit squashed in the back but the little tacker can squeeze in between the reverend and Mrs. Gordon and it's not as if we're going far, Maddocks?"

"Pasir Panjang." Maddocks, back in the passenger seat, shook out a map. "It's a villa on the Pasir Panjang Road, just before the kampong. Louisa said it's right on the beach and we can't miss it."

Harriet tied a scarf over her hat as Hume cranked the engine. It purred to life and with another honk of the horn they set off. Six miles on Singapore roads, even in the latest motor vehicle, could still take time and it was nearly one before they turned into the driveway of the pretty villa. Louisa came out on the verandah to meet them, like Harriet, dressed in a light cotton dress, her hair done informally. She had the look of a woman on holiday and determined to share her good fortune.

A table had been set on the wide verandah at the front of the house. Steps ran down to a stubby lawn and on to the beach beyond. Will let out a sigh of appreciation.

"The children are having a picnic lunch on the beach," Louisa said to Will. "Do you have a swimming costume?"

Harriet had taken him shopping on Saturday afternoon after tennis and he had all the appurtenances required for a seaside holiday. With barely an acknowledgment to Harriet, he changed into the blue wool bathing costume, grabbed his sun hat and bucket and spade, and ran down the front steps onto the beach, where the Mackenzie children were seated under a shady palm.

"Thank you for this," Harriet said, squeezing her friend's arm. "He is so excited."

Louisa patted her hand. "I'm just sad you can't join us too," Louisa said. "I will be a bit devoid of adult company. Euan said he has to go in to the hospital tomorrow morning. I swear the man doesn't know that he needs rest as much as his patients."

"He's here today and that's important," Harriet said as they joined the men on the verandah where Euan, clad in linen trousers and an open-neck shirt, appeared to be dispensing gin and tonics.

A sumptuous lunch of cold cuts had been set out, washed down with beer and lemonade. As the only two women present,

Harriet found herself seated at one end of the table with Simon Hume on her left and Euan Mackenzie on her right.

"I do hope you will find some time to spend down here with the family," Harriet said to Mac.

"Louisa nobbled you, has she?" Mac replied.

Harriet returned his smile with a shrug.

"Were you called out to the murder at Blenheim Barracks?" Hume asked.

Mac nodded. "Bad business, but then violent death like that is never good, is it? I'm afraid poor Curran's got his work cut out for him dealing with the army. He'll be keeping you busy this week, I wager, Harriet."

Hume turned to look at Harriet. "You're in the police force?"

Harriet laughed. "Good heavens, no. I am the shorthand typist for the Detective Branch."

"Hardly a job for a lady," Hume said.

"Ah, Harriet is not your usual lady," Mac said.

Harriet flicked him with her table napkin. "What does that mean, Euan?"

Mac held up his hand. "I meant only that were the police force to take women, Harriet would be your ideal candidate. What about you, Hume, how long have you been in Singapore?"

"Just a couple of weeks. I'm here on a posting for the *Argus*. Southeast Asia correspondent." He paused and looked from Harriet to Euan. "Anything you can tell me about the Blenheim Barracks murder . . . ?"

He looked so innocent and hopeful that Harriet laughed. "You're as bad as Griff," she said.

"Did I hear my name?" Maddocks, seated next to Euan, looked around.

"Your friend here was just trying to extract information on poor Sylvie Nolan's murder from us," Harriet said.

Griff raised an eyebrow at Harriet. "Sorry, Hume. Harriet's my source, not yours."

"I am nobody's 'source,'" Harriet said. "Journalists!" she added with a shake of her head.

Mac clapped his hands together. "That was an excellent repast, my dear. What say we go for a stroll to the beach and see what the youngsters are up to?"

The youngsters were having a splendid time. Patsy and Eddie frolicked in the passive crystal-clear waters that lapped the beach while Will and Roddy seemed to be engaged in building a sandcastle under the watchful eye of the Mackenzie's amah, Charita, who had come with them from India.

Perched on the solid trunk of a near-horizontal palm tree, Harriet watched her ward, noting the way he took charge directing Roddy on the construction of the ramparts. Will had endured the deaths of his siblings and both his parents in his short life, his father in particularly tragic circumstances, but in the six months he had been with Harriet and Julian, he had blossomed both physically and academically.

"May I join you?"

Harriet, startled out of her reverie, looked up from under the wide brim of her hat as Simon Hume took a seat beside her, the tree bending under his weight as he cautiously tested it.

"Is young William a relative?" Hume inquired.

Harriet had known Maddocks long enough to know that the journalist would have fully briefed his friend on the residents of St. Tom's House, but she said, "No. His father died in March and we have taken him on."

"Ah!" The journalist's sharp gaze turned on her. "I remember now. The affair of the Singapore sapphire. He was killed. Wasn't there some story that he may have been involved in the incident?"

Harriet swallowed. The story that had been spun around John Lawson had been constructed to protect his son and the last person she wanted to be talking to was a sharp-nosed journalist.

"I prefer not to talk about it," she said. "I hope you understand."

"Yes. I'm sorry. I didn't mean to pry." And he promptly went on to pry some more. "You told me yesterday that you were a widow. You didn't go back to England after your husband's death?"

"I did. I hated it."

"Can't say I blame you," the Australian said. "I had a few months in London a couple of years ago. Miserable weather, for starters."

Uncomfortable with the direction the conversation was going, Harriet changed the subject. "And what about you, Mr. Hume? Tell me about Melbourne."

"Best city in the world, bar none, but a bl . . ." He stopped himself. "A long way from anywhere important."

"And are you married?"

"It would take a special sheila to tie me down."

"Mr. Hume, you are practically incomprehensible. What is a 'sheila'?"

He smiled. "A girl. I need to remember I'm not doing the rounds in the Collingwood police court. I assure you I attended the best school in Melbourne and they taught me to talk proper."

Despite herself, Harriet laughed. "Learned you good, did they?"

Hume chuckled, a warm, rich sound that brought a tingle to Harriet's heart. It had been a long time since a man had made her laugh.

"Harri." Julian came striding up the beach toward her. "There you are. Griff and I were just saying that we need to be getting back before dark. Sorry to break up the party."

Hume sprang to his feet and held out a hand to assist Harriet from her perch.

"All good things must come to an end," he said. His grip on her hand tightened. "Would you care to join me for an evening out, one night? I believe they do a particularly good show at the Harima Hall."

Harriet reluctantly extricated her hand and smiled. "I would like that very much."

He offered her his arm and she slipped her hand into the crook of his elbow, an unfamiliar thrill running down her spine at the touch of an attractive man. A night out at the Harima Hall, one of the local music halls, with Mr. Hume, would be most enjoyable.

It had gone dark as Curran and Leopold turned into the driveway of St. Tom's House. The horse moved slowly as if it had been as long a day for him as it had for Curran. A kerosene lamp burned on the verandah and Julian and Harriet were enjoying their Sunday-evening whiskey. Curran allowed himself a smile. He had known them both long enough now to know their routines and a whiskey would not be unwelcome.

Harriet rose and came to the top of the steps, peering out into the gloom. "Curran!" She smiled, and for a brief moment, Curran did not recognize Harriet. She wore an unfamiliar but stylish white cotton frock and she'd done her hair differently.

"Sorry to call unannounced but I was on my way back from interviewing a witness and I thought I would come by to see if you could be in early tomorrow. I have a stack of witness statements to type up." Every word seemed to require an effort.

"Come and sit down and Julian will fix you a drink. You look like you need one," Harriet said.

With a supreme effort, Curran slid from the saddle, looping the reins of the weary horse over one of the stone finials that decorated the final sweep of the steps. As he climbed the steps to the verandah, his foot caught on a riser and he almost fell. Julian caught his arm and steadied him.

"I say, old chap, are you quite well?" Julian inquired.

"Bit of a headache," Curran lied. The anvils of hell were pounding inside his head. He pulled off his helmet and ran a hand through his damp hair.

He collapsed into the nearest chair and took the glass Julian held out for him.

"Which witnesses have you been interviewing today?" Harriet asked.

"The last of the officers present at the dining-in night. There were fifty-three people at that dinner and not just from the South Sussex." He closed his eyes and took a draught of the whiskey. It tasted oddly sour. Julian normally kept good-quality liquor. "Where have you two been?"

"The Mackenzies have taken a villa at Pasir Panjang for a couple of weeks and Louisa invited William to stay and keep Roderick company. We took him down and stayed on for lunch." Harriet glanced at her brother. "We were just saying how empty the house feels without him."

Curran nodded. In the six months Will Lawson had been living with Julian and Harriet, he had seen the boy gain in confidence and maturity. He would make a fine young man.

"How's the investigation going?" Julian inquired.

Curran pulled a face and shook his head. "It couldn't be worse. As if dealing with the army isn't difficult enough, Nolan has burned the contents of his wife's bedroom along with her journal and the adjutant has sent the only witnesses to his whereabouts to the farthest end of the island. On top of everything, I have Goff breathing down my neck—"

"Who's Goff?" Harriet asked.

A wry smile tugged at the corners of Curran's mouth. "A hungry ghost from my past," he said.

"Ah yes, hungry ghosts," Julian said. "Interesting how the Taoist beliefs echo our own All Hallows, isn't it?"

"Fascinating," Curran remarked drily.

"Maybe that's what Nolan was doing when he burned his wife's belongings?" Julian commented.

Curran coughed. "I doubt it."

Huo Jin appeared at the door. "Mem, supper is served. You want an extra seat?"

"You're welcome to stay, Curran. We had an enormous lunch so it is only a light repast," Harriet said.

Curran hauled himself to his feet. The mere thought of food made him feel nauseous. "Thank you, but I think I should get home . . ." He took two steps and the world began to pitch beneath his feet. "Sorry, I . . ."

He barely made the chair. As the world roared in his ears, he closed his eyes. Harriet placed a cool hand on his forehead.

"You're burning up," she said.

"It's malaria," Curran muttered. "Nothing I haven't had before. Just give me a moment."

He had been fighting the onset of the familiar fever for three days but he knew the moment he had succumbed to the shivers in the late afternoon exactly what it was that ailed him.

"Water!" Harriet's voice again.

She pressed a cool glass to his lips and he drank greedily.

From somewhere above him, Julian said, "If it's malaria, you're not going anywhere, Curran. You'll fall off your horse before you've got to the end of the drive. In fact, I'm surprised you got this far. Huo Jin, please fetch Lokman and Aziz, we need to get the inspector to a bed."

Curran tried to stand but his legs wouldn't work and he was cold, so cold that his teeth had begun to chatter. "Must get home," he said. "Can't impose."

"Rubbish." Harriet again. "Will's away. You can spend the night in his room."

From somewhere above him he caught snatches of a whispered conversation between Harriet and her brother. They could have been holding the conversation at the far end of a very long corridor.

"We need to send for Mackenzie," Julian said.

"But he's at the villa tonight," Harriet replied.

Their voices faded again.

All Curran wanted to do was lie down and sleep. He fought back the urge to let the dark take him and managed to say, "I don't need Mackenzie . . . I've quinine at home."

"Then we will send to your home to fetch it," Harriet said. "Curran, let's get you up. Lokman, can you take his arm? That's right. Julian . . ."

"I can get myself . . ." Curran began to sit up but fell back. "I'm so sorry . . ."

He had no fight left. With Julian and his cook's help, they managed to get Curran into the house, where they dropped him onto a bed. The pillow felt wonderfully cool beneath his cheek and he closed his eyes, only vaguely conscious of someone tugging at his boots. He didn't care. He just wanted to sleep.

Harriet turned the lamp down and dipped a cloth in the basin of water Huo Jin had placed on the table beside the bed. She wiped Curran's face, and while he turned his head away muttering, he didn't open his eyes.

Julian had taken Aziz and the pony trap and gone to Curran's bungalow to fetch the quinine, leaving Harriet alone with the sick man.

The men had stripped him of his uniform, leaving only drawers and the sheet for modesty. She ran the cloth down his neck and across a well-muscled, bare chest. He murmured, arching his back against her touch and throwing back the covers. As she pulled the sheet back up, the dim light picked up a shadow on his left side, just above his hip. A jagged scar, at least six inches in length. She traced it with her finger. A knife had been plunged in and drawn up. Her blood ran cold. She knew he had served in South Africa but that was nearly ten years ago. This scar looked newer, still livid. She glanced at his face, but he was lost in the fever. That was a question for another day.

She restored the sheet and bathed the insides of his wrists. His fingers curled around her wrist and he mumbled something unintelligible that could have been "I'm sorry."

She extricated her hand and set the cloth back in the basin. The last time she had nursed a man with this degree of intimacy had been her husband, James. He had apologized too, but all her tender care had not saved him or her child, who had followed his father to the grave within a week.

She subsided onto a chair and buried her face in her hands. In the three years since James and Thomas had died, not a day went by when she didn't think of those two lonely graves in the Sewri Cemetery in Bombay that she would never visit again. Sometimes grief threatened to overwhelm her, particularly in the dark of the night.

She took a deep steadying breath and dashed at the tears that had gathered in her eyes. Malaria was not typhus, but it could still kill, and she realized in that moment how much Curran had become part of her life and how much she valued his friendship. To lose him was unthinkable.

Curran muttered something and she heard Julian's voice in the front room. Gathering herself together she rose to her feet. A shadow passed in front of the light from the hallway and Harriet started as a slender young woman with long dark hair, falling unbound around a pale oval face, stood in the doorway.

"I have come to look after Curran," the woman said, taking a step into the room.

Julian poked his head around the doorway. "Harri, this is Li An. She's brought everything Curran needs."

The woman tossed back her hair. The light thrown by the kerosene lamp brought into sharp relief, a long, knotted scar that transected her left cheek, tugging the corner of her mouth up slightly so she seemed to be half smiling. Seeing Harriet's face, she turned away so the right, unmarked side of her face fell in the light and Harriet caught her breath. Khoo Li An had once been beautiful. Not just beautiful, exquisitely beautiful.

Still struggling to regain her composure, Harriet wiped her damp hands on the apron she wore and held out her hand. "Pleased to meet you at last, Miss Khoo."

Li An glanced down at Harriet's outstretched hand and her cool fingers brushed Harriet's.

"I am just Li An," she said. "I am pleased to meet you too, Mrs. Gordon. I have heard much of you."

"Oh . . . really? All good, I hope?" Harriet knew she sounded imbecilic but the broken beauty and the very stillness of the woman reduced her to a clumsy, incoherent elephant.

But Li An had no more time for Harriet. She crossed to the bed, running slender, elegant fingers across Curran's forehead.

"Curran?"

His eyes flickered open. "Li An. What are you doing here?"

"Reverend Edwards tells me you have the malaria again. If you cannot come to me, I have come to you." She glanced up at Harriet. "You need not trouble yourself with his care, Mrs. Gordon. I have everything I need."

Curran struggled up onto one elbow, his fevered eyes going from Li An to Harriet. "I'm sorry to be such a nuisance."

"It's fine, Curran. I will leave you in Miss . . . Li An's capable hands."

Curran collapsed back on the bed and Li An turned to Julian. "Where is my basket?"

"Oh . . . I left it on the verandah. Just a tick."

Julian returned with a rattan basket. Li An pulled out a dark bottle, familiar to Harriet—ammoniated tincture of quinine.

"There is water on that table," Harriet said. "I will ask Huo Jin to make up a bed for you out the back—"

Li An reared up, drawing herself up to her full height. She

looked Harriet, who was by no means short, in the eye, and even in the gloom, her dark eyes blazed. "I am not a servant to be confined to the servants' quarters."

The breath left Harriet's body and her hands fluttered in a vain attempt to placate the woman. "I didn't mean . . . oh Lord . . . I meant only we have a smaller room at the back of the house we use for visitors. It wouldn't even have crossed my mind to suggest . . ."

The two women stood facing each other across the sudden divide of complete misunderstanding.

To Harriet's surprise Li An began to laugh. "Do not trouble your amah unduly, I will just sleep here."

From the doorway, Julian put in, "I say, young lady, I'm afraid that's just not possible. We are a Christian household and well . . ." Julian glanced at Harriet, his eyes wide and appalled. "What if the bishop finds out?"

Harriet glared at her brother. "She doesn't mean she is going to share his bed," she said. "Anyway, he's hardly in a condition to offend anyone's Christian values at the moment."

Curran threw his arm over his eyes. "I just want to be left in peace," he mumbled.

Li An glanced from Curran to Julian. "I do not wish to cause you embarrassment, Reverend Edwards. If it is not too much trouble, a bed in the back room will be fine."

Harriet glanced at her watch. "If there's nothing more I can do, I'll leave you with your patient, Li An," she said. "If you need anything, please just ask me or Huo Jin."

Li An stepped out into the corridor and turned to Huo Jin, who had been hovering near the door.

There followed a rapid and, to Harriet's ears, heated conversation in Chinese between the two women.

Huo Jin turned to Harriet, pointing a finger at the younger woman, which even Harriet knew to be an extremely insulting gesture. "You should not have her in this house, mem. She is *dàng fù*."

Li An took a step back.

"What did she call you?" Harriet demanded.

Li An turned to her. "It doesn't matter," she said.

"She called her a . . . slut," Curran said. "Harriet, this is madness, I think it best we go home . . ." But even as he struggled to sit up, he fell back with a groan.

"Enough! We have a dangerously ill man in this house who needs peace and quiet." Harriet's temper snapped and she turned to Huo Jin. "While Miss Khoo is in this house, she will be treated as an honored guest. Understood?"

Huo Jin's eyes widened with indignation but she recognized defeat.

"Yes, mem," she replied, placing a particularly sarcastic emphasis on the "mem."

"Please make up a bed for Miss Khoo and bring her anything else she may need, and if you call her by that name or any other such name, you can find yourself another position."

Muttering to herself, Huo Jin stomped down the corridor, slamming the back door behind her.

Harriet turned back to Li An. "I'm sorry."

Li An shrugged. "I have been called worse. Thank you for your kindness, Mrs. Gordon. It is getting late and you have a busy day tomorrow."

"Are you sure? I am an experienced nurse . . ."

Li An shook her head. "Leave me, and if I need you, I will call upon you."

"Dr. Mackenzie will be back in Singapore tomorrow. I will leave a message for him to call in."

Li An nodded. "That would be good. Dr. Mac, he knows and understands about these things. For now, I will give him quinine and watch and wait. The fever must take its course."

With that she turned back into the bedroom, closing the door behind her.

"Well, I never," Julian said, pushing his glasses up his nose.

Harriet patted him on the arm. "No, dear, you never!"

❧ TEN

Harriet pushed open the door and let her eyes adjust to the gloom of the sickroom. Li An lay curled up on a sleeping mat under a light sheet. Even after a night of heavy nursing, she still looked beautiful. Her patient, on the other hand, looked like he'd been dragged through a hedge backward, his hair stuck up and his unshaven face appeared gaunt and gray beneath his tan. At the creak of the floorboard under Harriet's foot, his eyes opened.

"I thought I would just check in on you before I went to work," she whispered.

"Li An?" he croaked.

Harriet glanced at the sleeping woman. "She's asleep. She sat up all night with you."

Curran grimaced. "I don't think either of us had a pleasant night. Can I trouble you for some water?"

Harriet checked the jug by the bed. The water was tepid but still drinkable. She poured a glass and with practiced efficiency held it to his cracked lips.

"You've done this before," he said.

"You know my husband was a doctor. I often had to play the role of nurse to his patients . . ." *And to him*, she thought.

He lay back on the pillows and she placed a hand on his forehead. "You still have a fever," she said.

He grimaced. "I have work to do. I can't lie here all day."

She looked down at him. "It's going to be at least another twenty-four hours before you are capable of standing on two feet let alone conducting an investigation. Do you want me to speak to Cuscaden?"

Curran ran both hands up over his face. "Thank you. I would appreciate that. Hopefully he can deal with Nolan." Curran frowned. "Is my uniform jacket in here?"

Harriet lifted it from the back of the chair where it had been placed by Julian the night before.

"Right-hand pocket," Curran said.

She pulled out a paper bag, and as she did so, a piece of joss paper fell to the floor. She picked it up and put it in her own pocket. He'd probably picked it up off the street. It could go on Huo Jin's pyre later.

"What's this?"

"Sylvie Nolan's journal, or what's left of it." Curran sounded despondent. "Our one decent piece of evidence and Nolan burned it. It needs to go with the rest of the evidence. I forgot about it yesterday."

Harriet peered in the bag, the smell of burning pervading the room. "Not much of it left," she said. "Why would he burn it?"

Curran shook his head. "She was carrying a child. Probably six weeks. Maybe there were things she wrote Nolan didn't want the world to know."

Harriet gasped, overcome with the tragedy of not one but two lives lost in that violent attack. She glanced down at the journal again and a realization dawned on her. "Do you think Nolan may not have been the father?"

Curran closed his eyes. "I don't know what to think. Just get it back to Headquarters for me."

Li An stirred, her long dark hair falling across her face as she sat up. "Curran?"

"Not dead yet," he replied.

She rose to her feet and faced Harriet across the bed. Instinctively Harriet took a step back. There was something proprietary and challenging in Li An's dark eyes.

"I'll leave you with the patient," she said. "Do you want me to instruct Huo Jin to organize some tea . . . food?"

"No need," Li An said.

"See you this evening."

Harriet beat a retreat.

She found Julian on the verandah reading the paper, a cup of tea on the table beside him.

"How is Curran this morning?"

Harriet cast a glance inside the house. "Not well, but Miss Khoo seems to have matters in hand."

"Do I need to do anything?"

"If you could send a note to Euan at the hospital and ask him to call past. I think Curran should be seen by a doctor."

Julian pulled an envelope from his pocket. "This just came from Priscilla Nolan. Sylvie Nolan's funeral is this afternoon and Miss Nolan is hoping both you and I can attend."

Harriet sighed, thinking of the witness statements waiting for her to type up at South Bridge Police Station.

Her brother viewed her from over the top of his glasses. "Has it occurred to you your attendance at the funeral provides a splendid opportunity to assist your ailing inspector with his investigation?"

Harriet caught his meaning. "Oh, I suppose we could ask a few questions . . . report on who is there. That sort of thing. Very well, brother dear, I will see you this afternoon. What time?"

"Three at the British Cemetery."

South Bridge Road

Harriet's first task on arriving at South Bridge Road Police Headquarters was to inform Inspector General Cuscaden of Curran's indisposition. Cuscaden always treated her with unfailing courtesy, clearly uncomfortable with the presence of a woman in his employment and furthermore one over whom he exerted no real right of command. While quite progressive in many areas of police practice, the employment of females even in administrative roles was apparently not one he had ever considered. This weakness was one that Curran exploited shamelessly, dispatching Harriet with unpleasant messages he knew would cause his senior officer to thump his desk had it been Curran standing before him.

"This is dam . . . extremely inconvenient," Cuscaden remarked. "The bl . . . army will seize any opportunity to take over the investigation." He blew out a breath, "Well, if the army asks questions, I'll just say I've had to send him out of town on an extremely urgent matter. Don't let me keep you, Mrs. Gordon. You must have work to do."

At the door, Harriet turned back. "Miss Nolan has asked that I attend the funeral this afternoon."

"Are you asking me or telling me?" Cuscaden replied.

Harriet smiled. "Telling."

"Then I shall see you there. Close the door after you and send Singh to see me. He'll have to step up while Curran's indisposed." He rolled his eyes. "That'll please the army."

An air of gloom hung over the Detective Branch after Harriet's news of Curran's indisposition. There were no more witnesses to interview. Greaves had failed to find a single useful fingerprint and his plans to go back and redo the bedroom had been scuppered by Nolan's bonfire and thorough cleansing of the crime scene.

All they could do was stand around and stare at the blackboard.

Harriet removed the journal from her pocket and took it across to Greaves.

"Curran wants this logged as evidence," she said.

Greaves turned it over. It had burned right down leaving only a couple of inches of the cover and the spine intact. "Not much left of it, is there?" he said. "But let's have a look. It might yet tell us something interesting."

Fascinated by the work Greaves did, Harriet stood and watched as he laid out the journal on a piece of old newspaper and, using a pencil, turned the stubs of pages. What pages remained were unintelligible or blank. He gently fanned out the remnant pages, but nothing fell from the leaves except burned paper. Finally, he picked it up and held it up to the light and peered down the spine.

"Hello, what's this?" he asked no one in particular.

He picked up a pair of tweezers and everyone in the room gathered around his desk as he inserted the tweezers into the spine and pulled out an intact thinly folded piece of paper.

He looked up at Harriet and grinned.

"Why don't you have a look at it, Mrs. Gordon? What does it tell you?"

Harriet picked up the paper. "Poor quality writing paper," she began. "Green-blue ink. No identifying address or even a date."

"A man or woman's hand?" Greaves asked.

Harriet studied the spidery scrawl and shook her head. "Impossible to tell."

Greaves took the paper from her and studied it. "I think it is a man's handwriting."

"How can you tell?"

"The downstrokes are very firm and it's spiky rather than rounded, but"—he shook his head—"I'm only guessing. Graphology is not my speciality."

Harriet took the note from him. "One thing I can tell you, it is a love letter." She read aloud.

Dearest, It was a torment to be so near to you and yet so far away.

How lightly your fingers fly across the keys, creating sublime music for us all! I felt quite mesmerized, watching them.

Like your music, your very presence fills the air and gives me succor in this difficult world. When I am around you, I feel a weight lift from me momentarily; you free me from the burden of being alone in this world.

How I treasure our friendship! My dear, if you only knew how light my heart feels when I am in your presence . . .

She turned the paper over but the letter must have continued on a separate page.

"That's it," she said.

Greaves poked around the cavity in the spine with the tweezers. No more hidden pages came to light.

Greaves took the paper back and wrinkled his nose. "Bit prosy. I'd never write something like this."

Harriet tried to imagine the serious young man writing any sort of love letter . . . and failed.

"I do not think it was written by the colonel," Musa said.

"Neither do I," Harriet agreed.

Harriet returned to the dull transcription of statements that added nothing to the investigation, her mind racing with the possibilities the letter revealed. Was it proof that Sylvie Nolan was having an affair or did it date back to a time before her wedding? It obviously had a particular significance to have been so carefully concealed.

Among the reports on her desk, she found Dr. Mackenzie's account of the autopsy. Curiosity got the better of her and she scanned it before filing it, noting the observation that Sylvie Nolan had been at least six weeks pregnant. At the end of the report Mac had penned a short note:

The late Mrs. Nolan had borne a child within the last two years.

She stared at the perfunctory sentence. Mrs. Nolan . . . or Miss Gentry, as she had been then . . . had another child, presumably back in England. Miss Gentry had come to the marriage as "soiled goods." Was the author of the concealed letter the father of that child? No point speculating, she had work to do and a funeral to attend. She filed the letter and glanced up at the large clock. She had to leave now if she was going to make it home for a quick luncheon with enough time to change for the funeral.

On her return to St. Tom's House, she checked in on Curran.

He was asleep in a tangle of bed linen, Li An sat on Will's hard desk chair, flicking through a copy of *The Lady*, loaned to Harriet by Louisa Mackenzie. Li An looked up and acknowledged Harriet with a nod of the head and a finger to her lips.

Harriet returned to her bedroom. Being in the habit of emptying her pockets, she turned out the contents of her skirt pockets, her fingers closing over a scrap of paper . . . the joss paper she had picked up off the floor in Curran's room that morning.

She turned it over and drew a breath.

TCK. Sri Mariamman Temple. Monday 10 P.M.

She stared at it. Was this another important piece of evidence she should have left with Greaves? Curran hadn't mentioned it.

She sat on her bed and reread the note before setting it down on her dressing table. She would have to ask Curran about it later.

British Cemetery, Bukit Timah Road

Although Harriet and Julian arrived in good time for the funeral, a sizable crowd had already gathered around the graveside. Army officers in full regimental dress, wearing somber faces, their hats or helmets tucked respectfully beneath their arms, clustered together talking in low voices. A small group of younger women, dressed in black with heavy veils covering their hats and faces, clung to one another, weeping.

The coffin, resting on a wooden pallet and covered in the regimental flag, looked tiny.

Lieutenant Colonel John Nolan, resplendent in his scarlet ceremonial uniform with green facings, accompanied by his sister and son, stood beside the coffin along with a young officer Harriet did not know. From the images she had seen of Sylvie Nolan, she assumed him, with his fair hair and delicate features, to be Nicholas Gentry, Sylvie's brother. The young man looked shattered, his face blotchy and his eyes heavy and red with weeping. He seemed impossibly young, no more than a boy himself.

Like the other women, Pris Nolan wore heavy mourning and stood next to Lavinia Pemberthey-Smythe. The previous commanding officer's relict, unlike the other women, stood tall, straight and spare, dressed, for once, in conventional Western dress. Although her black gown appeared rusty in patches and harked back to a fashion of several years past, there could be no mistaking her rank and importance. The dowager colonel's lady.

The final member of the family, Jack Nolan, had been forced into a suit that seemed a size too small for him. He looked around and, seeing Harriet and Julian, gave them a tight smile and a small wave.

Curran had told Harriet that the funerals of murder victims often told the investigator more about the victim's life and death than days of investigation so he made a point of attending funerals. Although Curran was not here and in this rigid societal code, his men would not be welcome, it didn't surprise her to see Constable Greaves hovering on the edge of the crowd, dressed in his ceremonial police uniform. Although he was English, as a mere police constable, he had no better chance of penetrating the walls that surrounded Sylvie Nolan's social circle.

Julian excused himself to speak with Pris, leaving Harriet standing alone. Inspector General Cuscaden strode across the ground. He stopped to have a few words with Greaves, before falling in beside Harriet.

"Good afternoon, Mrs. Gordon," Cuscaden said.

"Good afternoon, sir," Harriet replied.

"You see that man?" He indicated a short, balding, slightly overweight army officer, who wore the single crown of the rank of major and carried his red-banded cap under his arm. "That's the military policeman Goff. Any excuse to see Curran off this investigation and he'll take it. We only have a few days to bring the perpetrator to civilian justice."

"Is there anything I can do?" Harriet asked, her blood quickening.

Cuscaden indicated the sobbing women. "Perhaps you can ask a few questions of her friends. They may know something. Do you know any of them?"

Harriet scanned the heavily veiled women. "I think the short one is Mrs. Chatham. Her son, Peter, goes to the school. Her husband is an officer in the engineers."

"Excellent," Cuscaden said. "Nothing like a bit of female chitchat. I'll leave you to it. Tell Curran I expect him back on deck tomorrow."

"Sir, I must protest. Malaria—" Harriet began.

"Pfft," Cuscaden responded. "He can indulge himself when

the miscreant is caught. Now I better go and soothe the ruffled feathers of the colonel."

Cuscaden strode off to speak with Lieutenant Colonel Nolan.

As Julian rejoined her, Harriet found her gaze drawn to the military policeman Goff. The man wore a scowl on his face as he in turn watched Cuscaden engage in polite formal conversation with Nolan.

"Cuscaden's no fool," Julian remarked. "He's making a point that Curran's his man and he will defend his right to investigate this crime."

Harriet nodded. "Excuse me for a moment, Julian. I must speak with Mrs. Chatham."

Picking her way through the graves, Harriet joined the group of women. "Mrs. Chatham?"

The woman looked up through her heavy veiling. "Mrs. Gordon. I didn't know you were acquainted with poor Sylvie?"

"I am a friend of Miss Nolan's and she wished me to attend to support her and young Jack," Harriet said. "I never met poor Mrs. Nolan in life. Such a terrible thing to have happened."

"She was an angel," one of the other women blurted out, followed by an outburst of sobbing into the shoulder of her friend.

Elspeth Chatham introduced the two other women as Mrs. Simpson and Mrs. Mclean, both of whom were the wives of army officers in other units. A fourth woman, introduced as Mrs. Hartwell, hovered on the edge of the group.

"Such a breath of fresh air," Mrs. Chatham said. "She was such fun. Everyone who met her couldn't help but be charmed by her."

Harriet glanced across at Sylvie's husband. "She was a little younger than her husband, I believe."

"Oh, twenty years at least, but she adored him," Mrs. McLean responded between sobs. "So sweet to see them together."

"Of course the younger officers all fell in love with her," Mrs. Simpson said, with a slight edge of acerbity.

Mrs. Chatham stiffened. "Of course they did. Silly things, but she had eyes only for her 'darling John,' as she called him. Things won't be the same without her." Mrs. Chatham dabbed her nose with a black-edged handkerchief.

The regimental chaplain cleared his throat and Harriet returned to Julian.

As she did so, the silent Mrs. Hartwell caught her sleeve. "A word with you later?" she said in a low voice.

Harriet nodded and a thrill of anticipation ran down her spine. Would this be the telling piece of female chitchat that had brought her here?

"Ashes to ashes, dust to dust . . ." the chaplain intoned.

The officers of the regiment lowered the little coffin into the dark, unforgiving clay of this foreign soil where Sylvie would rest in eternity, eventually forgotten, her name and memory obscured by moss and the passage of time, like so many of the graves around her.

The funeral party turned to leave as the resounding thud of dirt hitting the wooden lid of the coffin followed them.

Harriet hung back, ostensibly studying the inscription on a nearby memorial. A black-clad figure joined her, throwing her veil back.

"I'm Alice Hartwell," she said. "My husband is chief clerk of works. Pris and Lavinia have spoken about you and now I hope you are going to join us at our meeting tomorrow."

One of Lavinia Pemberthey-Smythe's suffragists, Harriet thought, any idea that Alice Hartwell had some new light to shed on the case evaporating.

"I haven't said I will—" she began but Alice Hartwell waved her hand.

"That's not why I wanted to catch up with you," she said, lowering her voice. "I know you work for the police and I rather hoped to see Inspector Curran here."

"He was unable to attend," Harriet replied diplomatically, "but if you have a message for him, I will pass it on."

"It's nothing really," Alice replied, her gloved fingers playing with the fringes on her sleeve. "I was not quite such an acolyte of Sylvie Nolan as the others. There was something devious about her I didn't like. Her professions of affection for 'darling John' were not matched by her eyes. They were for another person."

Harriet held her breath for a moment. "Who was that?"

Alice Hartwell's voice dropped even lower, her eyes darting right and left to ensure they were not overheard. "The adjutant of the regiment, James Hawke. That's him." Alice nodded her head toward a tall, handsome officer wearing the rank of captain and dressed in the same scarlets as the colonel who had remained at the graveside with Priscilla Nolan standing beside him. "You may not know this, but James Hawke had been courting Pris for years. In fact there was more to it than that. They had an understanding, if you know what I mean. Then Sylvie turned up and he could look nowhere else. Men are such fools," she added.

"Not all men," Harriet said.

Alice nodded. "My own George is very sweet so I shouldn't complain. He would never look twice at another woman, but Sylvie Nolan—" She straightened and readjusted her veil, drawing it back over her face. "Good afternoon, Lavinia."

Harriet turned to greet Lavinia Pemberthey-Smythe, curious as to how much of the conversation she may have overheard.

"Alice, Harriet. How nice that the two of you have met." Lavinia smiled.

"My husband is waiting. Good day to you, Mrs. Gordon, I look forward to meeting you in different circumstances," Alice said.

Lavinia Pemberthey-Smythe tucked her arm into Harriet's. "Let us walk together, Harriet." They strolled a little distance down a quiet path in silence. Out of earshot of the other mourners, Lavinia said, "Such a sad occasion."

"How is Miss Nolan?" Harriet inquired.

"She's holding up. John needs her to be strong if only to keep the household running."

So Pris gets her position in her brother's household back, Harriet thought. *Does she also get her suitor back?* At the carriages parked along Bukit Timah Road, she saw James Hawke hand Pris up into the carriage. Maybe their hands lingered a little longer than propriety demanded?

"Have you thought any more about my invitation?" Lavinia asked.

Harriet hesitated for a couple of moments, remembering her conversation with Julian. Despite her misgivings, with Curran incapacitated, perhaps her attendance could be useful for the investigation and maybe, just maybe, Julian was right, she did need to talk about her experience, share the pain.

As if reading her mind, Lavinia Pemberthey-Smythe said, "I know it's hard for you, Harriet, but I think you need us as much as we need to hear from you. I very much doubt you have spoken about what happened to you beyond the barest details and the doctors probably told you that it was best forgotten. Am I right?" When Harriet did not answer, Lavinia continued, "I think you will find unburdening yourself to a sympathetic audience will do more for the healing than holding the pain inside."

Harriet summoned a smile. "My brother said much the same thing. I only hesitate because it is not common knowledge and some people may not take well to the fact that I have a criminal conviction."

"I think you can trust to our discretion, Harriet. What we are doing is not universally popular either so we can keep your secret. We will gather at my home tomorrow at three in the afternoon. In the meantime, Pris has asked me to extend an invitation to you and your brother to come up to the house. She has few friends, Harriet, and would like to count you among them."

* * *

A smaller, subdued gathering crowded the elegant living room of The Cedars. The surly military policeman Goff was not among the red-coated officers. However, the handsome Captain Hawke held court over a group of younger officers, Lieutenant Gentry, Sylvie's brother, among them. Lieutenant Colonel Nolan stood with the older men while women flitted from group to group.

Pris sat alone on the daybed with Lavinia by her side.

Seeing Harriet and Julian arrive, Pris looked up and waved. As they approached, she patted the seat beside her. "Come and sit with me, Harriet. It is a great comfort having you here."

Harriet gave her brother a sharp glance and he tactfully withdrew to talk with the regimental chaplain.

Pris looked around the gathering and sighed. "Thank heavens that is over," she said. "I hate funerals at the best of times."

"Who was the young officer with you and your brother?" Harriet directed her glance to the young lieutenant.

"That's Nicholas. Nicholas Gentry. He is . . . was . . . Sylvie's brother."

"And the man he's talking to?" Harriet inquired, all innocence.

Pris's hand went to the brooch at her throat, a pretty gold-and-pearl design and Harriet wondered if it had some connection with James Hawke. A gift, perhaps?

"Oh, that's James Hawke, the adjutant of the battalion." Her gaze slid away from her former suitor and her hand dropped back to her lap, the fingers twisting the handkerchief she held. "He was a particular friend of Sylvie's."

As if aware that his name had been mentioned, James Hawke looked across at the women.

"He's certainly very handsome," Harriet said. "Have you known him long?"

Pris's well-corseted bosom rose and fell. "I thought I knew

him," she said cryptically. "Where is that nice police inspector? I hoped he would be here."

"He would but unfortunately he . . ." Harriet paused, remembering Cuscaden's story. "He has been called away on another matter today."

Pris seemed to accept that excuse and asked about Saturday's tennis tournament.

"Mr. Morris asked to have his very best wishes conveyed to you," Harriet said.

Pris looked up. "Did he? I suppose he was terribly disappointed at having to forfeit the game."

"He understood."

Pris nodded. "Of course. He is a very nice man."

James Hawke kept glancing their way and after ten minutes he broke away from his group and made his way across the room.

Pris extended a gloved hand, which he took in both hands. "Pris, how are you bearing up?"

Pris sighed. "John needs me to be strong, James. Have you met Mrs. Gordon?"

Hawke turned to Harriet, bringing his heels together in a stiff, formal bow. "Mrs. Gordon."

"Harriet works for the Straits Settlements Police, James," Lavinia Pemberthey-Smythe said.

James Hawke's eyebrows raised. "Really? How extraordinary. Are you, by any chance, in contact with that man Curran?"

"Yes."

"Then could you please tell him that I expect the platoon back from Seletar this evening. It is extremely inconvenient and I would appreciate his urgent attention in this matter or I will be sending them straight back."

Harriet had no idea what the adjutant was talking about, but she nodded. "I will pass your message on. Unfortunately, he is out of town today, but we are expecting him back tomorrow."

"Thank you," Hawke said. "Pris . . . Miss Nolan . . . if there is anything I can do to help you at this difficult time, please do not hesitate . . ."

Pris thanked him and he turned away. The three women watched his broad, red-clad shoulders as he was reabsorbed among his fellow officers.

"Is he married?" Harriet inquired.

Pris shook her head.

"I can imagine he has stirred the hearts of many a lady," Harriet continued.

"Handsome is as handsome does," Pris replied with undisguised acerbity. She turned to Harriet and, as if continuing the same thought, said, "Is it true that Sylvie was with child?"

This was not news to Harriet but it surprised her that Pris knew about Sylvie's condition.

"Did she tell you?"

Pris snorted. "Hardly! No, John told me."

"As a new bride, it can hardly be surprising," Harriet said.

Pris lowered her head. "It is if the bridegroom has never shared a bed with the bride," she said.

Harriet caught the sharp glance Lavinia shot her friend.

"That's enough, Pris," Lavinia said. "I see Mrs. Crawford coming this way . . . please excuse us, Mrs. Gordon. We will see you tomorrow."

Mrs. Crawford descended on them. "Miss Nolan, my poor dear. Aren't the flowers wonderful? Sylvie would have loved them. Are they from your garden, Mrs. Pemberthey-Smythe?"

Dismissed, Harriet rose to her feet and rejoined Julian. Time for them to leave. She had a patient at home she had to check up on and, if he was up to it, update on the things she had learned over the course of the afternoon.

Curran dreamed again of Deerbourne Hall in winter, the snow thick on the ground and the lake frozen. He had loved winter and a chance to show off his prowess at skating, something his odious cousin George had no talent for. He had been skating fast, so fast that the ice flew in chips from beneath his skates. The ice cracked and the solidity beneath his feet gave way and he plunged into dark, freezing water that filled his nose and lungs. He tried to call for help but the words wouldn't come out and he knew it would be only a matter of minutes before he was dead.

He woke gasping for breath, the sheets that covered him saturated, but not with the icy water of the lake. He lay looking up at the mosquito net suspended above the bed, tied in a neat knot. On a shelf on the wall an army of toy soldiers marched toward a stack of books. He took a shuddering breath and remembered where he was.

"You're awake." Harriet Gordon stood in the doorway, all crisp efficiency, a white apron over her familiar blue skirt and white blouse.

"I take it I'm still alive," he countered. He looked around the room. "Where's Li An?"

"She's asleep in the guest room. She sat up all night and most of today with you. As your temperature has fallen, I suggested she rest. Are you up to eating something?"

Curran thought about that for a long moment. Having spent most of the night throwing up, the thought of food made his stomach lurch.

"I'm not sure," he said.

"I'll fetch some tea and something light." She turned and left him to his thoughts.

All night and most of the day? Curran turned his face to the window. Beyond the elaborate grille, a troop of monkeys were chattering in the trees and a distant koel bird sent out its mournful cry. He could hear voices coming from the kitchen and the scent of something that must be Julian and Harriet's evening meal drifted in through the open window.

Harriet reappeared, holding a tray that she set down on the bedside table.

Curran struggled upright. Conscious of his state of undress and mortified to be in such a position with Harriet Gordon of all people, he pulled the sheet up as high as it would go. Harriet shot him an amused glance as she handed him a cup and saucer. He downed the warm liquid without drawing breath.

"What time is it?"

"It's just gone five. Julian and I have just returned from Sylvie Nolan's funeral. Try some bread and butter."

He took the plate she offered and picked up one of the bread triangles and smiled. "I haven't seen one of these since I left the nursery," he said.

"I didn't think I should offer you anything more challenging," she said.

He chewed the buttery morsel and looked around the room, evidently Will Lawson's bedroom. "What have you done with Will?"

"He's staying with Louisa and her children at the beach for a few days."

He had a vague recollection of that same conversation on Sunday night before he had collapsed. He found that memory mortifying.

He polished off another piece of bread, feeling slightly restored for the refreshment.

"What's happening with the case?"

She smiled. He knew her well enough to know she had something important to tell him.

"Cuscaden is not very happy with you."

He grimaced. "I can imagine."

"He told Nolan that you were called away on another case today."

"Did he?"

"I think he dislikes the army as much as you." She smoothed the front of her skirt. "I've been busy."

"Typing witness statements?"

"That was this morning." She pulled a face. "There are so many witnesses to absolutely nothing but Greaves found something interesting hidden in the spine of the journal you gave me this morning. A love letter or at least a portion of a love letter."

Curran's pulse quickened. "Who from?"

Harriet shook her head. "No signature. Nothing to identify the writer except the writing."

Curran's excitement faded, but a quick glance at Harriet's bright eyes and he realized she had more to tell him.

"What else have you discovered?"

She perched on the side of the bed. "I had a couple of very interesting conversations this afternoon at the funeral and afterward. You've met Captain Hawke, I presume?"

"Yes."

"Did you know that before Sylvie arrived at The Cedars, he and Pris had an understanding?"

Curran's fuddled brain did not immediately connect what she was saying. "What sort of understanding?"

She rolled her eyes. "I will put your lack of perception down to the fever. Not quite an engagement."

Curran picked up the last piece of bread and butter and handed her the plate as he digested this piece of information and the bread. "That is interesting. Is it over?"

"It ended shortly after the Nolans arrived from England. It seems the captain was one of Sylvie's most ardent admirers—of which there were many."

Curran grunted. That tied in with what Mayhew had said, although the quartermaster had not mentioned Hawke. If the adjutant was among the infatuated men who surrounded Sylvie Nolan, he would have to look more closely at him.

"There's more," Harriet said.

He raised a questioning eyebrow.

"The marriage was a sham. Nolan and his adoring wife had never consummated it. The baby cannot be Nolan's."

Curran stared at her. "Who told you that?"

"Pris. She asked about the baby and then said it couldn't be her brother's because they had never shared a bed."

Curran lay back on the pillows and, looking up at the mosquito net, took in the enormity of this piece of intelligence.

"I would wager that's why he destroyed the journal," Harriet continued.

Curran nodded. A mistake, he still had a headache.

"You've done well, Harriet. Did Priscilla give you any hint as to who the father could be?"

Harriet shook her head. "No, but . . . if I were to make a suggestion, the first person I would be looking at is the handsome Captain Hawke."

"She had a number of admirers among the younger officers. It could have been any of them."

Harriet shrugged. "Call it a woman's intuition."

"Unfortunately, I need a little more than intuition and it doesn't make him a murderer."

Harriet stood up. "There's one more thing. Hawke asked me to tell you that the witnesses you wanted to see will be back tonight. He is none too pleased about it and said if you don't interview them tomorrow, they're going back. I presume that means something to you."

"Yes, it does. Probably more than Captain Hawke realizes," Curran mused. "By the way, where's my horse?"

"In the school paddock with Mr. Carrots."

"That disreputable beast is no fit companion for Leopold."

"On the contrary, they are getting on famously," she said.

Curran smiled but the humor drained from him as he realized the importance of what Harriet had told him about the

Seletar contingent. "Damn this bloody malaria. It couldn't have happened at a worse time."

"I told you to keep taking the quinine."

Curran grimaced at the sight of Euan Mackenzie in the doorway. "Who sent for you?"

"We did," Harriet said.

As Mac advanced into the room, Curran said, "It's been a year since the last attack. I thought I was over it."

"You're never over malaria," the doctor said.

Mac glanced at Harriet, who took the hint and left them alone, shutting the door behind her. Mac conducted a quick examination.

"Good God, man, don't you own a nightshirt?"

"No, but Li An's here. She's looking after me."

Mac shook his head. "You know how this goes, Curran. You're not out of the woods yet. You'll have at least one more bout of the fever before this is over."

Curran nodded, regretting the tea and bread. He had no doubt both would make a reappearance in the next hour or so.

Mac took a bottle of quinine tablets from his bag. "Take a double dose tonight. As a doctor, my medical advice is a week of complete rest . . ." As Curran pushed himself upright to protest, Mac held up his hand. "As a friend, I know you have a murder to solve. If you come through the next round of fever tonight, give yourself twenty-four hours."

"I like the 'if,'" Curran remarked drily.

Mac frowned. "Curran, I don't use the word lightly. Malaria may be a fact of life here but it is also a fact of death. There are no heroics to be gained in not keeping up your quinine or going back to work while you're still sick."

"I consider myself chastened."

Mac snorted. "Hah. I know you of old, Curran. You are a bad patient and will take no notice of what I say and blame it all on Li An. You don't deserve her."

Curran looked away. "No, I don't," he said.

∞ ELEVEN

St. Thomas House
Monday, 15 August

Julian had a dinner appointment with the bishop, never one of his favorite social engagements, so Harriet ordered a light supper for herself and Li An, and as night descended on the garden, she lit a lamp and took a whiskey out onto the verandah, pausing to collect the cat and the curious scrap of joss paper she had found on the floor of Curran's room.

She was pleasantly surprised when Li An joined her on the verandah, curling up in one of the rattan chairs like a cat herself. She wore a simple dark-blue *samfu,* her hair dressed in a single braid down her back, which made the scar on her face more pronounced.

"Curran is asleep," she said. "Sleep is the best thing for him."

Li An picked up the book Harriet had set down on the table beside her: George Eliot's *Middlemarch,* borrowed from the library.

"At my school, we had to read such books," Li An said with a furrowed brow. "But they are not to my taste. What does it mean for a girl in the Straits to learn of English villages?"

Harriet held her breath for a moment, unsure as to whether this was an invitation to ask Li An something of her life.

"Where did you go to school?" she ventured.

Li An set *Middlemarch* back on the table. "The Convent Light Street in Penang. The nuns, they were very strict . . . and French," she added.

"But they taught English literature?"

Li An shrugged. "They preferred to teach French literature but the library contained only books such as this. My father, he believed that a woman had as much right to a good education as a man. That surprises you? You believe that we Chinese girls are brought up to be subservient to our fathers and husbands?"

Harriet shook her head. "I would have liked to have gone to university and become a lawyer like my father but my parents believed education beyond school was wasted on a girl," Harriet said, rising to her feet. "Whiskey?"

Li An nodded, and as Harriet busied herself pouring a glass, Li An said, "And that is why you are a . . ." She paused. ". . . suffragist?"

Harriet turned to face the woman. "Curran told you that?"

Li An gave a half smile and a shrug. "Curran tells me many things."

Harriet handed her the glass and resumed her seat. Shashti climbed onto her lap and eyed Li An suspiciously.

"And he tells me things too," Harriet said. "You do not like cats?"

Li An laughed. "They make me sneeze. Did Curran tell you that? What else has he told you about me?"

"Nothing," Harriet answered with an apologetic smile. Curran kept his private life . . . private. "But I am pleased to meet you at last."

Li An considered her. "And I you," she said. "He has great respect for you and he considers you a friend. He is not a man with many friends."

"Oh," Harriet said, unsure how to respond to that. Curiosity burned and she would have loved to have asked Li An in what circumstances she and Curran had met . . . and how they both came to bear such terrible scars, but she bit back the questions.

As if reading her thoughts, Li An touched her face and said, "You have been wanting to ask about my scar. Curran and I are bound by the blood my brother shed."

Harriet stared at her. "Your brother did that?"

Li An did not reply for a long moment, her gaze holding Harriet's. "Yes, my brother did this. I think you and I have much in common. We both bear scars." She touched her scarred cheek again. "I wear mine for all the world to see." Her hand went to her heart. "Your scars are here and you hide them well."

Harriet cleared her throat. "Perhaps." She found the other woman's directness and perception unsettling and she changed the subject.

"Li An, can you tell me if this means anything to you?" She passed over the joss paper. "I found it in Curran's pocket this morning."

Li An looked at the paper and shrugged. "Just joss paper," she said. "Nothing special. The characters are intended to make peace with the dead."

"Turn it over."

Li An held the paper to the light and read the penciled note aloud. She looked up at Harriet. "The Sri Mariamman Temple is in Chinatown," she said, "but I do not know who Curran intended to meet there tonight." She frowned. "Do you think it may have something to do with the death of the colonel's lady?"

Harriet shook her head. "I don't know if I was meant to hand it over as evidence this morning. Curran only mentioned the journal, not this paper."

Li An took a sip of the whiskey. "Should we tell someone?"

Harriet thought about whom precisely they should tell. Was

it worth bothering Curran's men over something that could prove to be trivial?

"The reverend?" Li An suggested.

"He is out for the night and likely to be very late. Perhaps we should ask Curran?"

Li An shook her head. "He is asleep. The fever will return tonight and he must be strong," Li An said in a tone of voice that brooked no argument. "I will go. Chinatown holds no fear for me."

"You can't go alone," Harriet said.

Li An cast her a scathing look. "I am a part of Chinatown," she said. "Who would question me?"

"It might be dangerous." Harriet hesitated. "Perhaps if we both went . . . ?"

This time Li An laughed. "A Western woman in your Western clothes? Do you not think that would be strange?"

"I have a *salwar kameez* from my time in India," Harriet ventured.

She referred to the loose tunic top and trousers favored by the women of the north of India.

Li An shrugged. "I must fetch clean clothes for Curran from our home. If you wish to accompany me, who am I to stop you?"

Harriet took her grudging acquiescence. "We can take the pony trap and Aziz," she said slowly. "Huo Jin can keep an eye on the patient."

Li An gave a sharp inclination of her head and rose to her feet in one swift, languid and elegant movement. "Very well. We will go at half past eight. That will give us time to visit my home first."

While Li An saw to Curran, Harriet asked Aziz to bring the pony trap around to the front of the house. She changed into the *salwar kameez* that she had sometimes worn on visits to the Bombay slums with James. She had forgotten she had it until she had seen Lavinia Pemberthey-Smythe effecting native dress and now she retrieved it from a forgotten drawer. She tied her hair in a loose chignon at the nape of her neck and draped the scarf over her head. Completing the outfit with a pair of practical Indian sandals.

She nodded approvingly at her reflection, and before leaving the room, she unlocked her bedside cabinet and pulled out the wooden case containing the .22 caliber Smith & Wesson revolver that had been her husband's. He had purchased it for "protection" during a period of civil unrest and had taught her the rudiments of shooting. Like the *salwar kameez* it had lain forgotten. Harriet had not taken it out of the box since leaving India and it badly needed a clean. She held it up to the light and grimaced—even she could see the rust spots. She had no ammunition but maybe the presence of the weapon would be sufficient to warn off any attackers.

"You are taking that?" Li An stood in the doorway, her eyes wide.

Harriet looked at the revolver. "The affair of the sapphire has taught me to be prepared for all eventualities," she said. She didn't mention that the weapon held no ammunition, and even if it had, she had no confidence in her ability to use it. She dropped it into the capacious pocket of her pantaloons.

She turned to face Li An. "Do I pass?"

Li An nodded. "You will do," she said. "Curran is still sleeping and that woman"—Harriet assumed she referred to Huo Jin—"will watch over him."

That woman stood in the corridor, her arms crossed. "Where you going dressed like that?" she demanded.

"I am accompanying Miss Khoo to the inspector's house to collect a clean uniform."

"And you dress like that?" Huo Jin bristled with indignation.

"It's comfortable," Harriet replied. "We'll be back before the reverend."

Aziz grumbled about having to hitch the pony trap and go out after dark. He grumbled even more when told where they were going.

"Chinatown? That is not safe, mem."

"Nonsense. We are only going to fetch a clean uniform for the *tuan* and Miss Khoo has suggested it is a good time to see some of the Hungry Ghost activities in Chinatown. We won't stay long."

Aziz rolled his eyes.

Mr. Carrots also seemed unenthusiastic about the nighttime excursion and leaving his newfound friend, Curran's magnificent chestnut, Leopold, but with lamps tied to the pony cart, they set off just after nine, intending to do exactly what they said they were going to do, collect a clean uniform and visit Chinatown.

They were well on the way before Harriet remembered she had left the joss paper note on the table on the verandah. Nothing to be done about it. If they went back for it, they would miss the assignation.

Curran's bungalow was off Cantonment Road tucked into the corner of the old Everton estate. Aziz muttered to himself as they made their way up the hill to the small, thatched bungalow.

They drew up outside the front door, where the air hung heavily with the scent of the huge frangipani tree that stood beside the steps up to the verandah. Li An jumped down from the trap and took one of the lanterns.

"Are you coming?" she said to Harriet.

Harriet climbed down from the pony trap and followed her up the steps onto a verandah furnished with a couple of elderly rattan chairs with colorful cushions. Li An unlocked the front door, which opened onto the ubiquitous living room, a simple combination of both living and dining. The furnishings were plain and obviously secondhand but everything had an air of being well looked after.

"Wait here. I won't be long." Li An lit a candle on the dining table and pushed open a door beyond which Harriet caught the glimpse of a white mosquito net knotted above the bed. She lifted up the lantern and crossed to a bookcase on the far wall.

Books did not survive long in the Singapore climate and the spines were mildewed and the pages felt damp to her touch, but it seemed Curran's reading ran to the classics—Dickens and Thackeray jostled with two volumes of *Halsbury's Laws of England* for space on the crowded shelves. She pulled out Volume 1 of *Halsbury's* and flicked through the index: Action, Admiralty, Agency . . . It reminded her of her father.

"Curran is a great reader," Li An said.

Harriet replaced the book and turned around.

Li An held up a bag. "I have everything I need. We should go now."

Aziz did not look happy when instructed to drive them down onto South Bridge Road. Even though Police Headquarters and the police courts were on the eastern fringes of Chinatown, Harriet rarely ventured into the maze of alleys and dark shophouses that were entered via the uneven five-foot walkways. To come here in daylight, let alone after dark, was to enter a foreign country, one where her white skin and Western dress did not belong. She pulled the scarf around her face, grateful she had adopted a simple disguise for this excursion.

The Hindu temple of Sri Mariamman had been on the same site for nearly a hundred years and Chinatown had grown up around it. It had never been explained to Harriet why, in the middle of this bustling, all-Chinese population, there should be a Tamil temple, but it rose up from the street, dominating the streetscape with its three-tiered *gopuram* surmounted by writhing demons and Indian gods adding to the general confusion.

They left Aziz and the pony trap across from the temple in South Bridge Road and continued on foot.

The smell of a thousand cooking fires mingled with the bra-

ziers and incense of the Hungry Ghost Festival and other un-
identifiable smells produced by a press of humanity forced into
close proximity. A Chinese opera in full voice drifted down
Temple Street, a large crowd of onlookers blocking the street.
The performance of operas was important during the Hungry
Ghost Festival but Harriet had yet to see any Chinese opera.
Huo Jin was, by all accounts, a much-sought-after celebrity and
had invited Julian and Harriet to attend a performance at a local opera in which she would be performing. Huo Jin's rehears-
als echoing from the kitchen had been intriguing.

"What is the time?" Li An asked.

Harriet glanced at her watch. "Nearly ten," she said.

At the heavy wooden doors that marked the entrance to the
temple, Harriet stopped to remove her sandals, grateful she did
not have laces or buttons to contend with. She had lived long
enough in India to know the correct protocol for entering the
sacred space and paused to ring one of the many bells on the
door. Li An followed suit and they entered the dark temple, lit
by braziers and oil lamps. A cloying scent of chrysanthemum
and jasmine hung in the heavy air, and at the altar to the god,
white-robed priests with bald heads officiated to a small congre-
gation of devotees. Harriet drew the scarf around her face but
no one gave the two women a second glance, and in the press of
people, Harriet wondered how they were supposed to recognize
the contact that had left the note for Curran.

They drew back into the shadows near the entrance to watch.

"Where is Curran?"

Both women started. The voice came from a shadowed re-
cess behind them.

"No, don't turn around." The man spoke so quietly Harriet
had trouble hearing him above the buzz of the temple.

"He is ill," Harriet said. "We have come in his stead. Anything you have to say to him, you can say to me."

To her surprise the man laughed.

Harriet turned in time to see the back of a tall man dressed in a *kurta* and *lungi* with a loose turban wrapped around his head, pushing his way through the worshippers to the door of the temple.

She hurried after him, catching his arm. "Who are you? What message do you have for him?"

He turned to look at them.

Beside her, Li An let out a sharp cry and said, "It was you who followed me."

The man glanced at Li An and brought his gaze back to Harriet. A youngish Indian man with a lean face and a dark moustache.

"My words are only for Curran."

He shook her hand free and ran for the entrance. Harriet and Li An hurried after him but they were fighting against a tide of people entering the temple, and by the time they had regained the street, the man had gone, plunging into the crowd that thronged Temple Street.

Harriet and Li An pulled on their sandals and went after him. The man's height betrayed him and he was easy to spot above the crowd. He glanced back and broke into a run, ducking and weaving in and out of the masses. Then quite suddenly he vanished.

They had reached a quieter end of Temple Street beyond the opera. Here the tall shophouses were shuttered and silent and there were only a few passersby who gave them curious glances. They stopped at the dark alley down which the man must have gone. A single lamp glowed at the far end.

Li An grabbed Harriet's arm, pulling her away from the yawning mouth of the alley. "This place is dangerous," she said. "We must not be found here."

Two darker shadows moved in the lane, coming toward the two women. As Harriet and Li An turned to run down Temple

Street, two burly men emerged from the shadows, one on each side of them, cutting them off in either direction.

They were both Chinese. Li An said something that sounded uncomplimentary and the men just laughed, closing in on them.

Harriet reached into her pocket, her hand closing on the butt of the useless revolver.

She pulled it out and held it up, moving the barrel from one man to the other and hoping they would not call her bluff.

Instead, the larger of the two men had the audacity to laugh, but they both raised their hands and drew back against the sagging, mildewed wall of an ancient shophouse.

"After you, Li An," Harriet said, her voice high and strained.

The women turned and ran, not looking back until they reached the relative safety of the crowd around the temple. Only then did Harriet slow, her heart pounding and her breath coming in short gasps. Even in the relatively short sprint, her tunic was soaked with perspiration and she had lost her scarf.

She swallowed hard and glanced at Li An, who, annoyingly, managed to look perfectly composed. Conscious of the crowd around her, Harriet returned the weapon to her pocket.

They found Aziz sitting on the edge of a five-foot way, the pony's reins looped around his arm. He jumped to his feet on seeing them.

"Oh, mem," he said. "I was worried."

So was I, thought Harriet. Instead she gave the boy a reassuring smile. "Nothing to be worried about, Aziz. We stopped to watch the opera. Now let's go home."

"What was that place? Who were those men?" Harriet said once they were both safely in the pony trap and crossing the Coleman Bridge, making for River Valley Road.

"It is an opium den," Li An said. "A place of much unhappiness."

Harriet lapsed into silence.

"It was as well you went prepared," Li An said.

Harriet's hand strayed to her pocket, her fingers closing on the cold metal of the pistol. "It wasn't loaded," she confessed.

Li An cast her a disparaging glance.

Embarrassed, Harriet looked away.

"The man in the temple, you recognized him," she said, turning back to Li An.

Li An shook her head. "It is the same man who followed me home from the market the other day and I have seen him watching the house."

"So, nothing to do with the Nolan murder?"

"No. I do not believe so."

What could she tell Curran? What distinguished the man from the others who thronged the temple? It had just been an impression, nothing more, but she could have sworn that one eye had a milky whiteness to it that the other, lost in the dark shadows, had not. The man was blind in one eye.

As the pony trap turned into the driveway of St. Tom's House, Harriet's heart sank. A lamp burned on the verandah and Julian sprang up from a chair and came to the top of the steps, his stiff posture every inch the headmaster. She felt like one of his students caught doing something wrong.

He waited until both women had alighted from the trap and Aziz had driven it away before he thundered, "Where have you been?"

"We went to fetch some clean clothes for Curran," Harriet said, indicating the bundle Li An carried.

"I got home an hour ago and Huo Jin said you left at nine. It does not take you that long to get to Cantonment Road and back," Julian raged.

"And I didn't need clean clothes so badly that it couldn't have waited until daylight."

Harriet swallowed. She hadn't noticed Curran, bundled in Julian's dressing gown, sitting hunched in one of the other chairs.

"You shouldn't be out of bed," she countered.

"You haven't answered Julian's question," the policeman said. "From the state of the two of you, I don't believe it was just a trip to Cantonment Road and back."

Conscious that her hair had lost a few pins and was falling around her face, Harriet tucked a lock behind her ear.

Curran still looked terrible, haggard and unkempt, but the eyes he turned on Harriet were bright and clear . . . and icy with anger. While it was hard to take an unshaven man in rumpled pajamas (also Julian's) seriously, Harriet now knew him well enough to know that he was seriously displeased with her.

Curran held up the now-familiar piece of joss paper that Harriet, in her haste and excitement, had forgotten. "Don't bother inventing some far-fetched explanation," he said. "You went to make this assignation."

"We . . . I . . . thought it might have some bearing on the case," Harriet said.

"Mrs. Gordon, I credited you with more sense than that. I don't know why you would take it upon yourself to make an assignation that I myself had no intention of making."

"It was only one man, an Indian, and he seemed determined to speak to you." Harriet knew she sounded defensive.

Curran shrugged. "I have hundreds of cases . . ."

"That's an exaggeration."

"I certainly have more cases than you necessarily know about and they include some very dangerous men involved in the opium trade that make the Nolan murder look tame. Whoever this man is or what he wants of me, it is absolutely none of your business, or yours, Li An. Do I make myself clear?"

Li An lifted her chin. "It was the man who followed me home, Curran," she said. "I think that gives me a right to know what his business is with us."

That seemed to give Curran pause. "Are you sure?"

"Of course I am," Li An replied in a glacial tone.

"Describe him," Curran said.

"Tall," Harriet said. "Midtwenties, at least six feet, dark hair and moustache and blind in the right eye."

"Are you sure?"

"It was dark and I only got a passing look at his face, but yes, I'm sure. Do you know him?"

Curran shook his head and sank back into his chair, running a hand over his face. "You are both safe, that is what matters. Now please excuse me, I am returning to bed. I can't afford another day off."

Harriet opened her mouth to protest that he was far from well enough to return to work, but from the icy glare he cast at her, she could see that he was still angry so she held her peace.

Li An glanced at Harriet. "I will see to him," she said. "It is the illness that makes him cross."

"As for you . . ." Curran turned to Li An.

She raised her chin. "Go to bed, Curran. We will talk in the morning," she said in a tone that brooked no argument even from a senior policeman.

Alone with her brother, Harriet sank onto the chair Curran had vacated and the foolishness of what they had done hit her, compounded by her brother's expression of wounded concern. She leaned forward, her head in her hands.

"Harriet Jane, what were you thinking?" Julian said, but the anger in his voice had died.

Harriet shook her head. "I don't know," she admitted. "I suppose I thought I was being helpful."

"Helpful?" His glasses slid down his nose in his consternation as he sat down beside her. "Dear girl, you could have been . . ."

She held up a hand. "Don't! I feel foolish enough."

He took her hand, patting it with his other hand. "When I found you gone, I was terrified. This isn't London and I don't need to tell you Curran was livid when he worked out where the two of you had gone. You are not a policeman, Harri. You had no right and no business going off on such an excursion. It was unbelievably stupid."

She rose to her feet, uncomfortably aware of the weight of the pistol in the pocket of her pantaloons. She sent silent thanks to Li An for not disclosing exactly how much danger they had found themselves in.

"I'm going to bed. Good night, Ju."

He stood up, laid his hands on her shoulders and kissed her forehead. "Good night, my mad, impetuous little sister."

Crushed with weariness she dragged her feet down the passage with no thoughts except bed and sleep. Across the corridor from her bedroom, the door to Will's room stood ajar, a soft light still burning.

She peeked around the door, wondering if Li An was still awake and if she should tell her that Julian had calmed down and not to say anything about the two men and her pistol. Curran lay on his side, one arm across Li An, who lay outside the covers, still fully dressed, curled against him. A memory stirred and Harriet's heart ached as she remembered the nights she had curled against James, felt the weight of his arm across her body . . . knew she was safe and loved.

She gently pulled the door shut. After she had washed, she climbed into her own empty bed and lay awake for a long time, curled up with her own arms around herself, nursing the gaping wound of loneliness in her heart.

❧ TWELVE

Curran dragged himself out of bed and dressed in the clean uniform Li An had procured from their home the previous night. She was still asleep, stretched out on Will's narrow bed, and he stooped and kissed her unscarred cheek. Her eyelashes fluttered but she did not wake and it occurred to him that she must be exhausted.

As he shaved, he leaned on the hand basin, scrutinizing his reflection in the mirror. He looked like a shade of death and felt like it too, but he had to keep going. He leaned closer to the mirror. What had Harriet said? The man in the temple had been blind in one eye? What did that man have to do with the Coward of Kandahar—Edward Curran, his father?

He stepped back and rinsed off his razor. This was a distraction he didn't need. Whoever wanted to speak to him would just have to bide his time, and if he chose to make contact again, hopefully the two interfering women would keep out of his business.

Li An had confessed the parts of the story edited out of Harriet's version, which had involved two large, burly men, a known opium den and the fact that Mrs. Gordon went to the liaison armed with an unloaded revolver. He vacillated between white-hot fury at their interference and horror at the danger in which the women had put themselves.

He found Li An's partner in crime taking breakfast alone at the table on the verandah.

She glanced up at him and had the grace to look embarrassed.

He scowled. "Good morning, Mrs. Gordon."

She visibly flinched at his deliberate use of her formal name. Curran was accustomed to employing the familiarity of her first name when they were alone, so reverting to formality emphasized his annoyance with her, and he was very annoyed.

"Julian had to go up to the school. He sends his apologies for not being here this morning," she said.

Curran reached for the teapot and poured a cup.

"What's this about you carrying a weapon on your little escapade last night?"

Harriet looked up, her eyes wide. "Li An told you?"

"Li An told me everything."

"It was James's pistol." Harriet's words came out in a rush. "It wasn't loaded. I don't even have any ammunition for it."

"Then why do you have it?"

"Since that affair back in March, I dug it out—just in case. It was a foolish thing to have done. I endangered both of us and have probably ruined one of your cases. I'm sorry."

Curran had no intention of letting her off with a mere apology. "Give me one reason why I shouldn't terminate your services," he growled.

He thought he detected a twinkle in her eye as she said, "Because the inspector general can't read your writing."

He bit back a smile. She had him on that point.

"Very well. Just promise me, you won't do anything like that again?"

"Of course," she said in a subdued voice, her eyes fixed on her plate.

He knew she meant it—for the moment, but he knew Harriet Gordon well enough to know that curiosity would always get the better of her.

He glared at her. "Do you know how to use the weapon?"

Her chin came up in that now-familiar gesture of defiance he'd come to know so well. "Yes . . . no. James taught me but it was a long time ago."

He held her gaze, forcing her to lower her eyes and fiddle with her serviette. "I hadn't even opened the box in four years," she admitted.

"Can I see it?"

She brought out the box and unlocked it for him. He took out the Smith & Wesson and grimaced as he turned it over. "It should have been stored in oil," he said. "If you'd tried to use this last night, it would have blown up in your face." Curran set it back in the box and locked it again. "May I take it with me? I will see what can be done about cleaning it up and then I suggest I take you out on the shooting range and run you through the basics," he conceded.

She looked up at him. "Would you?"

He grunted his assent.

"Toast?" She pushed the toast rack across the table toward him. He had no appetite but recognized he needed to eat something, so he took a piece of the cold, singed bread and spread it with honey.

As he ate, he watched her. In her white shirt and dark skirt, her hair neatly coiled on her head, she was the Harriet Gordon he knew, but last night he had seen a different woman in a *salwar kameez*, her dark hair falling around her perspiration-sheened face. In her dishevelment, she had looked vibrant and alive, and he understood why he valued her friendship—and her companionship.

"You really shouldn't be returning to work today," she ventured, a little of the old Harriet returning.

He set the unappetizing remnant of toast down on the plate. "I can't afford the luxury of lying around in bed. Goff only needs one small excuse to shut the door to this investigation in my face."

A familiar motor vehicle turned into the driveway, driven by Constable Tan bearing Gursharan Singh in the passenger seat. Singh left Tan in the car and bounded up the steps two at a time.

From his furrowed brow and tightly compressed lips, Curran knew his sergeant well enough to know something was not right.

"What's happened?"

"Oh, sir. Never was such a bad time for you to be unwell." Every hair in Singh's immaculate beard bristled with displeasure as he said, "I had word yesterday afternoon that the soldiers you had wanted to interview had returned to barracks, but when I went to interview them in your absence, Major Goff would not admit me. I cannot tell you, sir, the things he called me. I have not heard the like in many years. Worse even than that insolent corporal."

Curran rose to his feet and laid a hand on Singh's shoulder. "I'm sorry, old friend," he said. "I am sorry for my whole cursed race. If it is any consolation, he hates me too."

Singh coughed and his moustache twitched. "Ah yes, he was less than complimentary about you."

Curran's lips tightened. "We'll go and face him together and hopefully we can get these interviews over with."

Before I fall flat on my face, he thought.

Singh looked at Curran. "Are you sure you are up to it, sir? You do not look well."

"I'm fine," Curran said with more confidence than he felt. If they could deal with the military in the morning, he could retire to his bungalow in the afternoon.

He turned to Harriet. "Thank you to you and your brother

for your hospitality and I apologize for the inconvenience. I will send my syce to collect the horse."

Harriet nodded. "Do you need me in the office today?"

He frowned, just to let her know she still had not been completely forgiven. "Have you finished typing the statements from the weekend?"

"No. I had to go to the funeral."

"Then, yes. I do need you," he snapped, and started down the steps.

Curran climbed into the motor vehicle, and as they drove out of St. Thomas Walk, he wondered about the wisdom of bringing Harriet Gordon and Khoo Li An together. He suspected the two of them could cause him more trouble than each one individually. Life had been considerably simpler when he had been a confirmed bachelor, but, he conceded with a smile, it had also been extremely dull.

Blenheim Barracks

Curran stood fuming at the barracks gate while the guard went to fetch Goff. The military policeman took his time, a confident swagger to his step as he approached the two policemen, accompanied by a solid MP corporal. He ignored Singh and looked Curran up and down.

"You look half-dead, Curran," he remarked. "Your business out of town concluded satisfactorily?"

Curran fixed the man with a steely glare, hoping Goff didn't notice the residual tremor in his hands. "I'm here to interview the soldiers involved in the fracas that interrupted the mess dinner on Thursday night, a task that could have been accomplished yesterday had you let Sergeant Singh do his job."

Goff's gaze flicked to Singh. "I'm not letting a native interview Englishmen," he snarled.

Curran felt his sergeant tense but he knew Singh well enough to know he would not react to the deliberately provocative remark. That would be exactly what Goff wanted and Singh chose to ignore it.

With a jerk of his head, Goff indicated for them to follow him to the administration building, where he left them sitting in a hot, airless room for twenty minutes while the soldiers were fetched.

As Curran sat waiting, the fever began to creep back. He schooled himself to ignore it, silently cursing Goff. The perceptive Singh noticed his discomfort and stood up. "I will fetch you something to drink."

He returned with a cup of tepid black tea.

"You conduct the interviews, Singh," Curran said.

"They will not like that."

"They can go to hell," Curran said.

"Left, right, left, right, HALT." The tramp of boots and the familiar shouted commands brought both men to their feet as a corporal appeared in the doorway.

"Privates Jenkins and Sims, sir."

"And who are you?" Curran asked.

"Corporal Barnes, SIR," the man barked.

"Barnes, were you present on Thursday night when these two got into a scrap?"

"I was, sir. Disturbed me Thursday night, they did, 'orrible little maggots."

"In that case, I would like to interview you as well."

Barnes's eyes narrowed. "Me, sir?"

"If you could wait outside until we have finished with the private soldiers. Send in Private Jenkins."

Jenkins was a heavyset young man with a beetling brow, sporting a magnificent black eye and a cut lip. He scowled at the two policemen, sitting back and crossing his arms, belligerence written in every fiber of his being.

"Sit up straight, soldier, or I will make you stand." Curran assumed the long-practiced voice of command and the soldier obeyed instinctively.

Curran glanced at his sergeant. "Carry on, Singh."

Jenkins glanced from Curran to Singh and back again. "I ain't answering to no . . ."

"Enough!" barked Curran. "You will answer his questions or you will be answering to your corporal out there, and punishment duty at Seletar will be nothing in comparison to what I will be requesting."

Jenkins lapsed into sulky silence before answering Singh's questions with monosyllabic bad grace or simply refusing to answer.

By contrast Sims was small and wiry with a narrow face and a walleye. Unlike Jenkins, his face bore no sign of the fight, but he moved stiffly as if his ribs hurt. If these two were the pride of the First Battalion of the South Sussex Regiment, God help the rest of the regiment, Curran thought. At least Sims, to his credit, raised no objection to being questioned by Singh.

The story they both told smacked of concoction and rehearsal.

The two soldiers had got into an argument over a girl whose name neither could recall. Neither did they seem to remember what exactly had provoked the argument, only that Jenkins had hit Sims and they had fallen into a fight, only broken up when Captain Hawke had been summoned by their corporal. With straight faces they swore that Hawke had arrived sometime after ten and been with them until they were cast into the military police cell shortly after eleven.

Curran told Barnes to dismiss the two private soldiers and invited the corporal into the interview room.

In contrast to the two soldiers, Barnes addressed Singh politely in Punjabi. Singh's eyebrows rose and he responded in kind. Curran, whose Punjabi was limited, recognized the exchange as one of polite greeting.

"Served with the sepoys in India, sir," Barnes said, turning to Curran. "Best damn soldiers in the British Army."

Curran joined Singh at the table. He glanced at the door and said in a low voice, "And those two are not?"

Barnes frowned. "Scum of the earth, the two of them," he said. "If they weren't in the army, they'd be in Pentonville."

"You said you were present when they got into a fight last Thursday," Curran began.

Barnes scratched the side of his nose. "I was called in. By all accounts it was just a normal Thursday night before lights out. They'd been polishing their boots when all of a sudden Jenkins hit Sims and they was rolling on the floor. I had to send for the duty officer."

"Who was?"

"Captain Hawke. Had to haul him out of a mess dinner. I can tell you he wasn't too pleased."

"What did he do?"

"He ordered both men be taken off to the cells to cool off."

"What time was that?"

Barnes thought for a moment. "The fight broke out just before lights-out at ten. By the time he got there it would've been just after ten."

"How long was he present?"

Barnes looked up at the ceiling as if a clock had been plastered there. "Once he turned up, Jenkins and Sims went quiet as two lambs. He stayed long enough to see the two ninnies had been parted and then headed off so that couldn't have been much later than quarter past."

Curran stiffened. That contradicted the two soldiers' claim that he'd seen them into the cells.

"Are you sure he didn't escort them to the cells?"

Barnes drew his lip back. "Him? Not likely. Left it to me and a couple of the others to see 'em safely tucked up."

"Did Captain Hawke return to the dinner?"

Barnes thought for a long moment. "Dunno, sir. Couldn't say."

Curran let a silence lie between them. He suspected the corporal had more to say and he found silence most useful for prompting memory.

Barnes coughed. "He might've gone back to the dinner, but when I last saw him, he was heading toward the back gate."

Curran schooled his face to neutrality. Hawke had last been seen going in the opposite direction to the officers' mess. There were at least forty-five minutes of Hawke's alibi now missing. He just needed a little extra confirmation.

He thanked the corporal and asked him to bring both soldiers back into the interview room.

The two soldiers returned to the airless interview room together. Curran told the corporal to remain.

This time Curran did not invite Sims or Jenkins to sit and they stood facing him, casting side glances at each other.

"Stand at attention," Curran ordered.

Two pairs of feet were dragged into the attention position.

"Name and rank," Curran continued.

"Sims, private."

"Jenkins, private."

Curran left them both standing at attention.

"That's right. You're both private soldiers. They don't come much lower than you. What's your pay? Three shillings a week?" He allowed a significant pause before he said, "How much did Captain Hawke pay you to stage the fight on Thursday night?"

Sims swallowed, Jenkins's bruised face did not twitch. Behind them, Corporal Barnes shifted his position but kept quiet.

"Well?" Curran leaned forward on the table.

"One pound apiece," Sims said.

Jenkins cast him a hateful sideways glance. Sims looked at his comrade. "I ain't taking no more punishment details for Hawke. He can 'ave his poxy money back for all I care."

Behind them, Corporal Barnes snorted. "You two are in so much trouble, you'll be scrubbing the latrines till you're old and gray."

"Take them away, Corporal," Curran said.

The door slammed behind the furious corporal. "Left, right. Left, right . . ." The tramp of boots faded into the distance as Singh and Curran exchanged glances.

"Do you still want to speak to Lieutenant Cox?" Singh said.

Curran sank back into the chair and rubbed a hand across his eyes. He could barely think straight. Who was Cox again? Cox shared a room with Nicholas Gentry. Curran tried to draw his scattered thoughts together. What could Cox add to the story? Nothing he could think of for the moment, not when Captain James Hawke's alibi had just disintegrated.

"He can wait," Curran said at last. "I think we need to speak to Captain Hawke first. He has some explaining to do."

"You lied to me," Curran placed his hands on the adjutant's desk and glared at the officer.

"What the hell are you talking about?" Hawke leaned back so far in his chair, it almost toppled.

Curran straightened. His head throbbed and his vision was blurring. By rights he should be in bed with a cold compress and Li An's quiet, efficient nursing.

He subsided into the nearest chair and took a deep breath. "I have very little patience today, Hawke." He brought his gaze back to the adjutant. For the first time in their short acquaintance, Hawke's self-assurance had slipped. His forehead shone with perspiration and his red-rimmed eyes told of a man who was not sleeping well.

"I don't know what you mean?" Hawke tried bravado and failed.

"Those two idiots you paid a pound each to start a fight have confirmed their corporal's story that you had left them by quarter past ten," Curran said. "Where did you go between leaving the soldiers and returning to the mess well after eleven?"

Hawke wiped his face with a pristine white handkerchief. "Why in God's name would I lie about something like that? I just didn't keep good track of the time. That's all."

Curran narrowed his eyes. "Let me make a suggestion. You needed an excuse to leave the mess dinner to make an assignation with Sylvie Nolan."

"That's preposterous," Hawke said. "And quite improper."

"You have at least three quarters of an hour of your time unaccounted for and you were seen heading toward the back gate. As duty officer you had the key to the padlock. It gave you plenty of time to get to and from the Nolan residence before you were missed."

"And plenty of time to commit a murder," Singh added.

Hawke looked from one to the other, the color draining from his face. He straightened, his gaze flicking back to Singh. "I'm not saying anything in front of him."

Curran stiffened.

"Gentleman to gentleman," Hawke continued.

Curran turned to his sergeant, and much as it angered him, he nodded. He knew Singh wouldn't like it but he would understand the reason.

Gursharan Singh's eyes blazed but he turned and left the room without another word.

Hawke rose to his feet and walked over to the window. He stood for a long moment, his hands behind his back.

"Well?" Curran said. He'd given the man long enough to compose a plausible story.

Hawke gave a sharp inclination of his head. "Very well, I admit I set up Jenkins and Sims to stage a fight. I needed to get away from that damn dinner and the only way that would happen was if I got called out as duty officer. It wouldn't have been a problem if Sylvie Nolan hadn't got herself killed."

Curran refrained from pointing out that it was hardly Sylvie Nolan's choice to die that night.

"So why did you need the diversion?"

Hawke drew in an audible breath. "I got a message from Sylvie during the day to say she had to speak with me urgently. It couldn't wait. She wanted an opportunity to speak with me without John in the house and that night was the one night she knew he'd be gone for hours. But you know what mess dinners are like? There's no escaping them so I volunteered to be duty officer."

"Why did she want to see you?"

Hawke shook his head. "None of your damn business. Just take my word, as a gentleman. She was alive when I left her."

"I think it is my business and I am not a gentleman. This is murder we are talking about, Hawke."

Hawke said nothing, so Curran continued. "I will venture a guess," he said. "She told you she was pregnant and you were the father?"

Hawke turned to face Curran, his mouth agape. "How the hell . . . ?" His shoulders sagged. "Of course, the autopsy."

"Was it yours?"

Hawke swallowed. He staggered backward, a hand groping for the windowsill. His mouth worked but no words came out. All he could manage was a nod.

Curran let a long moment pass before he said, "Can you be sure?"

Hawke raised his head. "The colonel had a month in Penang. He asked me to keep an eye on her and, well, you know how these things go, Curran . . . We never intended . . . but . . ."

Curran regarded him without sympathy. "Did she have other lovers, to your knowledge?"

Hawke's eyes widened. "No! At least . . . no . . . she didn't, I'm sure of it. Loads of admirers among the younger officers but none would have dared . . ."

"Take matters beyond a kiss on the hand?" Curran suggested. "And how are you so sure the child was yours and not her husband's?"

This time a small smile lifted the corners of the adjutant's mouth. "Because, apart from the colonel's absence during the relevant period, as far as I know, the marriage was never consummated."

"She told you that?"

Hawke lifted his head and nodded.

Curran let several beats pass before he said in a low, calm voice, "So, did you kill her?"

Hawke let out his breath in a whoosh. "No! How could you even suggest that? I didn't kill Sylvie. I couldn't . . . I loved her."

Curran sat back in his chair. "But she'd just told you she was carrying your child, a child that could not be her husband's. What were you going to do about that? Did you lose your temper with her, pick up a candlestick and hit her?"

Hawke held up a hand as if to protect himself from an imaginary candlestick. "No! No!" He paced the width of his office. "I can't deny I wasn't pleased but we agreed . . . it could be managed."

"How?"

Hawke turned to face him, his mouth curled in a sneer. "How do you think? Sylvie would arrange matters so the colonel would think the child was his."

"To be born nearly two months premature?"

Hawke shrugged. "I'm a soldier. I don't know much about these matters. There was an alternative . . . there are places in Little India or Chinatown that can"—he swallowed—"make these matters disappear, but she wouldn't hear of it. Said it was murder. It left us very little choice. She wanted me to resign my commission and take her away with me."

"That would mean personal disgrace and a dishonor to the regiment."

Hawke nodded and sank back into his chair.

"I can't deny that it was a damnable mess." He looked up, his eyes bright and fierce. "But I didn't kill her, Inspector." He covered his face with his hands and Curran could believe his grief was real. "I loved her. Every time I close my eyes, I think of her lying there, her beautiful face . . . If I find the bastard who killed her—"

Curran hesitated to ask the next question. He didn't like asking questions to which he did not know the answer.

"Do you think it possible the colonel might have flown into a rage and killed her?"

Hawke looked up at Curran, his eyes wide with disbelief. "No! Not for a moment. It might have been an unsatisfactory marriage from his side but I have no doubt he loved her and I don't believe he knew about her condition."

When a man's pride was at stake, he could do anything . . . Curran let the answer Hawke had given sit.

"What time did you leave her?"

At the prosaic question, Hawke visibly relaxed. "Just before eleven. I knew I had to get back to the mess or questions would be asked."

"Where was she?"

"I left her sitting at her desk. She'd pulled out her journal." He lowered his head into his hands again and shook his head. "Oh, that blasted journal. I suppose it's all in there."

"We are still looking for the journal," Curran lied. "Did you see anyone at the house when you arrived or when you left?"

Hawke shook his head. "Sylvie was waiting for me by the front door and we went straight up to her bedroom. The rest of the house was in darkness. I assume Pris was asleep. The servants' quarters were also dark." He let out an ironic snort of laughter. "I didn't think I would need a witness—or an alibi."

The room was beginning to spin and Curran knew any further questions would have to wait. If he didn't get home soon, he would humiliate himself by fainting or throwing up on the adjutant's pristine desk.

Hawke looked up at him. "Am I under suspicion?"

Curran gathered his thoughts. "What do you think, Hawke?"

The man swallowed. "Does it all have to come out?"

Curran nodded and rose heavily to his feet. "You should have thought about the consequences before jumping into bed with your commanding officer's wife."

Hawke place his elbows on his desk and his head sank into his hands. "Oh God. What am I going to do?"

"To begin with, I need a proper statement from you."

Hawke groaned.

"Write it out and give it to my sergeant. I have to . . . return to Headquarters."

He left Hawke sitting slumped at his desk and found Singh and Tan waiting outside on the verandah.

"Walk with me to the car?" he said.

Singh fell into step beside Curran. "You do not look well," his sergeant remarked.

"I'm going home, if anyone needs me. Get Hawke's statement and have him sign it."

"Is he a suspect?"

"He bloody well is," Curran swore. "Motive, means and opportunity, but it's all circumstantial at the moment. I need to get my thoughts straight before we take any further steps with him, Singh, so make sure that statement is comprehensive."

"What about Lieutenant Cox?"

"He'll have to wait until tomorrow. Can you pass a message through Gentry that if Mr. Cox can spare the time, I would appreciate his attendance at South Bridge Road in the morning?"

Singh nodded and stiffened as the now-familiar figure of Major Goff rolled toward them. "Finished, Curran?" he inquired.

"My sergeant will finish up. I have to return to Headquarters on another urgent matter."

Goff shot Singh an unfriendly glance but Curran did not have the energy to deal with it. Singh could fight his own battles.

He waved a hand at Singh. "Go and do what needs to be done and I'll speak with you later."

"What's he doing?" Goff demanded as Singh turned back in the direction of the administration building.

"No concern of yours, Major. I am sure you have some traffic to direct."

Curran began to walk away but Goff grabbed his arm, swinging him back to face him.

"Don't walk away from me, Curran."

Curran met the man's hostile gaze. "Unhand me, Goff," he said as calmly as he could. "Brawling with me in full view of the entire barracks does not become your dignity or authority."

Goff let his hand drop.

"I'll remind you once again that I am in charge of this investigation and I do not appreciate you abusing and insulting and obstructing my officers in the execution of their duties," Curran said.

Before Goff could respond, Curran turned on his heel and strode toward the waiting motor vehicle, sincerely hoping he looked more authoritative than he felt at that precise moment.

❧ THIRTEEN

Scotts Road
Tuesday, 16 August

As she climbed the steps to Lavinia Pemberthey-Smythe's house, Harriet swallowed hard. Her stomach roiled with nerves and she'd already thrown up once that morning. The chatter of women's voices drifted out from the house and she told herself it was no different to a social gathering or a meeting to discuss the next charity drive, but she knew she was only lying to herself.

She had dressed in the uncomfortable "walking" outfit she had worn on her last visit to Lavinia Pemberthey-Smythe, and as she waited for the door to be answered, she fingered the pretty brooch she wore at her neck. She had hesitated in wearing it. In fact she had never worn it before. It had lain in its little box untouched since the day her sister, Mary, had given it to her.

It had been her last day in London before leaving for Singapore and Mary had taken her to lunch at the Savoy. Sitting across from her elegant but conventional sister, Harriet had felt, as she always did feel in Mary's company, gawky and out of place and ten years old. Even as grown women the six years age difference yawned like a gulf between them.

They had talked of trivialities—Mary's children, sixteen-year-old Fleur and fourteen-year-old Edward, and her stuffy, boring solicitor husband, Roger.

As the meal came to an end, Mary opened her handbag and produced a small jewelry box that she pushed across the table.

"Open it," she said.

Harriet had complied, almost dropping the box at the sight of the brooch. At first glance it appeared to be just a pretty circular floral arrangement, but the violet of the amethyst flowers, the green enamel of the leaves and the small seed pearls were the colors of the suffrage movement. Purple stood for freedom and dignity, green for hope and white for purity. Together the message was clear.

She looked up at her sister and saw tears in Mary's eyes.

"Do you know what this means?" she had asked her sister.

Mary's hand closed over hers. "I didn't know how else to say it," she said. "I am so very proud of you, Harri. Proud of what you have done, and what you will do."

"I don't understand?" Harriet said.

Mary withdrew her hand, rummaging in her handbag for a handkerchief. "I don't have your courage. I couldn't put myself into the fight the way you have or suffer what you have done. I have too much at stake—the children, Roger's career . . ." She dabbed at her nose, restored the handkerchief and brought her gaze up to meet Harriet's again. "But I send money when I can and I subscribe to the WSPU newsletter"—she paused—"and I have a sister I love more than life itself who has carried the fight to places I would never dare."

As Harriet had sat at her dressing table that morning, she had brought out Mary's gift. She thought of her sister and the sentiment behind the gift, and pinned it to the high neck of her white cambric blouse. If Mary thought of Harriet as brave, then brave she would be and not in the silly way she had behaved the previous evening, the memory of which, and Curran's subsequent anger at her foolishness, caused her to squirm.

Her fingers tightened on her handbag into which she had, with much reluctance, placed the one other object she had brought with her. If these women wanted to understand what was happening in England, then they needed to see it.

Lavinia's house servant met her and indicated for her to enter. In the cluttered living room, Lavinia Pemberthey-Smythe held court, dressed splendidly in a purple sari, her graying hair in a long plait down her back. A dozen women sat in a circle around her, teacups delicately poised, chatting among themselves. Again it reminded Harriet of a meeting of a charity committee.

Seeing her hovering in the doorway, Lavinia rose to her feet. "Harriet, my dear, do come in. Do you know everyone?"

A dozen faces turned to look at her. She recognized Pris Nolan and Alice Hartwell and a couple of "mamas" from the school. Seeing them, Harriet nearly turned and ran but Lavinia had her by the arm and propelled her to the front of the room. The presence of these women she knew brought all her fears of exposure back to her; she could only hope that the shared passion for the cause would, as Lavinia had assured her, ensure they kept their peace.

"Now our guest of honor is here," Lavinia said, "We can begin. My dear Harriet, do take off your hat and make yourself comfortable in that chair. Tea?"

Harriet took the proffered cup as Lavinia said, "Pris, the minutes of the last meeting, please."

Minutes of the previous meeting were read out and Pris moved to correspondence. She rose to her feet, brandishing a newsletter that Harriet recognized immediately as that of the Women's Social and Political Union. She had not seen one since she had left England.

"Unfortunately"—Lavinia leaned over to Harriet—"reliance on the mail does mean our news about our sisters in London is at least a month old. Carry on, Pris."

Pris provided a summary of the main news in the journal

concluding, "And in concerning news, it would appear our sister Lady Eloise Warby, recently released after three long months in Holloway, is in failing health. Sources report that she endured a hunger strike and force-feeding over thirty of those days. Her husband, an ardent supporter of the suffrage cause, has removed her to the country to recover, but he believes her health has been broken by her ordeal and suffering. Lady Warby and her family are in our prayers."

Harriet's breath caught. Not only did she know Eloise Warby personally but she knew someone else in Singapore to whom such news would bring nothing but concern.

Aware of Lavinia's sharp eyes on her, Harriet straightened. "I was closely acquainted with Lady Warby," she said. "This is worrying news."

"It is indeed, but it brings us to why we have invited you here, Harriet."

Harriet laid a hand on her arm. "Please, before we go any further," she said, "I need your assurance that what I will say today goes no further than this room. It is not widely known that I have a . . . a history, and if gossip about what I am to tell you today reaches the ears of my employers, both myself and my brother could well lose our employment."

She looked around at the other women, particularly the school mamas.

Mrs. Wilson, mother of Theodore Wilson of the upper fourth, rose to her feet. "Mrs. Gordon, we are here today because we believe passionately in the cause of women's suffrage and we do so in the knowledge that our own husbands and families do not approve. I think I can speak for all of us when I say not one of us would do or say anything that will reflect upon you or your brother."

Lavinia nodded. "My dear Harriet, of course you can rely on our discretion. Ladies, you may not be aware but our sister Harriet was arrested during a peaceable demonstration outside the

Houses of Parliament in June last year. Like Lady Warby she endured several months' incarceration and was among the first of the courageous suffragettes to undertake a hunger strike." She turned to look down at Harriet. "I know how difficult this is for you, but our sisters are anxious to hear firsthand what was done to you."

She gave Harriet an encouraging smile and resumed her seat. Harriet took a breath. With shaking fingers, she opened her handbag and pulled out the small flat box that lived in her glove box. She opened the lid to reveal the medal on its purple, white and green grosgrain ribbon. At first glance it resembled a military service medal, an impression reinforced by its simple inscription FOR VALOR on the bar of the pin, but on the medal itself were inscribed the words HUNGER STRIKE.

"This is not easy for me," Harriet began. "I returned to England after the death of my husband and son in India." She drew breath as a murmur of mingled horror and sympathy went around the gathering. "It was expected that I would live out my life in my parents' house, content with domestic matters. That was when I took a course in shorthand and typing and I was on my way back from the college when I came across a rally in Hyde Park. Lady Warby was speaking and everything she had to say went straight to my heart. I joined the WSPU and to my family's dismay became actively involved in what were intended to be peaceable demonstrations."

She steadied herself for what was to follow. "We were protesting outside the Houses of Parliament when a crowd gathered around us and began taunting us, throwing stones. We tried to defend ourselves but that was all the excuse the police needed and they moved in on us with their batons."

Seeing her hesitation, Lavinia touched her hand. "Go on."

Omitting the accusation of her alleged assault on the policeman with an umbrella, Harriet continued, "We were arrested and tried. I was sentenced to three months in Holloway. We thought when we began our hunger strike that they would let us go as they had others before us, but the policy had changed and the prison authorities had orders and authority to feed us by force if necessary." She swallowed. "It took five wardresses to hold me down, while the doctor . . ." She broke off, conscious that she had begun to shake at the memory of the man who had called himself a doctor, probing her mouth with his big, ungentle hands.

"They strapped me to a chair which they tilted back. The doctor inserted a metal gag into my mouth to hold it open. It tore my gums . . ." Harriet closed her eyes as Lavinia's hand closed over hers. She took a deep breath. "Then came the rubber hose which they forced down my throat, and when I coughed it up, they had to repeat the process." She did not mention how it had torn her gullet as her body writhed and retched to expel the foreign object. "When the doctor was satisfied it was in place, they poured the gruel or soup down. Only when it was all gone did they withdraw the tube and the gag." Leaving her with torn flesh and nothing but the taste of blood in her mouth and the sense of violation in her heart. "This process was repeated twice a day. I endured it for two weeks." She swallowed, conscious that her voice had dropped to barely a whisper and the women were leaning forward to catch her words. "They occasionally changed the method, inserting a tube down my nose instead. It was on one such occasion that the tube was misplaced and went into my lung. Fortunately they realized before they had gone too far."

Yes, they had realized as she had begun to convulse and choke beneath their hands.

Mrs. Wilson gasped, her hand going to her mouth. "Oh, my dear . . ."

Alice Hartwell asked, "What happened?"

"They released me the following day. I was bedridden for a

month. My mother told me afterward that our family doctor had despaired of my life."

She could say no more.

She closed her eyes, her breath coming in short gasps. The effort of articulating the horrors of those two weeks had brought it all back. Her body ached as it had done after the cruel torture, curled up on the unforgiving cot in Holloway, tasting once again the blood and bile.

"Harriet?" Lavinia's gentle concerned voice returned her to the present and she raised her gaze to meet the horrified eyes of the dozen women, all fixed on her.

Lavinia had not released her hand, now she tightened her grasp and her voice shook as she said, "Harriet, my dear, words fail me. We knew it was bad, but not even in our worst imaginings . . ."

The room had begun to spin. Harriet extricated herself from Lavinia's grip, rose to her feet and excused herself. She stumbled to the bathroom, where she subsided onto the cool tiled floor with her head between her knees. She had only ever spoken of what had happened to her family, and of them, only her father and Julian knew the full horror. And Julian was correct, she had pushed the near-fatal violation of her body to the back of her mind, obedient to the doctor's advice to forget all about it and get on with life.

She took a deep shuddering breath and rose on shaking legs to inspect her appearance in the mirror. Her face was blotchy, her hair beginning to escape its roll. With trembling fingers, she restored the strands of hair and splashed her face with cold water. Only when she was satisfied that she made a presentable appearance did she straighten her shoulders, her fingers once again playing with Mary's brooch.

Taking a deep breath she returned to the gathering.

Lavinia handed Harriet a clean lace-edged handkerchief and she wiped her eyes and blew her nose.

"But it's still going on," Alice Hartwell said, continuing a conversation that had evidently begun in Harriet's absence. "Look at poor Lady Warby? How can the authorities permit this inhumanity? How can they call themselves Christians?"

Harriet took a breath. "My father is a crown prosecutor. Trust me, he just about knocked down the door of the Home Secretary and my doctor lodged a formal complaint with the medical authorities, but nothing came of it. The truth is, ladies, they fear us," Harriet said, conscious that for the first time in nearly a year she had said "us." "They will do anything to humiliate and break us. They are afraid they are losing control and by losing control they are losing power."

"But what can we do? We're so far away?" Alice Hartwell said.

"We have to continue in our efforts to raise money," Lavinia said. "Write to our families in England, tell them what is happening and, if any of us have relatives that wield any sort of influence, exhort them to stop this madness. Minute that, please, Pris."

The women began to talk in outraged tones among themselves. Lavinia let them go on before clapping her hands and bringing the meeting back to order.

She turned back to Harriet. "Thank you for sharing your experience with us, Harriet. I understand the courage it took to come and speak with us today, and I want to reassure you that you are among friends . . . sisters. I hope you will consider yourself one of us."

"But do you still believe in the cause?" Pris said. "Votes for women . . . suffrage."

"Of course I do," Harriet said, and meant it. "But please understand"—she looked around at the earnest faces—"I came to Singapore to start afresh, and if word of what happened to me becomes public knowledge, I really do fear that it could jeopardize my brother's position at the school and my work with the police, which is why I plead for your discretion."

But she had known that once she spoke openly of her experience, the chances of keeping her "criminal" past concealed from the close-knit European community was now an impossibility. It had taken a huge leap of faith to speak out and she just had to trust that there would be no repercussions.

"How can you work with the police after what they did to you?" Pris could barely contain her outrage. Her nostrils flared and color rose to her freckled face.

It was Lavinia who answered. "Don't you see, Pris, that Harriet has struck a blow for equality. She is the first woman to be employed by the Straits Settlements Police and for that she should be applauded. Sometimes change is best effected from within the system."

The assembly clapped.

Harriet, who hadn't thought of her work with the Detective Branch as "a blow for equality" said, "I am merely an underling. Equality will come when they allow women to become police officers."

"And indeed, what of our sisters in the other communities? The Chinese, the Indians, the Malays?" Alice Hartwell said.

"The politics of women's equality in the colonies is complicated," Lavinia conceded. "But rest assured, Harriet, we have no intention of chaining ourselves to the railings of Government House. We can take heart that our sisters in Australia and New Zealand now have the vote. Our time will come and in the meantime we will continue to work quietly to help like-minded sisters in the coming weeks . . . months . . . or however long it takes." She looked around at the assembled women. "If there is no other business, I declare the meeting closed."

Tea and cake had been served in her absence. Harriet accepted a restorative cup of tea and nibbled, without tasting it, on the cake as the conversation descended to mundane discussions of children, absent husbands and the latest fashion. When civilities were satisfied, she announced she had to leave.

Lavinia walked with her to the pony trap, where Aziz waited for her.

"Thank you for coming, Harriet," she said, taking both of Harriet's hands in hers. "I can only begin to imagine how hard it must have been."

Unsure whether Lavinia referred to her time in Holloway or the recent meeting, Harriet replied, "Perhaps I should thank you. The doctors said I was to put it behind me and not to talk of it, but in a way it is a release, however difficult."

Lavinia smiled and embraced Harriet as if she were an old and dear friend, not just the acquaintance of a couple of days. When Lavinia released her, she said, with a smile, "It never does to bottle things up. Secrets can eat away at you like a canker until you have nothing left on the inside."

Harriet climbed into the pony trap, and as they turned into Scotts Road, Aziz said, "Home, mem?"

Harriet shook her head. "No. South Bridge Road, please, Aziz."

She had to see Curran.

In the daylight, the bungalow off Cantonment Road did not feel quite so isolated as it had the previous night, when she had accompanied Li An. She left Aziz and the pony in the shade and walked up the steps to the front door, passing the magnificent frangipani. She inhaled the sweet scent that transported her to her own home in Bombay. A huge frangipani had grown in the front garden of the Gordons' bungalow. Thomas had delighted in collecting the fragrant blooms from the ground, twirling them in his small fingers until they were a blur of yellow and white. It had been a day for bittersweet memories.

Li An met her at the door, neatly dressed in a blue *samfu*, her hair in one long, dark plait. Without hesitation she stood back and invited Harriet into the home she shared with Curran.

"They told me at South Bridge Road that Curran was here," Harriet said. "Can I see him?"

Li An's glance went to the bedroom door. "Can it wait? He must rest."

Harriet shook her head. "No, it can't wait."

Li An stood aside and Harriet opened the door to the bedroom. Curran lay on the bed, dressed only in a loose pair of baggy cotton trousers, his chest bare and his feet crossed at the ankles, a damp cloth over his eyes.

"Go away, Harriet," he said without moving.

"How did you know it was me?"

"I recognize the perfume you use. Lily of the valley."

Harriet opened her mouth to protest that she did not use perfume but remembered her favorite lily of the valley soap.

"It can't wait, Curran."

He groaned and threw off the cloth and swung his legs off the bed. "Go and chat to Li An. I'll join you shortly."

Li An had set out a Chinese tea set on the table.

"You English do not know how to make tea," she said. She caressed the earth-brown teapot, which shone with the glaze of long use. "Sit down, please, Mrs. Gordon."

Harriet sat, watching the quick, deft choreographed movements of sweet-smelling jasmine tea and hot water, before Li An set the tiny cup before her, watching with a sharp gaze as Harriet took a sip of the beautiful, refreshing liquid.

Harriet set the cup down and smiled. "Thank you. May I have some more?"

She was on her third cup before Curran appeared, looking haggard and gray. He had pulled on a loose Indian top over the trousers but his feet were still bare. She rarely saw him out of uniform and the transformation always surprised her.

"I'm sorry to disturb you when you should be resting," Harriet began, conscious that she was already in disgrace with the policeman and now she had just compounded her crimes by invading his home.

"What is so important?" he grumbled, taking the cup of tea Li An proffered.

"I attended a meeting of the Singapore suffragettes this morning."

"The what?"

"I don't know if that's what they call themselves, but Lavinia Pemberthey-Smythe and Pris Nolan seem to be very much the leaders."

Curran's eyes narrowed. "Harriet . . ." His voice held warning.

She bridled at the implication that she was interfering again. "I had been asked to speak about my time in Holloway."

Curran nodded. He was one of the few she had trusted with her history.

"Curran, I have some news of Lady Eloise Warby . . ."

Curran stared at her. "It can't be good news. I can see it in your face. Is she . . . ?"

Harriet held up her hand. "She's not dead, but she's gravely ill. She was released from Holloway after days, if not weeks, of force-feeding. Her husband, Sir John, has taken her to their country estate."

Curran sat back in his chair, his brow creased in distress. "How old is this news?"

"At least a month."

"Ellie . . ." He said the name with such affection that Li An straightened.

"Curran? Who is this Eloise?"

"She is my cousin," he said, catching her hand. "More like a sister. The only one of my family I have any time for. Harriet, can you do me a favor? I need to telegram John and find out how she is. Can you send it for me?"

He scrawled a short note, folded it, and as he handed it to Harriet, her fingers closed over his for a fleeting moment. "I'm sorry, Curran. I would never have disturbed you if I thought you didn't want to know."

He shook his head. "Thank you for telling me. You know her. Ellie is Ellie. I just thank God she has a sympathetic husband."

"Your family has influence, can't they do something?"

Curran's mouth twisted. "You haven't met my uncle, and as for my useless cousin, George . . . let's just say they are probably glad Ellie is married and not dragging the Bullock-Steele name into Holloway with her." He managed a smile.

Harriet stood up. "I will go straight to the post office," she promised. "Will we see you tomorrow, Curran?"

"I have to . . ." He grimaced. "Excuse me for not standing," he said. "Li An . . . I'm going back to bed."

He hauled himself out of his chair like an old man, threw off Li An's proffered hand and staggered back to the bedroom, shutting the door behind him. Li An and Harriet exchanged a sympathetic glance. "He is a terrible patient," Li An said.

"Aren't most men?" Harriet said.

At the door, she turned to Li An. "Miss Khoo . . . Li An . . . I was wondering if you would care to join me for afternoon tea at John Little's on Friday afternoon?"

Li An looked genuinely surprised. "Me? Why?"

Harriet shook her head. "Do I need a reason? I would like to get to know you better. I don't have many friends in Singapore."

Li An stiffened. "Why do you think I can be your friend? You know nothing about me."

"And you know nothing about me," Harriet countered. "But I think two people who nearly got themselves killed on Monday night may find something else in common."

Something that might have been a smile caught the unscarred corner of Li An's mouth. "We were never going to be killed, Mrs. Gordon."

"Harriet."

Li An considered her for a long moment. "Very well . . . Harriet . . . I will join you for tea at John Little's. Very proper. You will find the nuns taught me well."

Aghast, Harriet stared at her. "I didn't think for a moment that you . . ."

Li An nodded. "No. You didn't and for that I like you."

"Three in the afternoon?" Harriet suggested.

Li An nodded and inclined her head. "I will look forward to it."

❧ Fourteen

Curran woke with a start. He lay in the dark, stuffy cocoon of the heavy mosquito net, sweating and breathless. It took a moment for his heart rate to return to normal and for him to recall what had woken him. A feverish nightmare, the one that always crept into his dreams when he felt at his lowest ebb. The dark night that he had thought would be his last on earth. The tang of the ocean, the soft wash of the waves beneath the wharf and Zi Qiang's laugh followed by the flash of light on the razor-sharp knife. Li An's scream cutting through the darkness . . .

But Li An lay sleeping beside him and they were safe and hundreds of miles from Khoo Zi Qiang.

He touched her shoulder to assure himself and she stirred.

"Curran?"

He put his arm across her, drawing her to him. "Just a bad dream," he said.

"What did you dream about?" she murmured sleepily.

He turned to face her, marveling at her dark eyes, still filled with sleep, softened in the gray, early-morning light. "Zi Qiang. It's always your brother."

Li An closed her eyes and he sensed rather than saw her tears.

"And I," she said at last. "Will we ever be free of him?"

There was no answer to that question and they lay side by side in silence, their fingers twisted together until daybreak, when Curran rose and dressed for the difficult day ahead.

Mahmud had still not retrieved Leopold from the school so he was left with no alternative but to walk into town. Despite Li An's strenuous protestations and exhortations to take the first ricksha he encountered, he found the brisk walk in the relative cool of the morning gave him time to think.

Today he would arrest James Hawke. The man had motive, means and opportunity. An angry man who could see his career destroyed by a woman could easily be forced to violence. Only one thing nagged at the back of Curran's mind. The killer would have been covered in blood spatter. Unless Hawke had somehow contrived to change his clothes, surely someone would have noticed if he had returned to the mess covered in gore. He'd have to check but it would be unusual for an officer like Hawke to have more than one set of mess dress, so changing before re-entering the mess would be unlikely.

However, it was not beyond the realms of possibility, given their relationship, that he could have been in a state of undress when the act was committed—if Sylvie Nolan had used her charms to soften the news she had to break to him.

If nothing else, away from the security of the barracks and under lock and key, James Hawke might be somewhat more cooperative.

As he passed the Sri Mariamman Temple, he paused, standing with his hands on his hips, looking up at the brightly painted images of the Indian deities twisting and writhing around the *gopuram*.

What had Harriet and Li An been thinking when they made the assignation with the unknown note writer? They had put themselves in unnecessary danger, compounded by Harriet's foolish decision to take an unloaded and unserviceable revolver with her. He would send it to the police armorer and she would not be producing it again until he was satisfied she knew how to use it properly.

Chinatown at this hour of the day still drowsed. Only a few street vendors were gathering, casting him hopeful glances, but despite the tempting smells coming from their baskets, he had no appetite for anything more exciting than the tea and toast he had managed to eat at home.

Beyond the temple the crowded streets and laneways of Chinatown hid many secrets. Li An had told him which laneway the mysterious Indian had disappeared down. At the far end could be found one of the most notorious opium dens on the island, a place known all too well by the police. Only a few short steps and he would be at its door but it would be the height of foolishness to go barging into such a place, particularly in uniform and without due cause.

He thought about sending in Constable Tan, who excelled at undercover work, but this was not a police matter and he would only be putting the young man in danger. Li An herself had offered to make inquiries, but he shuddered at the thought. Her brother's tentacles in the opium trade stretched far and wide and Curran could never, in all conscience, knowingly throw her back into his path.

He shook his head and turned on his heel, heading for the solid, colonial masonry of the South Bridge Road Police Headquarters. Whatever the identity of the man in the temple and his reasons for seeking him out, Curran had no intention of pursuing him.

Curran found everyone at work; even Harriet Gordon was seated at her typewriter, typing the handwritten statements and reports that had accumulated over the past few days. She looked up as he entered.

"You look better," she said.

"Nothing like a good night's sleep," he lied, the memory of

his nightmare still perched on his shoulder with Zi Qiang's grinning face.

He gathered his staff and they stood around the blackboard set up in the center of the room and went through the evidence piece by piece. The certainty with which Curran had started the day was confirmed by the agreement of the others. Leaving aside the question of bloodstained clothing, James Hawke remained the best suspect in the case.

"What now?" Singh inquired.

"I think we should bring him in here for further questioning," Curran said.

He ordered Tan to bring out the motor vehicle and, taking Singh, they motored out to the barracks.

Thankfully they were admitted without hindrance, but at the administration block, the sergeant who staffed the orderly room came out to meet them.

"Your business?" he demanded.

Curran identified himself and his sergeant and stated their business was with the adjutant.

"Ah yes, the police officers. Wait here."

Curran and Singh exchanged glances as the sergeant scurried down the corridor to the commander's office. When he returned, he said, "Colonel Nolan has requested to speak to you, Inspector. If your sergeant would care to wait here."

Chafing with impatience, Curran followed the man. Nolan stood at his window, looking out over the military complex, his hands behind his back. He turned as the orderly sergeant shut the door behind them.

"Ah, Curran. I saw you arrive. What brings you back here this morning?"

"I've come to request your adjutant accompany me back to South Bridge Road for further questioning."

Nolan frowned. "Hawke? Is he a suspect?"

No point in prevarication. Curran had no intention of making this easy. Besides which he had had his fill of the regiment. "Yes. He admitted to me yesterday that he slipped away from the dinner to make a tryst with your wife and he confirmed that they were having an affair."

As he spoke, he studied the colonel's face, looking for shock, horror, surprise—but he saw nothing, nothing except a dull resignation.

"You knew?" he said.

Nolan's lips tightened. "Yes, of course I knew. There are precious few secrets in the regiment, Curran, and I am not the blind old fool they might have thought me."

"Is that why you destroyed her journal?"

Nolan's eyes flashed. "Yes. While she had the sense to keep the sordid details of her affair off the pages, she made it clear what her feelings toward me were and, call it pride, I didn't want the world to read what she had written. As to the affair, she kept her secrets elsewhere, Inspector." He sighed. "So how did I know? I saw the glances, the whispered conversations, the notes she passed to him and the way they used young Nicholas as their go-between was shameful."

"Did her brother know what was in those notes?"

Nolan shrugged. "You would have to ask him. She flirted outrageously with the subalterns but her eyes were only for Hawke. Don't think I am not aware that every man in this battalion knows I wear a cuckold's horns. So you see, Inspector, her murderer could just as easily have been me.

Curran stared at him. "And was it you?"

Nolan shook his head. "No." He waved a hand at the door. "Go ahead and arrest Hawke if you must. I shall be glad just to see this matter concluded."

Curran collected Singh and found Lieutenant Gentry, at work at his own desk outside the adjutant's office. Through the open door behind him, Hawke's office was deserted.

"Where's Hawke?" Curran demanded.

Gentry shook his head. "Don't know. Haven't seen him since dinner last night. Is there a problem?"

"No," Curran said. "I just have some questions for him."

"Try the mess, his batman may know where he is."

Hawke's batman, Lewis, a lance corporal in his late middle age, told Curran that on his return to his room about ten the previous night, Hawke had dismissed him with orders he was not to be disturbed. The corporal had returned to his own quarters. At six he had gone to wake the adjutant with the usual cup of tea to find the room locked and, receiving no response to his knock, had assumed the adjutant would prefer not to be disturbed.

It was now ten in the morning. Using the batman's key, Curran opened the door to the adjutant's room to find it empty, the bed still turned down for the night and unslept in. Curran cursed. Had Hawke taken fright, foreseen his imminent arrest and fled?

Curran and Singh gave the room a cursory search. If Hawke had fled, he had taken nothing with him. According to the batman, all that was missing was one set of Hawke's uniform, his Sam Browne and his forage cap. Wherever he had gone, he had been wearing his uniform.

A search of the room revealed a man whose life was the regiment. A few family photographs, books on military law and old campaigns seemed to be his most treasured possessions. Curran found no personal correspondence, beyond a few letters from the man's bank. James Hawke was nothing if not thoroughly ordinary and a little dull.

Curran found the only incongruous item in the whole room in the pocket of the man's dressing gown, a delicate, lace-edged handkerchief embroidered with the letter *S. S* for Sylvie? Such a small, fragile object with so much meaning.

It galled him but he had no choice but to seek out the help of the military police to aid in the search for Hawke. He found

Major Goff in his office and asked him, as politely as he could, to organize a thorough search of the buildings and grounds. To his credit, the provost marshal did not argue, his concern for the missing adjutant greater than his antipathy to Curran.

They found no trace of the man within the barracks area. However, under intense questioning from Singh, the sepoy sentries on duty the previous night admitted to coming across the adjutant in the barracks area around eleven in the evening in the vicinity of the back gate. If Hawke had a copy of the key to the back gate, he could have left the barracks by that route and there would have been no one to see him.

In a vile temper, Curran returned to South Bridge Road, where Nabeel informed him a Lieutenant Cox had attended, waited an hour and left. Curran had no time to follow up on Cox. He gave orders to Singh to interview every ricksha driver in Singapore if necessary, to see if any of them had picked Hawke up.

Unable to settle to paperwork and lacking anything else he could constructively do to occupy himself, he stood for a long time looking at the blackboard with the timeline of the crime.

"Staring at the board won't help you," Harriet said from behind him.

Curran jumped. "I'm a damned fool. I should have acted on my instincts yesterday when I had him sitting in front of me. If he intended to disappear, why leave empty-handed and in uniform? Something's not right, Mrs. Gordon."

"He can't have gone far. An English Army officer in uniform is not going to go unnoticed." She paused. "If he has deliberately disappeared, it does point to his guilt, doesn't it?"

"Maybe," Curran conceded.

The telephone on the wall jangled and Nabeel, the clerk, answered it. He balanced the hearing piece between his shoulder and ear, as he scribbled on the paper kept by the telephone.

When he hung up, he picked up the paper and approached Curran, who glared at the man.

"Well?"

"I am sorry to bother you, *tuan*," he said, "but that was the Orchard Police Station. A dead body has been found in the Botanical Gardens." He paused for dramatic effect. "They say he is wearing the uniform of a soldier."

The pretty octagonal gazebo in the center of the Botanical Gardens, with its white-painted trelliswork and pointed fairy-tale roof, should have been, and probably was, the place for lovers' trysts. Now uniformed constabulary blocked the path and a crowd of onlookers, European and local, had begun to gather.

On seeing Curran approaching, a European man dressed in a crumpled linen suit and broad-brimmed pith helmet, detached himself from the crowd and came hurrying down the path.

"Are you in charge?" he demanded.

Curran looked down at the anxious little man. "I am Inspector Curran and you are . . . ?"

The man tugged at his overlong moustache. "Ridley, Henry Ridley. I'm the director of the gardens and I would very much appreciate you removing that"—he waved a hand in the direction of the gazebo—"that poor man as soon as possible. It is upsetting the staff."

"Death is upsetting," Curran replied. "Unfortunately, there is a procedure to be gone through, but I assure you we will be as quick as we can."

Ridley whipped his hat from his balding head and mopped his brow. "It's so inconsiderate," he said. "If you're going to take your own life, then do it in the privacy of your own home, not in public where it inconveniences everybody."

Curran knew Ridley by reputation but had never met him before. "Mad Ridley," as he was called, had single-handedly been responsible for the introduction of the rubber industry into the Malay Peninsula in the face of stringent opposition. While he admired such dogged enthusiasm for botany, at this moment Mr. Ridley was holding him up.

He excused himself and passed the police cordon. Mac had already arrived and knelt on one knee on the ground beside the uniformed figure. One glance was enough to satisfy Curran that the dark-haired officer wearing a captain's rank was the missing James Hawke.

From the position of the body, it looked as if Hawke had been kneeling. He'd fallen forward, and lay facedown, a service revolver still clutched in the fingers of his right hand. A shot to his right temple had done the deed, the force of the bullet causing considerable damage to the left side of his head. A grisly sight for the pretty setting.

Mac looked up at Curran. "You can see for yourself. Not much I can add," he said.

"Suicide?"

Mac shrugged. "Looks like it."

"Let's turn him over," Curran said.

Singh and Mac did so with infinite care. The shot had left his face mostly intact. Hawke's eyes were closed and his handsome face, now slack, was almost peaceful in death.

Curran looked around the gazebo. A Sam Browne belt with an empty holster had been folded on a bench beside Hawke's hat. Nothing in the gazebo indicated any sort of trouble and a quick search revealed no note had been left with his belongings. When Curran and Singh had searched his room a few hours earlier, they'd found no note or any indication that the army officer intended to end his life, but then not all suicides were that obliging.

"That's it, then. You got your man?"

Curran turned to face the intruder, the military policeman Goff.

"What are you doing here? Who let you through?"

Goff didn't move. "I may remind you that James Hawke is . . . was . . . a serving officer in the South Sussex. His death is very much my business. This"—he swept a hand at the corpse—"is all the evidence of guilt you need, Curran. As far as I am concerned, the case is closed and I will advise the colonel accordingly. Well done for hounding the man to his death."

"If he was guilty, he would have hanged and I was yet to be entirely convinced of his guilt," Curran said.

Goff snorted. "Do you think an innocent man would shoot himself in the head?"

"Unfortunately, Captain Hawke's death denies me the opportunity to question him further," Curran said. "And it is my responsibility to report to the colonel, not yours."

Goff's eyes blazed but Curran held his tongue. He was not going to get into a public spat with the military policeman. Goff glanced around at the interested crowd of onlookers and must have decided discretion was the better part of valor. He glanced down at the dead man.

"Whatever his guilt or innocence, he was a bloody fool," Goff said. "Suicide is never the easy answer."

Privately Curran agreed but he kept his peace. "Wait outside," he told Goff. "We'll both go to the colonel."

Curran remained long enough to give Singh his orders regarding the removal of the body and recovery of any evidence, but he had some questions for the director of the Botanical Gardens before he left the scene.

He found Ridley with the onlookers, fidgeting with his hat, and drew the man to one side. "Do you live nearby?" he asked.

Ridley gestured in the direction of the north side of the park. "On-site, Inspector."

"Did you hear anything unusual last night, like a gunshot?"

"No . . ." Ridley began. He frowned. "Wait—I was working in my study on an article on the cultivation of gambier and I heard a crack. Didn't think anything of it. Just thought it was lightning."

"What time was this?"

"Just past eleven. I know because I looked up at the clock."

Curran thanked the man and assured him that the scene would be cleared within a couple of hours. He found Goff smoking a cigarette, under a nearby traveler's palm. Seeing Curran, Goff dropped the half-smoked cigarette on Ridley's impeccable grass and ground it down with the heel of his boot. Curran gained the distinct impression that Goff wished it was Curran he had under his boot.

≫ FIFTEEN

Blenheim Barracks
Wednesday, 17 August

The ten-minute walk back to the barracks felt like a lifetime in Goff's company. The man's antipathy oozed from him, and as far as Curran was concerned, the feeling was mutual.

Nolan looked up from some papers he had been reading at his desk, as the two men entered his office.

"Well? Who was it?"

"Hawke." Goff cut across Curran. "Looks like he shot himself."

Nolan leaned back in his chair. "Did he, by God? Was there a note?"

Curran shook his head. "Not with his body, but I would like to search his room more thoroughly."

"Is that necessary?" Goff said. "Haven't you already done that?"

Curran glared at him. "I was only dealing with a missing man, not a dead one. A report will need to be made to the coroner, whatever the feelings of the military."

"Sir—" Goff began appealing to Nolan.

Nolan waved a hand. "You heard him, Goff. Hawke's got

nothing more to hide and the quicker Curran finishes his investigation, the quicker he'll be gone."

At the door Curran turned back to the colonel. "I will have some questions for you, sir. When I am done with Hawke's room, I'll return."

Irritation flickered in Nolan's eyes. "If you must. I've lost my wife and now a friend. Just bring this all to a close."

Unsurprisingly Curran found nothing new in Hawke's room and he ordered the room to be locked, taking custody of the key from the reluctant batman.

Goff, who had watched the search from the doorway with obvious impatience, dogged Curran back to the administration building.

"That's it then, Curran. Seems clear to me. Hawke's death brings the investigation to a close," he said as they entered the cool building.

Curran turned and glared at the provost marshal as he strode down the corridor back to Nolan's office. "It is over when I say it is over, Goff. Now leave me to talk with the colonel. I don't need you."

"I should . . ."

The door opened as they approached and Nolan himself stepped into the corridor. He looked from one to the other and held up a hand. The man looked tired and defeated. "Major Goff, I appreciate your concern but I wish to speak with Curran in private."

Goff scowled but, with a quick and somewhat insubordinate salute, stomped down the corridor.

Curran entered the colonel's well-appointed office and Nolan indicated a chair.

"I've heard Goff's opinion. Do you think it was suicide?" Nolan took his own chair behind his imposing desk.

"At this stage, I have no reason to think otherwise," Curran began carefully, "but I would appreciate it if you could be honest with me, Colonel."

Curran took out the handkerchief he had found in Hawke's dressing gown and passed it across the desk to Nolan. To his surprise the man picked it up and pressed it to his nose, closing his eyes as he inhaled.

"It still carries her scent," he said. "Where did you find it?"

"In Hawke's room."

Nolan set the handkerchief down on his blotter and folded it neatly into a square before passing it back to Curran. He looked out of the window through which came the shouts and crunch, the familiar sounds of soldiers being drilled.

"Sir, this is difficult but I have reason to believe Hawke had to have been the father of the child your wife was carrying."

Nolan sat quite still, rigidly to attention. He could have been a statue or an oil painting—the very epitome of an army officer.

"You may be correct. What else do you know?" he said at last.

Curran hesitated. He had to choose his words carefully. "I am led to believe yours may have been a marriage of convenience."

Nolan brought his gaze back to Curran. "What makes you say that?"

"Your wife had borne another child."

Nolan's face still betrayed nothing. "I am not a particularly old man," he said at last. "I loved my first wife and never thought I would marry again. Despite everything you may have been told or you may believe, Curran, believe this. I loved Sylvie and I would not have abandoned her if she had told me she was carrying a child . . . even though the child could not have been mine. I would have preserved her honor at all costs. I would have raised the child as my own."

Looking into the man's eyes, Curran believed him. He wondered if Sylvie Nolan knew that or had she thought he would turn her out? Whatever had happened to her first child may have scarred her deeply to the extent she did not trust the men in her life.

"As to the matter of whether she was damaged goods," Nolan continued, "that is none of your business and I will not have her past brought into this matter. It has no bearing on her death." Nolan pushed his chair back and stood. "I will telephone Cuscaden today and tell him I want the investigation ceased immediately. As far as I am concerned, Hawke's suicide is tantamount to an admission of guilt on his part and the matter of my wife's death is now closed. I trust your report will reflect these findings."

Curran stood up to face the man, circling his helmet in his fingers. "That is your prerogative, Colonel, but ultimately it is my decision what goes in my report, and Cuscaden's to say whether the case is closed. There will still be a coroner's hearing and certain matters will need to be revealed."

Nolan's eyes blazed. "Let me be quite clear, Curran. I have tolerated you poking around in my private business in the interests of finding Sylvie's killer. That question has now been answered and after today you and your men will have no further access to these barracks or any of my officers and men, is that understood?"

The door to the colonel's office all but slammed behind Curran. He stood in the corridor gathering his breath and deciding on his next move when the door to the office next to Hawke's opened and Nicholas Gentry poked his head out and gestured for Curran.

"I didn't want the colonel to hear me," he said in a low voice, shutting the door to his office behind them. "Is it true?"

"Is what true?"

"Hawke blew his brains out in the Botanical Gardens?"

"He is dead, yes," Curran concurred.

Gentry sank back against his desk and wiped his sweating forehead. "Poor old Hawke. I knew something was bothering him, but I had no idea . . ." He looked up at Curran. "Did he . . . did he kill Sylvie?"

"In the absence of a confession or a note of any kind, I can't possibly say," Curran said. "Were you aware of their relationship?"

Gentry smiled, a small, grim smile. "Of course. Sylvie had me acting as a courier, taking notes between them. I don't know what sort of fool she thought I was."

"Did you mind?"

Gentry shrugged. "She was my sister and I loved her. I'd do anything for her."

Curran considered the young man for a long moment. "You only came out to Singapore with her early this year. Where were you based in England?"

"At the regimental headquarters."

"What can you tell me about the relationship she had before her marriage to the colonel?"

Gentry looked up. "What relationship?"

"Sometime in the last couple of years your sister bore a child."

Gentry's mouth fell open. "You're wrong."

"The medical evidence doesn't lie, Lieutenant. Don't tell me you, as one of her closest relatives, didn't know?"

The young man shook his head. "I didn't. She spent a few months up in Scotland with relatives last summer. Are you saying she went there to hide?"

"Very likely."

"I didn't know. Remember, I lived in the barracks and I only saw her at weekends or parties or the like."

"So, you don't know who the father of the child might have been?"

Gentry shook his head. "No idea. She was young and beau-

tiful and she had admirers by the basketful, but one particular
relationship . . . ?" Something flickered in his eyes. "Well, there
was Rupert . . ."

"Rupert?"

"Rupert Allen. He was a subaltern in the Second Battalion."
Gentry swallowed and he cleared his throat. "But he's dead,
Inspector. Died a year ago."

"How?"

Gentry stared at a point somewhere beyond Curran's shoulder. "Took his own life."

"Was he a friend of yours?"

Gentry gave a barely perceptible nod.

"In what way did your sister and Mr. Allen have a particular
friendship?"

Gentry shook his head. "You know how these things go . . .
He always seemed to get more dances, escort her into dinner,
partner her at tennis."

"You never saw anything else between them?"

Gentry shook his head. "No . . . Yes . . . Allen told me that
he was plucking up the courage to ask Father for her hand."

Curran raised his eyebrows. "Bold? A mere second lieutenant?"

Gentry shrugged. "Father liked him, he probably would have
said yes, but then Allen went and did what he did."

"Did he leave a note?"

Gentry shook his head. "No, and now Hawke's gone and
done the same thing. I don't believe for a minute he would have
hurt Sylvie." The sudden passion in the young man's voice broke
and Nicholas Gentry looked younger than his nineteen years.

Curran brought the subject back to Hawke, asking Gentry
when he'd last seen the adjutant.

Gentry blinked rapidly as if trying to refocus at the rapid
change in subject. "Hawke? Last night at dinner. He left the

mess about ten after port and cigars. That's the last I saw of him."

"What was he wearing?"

"Tropical dress. We always dress for dinner."

"How did he seem to you?"

Gentry thought for a long moment. "He's been out of sorts since Sylvie died but so have we all, and given they were more than just friends, I don't blame him. I suppose he knew it would all come out." His eyes widened. "Do you think he took the honorable way out?"

Curran kept his opinion to himself. Had Hawke done the "honorable thing" so beloved of nineteenth-century storytellers or had it been a cowardly act, intended to avoid the dishonor that would follow the revelation of his affair with his commanding officer's new young wife?

"Where was the colonel last night?"

"At home, as far as I know. You'll have to ask Pris." His eyes widened. "Oh, Pris. She'll take it badly. She had been engaged to him, you know?"

"Officially?"

Gentry shook his head. "I don't think so. More like an understanding. It was all off when Hawke met Syl. Poor Pris. She must have hated Sylvie."

"What makes you say that?"

Gentry shrugged. "I know she was my sister but Sylvie could be a little careless of other people's feelings."

Including those of her brother, Curran thought.

"What about you? What was your relationship with Captain Hawke?"

"Apart from being my senior officer?" Gentry quirked an eyebrow. "I'd like to think we were on good terms, friends even, as much as one can be." He straightened. "I've said enough. If you're done here, I'll see you to the front gate. Do you have transport?"

As Curran headed for the stairs, the door to Nolan's office opened and the colonel looked out. "I thought I heard your voice, Curran," he said. The anger had gone from his face and his tone was civil when he asked, "What are you still doing here?"

"My fault, sir. I waylaid him," Gentry said.

His commanding officer cast the young man a withering glance. "As you're still here, perhaps you could do me a small favor. I have to break the news to Pris. Might help if you're there. She seems to like you."

"Of course, sir," Curran said.

The colonel fetched his hat and they stepped outside into the heat of the day. Walking in silence, they skirted the parade ground, where a platoon of sweating soldiers was being drilled, heading for the back gate and the laneway to Blenheim Road. Private soldiers stopped what they were doing to salute their commanding officer as they passed. Nolan returned the salutes but didn't slacken his pace.

"You must think I was a little hard on you," Nolan said as they passed the sentry on the gate.

"Your prerogative, sir. Your wife has been murdered and a friend has betrayed you."

"Put like that," Nolan said with a shake of his head.

"It would have saved me a great deal of trouble if you had told me about their relationship at the beginning."

Nolan shrugged. "A man has his pride, Curran."

They walked in silence for a little while before the colonel spoke up. "Explain your conclusion about Hawke's guilt."

Curran took a deep breath. "He engineered an excuse to leave the dinner to meet with your wife. Of course we don't know what was said . . . or done . . . but it is possible she told him about the baby and he became enraged and hit her."

"And he returned to the mess completely composed without a trace of blood on him?" Nolan said.

Curran paused. "He may not have been fully dressed at the time the crime was committed."

Nolan fell silent, digesting the implication of what Curran had just said. "It sounds plausible enough, except for one thing, Curran. I believe Hawke loved my wife."

"It is a very fine distinction between love and hate, Colonel, and love is often as much a motive for murder as hate," Curran said.

Nolan's shoulders slumped and his face lapsed into deep lines, the strain of the past week telling on him.

"When did you suspect the affair?" Curran ventured.

"As soon as it began. You only had to look at her to know she was in love and it wasn't with me. She was young, pretty and vivacious. Whatever hope I may have entertained that she had feelings for me existed only in my own aspirations, not in reality. She'd strayed before, why should I be surprised that she strayed again?"

Curran seized the opportunity. "What do you know about her previous relationship?"

Nolan's eyes flashed. "I told you . . . nothing." He drew a breath. "I'm telling you this in confidence, Curran, because I need you to understand how things work in the regiment. When I arrived in England just before Christmas, the colonel told me his daughter had been indiscreet and he was anxious to hush up the faintest breath of scandal. How better to do it than to marry her off to an old, reliable comrade?"

"And you agreed?"

"Of course. Jack's been too long without a mother and I needed a lady to grace my table, amuse the wives. That sort of thing."

"And was she happy with the arrangement?"

Nolan shrugged. "She agreed on the condition that it was marriage in name only and she played her part, as long as I complied with her whims and wishes." He shook his head. "If I dared to deny her, she had a temper, Curran."

"That must have been hard for you," Curran said.

Nolan drew his shoulders back. "As far as I was concerned, what had happened in the past was no concern of mine. That's what I told her. She in turn assured me that it was all forgotten. I entertained the hope that given time she might come to me of her own volition."

"What became of the child?"

Nolan shrugged. "What do you think happens to children in those circumstances, Curran? He or she is probably being raised by some respectable family somewhere in England. Her father would have seen to that."

"And Sylvie's feelings?"

"Wouldn't have entered into it. She made her bed, metaphorically and literally, and I was her salvation. She knew it and was grateful for my offer subject to the conditions she set out."

Curran stared at the road ahead. Nick Gentry had told him Sylvie had spent several months in Scotland, where, no doubt, she had borne the child away from the snapping tongues. As soon as the child drew breath, it would have been taken from her and consigned to its fate as the foundling child, the cuckoo in the nest of some other family, paid well for the privilege. Sylvie would have returned to society, having recovered from her indisposition and extended holiday, but with her chance of making a good marriage forever marred. The widowed Lieutenant Colonel Nolan would indeed have been her only salvation.

And what did Nolan get in return? Nolan hadn't admitted it, but Curran guessed promotional preferment was a certainty, possibly . . . probably . . . anointment as the next commanding officer of the regiment.

That was how these things worked.

"What can you tell me about Rupert Allen?" Curran asked.

Nolan stopped in his tracks. "Allen? What's he got to do with it?"

"He took his own life, I believe. Was that before or after she returned from Scotland?"

Nolan stared at him. "You're not suggesting Allen had anything to do with . . . with what happened to Sylvie?"

"I don't know, did he?"

Nolan snorted. "He was just one of the young officers who floated like moths around her flame, Curran. Trust me, the reasons for his death had nothing to do with Sylvie. And to answer your question, he died in July—before Sylvie returned from Scotland."

They had reached The Cedars. The front door stood open and the sound of women's voices drifted out of the living room. As the two men entered the room, Pris rose to her feet, her hands clasped together at her throat.

"Oh, John, thank heavens. Have they found James?"

Curran's gaze went to the other woman in the room.

"Good afternoon, Mrs. Gordon."

Harriet Gordon smiled. "Good afternoon, Inspector."

Harriet had been wrestling with Curran's appalling handwriting when a telephone call had shattered the peace of the Detective Branch. The clerk summoned Harriet.

"For you, mem," he said.

"Is that you, Harriet?" a female voice said.

"Yes," Harriet said slowly. She had little experience with telephones and was never sure if she was holding the earpiece correctly.

"It's Pris Nolan. I was hoping you might come out to The Cedars."

"I'm at work. Is it important?"

The voice on the other end gave a choked sob. "Nicholas just sent me a message that James Hawke is missing. I fear the worst, Harriet, and I would like someone to sit with me for a while. The house is so quiet and empty and Lavinia can't be reached." Her voice cracked. "I have no one else."

Harriet rolled her eyes, her gaze drifting in the direction of the pile of papers on her desk. "I'm not sure I can get away," she said.

An audible sniff. "I'm sure that nice Inspector Curran won't mind."

Harriet was not quite so sure that the "nice Inspector Curran," who needed his notes typed, would understand, but a friend in need . . .

The reflective chords of a Chopin nocturne greeted Harriet as she alighted from the gharry at the gate to The Cedars. The majordomo, Abdul, answered the door and showed Harriet through to the living room, where Pris sat at the grand piano. Harriet, who had not a musical bone in her body, thought the playing quite accomplished. She appreciated such talents.

Pris looked up and, seeing Harriet, broke off, rising to her feet. She ran over to Harriet and threw her arms around her.

"Oh, you came. Thank you, thank you."

"What's happened?" Harriet said as she disengaged herself from the clinging arms.

Pris recovered herself and sent Abdul for tea, gesturing for Harriet to join her on the settee.

"We were expecting Nicholas to join us for dinner tonight. It's not even been a week since . . ." Her voice cracked and she fished a crumpled handkerchief out of her sleeve and dabbed her eyes. "But he sent a message this morning to say James Hawke could not be found and as assistant adjutant he was going to be extremely busy."

"Why would James Hawke go missing?" Harriet mused aloud, although she knew the answer. It had been in Curran's notes. The man had admitted to being Sylvie Nolan's lover and he had been possibly the last person to see her alive—if not her actual murderer.

"I don't know." Pris blew her nose. "He was terribly upset by Sylvie's death." Pris looked down at the damp, crumpled handkerchief and continued, "James and I had an . . . understanding. He had actually proposed to me at Christmas but John was in England and we needed his permission, of course. Then he arrived home with Sylvie and James . . ." Her lips tightened. "James started to behave like a giddy schoolboy. Anyone with one eye could see he was besotted with her. Always at her beck and call, the first to take her in to dinner, to dance with her. I think he stopped noticing me altogether."

Harriet laid her hand on the other woman's hand. "How dreadful. Some men can be so easily led astray."

Pris took a shuddering breath. "And now he's missing." Her lip trembled and the tears dribbled unchecked down her face.

Abdul, entering with the tea, cast an inquiring glance at Harriet.

"Can you tell Indira to fetch some clean handkerchiefs?" Harriet said.

As she comforted the weeping woman, Harriet thought, under the circumstances, Lavinia Pemberthey-Smythe would be a much better friend and confidante. Soggy women, as Julian called them, tended to try Harriet's patience.

A clatter of claws on tiled floors and a shout of "Rufus, no!" interrupted the two women as a large brindled dog with floppy ears and friendly brown eyes skidded into the living room, its gaze fixed on the biscuit plate. Jack Nolan came rushing in after the dog, seizing it by the collar just before the tray and table went flying.

"Jack. Keep that animal under control," Pris scolded.

"Sorry, Aunt Pris. He's just so pleased to be home."

Rufus sauntered over to Harriet and put his big head in her lap, looking up at her with pleading eyes.

"Papa didn't kill him," Jack said. "He's been living with one of the sergeant's families. Now Sylvie's gone and the dratted Pansy has gone to live with Aunt Lavinia, I can have him back. He's been spoiled rotten."

"And is Pansy's relocation permanent?" Harriet asked.

"Pansy is a woman's dog and she will be happier there. Only room in this house for one dog. Jack, do take that revolting smelly beast out of here," Pris said.

Rufus lolled his tongue and grinned at the women. Harriet gave in and tossed him the remains of her biscuit, which he caught deftly and swallowed in a noisy gulp.

"Back to school soon, Jack. Will you still be boarding this term?"

Jack shrugged. "Papa hasn't said."

Harriet glanced at Pris, who shook her head. "I think John has other things on his mind." She stiffened and glanced out the window. "I thought I heard his voice . . ." She rose to her feet, her hand going to her throat. "It's John and your inspector. Jack, be a good boy and leave us."

With a narrowed glance at his aunt, Jack took Rufus by the collar and they both skulked out of the room.

The grave countenances of both men left Harriet in no doubt that the news they bore was not good.

After the initial greetings, the colonel cleared his throat. "Please sit, Pris."

Pris obeyed, her hand scrabbling for Harriet's. Harriet glanced up at Robert Curran and his cool steady gaze met hers.

John Nolan cleared his throat. "I'm sorry, Pris. James is dead. Looks like he took his own life during the night."

Harriet braced herself, waiting for another onslaught of tears. Pris took a deep, shuddering breath and her fingers momentarily tightened on Harriet's.

"I had a bad feeling about James," she said in a voice that was quite controlled and calm. She rose to her feet and walked over to her brother. "Sylvie has a lot to answer for in hell or wherever she has gone, John. I curse the day you ever brought her into this house."

Pris walked out of the room without another word, her shoes echoing on the stairs as she hurried up them.

Nolan glanced upward at the sound of footsteps on the floor of Pris's bedroom.

"Should I go after her?" Harriet suggested.

Nolan shook his head. "No, leave her be. It's Nicholas I worry about. He had a friend who took his life last year. Now to lose another friend in similar circumstances . . ."

"I just spoke with him. He seemed to take the news as well as could be expected," Curran said. "We won't take up any more of your time, Colonel. There may be a few loose ends before I can finalize my report."

Nolan nodded. "Of course. Whatever you need to finish off this business, Curran." He cleared his throat. "I spoke harshly before but I meant what I said. As far as I am concerned, you have no further need of access to my barracks or my men. If you have any further questions, direct them to me through Major Goff."

Curran circled his hat in his hands. "Mrs. Gordon, would you care for a ride back to town? I have the motor vehicle."

Harriet stood up, straightening her skirt. "Thank you."

At the door, Curran turned and looked back at the colonel. "How did Rupert Allen take his life?"

Nolan seemed distracted. It took him a moment to register the question. "I believe he hanged himself in the clock tower at headquarters. Nicholas Gentry had the misfortune to find him. No explanation as to why Allen did what he did, but he never was cut out for the army, that one."

Tan had brought the motor vehicle around to The Cedars and Harriet and Curran rode back to South Bridge Road in silence.

"Odd reaction from Miss Nolan," Curran said at last as they turned onto Napier Road.

"Pris? Not really, she told me she and Hawke had an understanding. He'd actually proposed to her at Christmas."

"That confirms what others have said. Miss Nolan had a lot of good reasons to dislike her sister-in-law," Curran mused.

"Disliking is a long way from wanting to murder," Harriet said. "Besides, Hawke . . ."

"Yes, Hawke." Curran sank down in the seat of the motor vehicle. "Something is not right, but I can't put my finger on it."

"But surely the case is closed."

"Not in my mind," Curran muttered.

As they climbed the wooden stairs to the Detective Branch offices, the sound of voices came drifting out of the half-open door. The inspector general himself stood in the middle of the outer office, in conversation with Musa, who appeared to be demonstrating the use of the blackboard Curran prepared for his cases.

Cuscaden greeted Harriet with scrupulous politeness and she slid into her place behind the typewriter.

"News travels fast?" Curran said, throwing open the door to his office.

The glass-partitioned office was hardly soundproof and Cuscaden had only one volume. Harriet turned to her work while keeping one ear on the conversation.

"Suicide. That's it, then?" Cuscaden demanded.

"Looks like it, sir. Nolan doesn't want the matter investigated further."

"What do you think?"

A pause before Curran replied. "He had motive and opportunity and the means were on hand but there are inconsistencies that make me uncomfortable."

"So, what are the other options?"

Another long pause. "None," Curran said.

"Then the case is closed," Cuscaden said. "Good. Can't stand dealing with the bloody army. Write up your report for the coroner and we'll get both deaths off our desks."

"Sir," Curran concurred.

The door opened and Cuscaden stomped out, bidding Harriet, apparently intent on her typing, a curt good day.

The bungalow Curran rented from the owner of the Everton estate had a paddock adjoining it with a stable where he kept Leopold. He paused to greet his horse and apologize for the lack of exercise during the week. Leopold seemed to accept the apology and the proffered carrot and, with a shake of his mane, retired to the far end of the paddock.

"He is lonely." Mahmud, Curran's syce, came to stand beside him. "He and that pony at the school, you would think they were old friends."

"Herd animals," Curran agreed. "But I'm not getting another animal just to keep Leo company."

Inside the house, there was no immediate sign of Li An. He followed the sound of rustling paper and sighing to the bedroom and came across her, standing in front of the mirror, holding a European dress of a pale-yellow fabric to her slight body.

The sight of the dress hit him like a blow. "You were wearing that when I first met you," he said.

She turned to look at him, still holding the dress against her.

"I am afraid it is now no longer the fashion," she said.

But Curran was not thinking of fashion, he was remembering the glimpse of butter yellow among the dull dresses of the European women at the tea party given by the governor of Penang. She had been the most beautiful girl present, her dark hair coiled demurely at the nape of her neck and her lace-gloved hand tucked into the crook of her brother's elbow.

Khoo Zi Qiang had been introduced as one of Penang's influential businessmen. Curran had not known at the time when he was shaking hands with the smiling Zi Qiang that he was meeting one of the most dangerous men in Penang.

Zi Qiang in turn had introduced his sister . . .

Curran took the dress from her and pressed it to his face. It smelled of the sandalwood chest in which it had been stored and he wondered why he had not seen it before. As far as he knew, Li An had left everything to do with her old life behind when she had fled Penang.

She took the dress from him. "You will crush it," she scolded.

Curran shook himself out of the reminiscence that brought such bittersweet memories. "How do you come to have it?"

"My mother sent it," she said, her chin lifting defiantly.

He didn't ask her when the clothes had been sent. Despite her mother's public disavowal of her daughter, he suspected Li An had been in regular contact since she had left Penang, enough contact to know her mother had been ill. The fact her mother knew her daughter's whereabouts did not concern him. If Zi Qiang wanted to find them, he would not have to look too hard.

"Why have you got it out?" he asked.

She laid the dress on the bed, beside a fine lawn petticoat and a pair of white silk stockings, smoothing the creases from the delicate fabric. "Mrs. Gordon has invited me to take tea at John Little's tearoom on Friday afternoon."

"Has she indeed?"

Li An looked up at him, catching the surprise in his voice. "You don't approve?"

"Who you meet is none of my business," he said, conscious he must have sounded sharper than he intended.

She fingered the soft cloth of the dress. "Harriet is your friend. I would like her to be my friend too." She lowered her head, a curtain of hair falling around her face. "I miss my friends, Curran, but if you do not approve, I will not go."

It hadn't occurred to Curran that Li An could be lonely.

Their self-imposed exile from society, both European and Chinese, must be much harder on Li An than him.

He took her in his arms and kissed her forehead. "I'm sorry, Li An. I'm a blind fool sometimes. Of course you should go. Harriet Gordon is an unusual woman and I think she would be a good friend. Just make sure she's not carrying weapons this time."

Li An's shoulders lifted with silent laughter and she raised her face to look at him. "I think you are making a joke," she said.

He smiled down at her. "I am."

She stroked his cheek with her slender hand. "And will I be dressed properly for John Little's tearoom?"

"You are always dressed properly and you are beautiful whatever you wear."

Li An leaned her head against his chest. "You are a man. You cannot understand," she said with a sigh.

"No," Curran conceded. "I don't understand."

❧ Sixteen

South Bridge Road
Thursday, 18 August

It was not in Curran's nature to maunder, but a bad week and the brush with his recurrent malaria, which he still hadn't recovered from, had left him flat and unsatisfied with the outcome of the case. On Mac's advice he had delegated Singh to attend Hawke's autopsy. Apparently, Mac did not think a morgue a healthy place for someone recovering from malaria and Curran spent the morning shut in his office, drafting his report for the coroner.

His pen hesitated over the words:

The evidence would indicate that Mrs. Nolan met with death at the hand of Captain James Hawke, adjutant of the First Battalion South Sussex Infantry Regiment. From Captain Hawke's subsequent suicide, although without an admission of his guilt, such guilt can be inferred from the following evidence.

"Is Inspector Curran available?"
Curran looked up. Through the glass panels of his office, he

saw a young man in khaki uniform, his hat under his arm, talking to Nabeel, the department's clerk.

"I will see if he is available. Who shall I say wishes to speak with him?" Nabeel cast a glance at Curran's firmly closed door.

"Cox, Lieutenant George Cox."

Curran was on his feet and at the door to his office before Nabeel could reply.

He introduced himself and held out his hand. The young man took it, shaking it firmly. For his junior rank, he looked older than Curran would have expected. Midtwenties rather than a youth like Nicholas Gentry.

"I got a message that you wished to speak with me." Cox spoke with a strong London accent at odds with the clipped tones of his brother officers. What had Mayhew said? The son of the battalion sergeant major?

"Thank you for coming down here," Curran replied. "I apologize for inconveniencing you yesterday."

"From what I hear, the case is closed. Old Hawkey murdered the old man's wife and then did himself in. Not sure I can add anything you don't know already."

"Nevertheless, I would be interested in hearing from you before I finalize my report."

Curran ushered him into his office, shutting the door behind him. Cox sat down, crossing his legs. He had an easy, relaxed air about him and a strong, confident face.

Cox offered him one of his cigarettes. Curran declined, waiting patiently while the young man went through the ritual of lighting his cigarette and taking the first draught.

"You may have already been told this but before you ask, let's be clear, I'm not one of *them*," Cox said. "My father was the battalion sergeant major."

"Was?"

"He died in South Africa. Same affair that took the CO of the time, Pemberthey-Smythe. The reward for his bravery was my commission, but memories are short, Inspector. Now I'm just an embarrassment who doesn't know his soup spoon from his fish knife."

Curran knew exactly what Cox meant. While he was certain Cox did know his soup spoon from his fish knife, as the son of one of the "other ranks," he didn't come from the officer class, and like Captain Mayhew, the quartermaster, acceptance, preferment and promotion would come slowly . . . if at all.

"I was led to believe you were not an admirer of the late Mrs. Nolan?" Curran said.

Cox studied his cigarette and huffed a humorless laugh. "It was hard not to be dazzled, but she was just using them for her own amusement—playing them off against each other. Besides which I like the old man and it galled me to see him being played for a fool."

By "old man," Cox meant Nolan. It was a common, and affectionate, description of the most senior ranking officer in a battalion.

"Were you aware of any deeper relationship between Hawke and Mrs. Nolan?"

Cox snorted. "They were hardly discreet. The lowliest kitchen coolie must have been aware."

"In what way?"

"Mrs. Nolan would throw little afternoon tea parties at The Cedars and Hawke would be at her elbow, dancing attendance while she simpered and giggled and made cow eyes at him."

Cox really did not like Mrs. Nolan, Curran thought, and wondered if Cox's own attraction to the woman had been thrown back at him with a careless word or dismissive gesture.

He changed the subject. "Tell me about the mess dinner?"

Cox stubbed out his cigarette in Curran's ashtray and sat back, his hands behind his head. "God, I hate those shows."

"I did too," admitted Curran.

"You were in the army?"

Curran nodded. "Ten years in the Mounted Military Police."

"My problem is I don't drink," Cox said. "Methodist mother. Just not done, old chap. The whole idea of a mess dinner is to wipe yourself out on alcohol, make a complete idiot of yourself and spend the next day throwing up. Not my idea of fun."

Curran's pulse quickened—a sober, reliable witness at last.

"Did you see Hawke leave the dinner?"

"Yes, about ten. Trust me, I was counting the minutes," Cox said.

"When did he return?"

"We had retired to the anteroom so it would have been at least an hour later."

"Did you notice anything unusual about him?"

Cox considered this question. "He was sweating like a pig. Looked like he'd been running. He downed several whiskeys in quick succession, which I thought was odd for a man who was duty officer."

But consistent with a man whose married lover had just told him she was carrying his child, Curran thought.

"What about his clothing?"

Cox shrugged. "Mess dress. Nothing unusual about it. If you want to know if he was covered in blood, the answer is no."

"And when did he leave the festivities?"

"None of us could leave until the old man went, and he was in the mood to stay." Cox pulled a face. "It was tedious."

"Did anyone leave before Nolan?"

"Yes."

Curran feigned disinterest but his pulse quickened. "Who?"

"Nick Gentry."

Curran had not been expecting this. There had been mention of Gentry getting himself into a state and having to be escorted to his room, but Curran had failed to ask what time this had been. He cursed his inattention to that small detail.

"Go on."

"I was standing close to one of the doors leading onto the verandah, watching the fun and games. I heard Gentry and Hawke outside arguing."

"About what?"

Cox shook his head. "Too much noise in the anteroom, but it was clear that the situation was escalating. Nick had drunk way too much. He could barely stand upright. I thought it best to discreetly remove him before he made a complete and utter ass of himself."

"So you took him out?"

"Yes. Managed to get him upstairs and left him with Billings. Unfortunately, I had to return before I was missed." Cox shuddered. "As it was, I got a bollocking from Hawke the next morning for not playing up and he sent me off to Seletar with the punishment detail. My lot in life, Inspector."

"What about Hawke?"

"He looked like a man who was not in the mood for conversation, so I told him I had dealt with Gentry and left him alone."

"So what time did you leave?"

"The moment the old man left. Just after one."

"And Gentry was in his bed?"

Cox nodded. "Snoring like a pig."

"What time had you removed him from the mess?"

Cox shrugged. "I can't be sure. It was just after twelve because the clock in the anteroom struck when we were in the middle of some ghastly drinking game." He blew out a breath. "I should do what you did, Curran. Leave the bloody army and take on a sensible job."

Curran smiled. "I hate to say it, but we still have the equivalent of mess dinners every now and then."

Cox shook his head. "I think a high street greengrocer would suit me just fine at the moment."

"When did you last see Hawke?"

"Tuesday night? I saw him at dinner, but not after that. I went up to my room about ten."

"And your roommate?"

"I left Gentry in the anteroom. I wrote a letter to my mother and was in bed by eleven. Gentry came in a little later."

"Who else was in the mess on Tuesday night?"

Cox shrugged. "I couldn't tell you, to be honest. Mayhew was there quietly drinking himself into oblivion. Goff was there for a short while, but it was a quiet night. The mess staff may have a better idea. Is there anything else you want to ask me?"

Curran shook his head. "Not unless you have something else to tell me?"

Cox shook his head. "No one ever tells me anything, Curran. Bottom head on the totem pole is the one that gets pissed on and all that."

Cox leaned forward and picked up Harriet's Smith & Wesson revolver that had been returned from the police armorer that morning.

"Nice little piece," he said. "American."

"It belongs to Mrs. Gordon." Curran's gaze moved to Harriet, who clacked away at the typewriter, apparently oblivious to their conversation.

Cox followed his gaze. "So that's Mrs. Gordon. Heard her name around the mess in the last couple of weeks. Friend of Miss Nolan's, isn't she?" He set the weapon back on the oiled cloth. "Remind me not to cross her," he said.

The young officer took his leave and Curran sat back, going through the statements of the other people present in the anteroom on the night Sylvie Nolan had been killed. He wasn't imagining it. Beyond Hawke's brief mention of Cox taking Gentry up to his room, no one, it seemed, had missed Nick Gentry.

He rummaged through the papers on his desk, looking for Gentry's statement. He read it through and shook his head.

Gentry himself made no mention of a row with Hawke or being put to bed early.

He cursed the oversight of not speaking to Cox earlier and not asking that one question. Now he needed to speak with Gentry again and Billings, the young man's batman, before he could consider his report to be finalized.

Harriet looked up from her typewriter as the young officer left Curran's office. She hadn't met Lieutenant Cox in her dealings with the regiment and he intrigued her. He had a sharp, clever tanned face, sandy hair and languid dark eyes. Unlike many of the other officers he was clean-shaven.

Seeing her, he inclined his head and smiled. Harriet acknowledged the greeting.

As the door shut behind the officer, Curran came out of his office and handed Harriet her Smith & Wesson and a small box of ammunition.

"The police armorer has cleaned it."

"How kind of him," Harriet said.

Harriet unwrapped the oily rag in which her little revolver had been nestled. It glistened with oil, and a thrill of excitement ran through her. James's few desultory lessons had been conducted on a piece of barren land not far from where they lived and had involved tin cans and a great deal of bad temper—mostly on James's part. She rather liked the idea of learning how to handle it properly. Singapore had a very active Ladies Shooting Club. It would make an interesting change from tennis.

Curran picked the revolver up and turned it over in his hand. "He did a good job but I think I have expended any favors I might have from him."

Curran handed the weapon back and she wrapped it tightly in its cloth, stowing it in her bag to take home.

"Was Cox helpful?" she asked.

Curran blew out a breath. "If anything, he's raised more questions. I'll have to go back out to the barracks this afternoon. It seems young Lieutenant Gentry has not been entirely forthcoming about his actions on the night his sister died. If Cox is right, he would have had the time to go up to The Cedars to talk to his sister."

"Really, Curran? But what motive would he have to kill her?"

Curran shook his head. "If Hawke told him that she was pregnant, he may have gone to confront her, but you're right, is that a motive to kill her?"

"And if he was so drunk he could hardly stand upright, I can't see him staggering up to The Cedars," Harriet continued.

Curran narrowed his eyes. "You were listening! You're right, but the questions need to be asked." He glanced at the door. "Something smells good."

The tantalizing scent of curry wafted into the large room as Sumeet Kaur, Gursharan Singh's wife, entered, carrying the stacked tiffin boxes with Singh's lunch. She came every day, slipping in and out with a nod to anyone present in the room.

Curran bade Sumeet Kaur good morning and she returned his greeting with a soft response.

"Gursharan is not here?" she asked.

"No, he's at the hospital." Curran glanced at his watch as he walked back into his office. "He won't be long."

"I leave his lunch, then."

She placed the tiffin boxes on her husband's desk, the scent of the curry permeating the room. Musa bin Osman and Ernest Greaves looked up from the fingerprint records they were sorting, no doubt reminded that the lunch break was coming up. Sumeet Kaur stopped in front of Harriet's desk.

"Mrs. Gordon?" She had a soft, lilting voice that took Harriet back to Bombay and the happy days with James.

Harriet smiled. "Good morning, Mrs. Gursharan. How are you today?"

Sumeet Kaur smiled and tugged her bright red-and-green cotton sari higher across her head. She placed a cotton-wrapped bundle on Harriet's desk.

"You work so hard, Mrs. Gordon. I bring you some samosas for your lunch."

Harriet's nose twitched at the scent of freshly cooked samosas, the meat- or vegetable-filled pastries she had loved so much in India. She thought of the wilting cheese sandwich she had brought with her for her lunch and her stomach growled.

"That is exceedingly kind of you, Mrs. Gursharan. They smell wonderful. Do you have to hurry away or can you take a few moments to step outside and share them with me?"

Sumeet Kaur blinked. "Share them? I suppose I could, but I would hate for you to go hungry."

From the size of the bundle and knowing the generous portions of Sergeant Singh's usual lunch, Harriet did not suppose for a moment she would go hungry.

"There is a bench under the rain tree in the yard behind the building, shall we go and sit there?" she suggested, and the woman nodded.

Harriet retrieved her flask of tea from her capacious handbag and the two women settled in the shade of the tree. Normally this spot was a popular lunchtime gathering place, but they were early and alone.

Harriet had been correct about the samosas. Six golden, flaky pastries nestled together in the cloth. She bit into one, savoring the delicate spicy flavor of the still-warm vegetable filling.

"This is delicious," she said, spitting pastry crumbs in a most unladylike manner.

"Gursharan tells me you have lived in India?" Sumeet Kaur ventured.

Harriet nodded. "Ten years in Bombay. My husband was a doctor and always busy so we didn't travel as much as I would have liked. I believe the Punjab is a very interesting place."

"I am from Amritsar, the holiest city of the Sikhs. It is very beautiful."

"When did you come to Singapore?"

Sumeet Kaur smiled. "I came to marry Gursharan. We had never met, but my father knew his father and the marriage was thought to be a good one."

"How old were you?"

"Fifteen."

Harriet had lived in Asia too long to be shocked or surprised at the thought of a fifteen-year-old girl traveling thousands of miles to marry a man she had never met. From what she had observed of Gursharan Singh and his wife, the marriage seemed a happy one.

"Do you have children, Mrs. Gordon?"

Harriet brushed the crumbs of the samosa from her fingers and laid her hands in her lap as she shook her head. "No. My husband and son died in Bombay, Mrs. Gursharan."

Sumeet Kaur's face crumpled and her hand closed over Harriet's. "I am so sorry."

"Time heals," Harriet lied, and knew the woman did not believe her for a moment. "What about your family?"

"Does Gursharan not talk of our children?"

"Sergeant Singh is a policeman, Mrs. Gursharan. He shares nothing he doesn't have to."

At this Sumeet Kaur laughed and pulled her hand back. "That is true. Our pride and joy is our son Arjan. He has just turned sixteen and will be a policeman like his *pita* and his *baba*, and then there are the jewels of our lives, our daughters Jasmeer, who is fourteen, and our baby, Sarna, who is ten."

"The same age as . . ." Harriet bit back the words *as my son would have been* and said instead, ". . . as my ward, Will Lawson."

Sumeet Kaur nodded. "Gursharan has told me of the boy. He has had a sad life, but he is happy with you and the reverend?"

"We think so. This is his last year at St. Thomas so we have to think where to send him for the rest of his schooling."

"He will go to England, no?"

Harriet shook her head. "No. We can't afford to send him to England. There are good schools closer to home and my brother is making inquiries."

Sumeet Kaur looked at the remaining samosas and cast Harriet a reproachful glance. "You are too thin, Mrs. Gordon. Eat up."

Out of politeness, Harriet ate another samosa, washed down by tea. Sumeet Kaur produced some succulent pieces of jackfruit from her basket, which made the perfect ending to the impromptu meal.

"I must get back to work," Harriet said, brushing crumbs from her skirts.

Sumeet Kaur pressed the bundle of remaining samosas into Harriet's hand. "Give them to the inspector," she said. "He also needs some meat on his bones."

Harriet smiled. "Thank you. You are very kind and a most excellent cook."

Sumeet Kaur beamed and ducked her head. "We would consider it our honor to invite you to our home for a meal, Mrs. Gordon. Maybe you and your brother and young William?"

"Oh, that would be wonderful."

"We have rooms above Gursharan's brothers' tailor shop in Serangoon Road. Come during Deepavali."

Harriet smiled. Deepavali, the festival of lights, one of her favorite times of year during her time in India. "I would truly love that. I don't think Julian has ever experienced a proper Deepavali."

Sumeet Kaur nodded. "Oh yes. It will be wonderful."

It lacked a few months until the festival, which fell in late October, and as Harriet took her leave of Sumeet Kaur, she hoped the woman would remember her kind invitation. Somehow she thought she would.

Back in the office, she knocked on Curran's door and, with-

out waiting for an invitation, entered and set the remaining samosas on his blotter.

"You need to eat something," she said. "And these are good
and fresh."

Curran turned back the cloth and sniffed. "Hopefully I can
keep them down."

Harriet shook her head. "You really should not be at work."

Curran looked up. "Don't you start. Li An lectured me this
morning but here I am."

Curran pushed a hand-scrawled paper across the desk at her.
"Those are my notes on my interview with Cox, if you don't
mind typing it up for me."

Harriet picked the paper up and read through it. Even though
she had been working for Curran for several months, his writing still confounded her at times and she had to query a couple
of words.

"If Gentry did slip out to see his sister, how would he have
got out of the barracks?"

Curran shrugged. "He would know where the duty officer's
keys were kept. I presume Hawke would have hung them up
when he returned to the mess. Easy enough to pocket the key to
that back gate."

"You're not convinced about Hawke, are you?" she asked.

Curran shook his head. "Something is not right."

And the answer came marching in through the door in the
person of Sergeant Singh carrying a large paper bag that he set
down on Curran's desk. Behind him, Euan Mackenzie, flushed
and sweating, took off his hat and fanned himself.

Curran looked from his sergeant to the perspiring doctor.

"Mac? What are you doing here? I thought the autopsy was
straightforward."

Mac smiled a thin, humorless smile. "Nothing is ever straightforward, Curran, as well you know, and Singh thought I should
talk you through what I found."

Curran frowned. "And what did you find?"

"He died from a shot to the head, just behind his right ear."

"I could see that for myself."

"It doesn't ring true to me, Curran."

Curran glanced at Harriet. "Excuse us, Mrs. Gordon."

Harriet took the hint and left the office. It really didn't matter, Curran's office was hardly soundproof.

After the door closed behind the department's stenographer and typist, Curran turned his attention back to the doctor. "What do you mean? It looked like suicide to me. Are you suggesting something else?"

"That's for you to decide. Singh, do you have your notes?"

Curran took his sergeant's notebook and flicked over the pages. Singh had drawn a rough diagram of the trajectory of the bullet from the angle of the entry and exit wound. Mac leaned over him, indicating his conclusion with a pencil. "Hawke was kneeling when he was shot. As you can see, the entry point is behind his right ear and angled downward slightly as if he were holding the gun up. You try shooting yourself from that position."

Curran obliged, kneeling on the floor of his office. He found it an awkward but not impossible position using his right hand.

He looked up at Mackenzie, a realization burning in his mind as he said slowly, "Hawke was left-handed."

Mackenzie nodded. "Now try it with your left hand."

Curran rose to his feet. "Impossible, but I'm not sure it proves anything. He just may have preferred to shoot himself with his right hand."

Mackenzie shrugged. "Aye, but there was no powder on his right hand . . . or his left."

Curran studied the diagram again. "Are you suggesting someone stood over him and fired that shot?"

"I'm a doctor, not a policeman. Let me just say that the evidence from the autopsy would indicate that Hawke did not take his own life. Draw your own conclusions, Curran."

Curran nodded. "Was there anything else?"

Mac pulled out a handkerchief from his pocket. A large knot had been tied in one corner, which he undid, letting the object it held secure fall onto the blotter on Curran's desk.

Curran drew a sharp breath at the sight of the tarnished silver object.

"I found this clutched in Hawke's left hand. Recognize it?"

"It's a regimental button, South Sussex Regiment," Curran said. "What about it?"

Mac smiled. "All the buttons on Hawke's uniform were accounted for, so he either grabbed it off another person—"

"Or it was placed there." Curran glanced at Singh. "Fetch me the box with the evidence from Mrs. Nolan's bedroom."

Singh set the box on the desk and Curran pulled out the envelope containing the button he had found under Sylvie Nolan's bed. He set it down beside the second button. It seemed that all three men held their breath.

Mac broke the silence. "Dear God."

Curran pulled out the pictures Greaves had taken of the crime scene at The Cedars. Sylvie Nolan's left hand trailed over the side of the bed, the fingers uncurled.

"Is it possible she was holding this button and it fell from her hand as the body relaxed?" Curran asked.

Mac shrugged. "I couldn't say for sure, but yes, it's possible."

Curran felt the prescience of something monumental. There were no threads attached to the buttons, they had not been torn accidently from a uniform. They had been deliberately placed on the bodies.

If Mac was right, he was looking at two murders. Two connected murders.

Mac left them to it and Singh and Curran stood at the evidence table where the evidence collected from the pavilion had been laid out. Curran recoiled from touching the man's uniform jacket, a grisly object, soaked through with Hawke's blood that had now turned stiff and dark brown, but needs must. Swallowing his revulsion, he searched the pockets but they were empty except for an unused handkerchief. All the buttons, secured by a split pin at the rear, were intact. The only other objects from the scene, Hawke's forage cap and Sam Browne, were spattered with blood and gore but were otherwise unremarkable.

He picked up the Sam Browne. Every officer wore this practical brown leather belt with the cross strap. He wore one himself, and like his, Hawke's had a holster for his service revolver, now empty, the weapon presumably the one found in his hand. However, unlike Curran's meticulously polished Sam Browne, Hawke's was in very poor condition. It did not look like it had been polished in months and the brass fittings were tarnished and dull.

Curran frowned. He remembered the adjutant as a man who took particular pride in his appearance, every inch of his uniform immaculate. He would have been keen to set an example to his men, and if a soldier had appeared in such a shabby piece of kit, he would have been on a charge.

He buckled the belt in the position the wear in the leather indicated it was customarily fastened and held it up, frowning.

"Does this look odd to you?"

Singh nodded. "The captain was a well-built man. I do not think that belt is his."

Curran nodded. "I have to agree. The one I saw him wearing was polished to a mirror finish. This"—he swept his hand across the table—"asks more questions than it answers. I am going to have to go back to the barracks and speak with Nolan's batman."

"The colonel will not be pleased," Singh remarked.

"I don't really care what the colonel thinks," Curran said with slightly more courage than he felt.

✇ SEVENTEEN

The colonel was not pleased. He stood behind his massive desk, his hands behind his back, glowering at Curran.

"What do you mean you have more questions?" he said in a low voice.

"I advised you that I still had loose ends before I could finalize my reports on the death of your wife and now Captain Hawke."

The colonel's jaw worked but his voice was even as he asked, "What questions? Come on, man, get them over with."

Curran withdrew from his pocket one of the two envelopes he carried and held out the button that Hawke had been holding. "Have you ever seen this before?"

"Of course I have. It's the regimental button. Damn it, man, I'm wearing them myself."

"Captain Hawke was holding this button in his left hand when he died."

Nolan leaned on his desk. "Was he, by God?" he said with the last trace of defiance. He straightened. "The answer is simple, Curran. That is Hawke's suicide note."

"*Honorem ante omnia?*" Curran quoted the regimental motto.

"Precisely. Honor above all."

"Honor before all," Curran corrected, and before the colonel could take offense at his correction, he continued. "And did you order him to do the honorable thing?"

Nolan snorted with something that might have been laughter. "Good Lord, man. This is the twentieth century. I can't order a chap to take his own life, however much I would have liked to. Isn't it enough that my own honor has been dragged through the mud in this investigation?" His voice had taken on an edge of desperation. "Can't you let it be, man?"

Curran persisted. "So, whose button was he holding?"

"No idea. Stands to reason he had a spare one. Really, Curran, this will get you nowhere."

Curran let a few moments pass before he said, "I beg to differ, the button means more to you than just Hawke's last words, doesn't it?"

Nolan hesitated. "It may be nothing. I told you about young Allen yesterday." His face drooped, the lines deepening. "He was found holding a regimental button. That's it. That's all there is to it."

"Why did Allen take his own life?"

"Who knows?" Nolan all but threw his hands in the air. "Ask Gentry. They were friends. As far as I know Allen didn't leave a note either—just the bloody button. Gentry took it badly. In fact it was one of the reasons his father transferred him over here. Thought the change would do him good. Make a man of him."

Curran pulled out the second envelope and handed it to the colonel. The man read the inscription on the front of the envelope and opened it, the color draining from his face.

"You found this in Sylvie's room?"

"Yes. It had rolled under the bed. I believe she may have had it in her hand at some point."

All the bravado leeched from Nolan and he sat down heavily, looking at the two buttons on his blotter.

"A coincidence?" Curran asked.

Nolan shook his head. "I don't know what to think."

"Was your wife acquainted with Lieutenant Allen?"

Nolan looked up. "Of course, she must have been, but I wasn't in England when Allen died so I can't tell you anything about their friendship." He waved a hand at the buttons. "What does this mean, Curran?"

"I don't know," Curran admitted. "I was hoping you might tell me. I am beginning to wonder if the three deaths are connected by more than just the honor of the regiment."

Nolan shook his head and sat back in his chair as Curran replaced the buttons in their respective envelopes.

"What do you want to do?" Nolan asked, all his bluster having evaporated. He looked old and tired.

"I would like to have another look at Hawke's room at the mess and I also need to interview his batman and Corporal Billings."

Nolan nodded. "Carry on," he said.

At the door, Curran turned back to look at Nolan. "One last thing, sir. What were you doing on Tuesday night?"

Nolan's eyes flashed. "Me? You're not suggesting—"

Curran held his hand up. "Not for a moment, but if Hawke's death is connected to that of your wife, it will be helpful to know where everyone was."

"If you must know, I was at home. Lavinia Pemberthey-Smythe joined Pris and I for dinner and we played three-handed bridge."

"What time did the party adjourn?"

"Lavinia left around eleven and Pris and I went to bed. Ask any of the servants."

Nolan rose to his feet and threw open the door to his office. "Gentry!" he called out, and the young officer appeared at the door to the adjutant's office.

"Sir?"

"Escort Mr. Curran to the officers' mess and give him every cooperation."

Gentry looked like he hadn't slept all week and the hand he held out to Curran shook.

"Why are you back, Inspector? I thought it was all cut-and-dried. Should I inform Major Goff?" Gentry asked as they strode across to the officers' mess.

"No need to bother Major Goff," Curran replied.

At the mess, Curran handed Gentry the key to Hawke's room and let the young man open the door. It was just as Curran remembered it and another examination of the room, conducted while Gentry went to fetch the officer's batman, proved as fruitless as the previous searches.

The batman knocked on the door and entered, followed by Gentry.

"You wanted to see me, sir?" Lance Corporal Lewis stood rigidly to attention.

"Stand easy, man," Curran said, and the old soldier snapped into the at-ease position. "Can you assist me with piecing together Captain Hawke's movements on Tuesday night?"

Lewis's eyes flickered with something that might have been grief. "He came upstairs after dinner and changed into his khakis. Told me he had to go out and I wasn't to wait up for him."

"What time was that?"

"About ten, I think."

"And did you see him again?"

"No, sir. Retired to me own billet as he'd told me. Went to wake him with his tea in the morning. He was most particular about his tea . . ." He gave a shudder. "Well, you was here. You saw his bed hadn't been slept in."

"Was there anything troubling him?"

Lewis shook his head. "Mrs. Nolan's death had shaken him. They was good friends, but no, sir, nothing to indicate that he wanted to end it all. I've been 'ere long enough to recognize when a man's 'ad enough of life and I'd no reason to be concerned."

Curran nodded. He believed the old soldier.

"Did he say why he was going out? Was he meeting someone?"

Lewis shook his head. "He didn't say and not my business to ask."

Curran opened his satchel and pulled out the Sam Browne that had been found with Hawke's body. "I was just wondering if you can confirm that this is Captain Hawke's?"

The batman looked at the object and recoiled, not so much from the blood spatter but from the general state of this key piece of uniform. "It most certainly is not. Mr. Hawke was most particular about his polishing, sir. Said he had to be able to see his face in it. This hasn't been touched for months." Lewis took it and turned it over in his hands. "Definitely not Mr. Hawke's. His had a nick out of the shoulder strap, just there." He indicated. "And it's set up for a much slimmer gentleman than Mr. Hawke." He demonstrated the settings on the buckle that Curran and Singh had observed. "It would barely fit Mr. Gentry here, let alone Mr. Hawke," he concluded.

Gentry, standing by the door, stared at the Sam Browne.

Curran turned to him. "Do you know who this belongs to, Gentry?"

Gentry shook his head. "It's not mine," he said, rather too quickly.

"Never said it was," Curran replied.

"No idea. May have been an old one of Hawke's?" Gentry suggested.

Lewis shook his head. "I've not seen it before."

Curran returned the mystery Sam Browne to his satchel. "One last thing, Lewis. Are any of Mr. Hawke's regimental buttons missing?"

Lewis opened the top drawer of the chest of drawers and

took out a wooden box, containing the highly polished buttons and insignia. He did a quick tally and shook his head. "Save for those what was on his jacket when he died, all in order, sir."

After the batman departed, Gentry sank down on the neatly made bed and ran a hand through his hair. "Why'd he do it, Curran?"

Curran studied the young man. Young Nicholas Gentry was carrying more than just the grief of his sister's death. Confession would be good for his soul, he thought.

Curran sank into a comfortable armchair and crossed his legs. "I think you and I need to have a talk, Mr. Gentry."

Gentry's eyes flickered. "What about?"

"Let's begin with the night of the mess dinner. I don't believe you have been entirely truthful with me."

Gentry blinked. "I told you—"

"You omitted mentioning the fact that you had words with Hawke and left the anteroom early, apparently so drunk you could barely stand."

Gentry's eyes widened although from fear or surprise at being caught in the lie, Curran couldn't say. "Oh yes, that's right," he mumbled. "I'd had too much. Must've forgotten."

"What did you and Hawke argue about?"

Gentry swallowed. "Regimental business."

"Concerning your sister?"

"No. Absolutely not." Gentry's eyes flickered to a corner of the room. "It was to do with securing the soldiers who had been fighting. That was it . . . nothing else."

Curran let the lie pass. "And after Cox left you and returned to the anteroom, did you go up to The Cedars to talk to your sister?"

"At twelve thirty in the morning? Don't be ridiculous. I was, as you said, so drunk I couldn't see straight."

"But you knew what time it was?"

"Billings must have told me. You ask Billings, he'll vouch for me."

"I'm sure he will."

"Is that it?" Gentry's tone had taken on an angry belligerence.

"No. Tell me about Lieutenant Allen."

Gentry stared at him. "Allen? What about him? What's he got to do with this?"

"He was a friend of yours, I believe?"

Gentry gave a short inclination of his head. "We were at Sandhurst together and he joined the South Sussex with me. Top chap."

"Why did he kill himself?"

The belligerence returned as Gentry looked Curran in the eye. "No idea. He didn't leave a note."

"You hadn't noticed anything unusual in his behavior?"

"No. I'd been out on exercises on Salisbury Plain for a couple of weeks before he . . . before he . . ."

"Who found him?"

Gentry swallowed. "I did. He hadn't appeared for parade. I found him in the clock tower of the barracks. He'd hanged himself." Tears filled the young man's eyes. "I . . . it was horrible. I'd never seen anyone dead . . . not like that."

Curran refrained from commenting that a sensitivity to violent death was not conducive to a career in the military, but Allen had been a friend and suicide was particularly brutal—and unnecessary.

"I believe there was something unusual found with the body."

Gentry frowned. "What do you mean?"

"A small item found in his hand?"

Gentry's mouth fell open. "Oh, you mean the button? He had it in his pocket, not his hand. It seemed a little odd given none of his buttons were missing, but not that odd if you consider the motto of the regiment. The MPs concluded it was tantamount to a suicide note."

"He died for the honor of the regiment? What had he done to compromise the honor of the regiment?"

Gentry shrugged. "No idea."

"But he was your friend. Surely he confided in you?"

Gentry shook his head. "Chaps don't talk about things like that," he said. "Look, he wanted to get out. Army life didn't suit him. He liked books and theater and things like that but he didn't know what else to do. I certainly don't think that would be a reason to take your own life though."

"You told me yesterday Allen was more than just a friend of your sister's. Was it something to do with her?"

"No! He wanted to marry her and Father would probably have agreed. He had all the right credentials. Son of the regiment and all that?"

"What do you mean?"

"His father was an officer in the Second Battalion. Died in India."

He rose to his feet. "Will that be all, Inspector? I have duties."

"Before you go, find Billings for me."

Gentry nodded and left Curran alone in James Hawke's room. Curran looked around the room. James Hawke had been an exemplary but unremarkable officer, bound for a solid career in the regiment, probably married to the CO's sister, which would have furthered his chances of advancement.

Until he had met Sylvie Nolan and then it had all gone wrong.

"Who did you go to meet on Tuesday night?" Curran asked the empty room but received no reply.

He closed his eyes, suddenly exhausted.

"You wanted to see me, sir?" Corporal Billings pushed the door open.

"Come in, Billings." Curran, too tired to stand, waved at the desk chair. "Sit down and take the weight off your feet."

Billings perched on the edge of the chair, clearly discomfited by the informality. Curran took a moment to study him. Another old soldier who had carved a comfortable niche for himself as an officer's personal servant. The batman was as ubiquitous in any officers' mess as the silver. In a peacetime army their duties were general in nature and mostly involved taking care of their assigned officer's, or officers', equipment and uniform. It was a comfortable billet, particularly for an older soldier who had done his time in the ranks.

"I think you were not entirely honest with me, Billings," Curran said.

Billings opened his eyes wide with apparent shock at the suggestion. "Me, sir?"

"You failed to mention that on the night of the mess dinner, Mr. Gentry retired early from the anteroom."

Billings chewed his lip. "I didn't want to embarrass the young gentleman," he said. "He was a bit the worse for wear, and if the colonel found out, he'd have given him what for."

Curran studied the batman. "Surely not? Lieutenant Colonel Nolan was a young officer himself. There must have been times he disgraced himself."

A small smile caught at Billings's mouth. "Oh yes, sir. There were times, but when it comes to Mr. Gentry, the colonel doesn't want him making a fool of himself. Lot to live up to there."

"And is Mr. Gentry living up to his father's expectations?"

"Not for me to say," Billings said.

Curran let that pass. "And after you put Mr. Gentry to bed, did he stir again?"

Billings shrugged. "Couldn't say, sir. I left him in peace and retired to me own bed. I just know he wasn't that pleased to see me in the morning when I brought him and Cox their tea."

"His uniform, his clothes, was everything in order? Was there anything that might have led you to suspect he'd been out after you'd put him to bed?"

"Nothing, sir. State he was in, he could barely stand upright." Curran wondered if he detected the faintest flicker of hesitation before the old soldier concluded, "No, sir, he couldn't have found the latrine, let alone the back gate."

Curran quirked an eyebrow. "Why do you mention the back gate?"

Billings shrugged. "Just a figure of speech, sir. Is that all?"

Curran nodded and let the man go. He sat for a long, long moment breathing in the lingering scent of sandalwood soap and tobacco, reflecting on where to go next with this case.

One thing now seemed clear: whoever had killed Sylvie Nolan had also killed James Hawke. They had both been left with a tarnished silver button, just as another young man, who had died in England twelve months earlier, had a silver button in his pocket.

Honorem ante omnia—Honor before all. The buttons were a clear message, but what did they mean?

With a heavy sigh, Curran hauled himself to his feet and secured the adjutant's room once more. He didn't want a repeat of the destruction of evidence that had occurred with Sylvie Nolan's possessions, although he doubted there was anything more to find among Hawke's things.

To complete his perfect day, he found Goff waiting for him in the tiled entrance to the officers' mess. From the military policeman's florid complexion and perspiration-soaked uniform, he must have been told of Curran's presence and come running to intercept him.

"What the hell do you think you are doing?" Goff roared. "The case is closed."

"I have the colonel's permission to continue investigations," Curran said. "Good day to you, Goff."

He left Goff standing on the steps to the mess, his fists balled at his side.

Curran's pace quickened as if he could feel the ranks of the

South Sussex closing behind him. Maybe there was one person who might be able to shed some light on the inner workings of the regiment and that was a daughter of the regiment.

Lavinia Pemberthey-Smythe stood at a table in her conservatory, repotting orchids. She wore an apron over a loose robe and her graying hair had been tied back in a long plait and wound around her head like a coronet. She looked up as Curran entered.

"Inspector? To what do I owe the pleasure? It is my understanding that the investigation concluded with the death of poor James?" She shook her head as she continued with her task, her hands working with skill and speed. "People never cease to surprise me."

Curran came straight to the point. "Did you know of his affair with Mrs. Nolan?"

Lavinia shrugged. "I'd heard stories but I am somewhat removed from the day-to-day scandals of the regiment, Inspector." She turned and smiled at him. "The regiment . . . the battalion . . . they are like any close community. There are petty grudges, infidelities, scandals."

"But they are kept behind closed doors?"

"Precisely."

"Until they can no longer be contained."

She paused in her work, without looking at him. "What do you want to know, Inspector?"

"Did you know a young subaltern by the name of Allen? I believe he died last year."

Her hands stilled and she set the pot she held down. She leaned her two hands on the bench top and looked up at him. "You are being kind, Inspector. Rupert Allen took his own life."

"I was told he hanged himself—"

"In the clock tower of the Marlborough barracks on the thirteenth July 1909." He saw tears in her eyes. "Yes, I knew him. He was my sister's son. After my sister and her husband died of cholera when the battalion was stationed in India, my husband and I took him in. An orphan at five years old."

"I had no idea . . ." Curran stumbled, aghast at his callous questioning.

She shook her head. "How would you have known? Bertie and I were not blessed with children, so Rupert was as much a son to us as any child of our own." Her lips tightened. "My brother-in-law was an officer of the South Sussex and my husband, of course, rose to the rank of the commanding officer of the First Battalion. There was no question of the boy pursuing any other career than the regiment, but not all men are suited for it. I am sure you understand, Curran."

He nodded. During his time in the army, he had come across sensitive young men, forced into uniform because family demanded it. It rarely ended well.

"Could I ask if you know why he killed himself?"

"You can ask but I can't tell you. I was here, Inspector. I had only his letters and they said nothing I would not expect from a young man of nineteen. The obligatory notes one sends aunts of whom one is fond." She brushed her hands on the apron and undid the strings. "You are welcome to see them."

"Thank you. I would appreciate that."

He followed her onto the verandah and she left him standing there while she went inside, returning with a small pile of envelopes tied together with black ribbon. She handed the packet to him and he took them with a promise to return them as soon as he could.

He did not expect anything earth-shattering to be revealed, but it might help him understand Rupert Allen and hopefully make some sort of connection with his death and those of Sylvie Nolan and James Hawke.

"I've been told he left no note at the time but something un-usual was found on his body," he said.

Something sparked in Lavinia Pemberthey-Smythe's calm blue eyes. "You mean the button?" He nodded and she shrugged. "You know the regimental motto? It may just as well have been a farewell note."

"You think he died for the honor of the regiment?"

She rolled her eyes. "Really, Inspector. I know nothing. Now, if you'll excuse me, I would like to return to my potting."

She turned and walked along the verandah. She'd gone barely a few steps when she looked back. "On the subject of the honor of the regiment, come and take tea with me someday and I will tell you what I know about your father." She held up her hand. "But not now. You're not ready to hear."

Curran remained on the step for a long moment, watching her straight back as she walked away from him. At last he had met someone who knew his father's story, but would it be the legend of the infamous Coward of Kandahar, whatever that was, or something more nearly approximating the truth?

Back at South Bridge Road, Curran leaned back against the large table that dominated the center of the office, his feet and arms crossed, and considered the large blackboard on which he had just been writing. This method of thinking out aloud gener-ally cleared his mind, but for once it provided no assistance whatsoever.

"Let's start with who killed Sylvie Nolan," he said. "If not James Hawke, then who?"

"Her husband?" Gursharan Singh suggested.

"He had opportunity and motive. Without having a precise time for her death, we only have his word that she was possibly dead when he got home from the mess dinner. Cuckolded husband, forced into marriage with her for the sake of her respectability. Plenty of motive. What about his sister?"

"She took a sleeping draught," Greaves said. "It was definitely sleeping powders in the glass in her bedroom."

"Doesn't necessarily mean she drank it," Curran said. "Why would she want to kill her sister-in-law?"

"Jealousy. Mrs. Nolan had stolen her betrothed away from her," Greaves said.

"And her position in the household," added Tan.

"Nicholas Gentry." Curran moved down the list. "On the assumption Hawke told him about his sister's pregnancy, Gentry could have gone to confront her. We have no witnesses to the fact he remained in his bed from the time Billings put him there until Cox came to bed about one."

Singh shook his head. "If he was as drunk as they say, I doubt him capable of going up to the house and I do not see the boy bludgeoning his sister with such force and anger," he said.

"He was, as you say, drunk. We don't know how incapacitated he was," Curran put in. "And I still don't think we can entirely rule out James Hawke."

"But if that is so, then who murdered Hawke? It seems we would have two murderers on our hands," Singh said.

Musa, as the youngest and newest member of the Detective Branch, cleared his throat. "It was an execution," he said.

Everyone turned to look at him. Emboldened, Musa continued. "He was on his knees, the shot behind the ear?"

Curran nodded. "I hadn't looked at it like that, but you're right, Constable."

"So, are we looking at two killers?" Singh said.

Curran turned and looked at his sergeant. "Maybe," he began slowly. "So who could have committed the second crime?" He waved a hand at the board. "We know Hawke was killed around eleven on Tuesday evening. Every one of these people has an alibi."

Singh stroked his moustache. "Maybe. The young lieutenant

was at the mess and a mess full of officers attest to his whereabouts, and the colonel and Miss Nolan were at The Cedars
with Mrs. Pemberthey-Smythe."

"With a house full of loyal servants, all prepared to swear
they were sitting playing cards at the time Hawke died," Greaves
put in.

Curran ran a hand over his eyes. The aftereffect of the malaria still took its toll. He should have been at home with his feet
up and a good book. He turned to the evidence on the table: the
wrong Sam Browne, the two buttons.

"This is all pointing to a connection with the dead subaltern,
Rupert Allen," he said.

"It seems to me," Singh said, "that the answer is quite simple. The young man, Allen, was involved with Mrs. Nolan . . .
or Miss Gentry, as she would have been then. Maybe he was the
father of her first child?"

"Gentry tells me that Allen was sufficiently close to Sylvie
Nolan to be considering marriage, but I've read his letters."
Curran picked up the pile of envelopes Lavinia Pemberthey-
Smythe had given him. "If that was his intention, there is nothing in there to indicate anything closer than friendship with
Sylvie Gentry. It is curious that he was contemplating going to
the commanding officer of his regiment to ask for his daughter's
hand in marriage and yet says nothing to his aunt? It must have
been a hasty decision."

"It points to the marriage being forced upon him," Greaves
said, adding, "because he had got the girl pregnant."

Curran shook his head. "We can make all the suppositions
we like but nobody who knows the whole story is going to come
through that door to tell us. Greaves, did you have any luck
with the fingerprints?"

Greaves shook his head. "No. All the fingerprints in Mrs.
Nolan's bedroom can be explained. Family and servants." He
shrugged. "No strangers."

Curran shook his head. "I confess, I have no idea where to look next. I'm going home. Good night, gentlemen."

It had gone dark by the time Curran left the Police Headquarters. His head ached and he longed for a bath and his bed but Lavinia Pemberthey-Smythe's words still resonated and, on the walk home, he didn't hesitate to plunge into the maze of dark alleys and laneways that constituted Chinatown. His uniform afforded him some protection, but he still took the precaution of undoing the buckle on the holster of his Webley.

The fug of burning incense paper from the little piles on the roadway or braziers on the corners added to the already fetid air and his head thudded. He stooped and picked up a piece of joss paper that had escaped the nearest fire and turned it over, almost expecting a note on the back, but it was blank. He paused and, leaning against a nearby pillar, pulled out his pencil and wrote on the back.

At the entrance to the alleyway described by Li An, he paused. He knew the opium dens of Chinatown and this one had a particularly unsavory reputation. Once again fear and anger roiled in his mind as he considered the danger the two women had put themselves in.

Steeling himself he straightened his shoulders and strode into the blackness to be met by a heavy teak door. It had no grate but he knew he was being watched. He looked up in time to see the peephole, cut in the floor of the living quarters that hung over the entrance, shut with a soft snap. Many canny shophouse owners took such precautions. He thought of the old castle in the grounds of Deerbourne Hall. Above the gateway were the death traps, the holes through which boiling tar could be poured on the heads of invading troops. Despite the heat, he shivered.

The door opened as he raised his hand to the knocker. His

nose twitched at the sickly stench of burning opium rising from the bowels of the building and he turned his head away.

A heavyset man barred the doorway with his arms crossed. Although he lacked Curran's inches, Curran would not have liked to engage him in a fight. He looked Curran up and down, his lips drawing back in a snarl, revealing yellow, rotting teeth.

"What do you want, policeman?" he said.

"I want to speak with Madam Lim," Curran said.

"She not want to speak to you." The man's brows drew together.

"It's a personal matter, not police business."

"So why you come in uniform, scaring away my clients?"

A diminutive woman with gray hair, neatly secured in a bun at the nape of her neck, pushed the doorman aside. They had met before when Curran had conducted raids on the opium dens, and it struck him then, as it did now, that Madam Lim looked like she would have been more suited to making dumplings for a score of grandchildren than running a pit of vice and tragedy.

"Is there somewhere we can talk where I won't scare the clients?"

Madam Lim nodded to a rickety staircase running up the side of the building. "I meet you up there."

At the top of the stairs, Madam Lim opened the door to admit Curran into her inner sanctum, a pleasant living room, furnished simply in the Chinese style. A household altar stood in an alcove, an offering of oranges and burning joss sticks before the stylized ancestors. An elegant round rosewood table dominated the center of the room, set around with matching drum stools. Two beautifully carved rosewood chairs stood against a wall.

The woman stood with her back to the table, regarding him with her arms crossed. She must have barely reached five feet but she had an air of menace about her, and Curran had no doubt one of her trusty servants who had been deployed to see off Li An and Harriet lurked just behind the door that opened into the rest of the house.

"Say what it is that has brought you here," Madam Lim said.

"I am looking for a man."

The woman scoffed. "The sort of men I have here are no longer fit to call themselves that."

"An Indian man," Curran persisted. "He was seen entering your house on Monday night."

Something flickered behind the woman's flinty eyes. She shrugged. "Many people. They come and they go. I don't take notice of them all. As long as they pay their money and don't make trouble for an old lady."

Curran had no doubt that Madam Lim knew exactly who came to her door.

He gathered his courage. "You will know him. He is blind in one eye." He felt foolish even saying it.

Madam Lim's mouth tightened. "He has a name?"

"Not that I know."

"Is he in trouble?"

"I told you it is a personal matter."

Madam Lim tapped her foot, indicating the interview was over.

"If I see such a one, what do I tell him?"

"Tell him . . . tell him I answered his message. Give him this." He handed over the folded joss paper on which he had scrawled: *I want to meet you. C.*

Madam Lim glanced at the paper and her eyes narrowed in curiosity before she thrust the paper into her pocket.

"You go now," she said, indicating the door.

At the door he glanced back at the woman. "One more thing. Khoo Zi Qiang, is he trying to get into Singapore?"

The name of Li An's brother produced an interesting reaction. Madam Lim balled her fists and issued a stream of invective in a dialect unknown to Curran, punctuated by spitting on the floor. Curran gained the distinct impression Madam Lim did not think much of Zi Qiang.

"Well?" he said calmly.

The woman's lips twisted. "If he sets foot in Singapore, he's a dead man."

"Good to hear," Curran said as he placed his hat on his head and left the unpleasant company of Madam Lim.

✣ Eighteen

John Little's Tearoom
Friday, 19 August

With the school year due to resume within the fortnight, Harriet spent Friday morning at St. Tom's catching up with paperwork, compiling roll books and doing the dozen or so other unpaid jobs her grace-and-favor status required of her.

She returned to the house for lunch with Julian and pottered around, tidying Will's room for what seemed like the hundredth time. He would be staying down at the beach with Louisa for another week and she missed him. Shashti lay curled in a ball at the end of the bed, and Harriet sat down beside the little cat, picking up the disreputable stuffed rabbit that sat on Will's pillow, so lovingly made by Will's mother. Harriet pressed it to her heart, remembering another little boy whose shadow still tugged at her skirts.

A movement at the doorway startled her and she set the rabbit back down, making a pretense of smoothing the bedcover.

Julian stood at the door, his glasses in his hands.

"I miss him too," Julian said.

"I'm sure he is having a wonderful time," Harriet said, covertly wiping her eyes.

"How could he not? You know we need to talk about where he is going to continue his schooling. There is the Victoria Institute in Kuala Lumpur."

Harriet shook her head. "I don't want to send him to England or KL . . . or away anywhere."

Julian replaced his glasses on his nose. "The Prince Edward Academy here in Singapore is getting a new headmaster this year," he said. "With luck maybe we can wrangle a scholarship for him to go there."

"Do you think so?" The recently established PEA would mean that Will did not have to board away, and if a scholarship could be arranged, the fees would be affordable.

"A certain young man will have to do some work, but I have every faith in his ability," Julian said. "When the new head arrives, we shall be sure to make him welcome." He looked at his watch. "Aren't you going out?"

Harriet glanced at her watch. She didn't want to be late for tea with Li An.

She dressed in her linen suit and ordered Aziz to find a ricksha for her. Despite her best intentions with regards to punctuality, she found Li An waiting for her outside the fashionable department store, John Little's of Raffles Place.

It took her a moment to recognize the slender woman in a pretty lemon-colored muslin tea dress, clutching a small, intricately beaded purse in her white lace–gloved hands. Her blue-black hair had been coiled at the nape of her neck, with a wing of satin hair and an elegant hat, draped in silk ribbons and a fine veil, drawn down over the young woman's face, cleverly concealing her scar.

John Little & Co. had recently refurbished their popular tearoom, and although not as grand as Robinsons Department Store, the freshly decorated room, with its cane furniture and crisp white tablecloths, was a popular meeting place. Strategically placed potted palms added to the atmosphere and provided a modicum of privacy for those who desired it.

Even in her most fashionable suit, Harriet had never felt quite so tall, gangly and frumpy as she did walking beside the elegant and self-contained Li An. As they entered the tearoom, they attracted curious glances and she noticed that Li An pulled the veil lower on her face as a maid in a black dress and crisp white apron showed them to their table.

When they were seated and orders given to the maid who attended them, Harriet said, "You look quite different, Li An."

Li An looked down at her purse. "Do I look out of place?" she asked.

Harriet shook her head. "Not at all. That dress . . . it's French, isn't it?"

Li An looked up. "Jacques Doucet. My father imported it for my eighteenth birthday." She fingered the fine muslin of the draped sleeve. "It is a little outmoded now."

"It looks lovely."

Harriet had so many questions. She longed to ask about Li An's father and how he sourced the sort of money that provided haute couture for his daughter, about her schooling at the convent, her brother and how she and Curran came to be living in a tiny bungalow in Singapore . . . but she held her peace.

"Why have you invited me for tea, Mrs. Gordon?"

The directness of the question surprised Harriet, and while she stumbled around for a reply, Li An answered for her. "You are Curran's friend and I would like to be your friend too."

Harriet smiled. "So would I."

Over Li An's shoulder she noticed a woman enter the tearoom. Instantly recognizable in her plain black skirt and short black jacket over a white blouse—her nod to mourning—Pris Nolan looked around the room. Harriet smiled and waved but Pris seemed to freeze for a long moment before acknowledging that she had seen Harriet.

A meeting was unavoidable and Harriet stood to greet her.

"What a surprise," Pris said. "I thought you would be at work?"

"I am taking tea with my friend, Miss Khoo."

As Harriet made the introductions, Li An watched Pris from behind her veil, a cool smile on her lips.

"Nice to make your acquaintance, Miss Khoo," Pris said. "Please excuse me. My friend is waiting."

As she resumed her seat, Harriet caught a glimpse of a man, concealed by one of the potted palms, rise to greet Pris. The light caught a flash of spectacles and a shiny bald spot and Harriet recognized Pris's companion as her tennis partner, Clyde Morris. Unfortunately Harriet was seated with her back to the pair so any further observation would be difficult.

Li An peered around Harriet's shoulder. "Who is that lady?" she asked.

"She is the sister-in-law of Mrs. Nolan, the woman murdered last week."

Li An nodded. "And the gentleman?"

"Her tennis partner."

"And they have known each other a long time?" Li An continued.

"I suppose for as long as they have been members of the tennis club. Why?"

Li An leaned toward her. "I think they are more than just friends, Harriet."

"What on earth makes you say that?" Harriet inquired.

"You cannot see what I see. It is in the way they lean toward each other, whispering together. Not like you and I. Ah, see . . . Miss Nolan . . . now she touches his hand. I think she is seeking love and comfort."

"She has just suffered two violent deaths," Harriet said. "Of course she is seeking love and comfort, but . . ." She trailed off. She would never have thought that Clyde Morris would be the person Pris Nolan would run to. She itched to turn around.

Li An shrugged. "I may be mistaken. Now they just sit and talk like two good acquaintances." Her gaze shot to Harriet. "Like you and I."

The maid arrived with their tea and scones, and as Harriet poured the brew into delicate china cups, she found the courage to ask, "How did you meet Curran?"

Li An took one of the cups and lifted her veil enough to allow her to sip the tea. "In Penang," she said. "It was a tea party at the governor's house. I thought he looked very fine in his uniform, but I do not talk of Penang . . . Tell me about India, Harriet. Your husband . . . your son . . . ?"

"I don't . . ." Harriet began. "I prefer not to talk about that time. Nothing I say will bring them back."

"But they should not be forgotten. This is the month of the hungry ghosts. They should be spoken of and honored."

"Are you a Christian, Li An?"

A small smile caught at the woman's mouth. "I was schooled by the nuns," she said. "But I do not forget my own gods." She set the teacup down. "I cannot imagine what it is to lose a child." She looked up. "How do you, the mother, keep living?"

"You live because you have to," Harriet said. She forced a smile that she did not feel. "This is a grim conversation for a tea party."

Li An sat quite still. "I have lived too long in the shadows. I have forgotten that there is light as well as dark in life. Forgive me."

Li An glanced around the tearoom and Harriet followed her gaze. They appeared to be the center of attention.

"What do you suppose they are saying, Harriet? That a respectable lady should not be seen taking tea with a Chinese girl."

"Nonsense," Harriet said. "There are several other tables with Chinese ladies."

"And they also stare and whisper. They call me names, horrible names, like Huo Jin. I am Curran's 'native woman,' his mistress."

"But you love him."

"Love comes at a cost, Harriet, and I do not belong here in this world of tearooms, and polite chitchat."

"Li An—"

But the woman had pushed back her chair. She held out her hand. "Thank you kindly for the invitation," she said. "I have had a most enjoyable time, but I must return home now."

And she turned and walked . . . no, not walked . . . Li An glided out of the room, her head high, her back straight. The eyes of the women who had driven her out, followed her, before they leaned into each other no doubt to exchange more ribald gossip.

Harriet picked up her purse from the table, leaving a few coins for the waitress and discreetly glanced in the direction of Pris Nolan and Clyde Morris. As if aware of the movement, Pris waved and beckoned Harriet over. As she approached, Clyde rose to his feet.

"This is fortuitous, Mrs. Gordon," he said. "I have a small favor to ask of you." Harriet smiled encouragingly and he went on, "As you know, I'm on the social committee at the tennis club. I was rather hoping I could prevail on your considerable skills to type up a little notice for me about the Musical Evening and Tombola in a few weeks."

"Of course, I'll be delighted."

"Excellent, I have it with me. I was going to give it to Miss Nolan to pass on to you." Morris searched all his pockets before withdrawing a much folded and crumpled paper from the breast pocket of his jacket. Harriet took it and slipped it into her handbag.

"When do you need it? I won't be at tennis tomorrow. I have promised Julian I will come and watch the cricket."

Morris blinked behind his glasses. "I was hoping to have it done for the committee meeting next Wednesday."

Harriet nodded. "I'll make sure it is delivered to the club-house in time for that."

"You're very kind, Mrs. Gordon."

"Not at all."

She just hoped it wouldn't be the start of a steady stream of requests to type up this and that.

"Of course, the regiment is playing the Singapore Cricket Club tomorrow," Pris said with surprising animation. "John and Jack will be going, of course."

"And you?"

Pris shook her head. "I loathe cricket. There is a concert at Victoria Hall in the afternoon. Mr. Morris has offered to take me and I am glad of any excuse to escape the house." She glanced up at Morris and smiled.

Harriet looked at the little bank clerk. He seemed a kind man, with his mild gray-blue eyes and draggly moustache. He was also a married man with a wife and three children back in England, but life in the colonies could be a lonely place and the gesture was appreciated by Pris, so it was not Harriet's place to judge.

Harriet glanced down at the plate of untouched cakes and scones on the table between Pris and Morris and excused herself.

❧ NINETEEN

Singapore Cricket Club
Saturday, 20 August

In normal circumstances, sacrificing an afternoon of tennis for an afternoon of cricket would not have been Harriet's preference. However on Friday she had received a note from Griff Maddocks inquiring if, instead of tennis, she would care to join himself and Simon Hume at the Padang. It included an offer to collect her in Simon's car, which provoked a heady degree of girlish excitement, quite unlike her usual self.

With William still at the beach, she had no responsibilities and she decided to make the most of the afternoon, dressing carefully in a coffee-colored muslin gown and a matching hat—another of her sister Mary's choices. Hume and Maddocks duly arrived in the motor vehicle and conveyed her to the Singapore Cricket Club, arriving in great style and attracting the admiring glances of several of the other ladies.

She should have known better than to expect the company of two cricket-obsessed men to be anything special, and the crack of leather on willow, followed by the polite clapping that marked cricket matches around the world, was enough to send her to sleep. Harriet fanned herself and stifled a yawn.

Griff Maddocks turned to look at her. "You are a philistine," he said. "There's Julian playing his heart out and does he get any appreciation for the fine turn of the ball?"

"He's just been hit to the boundary," Harriet said. "That's four runs scored off him."

"You watch. It's all a ruse. He'll get his man on the next ball," Maddocks said with absolute certainty as Julian retrieved the ball thrown in from the man on the boundary and started his walk back to his mark.

Harriet looked around the packed pavilion, ruing her decision to come. She could have played singles at the tennis club. She could have spent the afternoon counting her knives and forks. Anything would have been more absorbing.

The South Sussex had turned out in force, the older officers sitting with their commanding officer. The younger men, dressed in flannels, ready to take to the field. She recognized Nick Gentry, already padded up, ready to go in on the next fall of wicket. Around the Padang, uniformed men lounged in the shade of the rain trees.

And in the very back row of the pavilion, a different khaki-uniformed figure sat by himself, his elbows on his knees, a pipe in his mouth, leaning forward, apparently intent on the game.

Harriet excused herself from her escorts and made her way up the stand, taking the seat beside Curran.

"What are you doing here?" she asked.

He straightened and removed the pipe from his mouth. "Working," he said.

She cast him a quizzical glance. "Really?"

"Really." He knocked the tobacco from his pipe on the heel of his boot. "I do all my best thinking at the cricket."

"And what are you thinking?"

He looked down at the pipe in his hand and gave it another knock. "I am thinking that I have no idea where to go to next with this investigation." His gaze moved to the officers of the

South Sussex Regiment. "They know who is responsible but they are never going to give up one of their own." He stuffed the pipe in his pocket and straightened. "Who's that with Maddocks?"

"That's Simon Hume. He's an Australian—friend of Griff's."

Curran gave her a sharp, appraising glance and she felt the heat rise to her cheeks. She cleared her throat. "Come and meet him. He's very keen on cricket."

"Lucky you," Curran remarked sardonically. He knew Harriet's thoughts on the game. "When are you going to meet a man who isn't keen on cricket and will take you to concerts and plays?"

Harriet thought of Pris Nolan and Clyde Morris. "Sadly that breed is in short supply. How is Li An? I fear I said something to upset her yesterday."

Curran cast her a quizzical glance. "Really? She told me she had enjoyed her time with you."

Harriet didn't respond. A man could not understand the effect the whispers and glances must have had on Li An. It had been foolish of Harriet to put her new friend in that position.

Below her Maddocks stood up and turned around, scanning the pavilion. Seeing Harriet and Curran he waved and indicated that they should join them. Curran rose to his feet and held out his hand for Harriet, assisting her down the steps to their friend.

"Last over before tea," Maddocks said as they joined him. "You're not playing today, Curran?"

"No. I've been a bit under the weather this week and the last thing I need is an afternoon in the sun," Curran said. "Besides which I've got enough on my plate."

"Ironic that they are playing the South Sussex today," Maddocks remarked. He cast a sideways glance at Curran. "So is it all nicely tidied up and put away? You are depriving me of some fabulous headlines: Colonel's lady brutally murdered by her lover who then takes his own life?"

"That," Curran said. "is journalistic speculation."

Maddocks grinned. "But it's all you've got, isn't it?" He straightened, remembering his manners. "Say, you haven't met Hume yet."

Simon Hume rose to his feet, held out his hand. "Simon Hume, Melbourne *Argus*. You must be Curran."

The two men shook hands with a degree of guarded reserve.

"So was the adjutant's death really a suicide?" Hume asked as they sat down.

Curran shot the man a sharp glance. "I'm here to watch cricket," he said. "I can't and won't discuss the case."

"Oh, well bowled!" Maddocks exclaimed as the last ball of Julian's over took the bails off the stumps. "That's tea. Let's go in and congratulate your brother on his four wickets, Harriet. Brilliant bowling."

As they made their way into the marquee that had been set up beside the pavilion, a short, stocky man in the uniform of an officer of the military police stepped in front of Curran. Harriet recognized him as Major Goff. Over the past week, she had seen the MP major at various uncomfortable occasions at The Cedars, lurking in the background, watching, always watching.

Now the man stood, swaying slightly in front of Curran.

"I want to talk to you," Goff said.

"Not now, Goff. It's neither the time nor the place."

Curran made to go around the other man, but the military policeman sidestepped to maintain his position in front of him. The crowd gathering in the marquee turned to watch the altercation.

"If you have anything to say to me, Goff, keep it till Monday."

Goff responded by jabbing a stubby finger into Curran's chest. "You always were an arrogant son of a bitch, Curran. Think 'cause your grandfather's some lord or another you're better than the rest of us, well, you're not. Your father was scum. A traitor and a coward."

Curran drew himself up to his full height, suddenly every inch an aristocrat in tone and bearing. "You've been drinking. Go home, Goff."

Goff swayed, his eyes narrowing.

"Don't think I don't know about you and that Chinese whore . . . I've seen her, Curran, and I wouldn't mind a taste of what she has to offer. Pity about the scar."

Curran stiffened and Maddocks, demonstrating admirable speed, caught the policeman's arm just as Curran raised a balled fist.

"Curran. Don't give him the satisfaction," Maddocks said.

Goff snorted. "Got to watch that temper, Curran. Got you into trouble before. Will get you into trouble again."

Curran's nostrils flared. "Get out of my way, Goff," he said, and pushed past the military policeman.

Harriet and Maddocks found Curran at the back of the pavilion, attempting to light a cigarette with a hand that shook. Maddocks extricated the matches from him and obliged, taking a cigarette for himself.

"Ever have one of those weeks?" Curran said after a couple of deep steadying draws. "I've got too much history with the South Sussex, Maddocks."

"What was all that about your father?"

Curran looked up at the sky. "They call my father the Coward of Kandahar."

"Very Kipling," Maddocks said. "What did he do?"

"That's the problem, I don't know. I was always told he died at the Battle of Maiwand. It's only since this case began that I have heard him referred to by that unflattering sobriquet. Now it's all I can think about." Curran took another deep draught of the cigarette.

"Isn't there anyone who can tell you the truth?" Harriet asked.

Curran shook his head. "I don't think anyone knows the

truth. Lavinia Pemberthey-Smythe may know something. Her father would have been a serving officer in the regiment about the same time as my father."

"But children hear things," Harriet said. "It will only cost you your pride to ask her."

Curran gave a snort of humorless laughter. "My pride comes at a heavy price."

Maddocks blew out the smoke from his own cigarette. "Well, it's not going to make your week any worse, is it, Curran?"

Curran rolled his eyes.

Harriet touched his arm. "The note you received? The meeting at the temple . . . was that to do with your father?"

He nodded. "I believe so."

"I'm sorry we made a mess of it. Li An and I . . . we didn't know."

He shook his head. "What's done is done. Whoever it was knows where to find me."

He stubbed out the cigarette and straightened. "I think I'd better leave before I cause any more scenes."

"You didn't cause the scene. It was that odious little major," Harriet said.

Curran smiled. "You're very loyal, Harriet," he said. "But if it hadn't been for Maddocks here, I would certainly have caused a sensation. Pass on my congratulations to the reverend for an innings well played. I want to see the South Sussex crushed by the end of the day."

Harriet and Maddocks watched him walk away, pushing his way through the crowd. Maddocks shook his head. "This case has got him rattled," he said. "It's too personal."

Harriet nodded. "I think you might be right, Griff," she said.

"Harriet . . ." Something in Griff's wheedling tone caused her to turn and look at him. "I have a small favor to ask."

"Go on," Harriet said.

"You see that girl over there. Do you know her?" Griff indicated a young woman with brown hair who stood with a group of other women, drinking tea.

"She's a nurse at the hospital, I think. What about her?"

Griff colored. "I've asked her to come to Harima Hall tonight and I was rather hoping you would come too. You and Hume . . ."

"Has she said yes?"

Griff nodded. "It's just I like her rather a lot and . . ."

"You don't want to be alone with her? Really, Griff." She turned to Simon Hume. "Do you mind playing chaperone to our friend?"

Hume smiled. "Not at all. Let's make an evening of it."

"Please, Harriet? Oh no, she's coming over." Maddocks had turned alternate shades of pink and white.

Harriet turned to greet the woman whom Griff introduced as Doreen Wilson. She had a pleasant, freckled face and a wide, curving mouth.

"I believe we are making up a party to go to the cinematograph this evening," Doreen said with a smile. "I've never seen moving pictures before. This should be fun."

"I'm not sure I approve of you going out unescorted."

Julian stood in the doorway to Harriet's bedroom watching as she put the finishing touches to her costume for the night out at Harima Hall.

She glared at him. "I don't care what you think," she said archly. "I am not a blushing debutante of seventeen. I am a respectable widow who makes her own decisions in life and I am having an evening out in the company of friends. If you want to come, you would be welcome."

Julian shook his head. "Not after a day of cricket and besides I have a sermon to finish for tomorrow. I'm preaching at the cathedral or had you forgotten?"

"Of course I haven't," Harriet snapped. "Why can't I have some fun occasionally or have you forgotten what that is like? It's high time you found yourself some nice, sensible girl who doesn't mind being a vicar's wife."

Julian's mouth tightened and Harriet instantly regretted her harsh words. She had forgotten Jane . . . the nice, sensible girl who would have been an ideal vicar's wife, now ten years in the grave.

"I'm sorry, Ju. I didn't mean it."

Julian shrugged. "I know you didn't and you're right."

She hadn't thought her self-sufficient brother could be lonely but the pain etched on his face said it all. At thirty-seven, Julian's chances of finding a nice, sensible girl seemed to have passed him by.

She crossed over to him and flung her arms around him, holding him tight. "We all deserve second chances," she murmured.

He patted her on the shoulder. "Hurry up and finish getting ready," he said.

"The pearls?" She held up the long string of pearls that had been her late mother-in-law's wedding gift to her.

"You look very nice," Julian conceded. "Is that dress another of Mary's choices?"

Harriet considered her reflection in the mirror. The gray silk evening dress was indeed another of Mary's fashion decisions. High waisted and narrowing at the ankles, even Harriet had to admit that she looked both fashionable and stylish, even if walking was rather impeded by the hobble skirts.

She looped the pearls around her neck and adjusted the gray feather in her hair. She didn't think Huo Jin had quite managed her hair properly, but their amah had been distracted by her forthcoming appearance in a Chinese opera, for which she had been practicing for months.

Simon Hume already had Maddocks and Miss Wilson in his

vehicle as he turned into the driveway of St. Tom's. He gallantly escorted her down the steps of the house and she turned to wave to Julian as they drove out.

In the dusk, the bright lights announcing Harima Hall as Singapore's first cinematograph spilled out onto North Bridge Road. A well-dressed crowd of Europeans, wealthy Chinese, Eurasians and Armenians were already filing in through the doors.

Simon Hume offered Harriet his arm as they dismounted from the vehicle. She hesitated momentarily before taking it, but in this foolish frippery of a dress with its narrow skirt and her unaccustomed gray leather evening shoes, a strong arm might well be needed in the crush.

They found their seats among the happy, multiracial crowd that thronged the hall. The men went to find refreshment, leaving Harriet with Miss Wilson. The woman sat back and fanned herself with the program.

"I don't think I'll ever get used to the heat," she said, her accent betraying a northern origin.

"How long have you been out here?"

"Six months," she said. "And you, Mrs. Gordon?"

"I came out in January," Harriet said, "but I have the advantage of some years in India."

"Oh aye, Griff said your husband was a doctor. Dr. Mackenzie is a friend of yours?"

"He is," Harriet said. "How did you meet Griff . . . Mr. Maddocks?"

"Bridge," Miss Wilson replied. "We found ourselves partnered and, well"—she glanced around and lowered her voice—"to be honest, I was rather taken by him. You're not . . . ?" She raised a questioning eyebrow and it took a moment for Harriet to realize what the woman wanted to know.

"Griff and me? Oh no . . . nothing of that sort. Just friends. He's my doubles partner at tennis."

Miss Wilson looked relieved. She smiled. "You must think

me very forward," she said, "but we're much of an age, Mrs. Gordon, and it's not often that nice men come our way."

Harriet didn't quite know how to respond to that statement but she wasn't Griff Maddocks's keeper.

The men returned with lime juices. Simon Hume settled down beside her and the lights dimmed. The first act was billed as Professor Fosbrook, "The World's Greatest Conjurer." Harriet felt that may have been a slightly exaggerated claim, but his tricks were clever and he earned a sturdy round of applause. He was followed by Miss Constance Cerito, a singer and dancer, famous for her "cakewalk," a dance craze from America. She inveigled a few willing volunteers from the audience and endeavored to teach them the steps to the great merriment of the audience. The final live act of the evening was Baby Ellen, described in the program as "six-year-old champion child singer." Harriet found the warbling of the precocious brat almost unendurable, but Miss Wilson came over all dewy-eyed and had to reach for her handkerchief with muttered exclamations of "What a darling child."

At intermission they took the opportunity to stretch their legs and Harriet found herself alone with Simon Hume. He offered her his arm and they strolled out into the night and comparatively fresh air.

"Enjoying the show?" he asked.

"I haven't had a night out for so long, I had forgotten what it is to have fun," Harriet replied.

"I've a confession to make," Simon said. He turned to face her, slipping her hand into his. "I inveigled Maddocks to invite you."

She made no attempt to remove her hand from his fingers. "Did you indeed?"

"I'm not sure how things are done here," Simon said. "But would it be out of order to invite you to supper at Raffles one evening?"

Harriet considered the question. "I am an independent woman, Mr. Hume. If I care to accept such an invitation, it will be entirely my decision."

He smiled, his teeth white in the dark. "That would be excellent. I—" Whatever he had been about to say was interrupted by the bell and they returned to their seats.

After intermission the real show began, the cinematograph with a series of short comedic moving pictures. The audience erupted in mirth at the pratfalls and contrived hilarity. The sheer silliness overcame Harriet's cynicism and she found herself laughing with the rest of them.

She arrived home to find Julian dozing on the verandah with Shashti on his knee. She tapped his arm with her fan and he jerked awake.

"Nice evening?" he asked.

"Very," Harriet said. She sat down and took off her shoes, stretching out her aching feet. "The cinematograph was most amusing."

"And how was Mr. Hume?"

She cast her brother a sharp glance. "He has invited me for supper at Raffles," she said.

"Really? Are you going to go?"

Harriet hauled herself to her feet and leaned over her brother, bracing her hands on the arms of the chair. "Of course I'm going to go, Julian." She straightened and gave him a sweet smile. "Good night."

❧ TWENTY

St. Thomas House
Sunday, 21 August

A lazy Sunday drowsed into the afternoon. Church in the morning, where Julian preached an excellent sermon on Lazarus, was followed by lunch and the nagging ache left by Will's absence grew stronger. Normally Sunday afternoons were spent on the verandah, reading books or playing board games.

Leaving Julian to doze, Harriet took out her Corona folding typewriter to write a letter to her sister. She knew it annoyed Mary to receive a typewritten letter, but as Mary was also the first to complain about Harriet's handwriting, it seemed there was no pleasing her elder sister. She recounted the doings of the past week, omitting any reference to reconnecting with a group of suffragists. The memory of the meeting at Lavinia Pemberthey-Smythe's house still caused her to wake in the middle of the night in a sweat, partly from the memories it had reawakened and partly through fear she had said too much.

She finished the letter, typed a couple of school-related letters for Julian and, remembering she had promised to type up the notice about the Musical Evening and Tombola for the tennis club's social club, she found the handwritten note Clyde Morris had left with her, still folded in her handbag.

She smoothed it out and huffed out a breath as she wound the paper into the machine.

LADIES LAWN TENNIS CLUB
MUSICAL EVENING AND TOMBOLA
ALL MONEY RAISED TO GO TO THE
CHILDREN'S WELFARE SOCIETY
Program will include a piano recital by Miss P. Nolan,
conjuring tricks by the Great Harold . . .

Harriet shook her head. She shuddered to think what conjuring tricks Harold Ramsey, the husband of the club's treasurer, had in mind. The man seemed incapable of hitting a tennis ball, let alone coordinating rabbits out of hats.

Her fingers stopped as she started to type Pris Nolan's name. The spidery hand and use of a blue-green ink seemed familiar. She had seen it before and it had not been on tennis club correspondence.

Harriet caught her breath—the note! The single page they had found secreted in the spine of Sylvie Nolan's journal. What had it said?

. . . How lightly your fingers fly across the keys, creating
sublime music for us all! I felt quite mesmerized, watching
them.
  Like your music, your very presence fills the air and
gives me succor in this difficult world. When I am around
you, I feel a weight lift from me momentarily; you free me
from the burden of being alone in this world . . .

There had been a talent quest at the tennis club a few months earlier that had been won by Pris Nolan with her piano playing.

Harriet stared at the notice about the tombola and the pieces of the puzzle tumbled into place. The note in Sylvie's journal had not been a love letter addressed to her, it had been a missive from Clyde Morris to Pris Nolan. As Li An had observed in the tearoom, their apparent friendship might be deeper than that of mere tennis partners.

Harriet folded the note and returned it to her handbag. Pausing only to fetch her hat, she woke her brother to tell him she was going out.

Julian frowned. "Where?"

"To find Curran," Harriet said, already halfway down the front steps.

"Don't forget Huo Jin's concert at five," Julian shouted after her.

Hazarding a guess that she would find the inspector at home, she ordered the ricksha wallah to drop her at his gate and ran up the path. Curran was indeed seated on the verandah, a book in one hand and his pipe in the other.

He rose slowly to his feet as she approached.

"Harriet? What's happened?"

She caught her breath as she fumbled in her handbag for Morris's note, which she brandished. "I know who wrote the letter we found in Sylvie Nolan's journal!"

He took the paper from her and scanned it. "The writing looks similar but I don't understand. We know it wasn't Hawke, the handwriting was not his. I assumed it was just one of her many admirers."

"It wasn't intended for Sylvie Nolan," Harriet said. "I spend a great deal of my life interpreting handwriting and I recognize this hand, but if you doubt me, I'm sure Greaves will have a better idea than me."

"So are you going to tell me who wrote it or keep me in suspense?" he asked.

"Clyde Morris," Harriet said.

"Who?" Curran frowned.

"Clyde Morris is the secretary of the social committee of the tennis club"—she paused—"and Pris Nolan's doubles partner."

"Was he acquainted with Sylvie Nolan?"

She could have hit him. "Curran! The note we found in Sylvie's journal wasn't written to Sylvie Nolan. I think it was written to Pris."

Realization flashed in Curran's eyes. "Pris Nolan and this Clyde Morris . . . ? Wait there, Harriet. I'll fetch my hat. We'll go and find the original note. Do you mind the walk?"

He returned a few minutes later with a battered pith helmet, locked the door and they set out down the hill toward South Bridge Road.

The hot afternoon sun beat down on them and Harriet began to regret the decision to walk the relatively short distance. After her experience in Chinatown the previous Monday, the bustling streets took on a sinister air even in the bright daylight.

As if he sensed her disquiet, Curran glanced at her. She smiled at him. "I was just remembering our stupidity of last Monday," she said.

"Ah . . . that."

"Do you really think it was someone who knew about your father?"

He shrugged. "Don't know, don't care particularly. My father was never part of my life. After my mother died, her family was quick to get rid of him."

"How?"

"My grandfather purchased a commission in the South Sussex Regiment for him and off he went. As far as I am concerned, he died at the Battle of Maiwand."

She studied his profile. The air of disdain he affected was belied by the crease between his brows and she knew better than to ask him any more questions.

In the quiet office, Curran rummaged through the box of

evidence. Finding the envelope he sought, he laid the single, torn piece of paper on the table.

> *Dearest, It was a torment to be so near to you and yet so far away.*
>
> *How lightly your fingers fly across the keys, creating sublime music for us all! I felt quite mesmerized, watching them.*
>
> *Like your music, your very presence fills the air and gives me succor in this difficult world. When I am around you, I feel a weight lift from me momentarily; you free me from the burden of being alone in this world.*
>
> *How I treasure our friendship! My dear, if you only knew how light my heart feels when I am in your presence . . .*

He set the note Harriet had given him next to it and let out a whistle. "I don't think I need Greaves to confirm that this is the same hand. The question is, if the love letter was intended for Pris, then what was it doing in Sylvie Nolan's journal?"

"Only one person can answer that question, Curran."

"Maybe two people . . . Perhaps I should start with Clyde Morris?" Curran glanced at his watch. "I'm not in uniform. It can wait till the morning."

"Is there anything I can do?"

Curran shook his head. "Harriet, while your insights are invaluable, I do need to remind you that you are not a member of the police force."

Harriet didn't need to be reminded but her disappointment must have shown on her face.

He shook his head and his tone softened. "If I am honest, I can't imagine what I would do without you, and if I haven't thanked you properly for everything you did while I was indisposed, then I apologize."

A warm glow spread through Harriet from her toes upward. "Perhaps I could speak to Pris?" she suggested.

"Of course not," Curran said, but she saw the light of doubt wavering behind his eyes.

"Li An and I saw Pris and Clyde Morris at the tearoom on Friday. Li An had a better view of them than I did and she said she thought there was more to the relationship," Harriet pressed.

Curran closed his eyes and took a breath. "Pris Nolan is your friend," he said. "It is none of my business what two women choose to discuss."

Harriet glanced at her watch. "Is that the time? I'm going to be late."

"What for?"

"Huo Jin's star performance in the local Chinese opera," she said. "Would you like to come?"

Curran raised an eyebrow. "I am sure the good Huo Jin will excuse me, but I think you might find Li An in attendance. She muttered something about an opera as she was leaving this afternoon. She's rather fond of Chinese opera."

Harriet frowned. "But she and Huo Jin—" She broke off.

"Whatever their differences, that is where she has gone today. Let me hail you a ricksha."

Harriet arrived home in time to change into a dress suitable for her night at the opera and she and Julian walked to the local temple. Compared to the big, well-funded temples in Chinatown, this one seemed little more than a roughly built shack, but tonight it burned with light, a huge brazier at the front circled with food offerings and burning joss sticks.

A makeshift stage had been set out on the vacant lot beside the temple and benches set in front of it. As she and Julian hovered on the edge of the crowd, wondering what they were required to do that would not cause offense, a slender woman detached herself from the group beside the brazier.

Harriet smiled with relief at seeing Li An. "Curran said you would be here," she said.

"Shall we sit?" Li An said, waving at the benches.

"There are some seats up the front," Julian said.

Li An gave a sharp intake of breath. "Those seats are occupied by the hungry ghosts," she said. "Come, we sit here."

At some urging from Li An, the patrons of the opera made room for them.

"This is Huo Jin's family troupe," Li An said. "They have been performing opera in Singapore for fifty years."

It embarrassed Harriet to realize how little she knew about her amah's life outside of St. Tom's House.

She looked around at the crowd, now standing as the last seats, save for those reserved for the hungry ghosts, had been taken.

"I know nothing about opera. It seems popular," she said to Li An.

"It is, but you must remember it is performed for the deities not the people, so it would not matter to the troupe if there were no one in these seats."

The orchestra, which seemed to consist of cymbals and drums, struck up and the troupe in their intricate costumes and intricately painted faces performed a mixture of stylized dance, acrobatics and some sort of martial arts.

It took a while to recognize Huo Jin in the guise of a wise scholar with a heavy beard.

"Huo Jin is playing a *sheng* role," Li An whispered. "A leading male role."

"She's very good," Julian said loyally. He leaned across Harriet. "What is the plot?" he asked Li An.

"It is about two heavenly stars who fall in love and come to earth so they can be together, but the queen of the heavens sends her general to bring the man back to the heavens and the lovers are forever separated except during the seventh month when they meet for one night across the river."

As she sat in the warm evening, caught up in the theatricality and the tragedy of the two separated lovers, Harriet thought about Pris and Clyde Morris. Were they the lovers, forever separated, who could meet only for the occasional night? It seemed so very sad, but the inescapable fact remained that Clyde Morris had a wife and children in England. Unless he was prepared to divorce, they could never be together. The scandal of such a relationship would shock the whole European community, let alone the strong bonds of the regiment. Little wonder Pris kept her secret tight.

When the performance concluded and they were able to take their leave, Harriet looked around for Li An but she had gone, melting into the crowd. Harriet and Julian walked back along the quiet country road to St. Tom's House and a strong whiskey.

⨴⨵ TWENTY-ONE

The Cedars
Monday, 22 August

Harriet tucked the neatly typed notice about the tennis club social event into an envelope, straightened her collar, pinned on her best straw hat and drove herself in the pony cart out to Blenheim Road and The Cedars.

The gentle notes of a well-played piano drifted out on the still air and the majordomo confirmed that Miss Nolan was at home. He showed Harriet through to the living room, where Pris sat at the piano, lost in her playing.

Harriet waited until the last note of the Chopin piano piece had finished before politely applauding.

Pris swung around to look at her. "Harriet, how long have you been there?"

"Long enough to admire your talent," Harriet said.

Pris moved along the piano stool and gestured for Harriet to join her. "Do you play?"

"Very badly," Harriet said. "My sister, Mary, was the musical one in the family."

Harriet took the seat beside Pris and let her fingers rest on the piano keys but no inspiration came. Pris laughed and took up a pretty melody. Schubert, Harriet thought.

"What brings you here today?" Pris asked as she played.

Harriet held the envelope up. "I brought the notice Clyde Morris asked me to type. I thought you would see him before I would."

Pris stopped playing and took the envelope. "Thank you. Clyde will be most grateful."

"Pris . . ." Harriet began. "Inspector Curran has a letter . . . or at least part of a letter. He found it in Sylvie's journal."

The woman beside her stiffened. "Sylvie wrote a lot of letters," she said.

"It was a love letter."

Pris snorted. "And she received a number of love letters too. Several of the boys in the regiment were smitten with her."

Harriet shook her head. "Not this one or at least not unless Clyde was one of her admirers."

"Clyde—" Pris began. Her fingers strayed to the keyboard again. "Clyde was not acquainted with my sister-in-law."

"I didn't think so. It was a letter addressed to you, wasn't it?"

Pris slammed her hands down on the keys with a discordant crash. She rose to her feet and glared down at Harriet. "I think you should leave, Harriet," she said. "You're not a police officer. I don't have to speak to you. In fact you're nothing more than an idle gossip, fishing for some juicy scandal to share with your friends."

Harriet stood to face the woman. Pris wrapped her arms around herself but the gesture did nothing to alleviate the trembling of rage and emotion. Two bright spots of color had appeared on her cheeks and she looked pointedly at the door.

Harriet steadied her own rapidly beating heart. "This is not about idle gossip. You were conducting a secret liaison with a married man and Sylvie Nolan knew about it."

Pris's chin came up. "I've done nothing wrong. Nothing I am ashamed of. I don't expect you to understand."

"I might surprise you."

Uncertainty flickered across Pris's freckled face. "I doubt it. I am a daughter of the regiment, Harriet. There are expectations about whom I should marry."

Marry . . . not fall in love with.

"Is that why you were engaged to James Hawke?"

"Of course. James was ambitious. He had an eye to the command of the battalion and ultimately the regiment and that is how it works. A marriage to the sister of the future commanding officer of the South Sussex Foot would have advanced his prospects significantly."

"And what about you?"

Pris swallowed. "Respectability. Children maybe. I'm not a fool, Harriet. I am old and plain and my chances of making a good marriage faded a long time ago."

"But then you met Clyde Morris."

"A married man with three children back home in Clacton," Pris concluded bitterly.

"Divorce is not impossible."

"It is for a Nolan. I would be shunned by society, the church would refuse to marry us. I would never be able to take communion again."

"But you're well and truly of age. What does it matter?"

"The scandal of his sister being the guilty party in a divorce would have finished John's career—if darling Sylvie didn't kill it first with her carryings-on. That letter . . . the one she had so cleverly hidden—she found it and threatened to show it to John. I searched her room but I couldn't find it. Where did you say she hid it?"

"In the spine of her journal."

Pris rolled her eyes.

"Was there a price for Sylvie's silence?" Harriet asked.

"Of course there was. I don't have much of a private income but Sylvie took it all."

"Blackmail?"

Pris screwed her face up. "Such a horrid word but I suppose that's what it was. Her silence for the cost of a few fripperies. That's not a reason to kill her."

Harriet let a moment pass before she said, "Isn't it?"

Pris's eyes widened. "Me? You think I . . ."

"To the police it may appear as good a motive as anyone. They know about the note. They know who wrote it."

Pris stared at Harriet, her mouth open. "But I didn't kill her. She made me miserable but I knew something about her that would have brought an end to the blackmail."

"What was that?"

"I knew, before her death, that her little affair with James Hawke had culminated in a mistake. I told you before, dear Sylvie was pregnant and John could not have been the father."

"Did you tell her that you knew?"

"That night, when we were alone over supper."

"What did she do?"

Pris shook her head. "Nothing. That was what was so strange. I expected tears and tantrums but she just rose from the table and told me that it didn't matter if I knew, she had a plan."

Harriet frowned. "And did she say what she planned to do?"

Pris's mouth tightened. "I assumed that she would see to the pregnancy. I believe these things can be arranged, but when James took his own life, I thought maybe she had told him and he had killed her and then taken his own life in remorse."

Harriet kept her peace. Curran had done a good job keeping the possible murder of James Hawke quiet.

"You were here in the house when she died. Did you see him kill her?"

Pris shook her head. "I was asleep, as I keep telling everyone."

"So why do you think it was James?"

"Because . . ." Pris threw her hands in the air. "Who else could it have been? James's career would have been ruined. He, more than anyone . . . more than me . . . had a reason to kill her."

"What on earth is going on?"

Both women turned to see Lavinia Pemberthey-Smythe standing in the doorway. Pris ran to her friend, falling weeping around her neck.

"She knows, Lavinia . . . the police know . . ."

"About what, my dear?" Lavinia said.

"About Clyde and the letter and the blackmail," Pris sobbed. "They think I did it! Me!"

Lavinia's hard gaze held Harriet's. "Do you?"

Harriet shook her head. "I don't think anything of the sort," she said.

"I suggest you leave, Mrs. Gordon." Lavinia's tone held an edge of ice. "This family has endured enough without further pain being brought to their front door."

Her face burning, Harriet took her leave, walking down the well-kept driveway to Blenheim Road, with her head high. Despite Curran's tacit agreement to her talking to Pris, she had the unhappy feeling that this was the second time in a week she had stepped outside the boundaries of her work with the police. She hadn't expected such a fulsome confession of Pris's adulterous affair and now, thanks to her meddling, Pris would be ready for any questions Curran would have for her.

Remembering his fury at her previous interference, Harriet fought the desire to run home to St. Tom's House and bury her head under her pillow. She had to speak to Curran before he confronted Pris.

Curran stood in the doorway of Clyde Morris's office at the Barclays Bank in Raffles Place and took a moment to get an impression of Pris Nolan's secret admirer. Morris was the sort of man one passed in the street without a second glance. With his mousy, balding hair, a too-long moustache and round tortoiseshell glasses, he hardly presented as an object of desire.

"What is it that you think I can help you with, Inspector?" He half rose from his chair, blinking nervously behind his glasses, reminding Curran of a schoolboy, overanxious to please.

Curran decided to come straight to the point. He set the love letter down on the blotter in front of the man. Morris sank back in his chair and picked it up, his hand shaking slightly. He read it through as if it were a statement of account and set it back on the blotter. Taking off his glasses, he proceeded to rub them with a large blue handkerchief.

"Is that your handwriting?" Curran inquired.

Morris cleared his throat. "You must know it is, or you wouldn't be here, Inspector." When Curran said nothing, Morris continued, "Yes, it's my writing. I wrote that note. A foolish notion. I don't know what possessed me."

"Are you having an affair with Miss Nolan?"

Morris sat back as if Curran had punched him. "An affair? Good heavens, no!"

"Then how would you describe it?"

"Miss Nolan and I are close friends but the fact is I am a married man, Inspector. My wife may still be in England, but that does not give me an excuse for indulging myself in any sort of amorous relationship outside the bounds of my marriage."

Curran leaned forward. "Morris, we both know it can be a lonely life out here for a single man, let alone one who is thousands of miles from hearth and home. Are you telling me that you have not been tempted?"

Morris blinked rapidly. "I am not going to deny that Miss Nolan and I are, as I have told you, good friends, but there is nothing more to the matter than that."

"So the relationship is not physical?"

Morris's eyes widened behind his glasses. "Physical? Oh dear me, no." He paused. "I have the greatest respect for Miss Nolan—and the sanctity of marriage."

Curran considered there were many ways to cheat in a marriage, not all of which required a physical union. Clearly from what he had written, Morris had, in his imagination at least, forgotten the inconvenient wife and three children.

"This"—Morris waved a hand at the letter he had written— "was a foolish whim for which I apologized at the time. Miss Nolan understood completely. In fact I'm surprised she kept it. She had promised to destroy it." His expression turned from one of innocence to one of resentment as he considered the incriminating document with a furrowed brow.

Curran said nothing. As he reached out to retrieve the paper, Morris brought his hand down on it. "You don't need this, Inspector. It is, after all, my property."

"Remove your hand, Mr. Morris. For the time being it remains evidence in a murder investigation." Curran met Morris's eyes without blinking, and with a show of reluctance, Morris took his hand away, pushing the paper in Curran's direction.

"I would hate word of its existence to get back to my wife. She would not understand."

"I am sure she wouldn't," Curran agreed.

"If there is nothing else, Inspector, I have work." Morris made a show of picking up a large ledger.

Curran didn't move. "Yes. Where were you on the night Sylvie Nolan was murdered?"

The question clearly took Morris by surprise. He blinked furiously behind his glasses and Curran reminded him of the date of the murder.

"I had a meeting of the tennis club social committee that Thursday," he said. "At my house."

"What time did it finish?"

"Ten thirty or thereabouts?"

"And after that?"

"I went to bed. I do work for my living, Inspector. Can't be doing with late nights."

"Anyone to vouch for you?"

"My house servants, but surely you don't need to bother them. I give you my word as a gentleman I was tucked up in my bed by eleven that night."

"What about last Tuesday?"

Morris pulled a small diary from his pocket and flicked through the pages. "I was at home, Inspector."

"All night?"

"Yes. Again, you can ask my servants."

"I will. Now, if you can provide me with their details? With your permission, I will arrange for them to be interviewed today."

Morris's face had taken on a sheen of sweat. "Really, Inspector, can't it wait? As their employer, I should advise them of their rights in respect of interviews."

"They are not suspects," Curran said. "Your address, please."

Morris scribbled an address on a piece of paper and handed it to Curran as the police officer rose to his feet.

"Thank you, Mr. Morris."

"I hope I have helped," Morris said, holding out a damp, clammy hand. Curran gave it a peremptory shake and smiled.

"You have been most helpful," he said.

Harriet found Curran sitting in his office in South Bridge Road, cleaning his unlit pipe, his booted feet on his desk. She knew him well enough now to know this picture of devil-may-care, in fact meant the exact opposite. Something troubled him . . . troubled him deeply.

He stood up as she entered his office and Harriet closed the door behind her. Without waiting for his invitation, she launched into an account of her meeting with Pris.

Curran glared at her. "Harriet, I might have intimated that I had no way of preventing you from an idle chat with Miss Nolan, but you had no authority to turn it into a full-scale interview."

Harriet bit her lip. "I know. I'm sorry. It's just that once she admitted to the affair with Morris, I couldn't just turn the conversation back to the tennis club or flower arranging."

Curran shrugged. "I'm not angry," he said. "It sounds like Miss Nolan's reaction was somewhat contradictory to what Morris told me."

Harriet leaned forward, conscious that her curiosity was once again getting the better of her judgment. She should just apologize once more and get back to her typing. Instead she asked what Morris had said.

Curran regarded her with an amused smile. "I suppose you will find out soon enough when I give you my notes to type. Morris maintains they were just friends. The letter was an aberration and he thought Pris had destroyed it. He certainly doesn't want his wife finding out about it."

"But that's not how they appeared on Friday," Harriet said. "I'm far more inclined to believe Pris than Morris, and if Pris is telling the truth, Sylvie Nolan certainly felt the relationship sufficiently far advanced to be worth a spot of blackmail." Harriet paused. "Do you think either of them capable of murder?"

Curran picked up his pipe again, tapping the stem on his blotter as he thought. "The blackmail gave either one of them a good motive to kill Sylvie, but why would they kill Hawke?" He sighed. "I've sent Singh off to interview Morris's household staff but they'll back up his story and what we'll have are two households of servants who will go to their graves swearing their master or mistress were in bed and asleep when the murders were committed." He set the pipe down and ran a hand over his eyes. "Thank you for your assistance, Harriet. Even if you did exceed your authority, it has been most instructive. Leave it with me and stay away from Pris Nolan."

Over supper that evening, Harriet filled Julian in on the events of the day.

"Good heavens," Julian said, pausing with his fork halfway to his mouth as Harriet shared the more salacious gossip about Pris and Morris. "I had no idea. Isn't he married?"

"Yes, but it's obvious Morris is lying to protect his marriage and reputation."

"Most men would," Julian agreed. "But why would he want to kill Sylvie Nolan? I mean, is he even capable of such a crime?"

Harriet shook her head. "No . . . I doubt it. He couldn't bear to get his hands dirty and it was a messy crime. Besides, whatever Pris may have thought of their relationship, I suspect Morris will be running straight back to his wife."

"Poor Pris." Julian paused. "But I wouldn't discount her as a murderer."

Harriet stared at her brother. "Julian!"

"Think about it, Harri. She more than anyone had more than one motive to do in both her sister-in-law and James Hawke." He forked up another piece of chicken and chewed thoughtfully. "Anyway, you don't need me to remind you that it is not your problem, old thing." He set his fork down. "I say, you're not in any danger, are you? I couldn't bear a repeat of what happened in March."

"No," Harriet said with a laugh.

Or at least I don't think so, she thought to herself.

❧ TWENTY-TWO

South Bridge Road
Tuesday, 23 August

Curran stood at the door to the holding cell beneath the Head-quarters building and looked through the grille at the miserable young man, curled up on the hard cement bench. The stench of stale vomit and urine hung heavy in the humid air.

Curran, who had woken with a headache, had to stop himself from gagging as he stepped into the cell. Li An's excellent congee that he had eaten for breakfast threatened to make a reappearance. Both symptoms could only mean one thing, the malaria was still lurking.

"Mr. Gentry," he said. "Are you awake?"

Lieutenant Nicholas Gentry stirred and groaned.

Dressed in flannel trousers and a stained linen shirt, he raised his head and with red-rimmed eyes blinked at Curran.

"Where was he found?" Curran asked Gursharan Singh.

"Drunk in a gutter in Battery Road at three o'clock this morning. He's taken a beating and he has no wallet or valuables on him so I am guessing someone took advantage of him."

"I am beginning to think this young man has something of a drinking problem," Curran observed. "Open the door."

The custody orderly stepped forward with the keys and opened the cell door admitting Curran into the stinking cell.

"Made quite a mess of our nice clean cell," Curran observed as Gentry pulled himself into a sitting position, leaning his head back against the wall. He had the makings of a black eye and his lip was cut and swollen.

"Any chance of a drink?" Gentry rasped.

"If you mean the alcoholic variety, no, but Constable Lee will fetch you a nice cup of tea." He nodded at the custody orderly and leaned back against the wall, his arms crossed. "What brought this on?"

Gentry shook his head. "Another death. Why does everybody I care about have to die?"

"Another death? Who?"

"Poor old Billings. He was all set to go back to the old man now that Sylvie's gone, but yesterday morning, Lewis found him dead in his bed. Doctor says it was his heart . . ." A single tear trickled down the young man's filthy, unshaven cheek.

Constable Lee appeared with a mug of hot black tea. He cast a glance around the cell and tutted. "I hope this young man is prepared to clean up his mess," he said.

Gentry groaned and buried his nose in the mug of hot liquid. Curran waited until he had drained the cup and raised his head once more.

"Tell me about Billings," Curran said. "Who did you say found him?"

Gentry shook his head. "Lewis. Thought it odd that Billings hadn't turned up for breakfast and went to rouse him. Found him stone-dead. Reckon he died during the night. He was a good stick. Knew how to keep a chap's secrets."

"And do you have any secrets you wish kept, Mr. Gentry?"

Gentry looked up, his eyes wide. "Me? Secrets?" He shook his head. "I meant Billings was the old man's batman for twenty years."

"And does your brother-in-law have secrets?"

Gentry jumped to his feet. "Stop it. Nobody has any secrets. He was just an old soldier with a weak heart. Now, are you going to let me go?"

"I've got no reason to detain you."

"Then why am I in this bloody cell?"

"To sober up. You appear to be relatively sober now so you are free to go."

Gentry looked down at himself. "I stink. Is there somewhere I can wash?"

"I tell you what, I'll give you a lift back to the barracks. I want to know more about Billings's death."

"Nothing suspicious about it, Curran."

"I didn't say there was."

Even after a wash, Nicholas Gentry made an odiferous companion on the drive back to barracks. The young man seemed lost in his own dark thoughts and stared moodily at the passing scenery.

Tan turned into the driveway of The Cedars and Pris Nolan came running out of the house as Gentry staggered from the motor vehicle. "Oh, thank heavens," she said, taking Gentry by the arm. "Nick, we were getting worried." She turned to Curran. "Thank you, Inspector."

Gentry brushed off Pris's hand and stalked toward the house, where he encountered his brother-in-law at the door.

"You are a disgrace," Nolan roared. "Look at you. Still drunk, I wager, and you stink to high heaven. Go and get yourself cleaned up and report for duty."

Gentry's shoulders stiffened momentarily before sagging. He mumbled an apology to Nolan and lurched into the house.

"Curran," Nolan said. "Where'd you find him?"

"He was picked up in Battery Road. He'd been beaten and robbed. As he had no identification with him, the constables brought him in to South Road to sleep it off."

Nolan shook his head. "To be fair to the boy, he's had a lot to deal with in the past week—his sister, Hawke and now Billings."

"Ah yes, he told me about Billings. Would it be possible to see the body?"

Nolan's moustache bristled. "Why? No need for you to be involved. The regimental doctor has confirmed his heart gave out."

"Colonel, this is, as you yourself say, the third death in ten days. I would like to satisfy my own curiosity that there is nothing sinister in this death."

Nolan snorted. "We're burying him this afternoon. You'll find him at Ravensway." He paused. "I owed the old chap a good send-off."

Curran thanked the colonel and returned to the motor vehicle.

Ravensway and Company in Orchard Road were one of the better-known undertakers in Singapore. Their public rooms were furnished with wood paneling and a plush carpet so deep, Curran thought he might sink to the ankles. One of the senior members of the firm, Adolphus Proctor, came out to greet Curran. Like all good undertakers, his face betrayed nothing when Curran asked to view the body of Fred Billings.

"You're in luck, Inspector. We were just about to dress him for the coffin. As it is you will find him through here."

The back rooms were clinical in comparison to the sumptuous public rooms. Like Mac's morgue rooms at the hospital, the stuffy room into which he was shown smelled of death and formaldehyde. Fred Billings lay on a marble table, covered with a sheet.

Proctor turned the sheet back. "Nothing remarkable," he observed. "His heart, the doctor says."

"Really?" Curran pulled the sheet down farther and took a breath. "Then what are these bruises?"

Proctor leaned forward and inspected the bruising on the man's chest. "Some injuries do not manifest until some time after death," he said carefully.

Curran leaned forward and, swallowing his distaste, pried open one eyelid. He let out his breath in a long expiration. "Do you see that, Proctor, the hemorrhaging?"

Proctor clucked his tongue. "That's unusual in a heart attack," he said.

Curran straightened. "But more usual in a strangulation or suffocation. I am sorry to do this, but I want this body sent to Euan Mackenzie at the hospital for a proper autopsy."

"But the funeral is this afternoon."

Curran shook his head. "It will have to be postponed."

"Colonel Nolan will not be pleased."

"I'll break the good news to him. Don't delay, Proctor."

Back at the barracks, Curran broke the news to Nolan that the funeral would be delayed and he suspected Billings's death needed to be investigated as suspicious.

Nolan's jaw tightened. "Really, Curran. You are boxing at shadows. It was widely known Billings had a heart condition. That's why he was employed as a batman and now you are obstructing the one thing I can do for him. Give him a proper funeral."

Curran was unrepentant. "There was sufficient evidence on the body to indicate that his death may have been hastened."

"But he had nothing to do with my wife's death or that of the adjutant."

"Nevertheless, three deaths in less than two weeks is something that needs to be looked into properly."

The colonel snorted. "I suppose you want to see his billet?"

"I do."

"I will have to advise Goff."

"Of course."

To Curran's relief it was not Goff who appeared to escort him to the batman's quarters but a large, humorless MP corporal. The officers' servants occupied a separate building behind the mess. In keeping with their status they had small individual rooms leading off a wide verandah.

Curran looked around the cell-like room and shook his head. As he had anticipated, it had been cleaned and tidied with military efficiency. The bed stripped of the mattress and pillows and no trace of Billings's personal possessions. He dispatched the MP to find Lance Corporal Lewis while he sat on the one rickety chair and tried to stop the world from spinning.

Lewis looked both hot and haggard. Curran reluctantly vacated the chair and waved the little man into it. Lewis sank down with a heavy sigh.

"I tell you, it fair did me in to find him cold and dead," the corporal said, mopping his face with a large red handkerchief.

"Describe how you found him?"

Lewis glanced at the narrow cot and looked away. "He was lying in his bed, his eyes wide open. He looked peaceful."

"How had he seemed over the past week?"

"Sounds odd to say but he was happy. With the mem dead, it meant he could return to being Nolan's batman but he had plans, he did. '*Lewis,*' he said to me only a few days ago, '*me fortune's made. I'm going to leave the army and buy that little house in Bournemouth I've been dreaming of.*'"

"His fortune? What did he mean?"

Lewis shook his head. "No idea, sir. Maybe he'd just been saving his pennies and the time had come."

"Everything in the room was in order?"

"Oh yes. He was a most particular man, Mr. Billings. Nothing out of place." Lewis frowned and glanced at the rickety chest of drawers. "Although I did think it odd that one of the drawers was still half-open. Not like Billings to be careless."

"Where's the mattress and pillow?"

"Burned."

"And the rest of his possessions?"

"I've got his box in my room, if you want to take a look?"

Like Billings, Lewis appeared to be a most particular man. His little cell was scrupulously tidy, the cleaning kit he used for leather and brass laid out on his table.

He pulled a metal trunk from under the bed and unlocked the padlock.

Curran went down on one knee and began pulling out Billings's meager possessions. He found little to show for thirty years in the military. A solitary life devoid of family photographs or letters from home. For men like Billings the regiment was their family.

He sat back on his heels and looked up at Lewis. "Did anyone visit Billings on his last night?"

Lewis shook his head. "Mr. Gentry had gone out for the night and Mr. Cox . . . well, Mr. Cox can't afford the services of a batman. Billings and I, we'd help him out every now and then, but mostly he does for himself. I do for a couple of the officers and I didn't get to bed until about midnight, Billings's room was dark."

"Locked?"

Lewis shrugged. "Couldn't say, sir, although it wasn't locked in the morning when I . . . when I found 'im."

Curran thanked the man and returned to Billings's room.

He stood at the door scanning every inch of the tiny cell. The whitewashed walls betrayed no possible hiding places. A gecko scuttled up the wall, a welcome sign of life in the silent room. The furniture consisted of nothing more than an iron cot, a rickety table and chair, and a well-worn half chest of drawers and half wardrobe. He pulled the chest away from the wall, inspecting the undersides of drawers and braving the insect life to see if anything had been hidden behind the stubby legs of the piece. He found nothing and checked the underside of the table. That too had no hidden clues as to Billings's death.

The floor had been laid with bricks, which had developed some unevenness over the years as the ground beneath had subsided. In the corner that had been concealed beneath the wardrobe, the bricks looked as if they had been freshly laid. A grouping of four bricks lacked any mortar between them. Curran knelt down and, scrabbling to get a purchase, lifted the bricks from their bed of fresh sand. He brushed the bedding sand away and his breath caught at the sight of the lid of a metal box.

Using his penknife he dug the tin out of its resting place and set it on the ground. It was a reasonable size, probably used at one time for army rations of some sort, but any identifying marks had long since worn off.

He almost let out a whoop when he saw the contents: a small carved wooden box and a Sam Browne.

The carving on the box looked Indian—hardly surprising considering the places the First Battalion had been stationed over the years. He opened it and frowned. It contained the shoulder and collar insignia of the South Sussex Regiment, four silver pocket buttons and one solitary silver regimental button from a jacket. The two silver pips, the Bath star, would indicate the insignia belonged to a second lieutenant, the most junior officer, who would wear one on each shoulder.

Among the jumble of military paraphernalia a pair of ruby earrings glinted at him. Curran lifted them out. They were pretty but unassuming, a simple ruby drop from a diamond stud. One of the screws that secured the earrings was missing and the other bent. He would need someone like Pris Nolan to confirm but he was certain these were the earrings Sylvie Nolan had been wearing the night she died.

He replaced the jewels and carried the box out of the room and showed it to Lewis.

"Who do these belong to?"

Lewis looked at the contents and shrugged. "Probably just spares. Any good batman carries spares."

"What about the earrings?"

"Not Billings's taste," Lewis said, and promptly apologized for his inappropriate joke before adding, "Never seen 'em before, but this . . ." He picked up the Sam Browne. His hands shook as he ran the well-polished leather strap through his fingers. "This is Captain Hawke's Sam Browne." He indicated a small nick in the shoulder strap. "I'd know it anywhere. Where'd you find it?"

"Hidden beneath the floor in Billings's room."

Lewis picked out the subaltern's pips and studied them. "Seems odd. Billings hasn't batted for a second lieutenant in all the time I knew him. In fact we don't have a second lieutenant in the battalion at the moment."

Curran took the pips back and returned them to the box.

"I just had word that Billings's funeral's been delayed," Lewis said.

"Just till tomorrow. I've ordered an autopsy on the body."

Lewis stared at him. "Why? You don't think he . . . who'd want to murder old Billings?"

"I don't know, do you?"

Lewis shook his head. "That's a rum thought, sir. He didn't do anybody any harm that I know of."

"It is indeed," Curran agreed.

He took his leave of the lance corporal and returned to South Bridge Road, stopping first at the hospital, where he found Euan Mackenzie in the autopsy room, staring thoughtfully at the body of Billings. The smell of carbolic and death did little to dispel Curran's nausea and he had to concentrate just to keep Mac in focus.

"You haven't started yet?" Curran said.

"He only just got here," Mackenzie said. "What are you thinking?"

Curran blew out a breath. "I am thinking that the bruise on his chest looks like someone heavy held him down. Look at his eyes, Mac. See the hemorrhaging? It looks to me like suffocation."

"Have you got his pillow?"

Curran shook his head. "The military has, as usual, beaten me to it. You should be able to tell me if he died of a heart attack."

"That won't tell you anything. If he was being suffocated, it's quite possible his heart gave up." Mackenzie shrugged. "I'll have a look and get some sort of report to you by tomorrow." Mac narrowed his eyes. "Are you all right, Curran?"

Curran summoned a watery smile and squared his shoulders. "Fine, Mac. Just fine."

"You're lying."

"Maybe," Curran mumbled as he turned for the door, "but I now have three murders to solve."

Back in his office, Curran set the metal box on his desk and studied the contents.

"What have you found?" Harriet Gordon leaned against the doorjamb, her gaze on the box.

"I found it in Billings's room," Curran said.

He sifted through the contents of the carved box that, in his mind, he called the button box. Harriet joined him, her woman's eye going straight to the earrings. She held them up to the light. "These are pretty. What were they doing in this box?"

Curran shook his head. "I don't know. I think they may be the earrings Sylvie Nolan was wearing on the night she died. I had assumed they had been taken along with the rest of the jewelry but it seems I was wrong."

Harriet shivered and set the earrings back in the box. "You mean, the murderer took them as some sort of trophy?"

"I think," Curran said. "They were torn from her ears after

she was dead." He picked one up. "There's blood caught in the screw at the back of this one."

"How awful."

Harriet separated out the two officer's pips. "A second lieutenant?"

Curran looked up at her. "Possibly and there's no second lieutenant in the First Battalion. The only second lieutenant I've come across in this case is Lavinia Pemberthey-Smythe's nephew, Rupert Allen."

"So is it possible that all these deaths are related to his suicide?" Harriet asked.

Curran shrugged. "If that is so, does that make Lavinia Pemberthey-Smythe a suspect?"

ᗉᗉᖛ TWENTY-THREE

Singapore Botanical Gardens
Wednesday, 24 August

Gursharan Singh stood on the doorstep of Curran's bunga-low early on Wednesday morning. "There has been another incident at the Botanical Gardens," he announced.

"Not another death?" Curran's blood ran cold.

"A hanging. I do not know if the victim is alive or dead," his sergeant advised.

Curran ran a hand through his hair and brought his scat-tered thoughts together as he issued his orders. He needed to wash and shave before he went anywhere.

He stared at his reflection in the mirror and swore as he cut himself. The hand holding the safety razor shook. His head pounded and his limbs felt like lead. No doubt about it, the ma-laria was returning.

Just have to get through the day, he told himself, swallowing quinine as he buckled on his Sam Browne.

At the Botanical Gardens, they were met by Ridley, the gar-den's director.

"This is intolerable!" Ridley blew out his raggedy mous-tache, his slight shoulders trembling with indignation. "I just can't tolerate people coming here to take their own lives. It took days to clean up the mess from the last chap. It's just not on. You've got to do something about it, Curran."

Curran ignored the indignant Ridley and stood with his hands on his hips at the entrance to the pretty pavilion where only a week ago James Hawke had been found dead.

A large, empty ceramic pot lay on its side beneath a cut rope suspended from the iron rafters. Two stretcher-bearers were lifting a young man in a khaki uniform onto a stretcher preparatory to carrying him to the horse-drawn ambulance that waited at the end of the path.

Euan Mackenzie, kneeling beside the unfortunate victim, looked up as Curran stepped into the pavilion.

"He's not dead," Mac said, rising to his feet, but his face was grim. "They got to him in time."

He may not have been dead but Nick Gentry was unconscious, his eyelids and lips blue and the livid mark of the rope harsh against the pale skin of his neck. Only the ragged rise and fall of the young man's chest beneath his jacket gave any hope that he might live.

Curran grimaced as he went down on one knee beside the young man. Of all the ways to kill yourself, Curran considered hanging one of the most unpleasant. There had to be that awful moment when you realized you could not breathe and the body instinctively fought to survive.

With professional efficiency he checked the contents of Gentry's pockets. He found a handkerchief, wallet, room key and in his jacket pocket, a piece of folded paper. No silver button.

As the bearers lifted the stretcher, a voice came from outside. "Stop. Where are you taking him?"

Lieutenant Colonel Nolan strode up the steps of the pavilion. Behind him Major Goff and Lieutenant Cox formed a phalanx barring the way to the ambulance.

"To the hospital, Colonel," Mac replied.

"No. I'll not have him taken there to be gawked at and talked about. Take him to The Cedars. We can care for him there," Nolan said.

"With respect, Colonel—" Mac began.

But the commanding officer of the First Battalion of the South Sussex would brook no argument so Mac shrugged. "Very well. I'll come and see him settled and we'll have to arrange for a nursing sister."

Nolan nodded. "Thank you. Goff, with me."

The two soldiers turned to follow the stretcher.

Mac picked up his bag and turned back to Curran. "Before I go, I had a look at that man Billings and I can confirm he died from heart failure."

Curran nodded, suppressing his irritation at being wrong, but Mac's eyes gleamed and he continued in a low voice, "Heart failure brought on by someone holding a pillow over his face."

Curran stared at him. "I was right?"

Mac nodded. "Someone knelt on him to hold him down while they did the deed. I found white fibers in his airways. No doubt in my mind, he was murdered." Mac nodded at the stretcher. "You better find who's doing this before they see to the entire First Battalion of the South Sussex Regiment."

Curran watched the stretcher party until it turned a corner with Nolan and Goff following.

Cox too turned to leave.

"A moment, Lieutenant," Curran said, and gestured for the young man to join him out of earshot of the crowd surrounding the pavilion.

"This is a sad thing to happen, Curran," Cox said. "I was on my way to inform the colonel he was missing when I heard the rumor about a body being in the gardens. I feared the worst and I was right."

"When did you last see Gentry?" Curran asked.

"This morning. He was up and dressed by six thirty and told me he was going for a walk before breakfast."

"Was he in the habit of going for early-morning walks?"

Cox smiled. "Now you mention, no. Mr. Gentry was not particularly fond of any form of exercise. He complained about the heat." Cox shook his head. "It never occurred to me that he had other intentions. I could have said something . . . helped somehow." He shook his head. "I feel so damn guilty."

Curran pulled out his cigarette case and offered it to Cox. The young man accepted a cigarette and Curran lit it from his own battered gold lighter.

"Had he talked about taking his own life?"

Cox shook his head. "No, but there's no doubt his sister's death affected him."

"He seems to have been stalked by death."

Cox nodded. "Hawke and Billings too. Poor chap."

"I believe he also found his friend's body, last year in England?"

"Oh, you mean Rupert Allen? I was in England when that happened. Sad business."

"Did you know him?"

"Of course. He was some years younger than me, but I knew him through Lavinia Pemberthey-Smythe. She was very good to both of us."

"What were you doing in England?"

"I'd been sent home to recuperate from a dose of yellow fever. I was seconded to headquarters and young Allen was a subbie in the Second Battalion. We met in the mess on occasion."

"What was the gossip about his suicide?"

Cox stiffened. "Army officers don't gossip, Curran."

"Yes, they do," Curran said. "Officers' messes are worse than a meeting of church ladies."

Cox's mouth curled in an ironic smile. "You're right, Curran.

I think everyone agreed that Allen was not cut out for the military. He should have gone to Oxford and got a classics degree and ended up as a vicar or schoolteacher. Anything but the army, but his father had been an officer in the South Sussex, and his uncle, Pemberthey-Smythe, was the CO of the First Battalion. He had no choice in the matter."

"What about lady friends?"

Cox ground his half-smoked cigarette out with the heel of his boot. "I don't know anything about that. He was a pal of Gentry's so he may be able to tell you more . . ." He paused. "God willing. Is that all, Inspector? I should get back to the barracks."

Curran watched the young man stride away with his confident swagger. Sergeant Singh came to join Curran. "Did he leave a note?"

Curran unfolded the paper he had found in Gentry's pocket. It said simply:

I cannot live with what I have done. NG

Curran handed Singh the note. "It would be helpful if people were to leave more detailed explanations," Singh remarked. "What do you think it means?"

"Hopefully Mr. Gentry will live long enough to tell us himself, but I think the implication is that Mr. Gentry was connected in some way with the death of his sister and possibly Hawke."

Returning to the pavilion, Curran addressed the crowd. "Who found him?"

A Tamil in a wide, straw-brimmed hat, holding a broom, stepped forward. "I did, sahib. I saw he was still alive." He mimed someone clutching at something around their throat. "I held his legs while my friend"—he indicated another gardener, who nodded in agreement—"fetched a ladder and cut him down. I stayed with the man while he went for help."

Singh stepped forward to take the men's names and details.

Back inside the pavilion, Curran upended the ceramic pot and stood on it. It gave just enough height to allow Gentry to have threaded the rope through the filigree-iron rafter and then kicked the item away. He had been wearing his complete uniform, no Sam Browne set to one side. His forage cap lay on a bench but there were no silver buttons anywhere in the pavilion and Curran concluded that, in this case at least, Nick Gentry had genuinely attempted suicide, although quite why he had chosen Mr. Ridley's pretty pavilion would remain an unanswered question for when, or if, the young man survived.

Curran pulled down the remnant of rope and coiled it with the noose in the ceramic pot, which he handed to Constable Musa along with the contents of Gentry's pockets. As the young man walked away, Curran rubbed a hand across his face. The fever had set in, his head throbbed and his joints ached. He leaned against the frame of the pavilion, wondering if he was about to be violently ill.

Dimly he was aware of Gursharan Singh asking something but the world had begun to roar in his ears and the filigree ironwork of the pavilion had begun to spin, and as he turned to face Gursharan, Curran pitched forward into the arms of his sergeant.

❧ TWENTY-FOUR

John Little's Tearoom
Wednesday, 24 August

After wrestling with her conscience, Harriet sent a message to Pris, asking her to meet her for tea at John Little's tearoom. She thought a meeting in a neutral, public setting may be more conducive to the apology she felt she owed Pris, rather than trying to confront her at The Cedars.

As the minutes ticked by and she sat waiting for Pris to arrive, she drank a small pot of tea and wondered if the woman would make the assignation or whether her friendship with Pris really had ended. She had just opened her purse to pay for her tea when Pris arrived, hot and flustered. She sat down across from Harriet, fanning herself with the menu and murmuring an apology about the difficulties of finding transport.

"The whole household is in uproar," she said. "Did you hear about Nick's . . . accident?"

Harriet shook her head. She had come straight from St. Tom's.

Pris leaned forward. "He tried to hang himself this morning."

"How awful," Harriet said, genuinely shocked. "You said 'tried.' Is he all right?"

Pris shook her head. "They brought him home but he's still unconscious. Dr. Mackenzie has sent a very efficient nurse. She won't let any of us into his room, even John. I thought I should not come but then again there is nothing I can do at home, is there?"

"Did you have any idea he was . . . ?" Harriet ventured.

Pris shook her head. "Of course not. Sylvie's death was a terrible thing to have happened and they had been very close, but no." She sighed. "I just wish he'd talked to someone."

The waitress brought tea and scones, and as the girl turned away, Pris raised her gaze to Harriet's, a challenge written in her eyes.

"So, what did you want to see me about?"

Harriet took a breath. "I wanted to apologize. It was not my place to question you about your relationship with Clyde Morris."

"No," Pris said, "it wasn't." She looked away and dabbed her face with her linen serviette. "But if you want to know, Clyde is leaving Singapore. I received this in the morning mail." She opened her bag and took out a folded letter, which she pushed across the table to Harriet. "Read it," Pris said.

Harriet unfolded the paper, recognizing Clyde Morris's spidery handwriting and blue-green ink.

My dear Miss Nolan,

It is beholden on me to write this note, apologizing sincerely for any misapprehension under which you may be laboring. While I have valued our friendship during my time in Singapore, the bank is returning me to England next month and I go with a glad heart, looking forward to a fond reunion with my beloved wife and children. I do not think it is wise for us to meet again but know that

I hold you in the highest esteem and wish you every
happiness for the future.

Yours sincerely,
C. Morris

Harriet looked up at Pris, whose face twisted in a mixture of anger and misery. "So it is that in her death Sylvie managed to achieve what she wanted to do in life. She couldn't bear for anyone else to be happy. Just because she had been forced to marry someone she—" Pris broke off. "That's unfair to John."

Harriet's curiosity roused, she asked, "Apart from James Hawke, had there been anyone else in her life?"

Pris fiddled with her serviette. "It's apparently no secret now that the lovely Sylvie was damaged goods. There must have been someone back in England, but she never talked about him." She leaned forward. "As for me, can I tell you, Harriet, that whatever he might say, Clyde and I were far more than just friends." Her hard gaze challenged Harriet to reach the conclusion that Pris and Clyde had been lovers in every sense of the word. Harriet looked at the impersonal little note Morris had sent his lover again and shook her head. She handed it back to Pris, who stuffed it into her bag.

"Laboring under a misapprehension," Pris spat. "Fond reunion with his wife and brats . . . He was going to leave them, divorce her. We had it all worked out. You know how these things are done? A discreet hotel in Brighton with a girl paid to be his companion for the night. I wouldn't be implicated and his darling wife would be free of him. He's a coward, Harriet. He used me!"

"Yes," Harriet agreed. "Shameful behavior."

All the fight went out of Pris and she sagged in her chair. "Now I have no one. James is dead, Clyde's left me. I am a thirty-five-year-old spinster with no prospects." She looked up.

"I've been such a fool, Harriet. I've told lies to protect a man who is not worth protecting. I don't care about myself anymore."

"What do you mean you've told lies?" Harriet asked.

Pris leaned forward. "I am telling you this in complete confidence, Harriet, but you may as well know the whole story. On the night Sylvie died I didn't take that sleeping draught. It was all a charade for Sylvie's sake. I didn't want her knowing what I was up to." Pris's eyes flashed. "I didn't kill her, if that's what you are thinking."

It had been the first thought that crossed Harriet's mind. She nodded encouragingly. "So why the deception?"

"I had arranged to meet Clyde. I knew John would be gone for hours and I thought once Sylvie retired to her bedroom and the servants had gone to their quarters, it would be simple to slip out. Our neighbors are away and they had taken their servants with them. I had a key to the house and it was the perfect place for a private tryst. We'd met several times over the past weeks at different places but there was always the fear of discovery. At the Pardews' we could be quite safe."

Her eyes gleamed at the excitement of the subterfuge involved in snatching those few precious hours, although Harriet had difficulty imagining Pris Nolan and Clyde Morris in a lover's tryst.

"We'd agreed to meet at the back door to the Pardews' house at ten thirty but I was delayed by James arriving to see Sylvie." She spat out her sister-in-law's name, her bitterness still raw. "They had a flaming row, which probably would have woken me even with the sleeping draught. I heard it all—the baby, the pleading to run away . . ." Pris rolled her eyes. "I had to wait until he left and Sylvie had shut her bedroom door. I could hear her crying so it was easy to slip out. I thought Clyde wouldn't have waited for me, but he was there." She fiddled with the catch on her handbag and pulled out a lace-edged handkerchief with which she dabbed her eyes. "That was the night he promised to leave his wife, arrange for a divorce and we would be married and to hell with John and Sylvie and everyone else." Her shoulders sagged. "We were so happy . . . or at least I was happy. When I left him, I thought I would fly back to my room."

"What time was this?"

Pris blinked. "I don't know . . . wait . . . it was before John came home so just before one in the morning. The clock struck after I was back in my room."

"Did you talk to Sylvie?"

Pris recoiled. "Good heavens, no. Her room was in darkness. I thought she'd gone to bed. I just went to my own bed and didn't know anything else till Indira started screaming."

"Did you see anyone else?"

Harriet wondered if she detected the slightest hesitation before Pris said, "No."

Harriet leaned forward and placed her hand over Pris's. "Pris, thank you for the confidence but it is important you are honest with Inspector Curran. You must tell him what you just told me."

Pris's eyes widened. "I can't. You can see that. It's much better he thinks I was in bed and asleep. If he knows I was with someone else, he may think that I killed Sylvie."

"But Morris is your alibi . . ."

Pris restored the handkerchief to her handbag, which she shut with a decisive snap. "Really, Harriet? Don't you see, he could just as well be my accomplice. You said yourself that Sylvie's blackmail gave me a motive to kill her and now you know that I could just as easily have killed her. No, I won't speak to Curran."

"What if I came with you?"

"No," she said, and rose to her feet, setting the serviette on her plate of untouched food. "I told you in confidence because I thought you might understand. Promise me you won't say a word to Inspector Curran?"

Harriet stood up. "For the sake of our friendship, I will hold my peace, until you feel it is the right time to talk, but I urge you to come forward with this."

They stood looking at each other and Harriet saw the light of indecision flicker in the woman's eyes before she straightened and shook her head.

"Good afternoon, Harriet. I shall see you at tennis on Saturday no doubt, although I shall have to find a new doubles partner."

Harriet sat down with a sigh and nibbled on a scone as she considered the dilemma she had been placed in. Curran had to know that far from being asleep in her bed, Pris Nolan had been very much awake. But exposing Pris's private life felt sordid and unworthy of her. Perhaps the correct course would be to continue to try to persuade Pris herself to go to Curran, despite the woman's misgivings.

Harriet found the office at South Bridge Road deserted except for Nabeel. He looked up and greeted her as she entered but returned to his work. Harriet crossed to the large blackboard Curran used to keep track of the most serious cases. He said he liked to see everything laid out in front of him.

She stared at the timeline he had drawn of the murder of Sylvie Nolan, mentally inserting the new information she had on Pris Nolan's whereabouts. Did it change anything? Not really, unless Pris was withholding other vital information, which was entirely possible. She had lied once, she could still be lying.

The clatter of boots and agitated voices on the stairs caused her to turn on her heel, moving away from the board to her desk.

Sergeant Singh strode into the office, followed by Constable Tan. From their grim expressions, Harriet concluded something was not right.

"It is a disaster." The normally phlegmatic Singh flung himself down on the nearest chair.

"What is?" Harriet asked.

"Curran collapsed. We have taken him home but it is the malaria again."

Harriet sank back against her desk. "Is he all right?"

Singh shrugged. "The doctor said he should go to the hospital but he refused. And this morning, Lieutenant Gentry tries to hang himself and we have three murders and I cannot ask questions of the great nabobs at the barracks." The bitter sarcasm in Singh's voice was so out of character, Harriet saw him in a new light.

"Cuscaden . . . ?" she ventured.

"Cuscaden is in Malacca," Singh said. He flung a hand in the direction of the blackboard. "All of this must stop until Curran is well again."

There were other Anglo police officers of the rank of Curran in the Straits Settlements Police but Curran would have come limping back into the office before he let any of his colleagues near his cases.

"I've just come from taking tea with Miss Nolan." She hesitated before divulging what Pris had told her but it was important, and despite her promise to Pris, she said, "You should know that Miss Nolan has admitted to me that she was absent from the house between eleven and one."

"Why?" Tan asked.

Harriet shook her head. "I can't tell you that."

Both policemen looked at her with narrowed eyes.

"I really can't tell you except to say she was not murdering Sylvie Nolan. You will just have to take my word for it."

With a shrug, Tan turned to the board and drew in the new information. The three of them stood staring at the board as if it would magically reveal the answers they sought.

Tan tossed the chalk in his hand. "What about Nicholas Gentry?"

"Ah yes, the extremely inebriated young Gentry," Singh said. "If he did go and visit his sister, we are looking at the time between

Billings leaving him about twelve and Cox returning to his room at one. That is the same time frame as Miss Nolan was absent."

"So Gentry effectively has no alibi for that time," Harriet said.

"And he left this."

Singh showed Harriet the note Curran had found in Gentry's pocket.

Harriet gasped. "Does this mean he is admitting to killing his sister?" she said. "But why?"

"That we will not know until the young gentleman recovers consciousness. They have taken him to the house in Blenheim Road, which makes it very difficult for us to interview him. If he were at the hospital . . ." Singh's mouth tightened again. "I have left Greaves at the house, but for the moment there is nothing we can do."

Harriet turned to the evidence table and picked up the carved Indian box Curran had brought back from the scene of Billings's death the previous day. She opened it, stirring the contents with her finger.

"Maybe I can help," she said.

Singh glared down at her. "You are not a police officer, Mrs. Gordon."

"No, but I have something you don't—easy access to the people you need to talk to." She held up the box. "If this did belong to Rupert Allen, then it is a simple matter of just asking his aunt, isn't it? I don't see how that would jeopardize your investigation."

Singh frowned. "I don't know . . ." He sighed and waved at the door. "Go, Mrs. Gordon. See what you can discover."

Harriet picked up the Sam Browne. "Can I take this too?"

Singh nodded and Harriet placed both items in her bag.

✤ TWENTY-FIVE

Scotts Road
Wednesday, 24 August

Despite the early hour, Harriet found Lavinia drinking a gin and tonic on her verandah, the little Cavalier spaniel, Pansy, curled up on the seat beside her.

"Mrs. Gordon, what brings you here?" she said.

"I came to tell you that I have apologized for upsetting Pris earlier and to ask you to accept my apologies too. I had no right to pry into Pris's private affairs."

Lavinia nodded. "No, you don't," she said, "but your apology is accepted. May I offer you a refreshment?"

Harriet eyed the gin and tonic but asked for tea.

"And the news keeps getting worse. Poor Nicholas Gentry," Lavinia said. "What a terrible thing."

"We can only hope he recovers consciousness," Harriet said.

"That is indeed what we pray for. As if that family has not been through enough."

The tea arrived, along with a fresh gin and tonic for Lavinia. Lavinia took the glass and raised it to Harriet. "I like to think the tonic water keeps the malaria at bay," she said. "It's all a myth, of course. Now, what brings you to my door, Harriet?"

"I was hoping you might help resolve a mystery," Harriet said.

She opened her capacious handbag and took out the wooden box Curran had found hidden in Billings's room and set it on the low table in front of Lavinia.

Lavinia Pemberthey-Smythe gasped. She leaned forward and picked up the object with a shaking hand, touching it with a forefinger as if she expected it to evaporate.

"You've seen it before?" Harriet inquired.

To Harriet's surprise a tear slid down Lavinia's face as she turned to look at her. The unexpected emotion from someone so controlled and calm took her by surprise.

"It was Rupert's." Lavinia's voice cracked. "My nephew, Rupert Allen. It belonged to his mother—my sister."

She set the box on the table in front of her and fished a handkerchief from a pocket somewhere in the *salwar kameez* she was wearing and dabbed her eyes. "Forgive me, Harriet. So silly . . . You think you can handle your grief and then something ridiculous like this box can set you off."

Harriet nodded. "I know only too well."

Lavinia patted her arm. "Of course, you more than anyone. Where did you find it?"

"It was found in Corporal Billings's room after his death," Harriet said.

"How extraordinary. It should have been with Rupert's personal possessions."

"Which are where?"

"Locked in a trunk in my box room. They were returned to me after Rupert's death. I don't understand how it would have found its way to Billings. Rupert had nothing to do with Billings for years." She paused. "Maybe he sent it as a present but I can't think why. It was one of the few possessions belonging to his mother that Rupert kept."

"Do you recognize any of the items in here?"

Harriet picked up the box and handed it to Lavinia. Lavinia took it from her, sifting through the contents. Her eyes widened and she pulled out the ruby earrings. "Good heavens, how did these come to be in there?"

"Do you recognize them?"

"Of course I do. They were Sylvie's. She wore them all the time, except on the odd occasion she wore pearls."

"Were they of some sort of sentimental value to her?"

Lavinia dropped the rubies back in the box and handed it to Harriet. "I've no idea. I never thought to ask her. The other items could belong to any officer of the South Sussex."

Harriet selected the single tarnished silver jacket button and handed it to Lavinia.

Lavinia turned it over in her hand and frowned. "Why are you showing me this? I've just said it's a standard-issue regimental button."

"How many should there have been?"

"The uniform jackets have four buttons."

"And one was found with your nephew's body."

"That's right." Lavinia nodded.

Harriet took back the single button and held it out on her palm. "This is the only one in the box. There were buttons left with the body of Sylvia Nolan and with the body of James Hawke. Is it possible they belonged to this set?"

Lavinia shrugged. "As I said, they are standard issue, Harriet. Who could possibly say if they came from the same set?" Her eyes widened. "Are you implying that these terrible murders are connected with Rupert's death?"

Harriet returned the button to the box. "It's not my place to say anything, Lavinia. I believe Sylvie Gentry and your nephew were engaged?"

Lavinia shrugged. "I'm not sure that 'engaged' is quite correct. He said nothing in his letters to me, but I have heard he and Colonel Gentry had discussed his marrying Sylvie. It would have been a good match, both children of the regiment."

"Rupert's father was also in the regiment?"

"Oh yes. We were all stationed in Cawnpore. My sister Margaret and I vied for his attention. Stephen Allen was a very attractive man."

"And Colonel Gentry was in India at the same time?"

"Of course. He was Captain Gentry then, of course, and, like the others, unmarried."

Harriet picked up the box, tracing the delicate carving of the elephant with her forefinger before placing it back in her handbag.

"Lavinia, do you think we could take a look in Rupert's trunk?"

"I suppose so. I've had no cause, or to be honest, no wish, to open it since it was returned to me."

Harriet followed Lavinia to a small room at the back of the house. Neat rows of boxes and trunks gave the room its name and Lavinia went straight to a solitary black-lacquered tin trunk stenciled with the name R. J. ALLEN. Kneeling, she flicked through the keys she carried on a ring, selected one and unlocked the lid. A year in the tropical heat had taken its toll and a bloom of green mold adhered to clothing and books.

Lavinia sat back on her heels, her hands in her lap and shook her head. "I can't, it's too painful. What are you looking for, Harriet?"

"A Sam Browne," Harriet said.

"It should be there."

Harriet flicked through the young man's possessions. Uniforms, shoes and books, a photograph of a younger Lavinia with a uniformed officer, no doubt her husband, and another photograph of a young couple, probably Allen's parents. Lavinia took both photographs and stood looking at them. Unspoken grief leeched from her.

Harriet found no personal papers or diaries and, significantly, no Sam Browne. She sat back on her heels and reached for her own capacious handbag. From it she pulled out the Sam Browne that had been found at the site of James Hawke's murder.

"Is this Rupert's Sam Browne?"

Lavinia took it from her, turning it over. "Possibly. I had hoped he would start to fill out a bit as he grew older but my sister had an impossibly slender build and I think Rupert had inherited it." She shook her head. "But there's no name. I couldn't be sure. How did you come by it?"

"It had been substituted for James Hawke's belt at the scene of his death."

Lavinia dropped the item as if it had scalded her. "How terrible. Why would someone do something like that?" Her eyes widened. "Do you mean James Hawke was murdered too?"

"That's for the police to say, not I," Harriet said.

"Oh, there you are, Lavinia."

Both women started at the man's voice coming from the doorway.

Harriet placed a hand under Lavinia Pemberthey-Smythe's elbow and helped her to her feet and they both turned to see George Cox standing in the doorway.

"George, what a lovely surprise," Lavinia said. "Are you acquainted with Mrs. Gordon?"

Cox brought his heels together and inclined his head. "Mrs. Gordon. I believe I saw you in the police department the other day."

Having seen him only on the one occasion in Curran's office, Harriet took a moment to study him. A man of average height with broad shoulders and a shock of sandy hair, he had a strong, well-proportioned face and an easy smile that some women would find attractive.

His gaze dropped to the Sam Browne she held in her hands. "What are you doing?"

"We were checking Rupert's trunk," Lavinia said.

"What were you looking for?"

"The strangest thing, George. Billings had Rupert's button box and I think this"—she held up the Sam Browne—"also belonged to Rupert."

"Really, can I see?" Cox asked.

He took the belt from Harriet, turning it over in his hands. "I didn't pack his possessions," he said. "As far as I know, it remained in the hold for the entire trip."

"Do you know who did pack it?"

Cox shrugged. "I presume his mess servant," he said. "Young Gentry was pretty cut up over his death. He may have helped."

Cox handed Harriet the belt and she returned it to her bag. Gentry—everything seemed to lead back to Gentry but something did not ring true and a small prickle of instinct told her that Gentry was not the answer.

"I believe you had the sad duty of bringing this box back with you from England, Lieutenant. What were you doing there?" she asked.

"I'd been sent home to get over a dose of yellow fever and they seconded me to headquarters for a couple of months while I recuperated. I couldn't wait to get back to Singapore." He straightened. "You almost made me forget why I came. I am the bearer of a message. Gentry has recovered consciousness and Miss Nolan has asked if you would come up to The Cedars, Mrs. Pemberthey-Smythe."

"Oh dear," Lavinia said. "It is so draining dealing with Pris." Her hand tightened over Harriet's forearm. "Would you come with me, Harriet? She seems to be a little less emotional when you are around."

Harriet nodded. "Of course."

"I have a gharry waiting outside," Cox said. "After you, ladies."

* * *

Ernest Greaves stood by the front door to The Cedars, shifting from one foot to the other as if he didn't quite know what to do next. General police duties were not his interest.

At the door of the house Cox caught Harriet's arm. "Nearly left this behind," he said with a smile, handing over her handbag.

Harriet smiled her thanks and turned to Greaves.

"Mrs. Gordon, I'm that pleased to see you. I have telephoned through to the branch and told the sergeant that the young gentleman had recovered consciousness. He's on his way."

"Where is Mr. Gentry?"

"He insisted on coming downstairs. He's with the rest of them in the front parlor." Greaves lowered his voice. "The colonel ordered me out here. At least you can keep an eye on them."

Lavinia and Cox had preceded Harriet while she spoke to Greaves and she followed them into the house.

Happy families, Harriet thought as she entered the living room, so quaintly referred to by Greaves as the "front parlor." Lieutenant Colonel John Nolan, clutching a glass of what appeared to be whiskey, stood behind the sofa on which Pris sat bolt upright, her eyes red-rimmed as if she had been crying. Nicholas Gentry reclined on the daybed, propped up by pillows, a light blanket over his legs. Standing over him, all brisk efficiency in her blue uniform with its starched white apron, collar and prim cap tied in a bow under her chin, was Maddocks's new friend, the nursing sister Doreen Wilson.

A flash of recognition caused the woman's professional mask to slip as she saw Harriet. She gave a quick smile and a nod of her head. There would be time to talk later. For now, Sister Wilson had a job to do.

Lavinia went at once to Pris, sitting beside her on the sofa and patting her hand. The odd man out, Cox, remained by the door, assuming an at-ease position.

"Cox, thank you for fetching the ladies, you can return to duties."

"Very good, sir. If there is anything else I can do," Cox said.

"Not at present," Nolan said.

Cox came to attention and left the room.

"Good of you to come, Lavinia—Mrs. Gordon." Nolan looked less pleased to see Harriet.

Lavinia looked up. "I asked her to come," she said.

"I can go," Harriet offered.

"No!" Pris reached out a hand and pulled her down beside her. "Stay, Harriet."

Nick Gentry's eyes flickered open and he raised his hand to his throat, circled by a neat white bandage. Any form of strangulation caused the blood vessels in the eyes to burst and Harriet flinched at the sight of those hideous red irises in his chalk-white face. He more closely resembled an evil spirit than a miserable young man.

Gentry swallowed. "I'm sorry to have caused such a fuss," he rasped in a voice so low, Harriet had to strain to listen.

Harriet could have pointed out that *causing a fuss* didn't even begin to describe the young man's actions. Gentry could be charged with the criminal offense of attempting to take his own life but that was Curran's decision, not hers.

"How about I organize some tea," Harriet offered, and went in search of the majordomo of the household, Abdul.

She found him sitting on the back step with his head in his hands. "Never has such a thing happened," the man said. "First the memsahib and now the young man. This house is cursed. I shall be leaving soon."

"I can hardly blame you for that," Harriet said. "In the meantime, please, could you organize tea and sandwiches?"

As Abdul rose to his feet and took himself, still muttering, to the kitchen, Harriet stood in the shade of the back verandah to gather her thoughts. She could hardly bring herself to return to the

living room with its heavy atmosphere of grief and recrimi-
nation.

"Mrs. Gordon?"

Jack Nolan peered around the corner of the house.

"Jack. How lovely to see you. How is Rufus?"

The boy frowned. "He's run off."

"Oh dear. When did this happen?"

"About half an hour ago."

"Shall I help you look for him?"

Anything for a diversion from the tense atmosphere of the
front room.

"That would be grand, thank you. I don't dare ask anyone
else. You've heard what happened?" Jack said.

"Yes. It is all very sad." Harriet murmured the appropriate
aphorism.

"I can't wait to get back to school," Jack said with feeling.

From the *ulu* at the back of the house came a frantic barking.

"Oh, there he is," Jack said, and set off at a run with Harriet,
skirts in hand, following.

They reached the large patch of jungle behind the married
quarters and pushed through the undergrowth to a clearing of
sorts where a rough shack, built of old packing cases and *atap*
leaned drunkenly against the solid trunk of a large tree. Above
them a troop of monkeys chattered their irritation at having
their peace disturbed. A hand-painted sign had been affixed to
the low crooked doorway from which a ragged piece of sacking
hung. The sign now teetered drunkenly from one nail. It read:
JACK'S DEN. PRIVATE. KEEP OUT.

Rufus bounded up to them with a *what a clever dog am I*
look on his face. He closed his jaws gently over Jack's hand and
tugged him toward the shack.

Jack went down on his hands and knees and crawled into the
hut while Rufus paced outside, barking happily. Harriet bent
down but all she could see were the soles of Jack's boots. The

boy appeared to be digging in the dirt floor. He backed out a few minutes later, clutching what looked like a bundle of rags to his chest. He dropped it on the ground and he and Harriet stood looking at it.

"There's something hard in there," Jack said at last. "Long and hard."

They both stared at the bundle, neither brave enough to unwrap it. The wrapping looked as if it had once been a shirt, the sleeves tied together to contain the contents. Even without touching it, she knew that the dark stains on the shirt cuffs were not mud and dirt. "I think you better fetch Constable Greaves," Harriet said. "He's standing by the front door."

The boy took off with the dog loping at his heels, returning with Greaves, his hat in his hand and his face flushed from the short run.

"What have you found?" he asked.

Harriet indicated the bundle, put her arm around Jack's shoulder, and they took several steps back. With infinite care Greaves undid the knot binding the two sleeves and opened the bundle. A pair of linen trousers had been loosely wrapped around a long, thin object. He untangled the legs of the trousers to reveal the missing silver candlestick and an embroidered bag, the sort of thing a woman would use for handkerchiefs.

Greaves peered into the bag and looked up at Harriet. "It's jewelry," he said. "Where did you find this?"

"It was buried in my hut." Jack pointed. "Rufus had already begun to dig it up. Whoever buried it, didn't do much more than cover it with dirt."

Greaves, for whom the proper handling of evidence was his reason for existence, carefully reassembled the bundle and peered inside the hut.

"What now?" Harriet asked as he straightened, pushing his glasses back up his nose.

He turned to look at her. "What should I do, Mrs. Gordon?

I really need Inspector Curran, but he's unwell and I know they won't talk to Sergeant Singh."

"To start with, whoever hid the evidence here, knew this place existed." Harriet turned to Jack. "Who else knows about your secret hut, Jack?"

Jack shrugged. "Father and Aunt Pris. I haven't used it for years. Aunt Pris helped me build it when I was little."

"Nicholas Gentry?"

Jack shook his head emphatically. "Nah. He wouldn't, not unless he was out here for some reason."

Harriet looked at Greaves. "You're the policeman, what would Curran do?"

Greaves swallowed. "He'd show it to the residents of the house and ask questions."

Harriet smiled encouragingly. "Then that is what you should do."

Behind his round wire-framed glasses, Greaves blinked. "But I'm not very good at that. I do bloodstains and photographs and fingerprints. I never know what to say to actual suspects."

"Ernest." Harriet used his first name. "Gursharan Singh is on his way, but here and now you are the only legitimate officer of the law and you are holding some important evidence. Evidence that someone in that house knows all about. You might like to begin by asking Miss Nolan about her movements on the night Mrs. Nolan died."

"Why?"

Taking a deep breath, Harriet told him.

❦ TWENTY-SIX

The Cedars
Wednesday, 24 August

Despite Harriet's prompting, on his return to the house, Constable Greaves held back with the excuse he would wait for his sergeant to arrive.

"I'll just wait outside," Greaves said, clutching to his chest the bundle found in the *ulu*.

But as Harriet entered the living room, it became clear that Greaves's hope of Gursharan Singh stepping into Curran's shoes would be in vain. Jack stood in the middle of the room regaling the assembled adults with the story.

"Is this true, Harriet?" Lavinia Pemberthey-Smythe asked. "Did that young constable recover the murder weapon and Sylvie's jewelry?"

Harriet looked around at the faces of the people in the room and asked Jack to fetch the policeman. Whatever Greaves might wish to do, in the circumstances, he needed to act now and act fast.

Greaves laid the bundle on the table. Pris gave a sharp cry and turned away.

"Have you seen this before, Miss Nolan?" Greaves asked.

"Pris?" Harriet said. "Is there more to the story than you told me in John Little's this morning?"

"You don't have to say anything, Priscilla," John Nolan said as Pris rose to her feet.

She turned to her brother. "Yes, I do. I've been hiding in the shadows so long, living in fear of what you would say . . . what the regiment would say. What people would think. I'm sorry, John, I'm not hiding anymore."

Her brother stared at her. "What are you talking about? What have you done?"

In a cool, clear voice, she repeated the story she had told Harriet, carefully omitting the name of the man with whom she had made the tryst.

Her brother's mouth fell open. "Priscilla, how could you . . . ?"

"Oh, it's all very well for you," Pris snapped. "I waste my youth looking after Mother and Father and I no sooner gain my independence when you send for me to be mother to Jack and your unpaid housekeeper. Then I meet a man who was actually interested in me, or so I thought . . ."

"Hawke . . ."

"Hawke?" Pris raged. "Let's be honest, John. He only saw me as a stepping-stone to advance his career. It would have been a heartbreaking marriage as I watched him chasing pretty young girls . . . just like your wife."

The barb hit home and John Nolan physically flinched.

"Who is this bounder?" he blustered.

His sister shook her head. "It doesn't matter. He's left me, John. He's going home to his comfortable life with his wife and children. It's just you and me again." The bitterness in her tone could have curdled milk. "I will freely admit that I hated her, John. Hated her for what she was doing to you. Making you the laughingstock of the regiment while she carried on with James Hawke but, believe me, I didn't kill her."

The silence that enveloped the room wrapped itself around everyone within it like a gathering thunderhead, ready to break.

Nick Gentry coughed and rose from the pillows. "Tell them, Pris. Tell them everything," he croaked.

Pris stared at him with wide, frightened eyes, as Sister Wilson gently pushed her patient back onto the pillows.

"I can't, Nick," Pris said.

"I don't care," he rasped. "Just tell them. Let's end it now."

Pris began to shake. Lavinia rose and guided her back to the sofa, where she subsided, trembling within the circle of Lavinia's motherly arm.

"Tell us what you know, Pris," Harriet urged.

She took a deep shuddering breath. "You were right, Harriet. I didn't tell you everything. When I came back from meeting with Cl . . . my friend, I saw the light was still on in Sylvie's room. I decided I was going to tell her there and then that she could do her worst, I didn't care anymore. My friend had told me he was going to leave his wife, file for divorce. This was my life. Nothing to do with the regiment." She swallowed. "Her door was ajar so I pushed it open." She shot a desperate glance at Nick Gentry. "Nick . . . I can't—"

"Do it," he said.

She swallowed. "Sylvie was lying on the bed and Nick was standing over her, covered in blood, holding the candlestick. He dropped it when he saw me."

All eyes turned to Nick Gentry but he had closed his eyes, his face creased in pain, and tears were running down his cheeks, soaking the pillow.

Harriet glanced at John Nolan, looking for a reaction, but the man could have been a statue. He stared at his sister without blinking.

Pris continued, "I could see Sylvie was dead. Nothing to be done for her so I asked Nick straight out if he had killed her."

"What did he say?" Greaves finally found his voice.

"He said he didn't know. He was drunk . . . or at least he had been very drunk. I could smell the alcohol on him from where I stood. I told him to go to the bathroom and strip off his clothes, wash and get into something clean from his own wardrobe. When he was done, I let him out of the house and went back to Sylvie's bedroom. I used Nick's discarded shirt to wipe the candlestick and then I"—she seemed to be struggling for breath—"I searched the room looking for the letter she had been using to blackmail me. I couldn't find it, so I took her jewelry to make it look like an intruder killed her. I wrapped the jewelry and the candlestick in Nick's clothes and buried them."

Greaves indicated the dirty bundle on the table. "Is this what you buried?"

"Yes."

"Tell me where you buried it?"

"In Jack's discarded shack in the *ulu* behind the house. The ground was so hard and I didn't have much time . . . After I dealt with those"—she waved at the items on the table—"I returned to the house. I had time to extinguish the light in Sylvie's room and lock the doors. I had just climbed back into bed when I heard John return. If he'd been any earlier . . ." She shook her head.

John Nolan groaned and sank into the nearest chair, his head in his hands. "Pris . . . what have you done?"

Pris rose to her feet and looked down at her brother, her back rigid with anger. "I have done precisely what you have always drilled into me, John. I have preserved the honor of the regiment."

Nolan looked from his sister to his brother-in-law. "But why?"

It was the first time Harriet had seen the man entirely discomposed. *Why* was the question they all wanted the answer to. She looked at Greaves. He looked at her. She gave him what she hoped was an encouraging nod.

"Oh yes, of course." Greaves cleared his throat, then addressed Nick Gentry. "Mr. Gentry, I have to ask. Did you kill Sylvie Nolan?"

The young man's mouth trembled. "I think I must have."

Greaves frowned. "You think you did? Surely you must know if you did or did not?"

Gentry closed his eyes. "It's all so confused. I'd had so much to drink. I remember someone took me up to my room. Cox, I think. Billings put me to bed, but I lay there thinking about Sylvie and Hawke and I got so angry." He paused, swallowing hard, his voice getting harder to hear. "I dressed in mufti and took the duty officer's keys from the cabinet where Hawke had left them. I vaguely remember trying to get the back gate open before the sentries returned but I don't remember what I did after that." He took a shuddering breath. "At least not until Pris was standing in the doorway and there was blood, so much blood. I had blood on my hands and I was holding . . . that thing . . . and Sylvie . . ." His face crumpled. "Sylvie was dead."

"Are you telling me you have no memory of hitting her?" Greaves persisted.

Gentry shook his head. "No. But I must have done, mustn't I." He turned away, curling up in a ball and crying uncontrollably, more like a small child than an officer of the South Sussex Regiment.

Sister Wilson straightened. "Constable, please, I think you have the information you need."

Greaves straightened, pulling together every ounce of authority he possessed. "In light of what you have just told me, Mr. Gentry, it is my duty to arrest you for the murder of Mrs. Nolan and, Miss Nolan"—he turned to Pris—"I have to arrest you for being an accessory after the fact."

No one spoke for a very long time.

It was Sister Wilson who broke the silence. "I appreciate you have a duty, Constable, but I too have a responsibility for this patient and I can tell you, he is in no state to be taken to a police cell."

Greaves scratched his chin. "I think in the circumstances," he said, "both Mr. Gentry and Miss Nolan should be considered under house arrest. That means we will arrange a police guard for the house and you are not to leave. Is that understood?"

Pris gave a snort of laughter. "This house . . . this life . . . it's my prison anyway. If anyone wants me, I will be in my bedroom."

Gathering all the dignity a woman of her disposition and class could muster, Pris rose to her feet and left the room.

"Pris," Harriet said, hurrying to the doorway. "Before you go. When you gathered up Sylvie's jewelry, did you take her ruby earrings?"

With her hand on the banister, Pris turned to look at her. "No. She wasn't wearing them."

❧ TWENTY-SEVEN

It had gone dark before Harriet returned to St. Tom's House. She paid off the hansom cab that had been summoned to transport her and trudged up the front steps. No lamp lit the front verandah and the house was in darkness. Belatedly she remembered Julian had a meeting of the school's governors.

She lit one of the gas lamps in the main living room as Huo Jin appeared from the back of the house with the announcement that now mem was home, supper would be half an hour.

Harriet carried her bag into her bedroom and set it on her bed as she unpinned her hat. Seeing it reflected in her mirror she remembered, belatedly, that she should have returned the button box and Sam Browne to Ernest Greaves to take back to Headquarters. She opened her bag and pulled out the Sam Browne, but even when she upended the entire contents of her bag, it was clear that the button box was missing.

Her stomach swooped and she swore aloud. Taking a deep breath she tried to recall when she had last seen it. It had been at Lavinia's house. Had she left it sitting on the table? No, she clearly remembered returning it to her bag.

The stuffiness of the evening threatened to overwhelm her and she rubbed her hand across her eyes. In the tension-filled house in Blenheim Road she had begun to develop a headache and now it throbbed in her temples.

She didn't want to have to explain to Curran that she had lost such an important piece of evidence. Even with Gentry's confession, he would not be pleased and it was beholden on her to re-trace her steps, beginning with Lavinia's house in Scotts Road.

She replaced the contents of her handbag, except for the Sam Browne, which she locked in her bedside table. To make room for it, she had to remove the little revolver, which she had not returned to its box. In her haste, and reluctant to leave the weapon unsecured, even unloaded, she thrust it into her pocket and asked Aziz to bring the pony trap around to the house. Huo Jin clucked her tongue and told her supper would be spoiled, but the tight knot in Harriet's stomach was getting tighter. She had to satisfy herself that the box was no longer at Lavinia's.

The Scotts Road house was uncharacteristically silent. Al-though a kerosene lamp burned on the verandah, there was no sign of Lavinia and no servant came out to greet her as Harriet climbed the steps and crossed the verandah. She could hear voices coming from Lavinia's bedroom and the hairs on the back of her neck prickled. They were not the voices of lovers. The man rapped out his words like a machine gun, and if La-vinia replied, she was inaudible.

Harriet crept forward. The bedroom door stood slightly ajar and through the gap she could see Lavinia seated in a cane chair, her hair coming out of its plait, and standing over her with his back to the door, a broad-shouldered man in a khaki uniform. The small uncertainty that had begun to prickle when Cox had held Rupert Allen's Sam Browne in his hands crystallized.

As she watched, the man leaned forward and hit Lavinia hard across the face.

"You're lying," George Cox said. "You knew. Of course you bloody knew and you had to tell her."

Lavinia gave a strangled cry, her hand going to her mouth to stem the blood that dripped from her cut lip.

Harriet stepped back, hurrying out as quickly as she could into the night to find the boy and the pony trap.

"Aziz, go to the police post in Orchard Road and get help. Now!"

"I am not leaving you here, mem."

Harriet hesitated. If she went with Aziz, then she could be too late. She now knew what had happened to the button box. George Cox had taken it from her bag, either in the gharry or in the Nolans' house. There had been one button left and she had no doubt it would be found in the morning with Lavinia's body.

"Go . . . go now," she said. "I'll wait here."

As Aziz turned the pony trap out onto the road, Harriet crept back onto the verandah, her fingers closing around the heavy object in her pocket. The foolish ruse had worked before; would it work now? She withdrew the little Smith & Wesson from her pocket, unwrapped it, and with her heart beating a tattoo of alarm, she crept back into the house. She heard another slap of hand on bone and Lavinia's choking sobs. Holding her breath, Harriet pushed open the door a crack. Lavinia now lay huddled on the floor, her arms over her head. Cox stood over her, his Webley drawn. With no plan, except to save the woman she considered her friend, Harriet flung the door open, holding the revolver in both hands.

Cox turned to face Harriet. Gone was the sardonic-but-charming young officer. A wild-eyed man who turned his weapon on her stood in his place.

"Don't move, Lieutenant," Harriet said. "Put your weapon down."

His lips drew back in a sneer. "You could no more fire that

weapon than fly to the moon, Mrs. Gordon. It's not in your nature."

"Are you willing to find out?" Harriet said, and for the first time hesitation flickered in his eyes.

Keep him talking . . . keep him talking . . . That's what Curran would do.

"Was the fourth button for Lavinia?" Harriet asked.

"It's no concern of yours," Cox said. "Now, please set that little toy down. I have no wish to kill you, but you've left me no choice. Your friend Curran will find two bodies in the morning, instead of one," he said.

Even if she had wanted to set her weapon down, Harriet realized she could not move. The revolver in her hand shook uncontrollably.

His mouth widened into a grin. "If you are going to shoot me, then do it, Mrs. Gordon. Go on, I dare you."

Harriet could see something that Cox, in his arrogance, had ignored. Behind the army officer, Lavinia rose to her feet. She raised her arms above her head and brought the ceramic chamber pot she had retrieved from under the bed down on Cox's head with a sickening crack. The chamber pot shattered into pieces and Cox went to his knees, a look of utter surprise on his face, before he pitched face-first onto the floorboards.

"Quick," Harriet said. "Tie his hands."

Lavinia already had the tie to her dressing gown in her hands and with surprising efficiency she wrested Cox's hands behind him and secured them. Cox had not completely lost consciousness and he groaned loudly at the manhandling.

Lavinia found another cord and tied his feet and then gagged him with a silk scarf. She sank into her chair, her hand going to her throat, while the man at her feet kicked and thrashed in an effort to free himself.

"Are you all right?" Harriet asked Lavinia as she rose to her feet.

Lavinia wiped a trickle of blood from her lip. She would have some colorful bruises in the morning. "Thank you. I believe I will live," she said.

"The police are coming," Harriet said, hoping that was the case.

Lavinia picked up the Webley and subsided in her chair. "You are an angel, Harriet. Do you mind fetching me a whiskey?"

"Where are the servants?"

"I think you'll find he locked them up in one of the back rooms. It's all right, I'm fine. You can leave him with me." She raised Cox's weapon, checked the safety catch was off and pointed it at him. "Do lie still, George, be a good boy."

Harriet looked at the weapon Lavinia held. Unlike her own trembling hand, Lavinia's grip was firm. There was no doubt that if Lavinia Pemberthey-Smythe fired the weapon, she wouldn't miss. Over the top of the gag, Cox's eyes widened and he stopped thrashing.

Harriet pocketed the Smith & Wesson. She had unfinished business of her own with Mr. Cox. Crouching down beside him, she went through his pockets. Her knees went weak with relief as she pulled out the button box. A quick check revealed the contents were intact, including the ruby earrings.

She straightened and looked down at Lavinia. "I'll release the servants. You're not going to kill him while I'm gone?"

Lavinia's eyes narrowed and she raised the weapon. "I should. He killed my Rupert. Didn't you, George? An eye for an eye." Cox had begun to sweat and for a moment Harriet thought Lavinia quite capable of carrying out her threat. She lowered the Webley and looked up. "Hurry up with my scotch, dear. There will be time for the full story later."

"So many secrets," Lavinia said, pouring herself another glass of whiskey from the rapidly diminishing decanter at her side.

She sat cross-legged in her favorite chair on the verandah, one hand caressing Pansy while the other held the glass.

Curran had arrived after the Orchard Road police constables had sent out the alarm to Headquarters and Harriet had never been so pleased to see him—apart from that time in Changi. He looked a little haggard but still managed to appear crisp and efficient and mercifully in charge.

Cox had been removed to South Bridge Road and now the three of them sat in the dark, warm night.

"Mrs. Gordon and I are waiting," Curran said.

"It's a question of where to begin," Lavinia said. "How much do you know, Inspector?"

"I know that the murders of Mrs. Nolan and James Hawke are connected to Rupert Allen's death," Curran ventured.

"You're right," Lavinia said. "Rupert was George Cox's first victim. He never took his own life."

"But what about the honor of the regiment?" Harriet suggested.

"Honor, maybe . . ." Lavinia said, and sighed. "It began when Cox was sent back to England to recuperate. As the good daughter of the commanding officer Sylvie used to visit him in hospital. Bear in mind, he'd known her all her life, but she was no longer a child; she was a beautiful and willful young girl and George was different from the other officers. He didn't fit the mold—you know exactly what I mean, Mr. Curran."

Harriet glanced at Curran, but his face revealed nothing.

"The attraction was mutual and, I am ashamed to say, acted on. The result was Sylvie's pregnancy. Sylvie was sent away and in her absence Cox went to Gentry to ask for Sylvie's hand but Gentry refused."

"Why would he do that? Cox may not have been the usual officer material but with Gentry's patronage he could have done quite well," Curran observed.

"Ah . . . there was a very good reason, which Gentry imparted to the young man."

"What was the reason?" Harriet pressed.

Lavinia held up a hand. "I'll come that. Gentry had another solution . . . my Rupert. Rupert came of good, solid regimental stock. He would go far in the regiment, whether he wanted to or not. It was agreed between Gentry and Rupert that the engagement would be announced when Sylvie returned from her extended stay in Scotland."

"How do you know this?" Curran cut in. "None of this was in the letters you gave me."

Lavinia shook her head. "The poor boy wouldn't have had time to write to me. Sylvie told me herself. She was so very angry with her father for denying her George. As you know, Cox had been sent back to Singapore immediately after Rupert's death so he had gone by the time Sylvie returned home." She paused. "From what Cox said to me, before your fortuitous arrival, Harriet, I suspect Rupert may have confided his good fortune to Cox and that enraged George. If he couldn't have Sylvie, no one else could. Rupert was a slight young man, no match for a man of George Cox's size."

"I suppose no one thought to question the means of his death," Curran said, and Lavinia shook her head.

"Cox always did have a flair for the dramatic and I think the idea of *Honor before all* appealed to him so he used the button from Rupert's own uniform as a suicide note, the implication being that Rupert killed himself in remorse for having deflowered the CO's daughter. Honor before all . . ." Her voice cracked and she took a sip of her whiskey.

"Poor Sylvie. Seventeen, pregnant, cut off and apparently abandoned by her lover and her family. Of course she was angry and hurt." Harriet frowned. "Why did Cox remove Rupert's Sam Browne and button box?" Harriet asked.

Lavinia shook her head. "I'm sure he removed them from Rupert's trunk before the voyage home, without any clear idea about what he would do with them. He'd already used one of the buttons, remember. I don't think in his wildest imagination he had anticipated that Gentry would marry Sylvie off to John Nolan, and I don't know what Gentry was thinking except Nolan presented as the answer to his prayers. Perhaps he thought Cox and Sylvie's affair was a thing of the past, and once she was married, she wouldn't look at the young man again."

"It must have been a terrible shock for Cox when Sylvie, the love of his life, arrived in Singapore on the arm of John Nolan," Harriet said.

"You must understand that her father had never told her why he refused to let her marry Cox." Lavinia took a swig of her whiskey. "She arrived in Singapore in the hope she would be reunited with her lover, but since his talk with Colonel Gentry, he rightly spurned her. His rejection had her in floods of tears." Lavinia rolled her eyes.

"So she punished him by taking up with Hawke and flirting outrageously with the other junior officers, particularly when Cox was around. I can only imagine his reaction when he overheard Hawke telling Gentry that Sylvie was once again pregnant," Harriet said. "He believed that the woman he once loved would bring dishonor on the regiment for a second time."

"So after Nick Gentry has been put to bed, Cox changes his clothes and goes up to The Cedars to confront her. They argue and he hits her with the candlestick," Curran said. "Probably leaving by the window."

"But he would have been covered in blood," Harriet said.

Curran continued, "Yes, but who was there to see him? I think when we look more closely at the clothes Gentry was wearing, we will find they were Cox's, not Gentry's. They are a similar size. Hopefully Gentry may begin to remember, but I wouldn't be surprised if Cox returned to the barracks, woke Gentry, telling him his sister wanted to talk to him, and in the boy's drunken confusion and with Cox's help, Gentry dressed in the bloodstained clothes Cox had been wearing. Gentry lurched up to The Cedars, found his sister dead and picked up the candlestick just as Pris walked in. The rest we know."

"How awful," Harriet said. "What about Hawke?"

"One of my men said that was an execution," Curran said. "Hawke had to die for the same reason Rupert Allen did. If Cox couldn't have her, no one else could."

"But there's no indication he intended harm to Nolan?" Harriet put in.

"Because poor John Nolan was a dupe. It was common gossip in the mess that the marriage was a sham," Lavinia said.

"So, Cox lured Hawke to the Botanical Gardens and killed him in cold blood, leaving the third button and Rupert's Sam Browne." Curran looked at Lavinia. "That was quite clever. It pointed us to you, Mrs. Pemberthey-Smythe."

Lavinia's eyes widened. "How terrible. I had no idea. I honestly believed Rupert had taken his own life. I have been blaming myself . . ." She looked away.

"And Billings died because he got in the way. I'm guessing, in his duties as batman, he found the button box and Sam Browne in Cox's possession, realized their importance and decided to try his hand at a bit of blackmail," Curran continued. "He didn't get a button because his death was incidental. The last button was intended for you, Mrs. Pemberthey-Smythe."

"He had set Nick Gentry up and his attempted suicide and note admitting his guilt should have closed the case, so why did he try to kill Lavinia?" Harriet asked. "It would have been obvious that Nick Gentry hadn't done it. He's under police guard and in no state to go about killing people."

"I don't think he really cared anymore. He wanted to kill me because I know his secret," Lavinia said. "The reason why he could never have married Sylvie Nolan."

Harriet leaned forward.

Lavinia swallowed the last of the whiskey. "Because Sylvie Nolan was his sister."

❧ TWENTY-EIGHT

The Cedars
Saturday, 27 August

Pris sat at the piano but the lid was closed over the keys and her hands rested on her lap. She didn't look up as Harriet entered the room.

"Play something?" Harriet suggested.

Pris shook her head. "I will probably never play again," she said, and a single tear rolled down her cheek.

Harriet could feel only pity at the sight of Pris's wan face. The freckles seemed to stick out in relief from her sunken cheeks and her eyes were lost in dark circles and swollen with crying.

"It's very quiet," Harriet said.

"John's taken Jack to the cricket and Nick is asleep."

"Is he better?"

Pris shrugged. "It will take time," she said. "Is it true?"

"What?"

"Everything Inspector Curran told us . . . about Sylvie being George Cox's sister?"

"Half sister," Harriet corrected. "Your Colonel Gentry was quite a lad when he was younger and didn't think twice about taking advantage of the wives of the other ranks."

"That explains why Cox's father was promoted to sergeant major," Pris said. "Repayment of a debt . . ."

"A debt of honor?" Harriet suggested, and for the first time something like a smile touched Pris's eyes.

"It all makes sense now. When she first arrived, Sylvie's eyes were only for George Cox but he was so rude to her. I suppose that was because he knew the secret but she didn't."

"That seems to be the case . . . until that last night when he confronted her about her affair with Hawke. He told her then and she flew at him in a rage. He picked up the candlestick and . . ." Harriet let the rest of the sentence pass.

"Poor Sylvie," Pris said.

Privately, Harriet agreed. What a terrible thing to have discovered about the man you thought you loved.

"Did your brother know the full story when he married her?" she asked.

Pris shrugged. "If he did, he will never say." She took a breath. "I just made it so much worse, Harriet. I really thought Nick had killed her and my only intention was to preserve John's good name—make it look like an intruder. That's why I hid the jewelry."

"To preserve the honor of the regiment?"

Pris shot her a quick glance. "For what it is worth." She frowned. "One thing I don't understand. Why did he take the ruby earrings?"

Harriet had the advantage of having typed up Curran's interview notes. "Gentry had given them to Cox's mother and Cox in all innocence had presented them to Sylvie. When she started wearing them, her father couldn't have helped but notice and he would have known their significance," she said.

"And by continuing to wear them, she was telling George that she still loved him?" Pris suggested.

Harriet shook her head. "I think it was her revenge," she said. "Revenge on her father, revenge on the lover who had apparently abandoned her. A reminder of what had been and how she had been betrayed."

Pris stared at the piano keys. "What a terrible story," she said. "I just feel sad for Sylvie and, in a way, for Cox too."

"What will you do now?" Harriet asked, changing the subject.

Pris rose to her feet and walked across to the window, wrapping her arms around herself. "John is sending me back to England. He says the tropical climate is to blame for . . . everything." She took a shuddering breath and turned to face Harriet. "Harriet, do you hate men?"

Harriet had not been expecting that question. She shook her head. "No. Why should I hate men?"

"Because of what they did to you in Holloway."

"What happened to me in Holloway . . ." Harriet began. "What happened in Holloway was a system and that is what must change. That is what the WSPU must continue to fight for. It was cruel but don't forget women were also involved. As for men, I consider myself very fortunate with the men in my life, Pris."

"You've been lucky," Pris said with undisguised bitterness. "You asked what I will do now. Well, it is all arranged. It has been decided that Jack will go to school in England and I am to accompany him," Pris said. "John will rent me a cottage near Jack's school where, no doubt, I will live out my life, giving piano lessons and arranging the flowers in the church. Jack will join the regiment as soon as he leaves school, and if I'm lucky he will write to me or visit me occasionally when he is home on leave from whatever corner of the empire he finds himself. That is what I have to look forward to."

And so the cycle continued. The sons and daughters of the regiment would go on perpetuating the myth of the "honor of the regiment," unless something monumental were to occur from which the world order would never quite recover. Harriet felt a shiver of premonition.

"What if Jack doesn't want to join the regiment?" Harriet said.

Pris turned to look at her. "Of course he will join the regiment. Just as Rupert Allen and Nicholas Gentry did. Nick is being sent back to England too. He will resign his commission." She shrugged. "I don't know what he'll do. This life has made him unfit for any useful occupation." A tear dribbled down her face. "What I can't forgive myself for is thinking Nick even capable of having killed his sister. I drove him to do what he did." She looked at Harriet. "It was his own doing, wasn't it, Harriet?"

Harriet nodded. She had no solace to offer. Even if it had been done with the best of intentions, Pris would have to live with her own guilt at perpetuating a lie that had driven a young man to the point of trying to take his own life.

"When do you leave?" Harriet asked.

"Thursday," Pris replied.

Harriet stood up and held out her hand. "Then this is goodbye, Pris."

Pris took her hand but Harriet sensed no strength in the lifeless grip. It was as if the events of the past week had taken from Pris all her life force.

Harriet walked away from The Cedars without a backward glance, conscious that Pris watched her from the window. On the ricksha ride back to River Valley Road, she pondered Pris's question. She had been fortunate with the men in her life and tonight she had been invited to dinner with Simon Hume at Raffles. Just the two of them.

No doubt that would set the tongues wagging but she didn't care. Despite the tragedies in her life, she had her ward, Will Lawson; a caring and understanding brother; a job that she loved and good friends. It may not have been how she would have planned her life but she had to admit that she was happy and maybe that was the difference between herself and Pris Nolan.

❧ TWENTY-NINE

Scotts Road
Saturday, 27 August

Curran rode through the gates of Lavinia Pemberthey-Smythe's home. He tethered Leopold in the shade and strode up the stairs to the pleasant front verandah, where he found the lady taking her leisure with a glass of something that looked suspiciously like a gin and tonic.

"Take a seat, Inspector. You look like a man who needs a drink. Gin or scotch?"

Curran accepted a whiskey and with a sigh leaned his head back against the bright cushions of the comfortable chair.

Lavinia leaned over and placed her hand over his. "You've done well, Curran. It can't have been easy. The regiment keeps its secrets close."

He smiled at her. "And you are the keeper of the secrets, Lavinia."

She nodded. "I admit I was wrong not to have told you about Cox's relationship with Sylvie. I'm sorry, Curran. At the time I didn't think it was relevant."

Curran fixed her with a hard look. "That should not have been your decision to make."

"I know. Now are you ready to hear what I know about your father?"

"Go on," he said.

"I remember your father visiting our house on several occasions. I was an impressionable girl of fifteen and I thought him rather dashing." She cocked her head to one side. "Yes, I think I can see a look of him in you, although he was a younger man than you are now. He told me once he had a little boy back in England." When Curran didn't respond, she set her glass down and wiped her hands on her skirt. "You must understand that they were wild times on the Afghan border. I was safe in Bombay with my mother and siblings and the story as I heard it was only whispered about in scandalized tones." She paused. "I may have been considered too young but I heard things and this is what I recall. Somewhere within the story of the Coward of Kandahar is the kernel of the truth but it is up to you to determine where the truth lies. Are you still sure you want to hear it?"

Curran took a deep draught of the whiskey, letting it burn the back of his throat. "As you say, I need to make my own judgment on my father's actions. I was told, and believed all my life, that he was dead, killed at the Battle of Maiwand."

"And maybe he was," Lavinia replied. "In the winter of '80, Lieutenant Edward Curran led a patrol out of Kandahar. They were ambushed and every man put to death. Every man but one. When a second patrol went out to recover the bodies, Edward Curran's corpse could not be found. At first it was presumed he had been badly wounded and crawled off to die. A search was mounted but no trace of him was found. In July of that year, Ayub Khan started to move on Kandahar and General Burrows was sent out to intercept him. They met at the Maiwand Pass and, as you know, it was a military disaster from the British side. Ayub Khan only had a small force but he still managed to defeat the British and Indian troops and he harried them all the way back to Kandahar. Kandahar came under siege and was only liberated by a relief force from Kabul. A thousand British and Indian troops died in the battle and its bloody aftermath and the colors of the First Battalion of the South Sussex Regiment of Foot were lost."

"And my father?" Curran asked.

"It was reported back by several of the survivors that a British officer, in uniform, was seen at the Battle of Maiwand, standing beside Ayub Khan." She paused, studying his face. "He was identified by eyewitnesses as your father, Curran."

Curran shook his head, not wanting to believe the implication. "Were the witnesses certain?"

Lavinia took a sip of her drink. "As sure as anyone in the heat of battle could be. It was said that when his patrol had been attacked, Edward Curran had begged for his life in exchange for information on the British strengths and dispositions. He alone was held responsible for the defeat at Maiwand."

Curran stared at the contents of his glass, not seeing the whiskey, just the blood and smoke and confusion of battle and a lonely figure in regimental scarlets standing at the right hand of the enemy. It was little wonder that anyone bearing the name of Curran encountered so much hostility in the regiment. So many dead and the loss of the colors, the ultimate dishonor.

"What happened to him?"

Lavinia shook her head. "Nobody knows. He was never seen again. I'm sorry, Curran. I wish I could tell you more and even what I have shared with you is all rumor and speculation. There could be no truth to any of it. The Afghans were quite capable of putting a man in British uniform on show to give the impression of a traitor."

Traitor . . . the word went to Curran's heart with the intensity of a knife.

"But it could be true," he said. "Charles Kent implied he had seen my father alive in more recent times."

Lavinia straightened. "Charles Kent? That unprincipled blackguard? He was cashiered and rightly so. I wouldn't believe a word he had to say on the subject. If he told you he believed your father to still be alive, it was said merely to gain some sort of advantage over you. Surely you realize that, Curran?"

Curran forced a smile. "My head tells me that, Lavinia—"

"But the heart tells you different? And you have a good heart, Curran. It is as well you listen to its counsel, even if it brings you trouble." She smiled and cocked her head to one side. "Why this sudden interest in your father?"

Curran was tempted to tell her about the mysterious note and the man who had frightened Li An and led Li An and Harriet Gordon into danger, but what was the point? It was only a hunch, his heart filling in blanks that may or may not exist.

As he took his leave of her and swung himself back into the saddle, he decided to let the dead lie where they had fallen. He couldn't grieve for a father he had never known. Like the story of the Coward of Kandahar, the real Edward Curran was a distant figure in scarlet, not quite discernible through the smoke and dust and confusion of the years.

❧ Thirty

Curran pushed his way through the evening crowd that drifted around the fringes of Chinatown. The air was thick with smoke from the braziers still burning offerings to the hungry ghosts and from several streets away came the drums and cymbals of a performance of Chinese opera. Li An had tried to explain the intricacies of the art to him but the cultural divide was too wide. He had no doubt Li An would feel the same way about *Tosca*.

A woman stood in his path, and as he made to go around her, she caught his sleeve. It took him a moment to recognize Madam Lim, the proprietress of the opium den. He stopped and took a step back from her, shaking her claw from his arm.

Without a word she handed him a small square of folded paper and she turned to be swallowed up by the crowd. Even in the dim light of the gas lamps, he recognized the red and gold of a sheet of incense paper and Curran toyed with the urge to toss it away.

He took three steps and curiosity got the better of him. Under a streetlamp he paused and unfolded the paper. Written in pencil on the reverse side, it read simply:

Collyer Quay by the entrance to Change Alley.
Tonight 10 P.M.

He glanced at his wristwatch. Eight P.M. He had time to go home and change into something less conspicuous. Time to lay this hungry ghost from his past to rest once and for all.

Collyer Quay was quiet, no large steamers waited to depart and most of the bigger cargo traffic had been diverted to the new docks at Tanjong Pagar. Curran took up a position at the entrance to Change Alley, propping his right foot against a wall as he lit a cigarette.

He smoked slowly, his left hand in the pocket of his trousers, watching the gently bobbing lights of the bumboats and more distant riding lights of the ships on Keppel Harbour. The tang of the sea and the lure of distant adventures called to him, until he remembered he suffered from seasickness. A life on the sea had never been an option.

The minutes dragged by and an hour drifted past the designated time on the note. He stamped the stub of his third cigarette under his heel and pushed away from the wall.

The man wasn't coming.

He took out the note establishing the abortive rendezvous and gave a huff of derisive laughter as he scrunched the paper. He held it balled in his hand as he turned on his heel for the walk home.

He passed the Thian Hock Keng temple on the waterfront in Telok Ayer Street and paused. A crowd had gathered around the brazier in the center of the yard and were tossing in their offerings to their ancestors.

Curran stepped over the lintel and the crowd parted until he stood beside the brazier. The ghosts, the hungry ghosts, had to be appeased. He opened his hand and looked at the scrunched paper he held. For a long moment he hesitated before tossing it into the fire. The ball of paper flared briefly as the fire of hell consumed it, dragging it down to appease his ancestor . . . his father.

He turned away and walked out into the street, feeling lighter than he had since Li An had first seen the mysterious man. He quickened his step toward his home and the life that he had built with Li An.

❧ THIRTY-ONE

St. Thomas House
Tuesday, 30 August

*T*HE FASCINATING TYPIST: *How She Is a Wrecker of Happy Homes: Delilah's Toils,*" Julian read aloud from the morning edition of the *Straits Times*.

Harriet stopped buttering her toast and looked up at her brother. "I beg your pardon?"

Julian tapped the paper. "The hysteria over the Crippen case shows no sign of abating. This article today is about the perils of employing a female secretary. Clearly if Dr. Crippen had not employed Ethel Le Neve, Mrs. Crippen would still be alive and treading the boards."

"You mean it was Ethel Le Neve's fault that Cora Crippen died?"

Julian resumed his perusal of the article, reading: "*The recent case of Dr. Crippen has brought one lady typist, and her calling in general, into prominence. One erring lady-typist, of course, does not brand the whole class as frail; but it is by no means an uncommon occurrence for the lady-typist, or lady-secretary, to come between husband and wife; and in America, at least, murder has more than once been the result.*"

Harriet stared at her brother. He glanced up at her from over his glasses, his eyes twinkling as he continued to read:

"Widows are dangerous to men's peace of mind, grass widows doubly so, and they abound in men's offices. Occasionally, a man is caught by a typist who is really a bad woman. She means to drag him down, and she succeeds. In other cases, blackmail is the object. The man is deliberately tempted, fails, and endures all the horrors of blackmail until at last he commits murder or suicide, or bolts, leaving a wrecked home behind him. It would be fair to represent the lady-typist as always the temptress, innocent or deliberate."

Julian looked up at his sister. "I say, Harri, I had no idea you were such a risk to the innocent, unsuspecting man."

"That's abominable." Harriet spat toast crumbs in her brother's direction. "Who wrote this rubbish?"

Julian peered at the article. "No one local," he said. "It would be one of those articles they've brought in."

"Nevertheless, I'm going to have strong words with Griff when I next see him, allowing such rubbish to be published." Harriet buttered her next slice of toast with such ferocity that it disintegrated under her knife.

Julian flicked through the paper to the cricket news. "I better warn Curran to beware the wiles of his lady typist," he said.

Harriet threw her serviette at her brother's head.

Author's Note

Fact and imagination mingle in the writing of this story. The South Sussex Regiment, St. Thomas School and the composition of the Detective Branch of the Straits Settlements Police are purely fictional or fictionalized for simplicity.

I have used the location of the Tanglin Barracks as the setting for the Blenheim Barracks. I was delighted to learn that Tanglin Barracks, under threat of demolition when I lived in Singapore twenty years ago, has been preserved and is now a popular meeting place with fashionable eating spots. However, I still retain happy memories of curries at Sami's (in what used to be the sergeants' mess), which is still in operation.

I served in the Australian military for nearly twenty years and endured many an officers' mess dining-in night with its rigid customs. Actually I always quite enjoyed them, except for the one time I was the designated "Mr. Vice" (really!) and I stood to say grace and the aged chair collapsed on me. So I have drawn a great deal on my own personal knowledge of life in the military as well as that of my father, who served as an officer in the British Army for many years, including stints in Singapore and (as it was then) Malaya.

The pretty little pavilion does exist in the Singapore Botanical Gardens and appears to be a popular spot for weddings.

"Mad" Ridley was the director of the Gardens at the time, and yes, he earned his nickname because he was thought to be mad for wanting to introduce the rubber industry into the Malay Peninsula. A very interesting man.

As always, I had a lot of fun trawling the contemporary issues of the *Straits Times*, and the fun and games of the cinematograph at Harima Hall is drawn from contemporary accounts as is the dramatic arrest of Dr. Crippen and the truly appalling article about the dangers of secretaries (you will find a full transcript on my website). Any errors in the spelling of names (Inspector Drew/ Dew), etc., were made by the original columnist and are reproduced accordingly.

Speaking of my website, I have not included a character list or glossary in this book, but you will find both on my website AMStuartBooks.com.

Singapore is a wonderful mix of different traditions and observances, and Hungry Ghost month (the seventh month of the lunar calendar) is still observed with the burning of incense papers, Chinese opera and reverence of the dead. It is considered ill luck to plan an important event during this month (marriage, children, house moves, business ventures, big trips). In fact there is a long list of dos and don'ts!

Finally, the views expressed by some of the characters in this book are not those of the author. This book is set in 1910 and intolerance shown to non-Europeans was real. As abhorrent as we, with our twenty-first-century glasses, might find it, this is how it was and it would be unbalanced for me to imply otherwise.

I hope you enjoyed this story.

A. M. Stuart

Acknowledgments

This story, more than any other, is drawn from my own personal experience of many years as an army officer in the Australian Army Reserve. The customs of even a modern army can still trace their origins back to times almost immemorial, and not much has changed when it comes to formalities such as dining-in nights (except provision for a comfort break!).

As always, the back issues of the *Straits Times* are my friend and are a serious rabbit hole down which I could spend hours. I love being able to incorporate snippets in the stories. Did you like the article about the dangers of the lady typist? I also have a rapidly increasing library of reprinted contemporary tourist guides and other references relating to life in colonial Singapore.

A huge shout-out to my cheer squad, support crew and writerly buddies, the Saturday Ladies Bridge Club, without whom my writing life would be a lonely one.

And thanks to my agent, Kevan Lyon; my editor, Michelle Vega; and the wonderful team at Berkley, most of whom I had the pleasure of meeting face-to-face during the writing of this book.

But most of all, thanks to my darling husband, David, also a former Australian Army officer and a keen military historian, who is my sounding board, chief researcher, brainstormer and beta reader—and who doesn't complain when I drag him to Singapore and Malaysia on research trips.

Helen Beardsley Photographer

Born in Africa, author **A. M. Stuart** has traveled extensively and has lived in Kenya, Singapore and Australia. She is the author of the Guardians of the Crown historical romance series published by Harlequin Australia, and her books have been nominated for multiple international awards.

CONNECT ONLINE

AMStuartBooks.com
AMStuartBooks
AMStuartBooks

Ready to find
your next great read?

Let us help.

Visit prh.com/nextread

Penguin
Random
House